The Secret Diary of a

BENGALI BRIDEZILLA

HALIMA KHATUN

A HAYAT HOUSE book
First published in Great Britain in 2021 by Hayat House.
Copyright © Hayat House 2021
The moral right of Halima Khatun to be identified as the author of this work has been asserted by her in accordance with the Copyright, Design and Patents Act, 1988.

Cover design by Felix Diaz de Escauriaza

Paperback ISBN: 978-1-9163183-3-5
A CIP Catalogue record for this book is available from the British Library

To Jasmine and Alexia, who were with me on this author journey from the beginning.

9th September
A Bengali game of thrones

As I sit on my makeshift throne, squirming at the sight of samosas that I'd devour on any other day, I notice a little mesh bag on the table above my untouched plate of starters. This tiny drawstring bag, aptly the same shade of green as the Bangladeshi flag, contains a date fruit, a single Cadbury's chocolate and a peanut brittle.

Then I remember. This small, unassuming drawstring bag has been the source of great angst over the last few months. This single, innocuous item threatened to drive me bat shit crazy as I threw myself headfirst into planning the biggest day of my life, leaving a debris of disgruntled loved ones in my wake.

Now, somewhat calmer, I wonder why the bag was such a big deal. Maybe it was my attempt at clawing back some control over what was supposed to be *my* day? Maybe I was clinging to the hope of pulling some strings behind the scenes. Maybe, just maybe, I wanted a small part of this wedding to be classy, expensive. You know, with some extra special touches.

I guess, just like mum, I wanted to keep up with the Mahmood's and have a big Bengali wedding that had all the trimmings and more. I always take the mick out of her for trying to compete with our almost-perfect cousins, but when it comes to the crunch, I'm the same. I'm every inch my mother's daughter and I want a wedding that people will talk about.

Now we've arrived at the day itself... I don't even care for peanut brittle, though I do like chocolate.

The point is, I'm not sure what the fuss was about. Why I was fretting so much over a bag of sweets?

Sorry, where are my manners? Allow me to explain...

Remember how I said you'd be invited? Well, pull up a chair. They're about to serve starters.

I'm getting married, you see. No, for real this time.

Eight months earlier
18th January
Modern minx

"So... has there been talk recently with this boy?"

Oh mum, you modern minx, probing me about this boy I'm seeing. Oh, and when I say seeing, I mean in the very prim, Bangladeshi sense with absolutely no funny business. Still, it astounds me that I can tell mum I'm *kind of* dating a boy without getting two slaps across the face. Middle sis was right, mum is the mistress of discretion and nosiness.

Then again, mum knows this isn't some flash-in-the-pan halal fling. When I told her about this boy two months ago, she knew I was serious. It wasn't a leap of faith like it was with Shy-boy, whose name (affectionately coined by me) pretty much sums up the entire issue with our one-date courtship. This time, it's much more than that. We've been on over a dozen dates. Most of which involved food. On one such occasion, I even paid the bill, though thankfully it was a Costa Coffee rather than a three-course meal. So, essentially, this is the real deal.

Mum doesn't really care when we speak, or what about. It's her way of asking if there's any progress on the marriage front. Which, by the way, she's been asking me every single weekend since she found out about him.

"No mum, there's nothing to report. I wish you'd stop asking. I told you already, if there's anything new, you'll be the first to know."

"What problem here? Can't a *maa* ask these things?" Mum always throws a bit of broken English into the Bengali mix when she's annoyed or on the defence. "You want be sure it be heading in right direction."

I'd like to head out of this conversation. "Like I said, I'll tell you when there's anything to tell. I better go, I'm getting late. Reena's nearly at the restaurant."

As I sit on the stairs to zip up my new, fresh-leather-smelling brown boots, mum leans over the bannister. "There's a rishtaa's details come through." She comes closer still to raise her eyebrows and whisper: "This boy be dentist. He got lots of hair." Mum rubs her head in a circular motion to emphasise her point.

Oh *come on*. Why do all the decent rishtaas come when I'm sort of off the market? I had a motley crew when I was single and looking. Yet, since meeting this boy, I've had to turn down a meeting with a surgeon (not even joking) and now this dentist. Where were they hibernating before, when mum was embracing the idea of a pizza boy from Bangladesh as a prospective son-in-law? Sometimes timing can be a right bitch.

"Mum, we've talked about this. Now's not the time to put rishtaas my way. Anyway, where did it come from? Are you still paying Mr Ashraf to find us boys?"

"Yes, I still use him. But this one from Mr Choudhury. He called to say sorry no rishtaa come good but he got new boy details and can send for smaller fee. Just £15."

"So you're paying two people to find me a husband when I'm no longer looking?"

For someone who once bemoaned the cost of hiring these professional busybodies when I was truly single and desperate to mingle, mum's behaviour is just confusing. Plus, her timing is terrible.

"It was *especial* offer and I thought it best keep these people in hand." Mum does her bottom lip grimace thing. "You know, just in case."

As I climb into my Ford Fiesta, I begin to wonder... why *hasn't* he told his parents about me yet? I told my mum as soon as she and dad had got back from Hajj. I've been paying the price ever since with mum's regular requests for a status update. I even told *him* my mum knows about us. I thought he'd do the same in return. Yet his parents don't know anything about me. Could it be that he's not as serious about me as I am about him? Is he still looking around? Maybe I was too hasty in telling my parents.

Bloody mum, she's infiltrated my head and is messing with my thoughts.

My phone rings. Crap! I bet Reena's already at the restaurant. This is embarrassing, as it's a 90-minute train journey from Birmingham and short cab ride for her but a quick 15-minute drive for me. I shouldn't be the one running late.

I'm getting my apology lined up but then I realise it's not Reena calling me, it's him. Him that I'm thinking I may marry. Him that makes frequent trips from London to see me. Him that will travel over an hour from the city to Heathrow Airport after work for a quick cuppa with me, while I wait for my domestic flight back home after a day at head office. Him that does all the legwork and never expects me to come down to see him on the weekend. Though to be fair, he comes up north to his hometown and visits his family when he sees me. If I went down to London just to meet him, I'd have to fork out on a hotel. This might also plant an unnecessary seed in the boy's head. So I keep it halal and keep him on his toes. Who knew I'd play such a blinder with my limited boy experience?

I'm not sure if I should answer his call and delay myself even further but I'm desperately keen to talk to him. My annoying mum has cast a shadow of doubt on this precarious union and I need to prove her concerns are unfounded.

"Hey, how are you?" I don't mean to sound so high pitched and enthusiastic.

"I'm good. What you up to?" He almost echoes my tone, out of solidarity I guess.

"I'm just about to meet Reena. You know, my friend from uni? She's got a hen weekend in Manchester but is squeezing in some lunch with me beforehand."

"Nice. How is she?"

"Well... I'll soon find out. Though I'm running late." Ooh, why do I sound so snarky?

"Ah... I'll leave you to it, then. I just called to see how you were," he trails off, sounding deflated.

"Oh no, it's okay. I can speak for a couple of minutes." I really can't and shouldn't but I'm slowly turning into one of those girls who prioritises their Misters over sisters.

"Nah, it's cool. You don't want to leave your friend waiting." He's obviously a more loyal mate than I am.

I still can't shake off mum's doubts. I must bring it up later. But then my words follow a different agenda: "Okay, but I just wanted to ask you, have you spoken to your parents about us?"

Me and my verbal diarrhoea. It is not the time for a deep and meaningful conversation. I have no filter or sense of timing.

He hesitates. This won't be good.

"Err, no I haven't, to be honest with ya. I've been meaning to but I'm waiting for the right time. If I tell my mum, she'll be printing out wedding cards the next day."

What does he mean, "if"? Surely it should be "when"?

"So I just want to be sure, to be honest with ya," he adds, making me now very *unsure* of our status.

"Are you not sure?"

Again, I have no idea why I'm bringing this up now. Not only am I late, there's also a real chance I'll be greeting Reena with ugly tears.

"No... no... no, I don't mean I'm not serious. I... Don't worry. I'll speak to mum. Anyway, you should go and meet your friend. I don't want her thinking I'm already taking you away."

I feel a faint sense of relief. My timing was terrible but I'm glad I asked. I just hope he tells his mum sooner rather than later so *my* mum can stop teasing me with the biodatas of very eligible bachelors.

Before I go, I have to do something. Yes, I know I'm already really, really late but to put my mind at ease, I go on the dating website to see if he's still online. It's become a weekly ritual of mine, to stalk the boy I'm seeing. It's astound-

ing how this website allows you to look at profiles without
even logging on or being a member. Obviously data protection pales in significance compared to enticing prospective
singletons with the vast array of talent on display at this halal
meat market.

My slow, buffering phone, which is groaning with too
many photos, finally wakes up. Right there, his profile is still
very much live, for all and sundry to see...

IN TRUE SELFISH FORM, I picked a lunch venue that's
super convenient for me. My trusty Italian restaurant is an
easy drive and serves the best rustic pizza. It's even got parking, which is a saving grace as I always get in a fluster when
having to find a space on the street. Yet I still managed to be
40 minutes late meeting Reena.

Plus I'm distracted. Why is he still online? Each time
I've had a snoop I've hoped, prayed and whispered positive
thoughts. *Today is the day... today is the day he'll take it down
and I'll know we're meant to be. Glass half full... glass half full.*
Each time, my heart would sink a little and I'd curse myself
for daring to dream.

My profile is still up too but that's different. It's free for
me to be on this website, so it's actually more hassle to make
the effort to close it down. It's not like I'm taking advantage
of this by hunting for guys.

For him, on the other hand, every single month he's reg-
istered with the site costs him the princely sum of £30. Surely
it wouldn't make sense to stay online unless he was still look-

ing? Was he chatting to other girls? Could I ask him to take his profile down? Is that too possessive?

Luckily, Reena's not overly aware of my distraction, or my lateness. She whiled away the time talking on the phone to Himesh, who she describes as her latest Mr Oh-you'll-do-I'm-bored-of-this-shit-now.

"This whole finding a man business is really starting to get on my tits." Reena is as charmingly unfiltered as ever. "But I have to tell you, Himesh is turning out to be the best of a bad bunch. I'm actually glad he slid into my DMs. I'm telling you, going online isn't actually that bad. You should try it."

I haven't told Reena I'm sort of no longer single. And I certainly haven't mentioned that I met the guy I'm sort of dating online. So far, only three people know about my Internet dating history:

- Middle sis - the more streetwise of my two older sisters.
- Sophia - my older, more worldly and twice-married mentor.
- Julia - my childhood friend who's more Bengali than most Bengalis.

I'd like to keep the *way* I met him confined to this small group. I don't know what mum would think if she found out and, as my sisters say, it's not how you meet someone that matters, it's who you meet. Also, despite my best efforts to be glass half full, I can't quite shake off my cynical nature. I'm scared of jinxing things with this boy by shouting about him from the rooftops. So my Facebook status is still single and I don't have any photos of M on my phone because I live in a home where privacy holds no value.

Though the temptation to share my news with Reena is huge. We rarely catch up these days. Our calls are sporadic and we meet once a year at most but each time, the manhunt is the hot topic of conversation. I'm usually put to shame as Reena always has something to report and is never not meeting/dating/being introduced. I'm always the one listening in awe at her ballsy, unrelenting determination to find a man. It's beyond annoying that the one time I truly have something to talk about, I feel it's too soon to divulge.

Our mains arrive. Reena gets to work lacing her pollo pizza with chilli oil. I suspect she'd rather have opted for a restaurant that serves up some spice.

"So what's new with you? How's the boy hunt going?" she asks the inevitable.

To tell or not to tell, that is the question.

I can't even look Reena in the eye so I start cutting at my vegetarian pizza. The crust is too crusty. I might lose a filling chewing on this one.

"Oh... it's not really. Mum's still paying a busybody to source suitable guys. But so far the pickings have been slim." In my defence, that bit is true.

Reena furrows her brow. "What's a busybody?"

"Oh, of course, I forget that your lot do things differently. It's basically someone who does matchmaking as a side-gig. Except they're as unregulated as they get and they only have a spreadsheet of about ten single guys to offer. None of whom are usually anything to shout about."

Reena, who comes from a community where the best things are free, is unimpressed. "So the cheeky bastards charge you for what nosey aunties have been doing since time began? That wouldn't fly with my mum. You know how tight us Gujis are!"

"Us Bengalis can be stingy too. However, in this case, mum thinks it's worth the expense. Who knew you could put a price on love? In our case, it's £30 a month."

"That's ridiculous! It costs me the same every month to be on the dating website. And I get to meet guys of my own accord. It cuts out the middleman. Or middle auntie. Though my one's exclusively for Hindus... but I bet there are sites for Muslims."

If only she knew. I spent half of last year on a Muslim-only dating site and courtesy of some slightly sexist rule, girls don't have to pay a thing while boys are charged a monthly fee. If I told Reena this, her stingy Gujarati heart (her words, not mine) wouldn't be able to take it.

Within minutes, Reena has managed to eat her way through half her pizza. Still chewing, she declares: "I really shouldn't be eating this."

"Why?"

"This stupid hen do is a spa weekend. So that means swimwear. The hen, Rakhi, is on some crazy Japanese diet and she's gone proper skinny. Do you remember her from my sister's wedding? The girl who tripped on the stage as she got her six-inch heels caught in her saree hem?"

"Oh yeah, that was the highlight of my day."

"Mine too. Well, she used to be a size 14 like me. But since her wedding diet she's literally shrunk. She's not much bigger than you now."

I could not imagine possessing such willpower. Luckily, my fast metabolism means I don't need to. "It's the bride's prerogative to crash diet and why should you care anyway? You look fab as it is. You've lost loads of weight since uni. Not that you were ever big. So you've got nothing to worry about."

"Yeah right. It'll be a long time before I'm bikini-ready. I might pretend I'm on my period to get out of Jacuzzi time."

She's splashed a drop of oil on her khaki blouse, which she hasn't even noticed. I think a speck of flour has also landed in her short, choppy hair. I love her lack of self-awareness. It makes me feel better about my un-ironed jumper with a crease down the front.

"Anyway, back to my main point. You should look into online dating. It's worth trying everything. A guy won't just fall into your lap."

Ooh, now I really want to smugly rebuff Reena's pearl of wisdom. My phone flashes with a new message. It's from him.

"Or maybe you *have* got a secret man." Reena glances at my phone from across the table before I snatch it away.

"Yeah, right, it's probably my mum." I scan the message quickly. It says something about his mum and if I can call him back. I'll have to deal with it later.

I put on my best poker face to stop myself from smiling. Every time I get a message from him I feel a flutter of excitement.

With a shared profiterole dessert obliterated, Reena and I grab the bill.

"I'll get this," I offer.

"Nah man, lets go halves."

"I insist, it's the least I can do for making you wait so long."

"Oh be quiet! We can still split the bill. You don't have to pay." Reena reaches for her purse.

This bill-fight goes on for a while. Despite us being from different countries and practicing different religions, Reena and I have many of the same Asian sensibilities. One of which is that we constantly argue over the bill. This same pretend fight was played out whenever I'd visit a relative's house when I was younger. The elders would always insist on giving me £10 as a thank you for coming over. My mum or dad would flatly refuse and sometimes it got into a full-on tussle. I, of course, would stay quiet and hope that I get to keep the money, which inevitably I would. I think I saved up for my first pair of proper branded trainers with the money from distant relatives whom I barely knew.

As Sergio the waiter arrives with card reader in hand, we're still arguing the toss.

Reena points her card at him. "Could you put half on this?"

I pull out my plastic too. "No, ignore her Sergio. Put the full amount here."

Sergio laughs. He's probably confused as I never insist on paying the bill when I'm with my usual company of Julia. I'm sure he'll figure out that it's an Asian thing.

Reena has the final word: "Right, don't be such a polite brownie and just go halves!"

I stand down, secretly pleased that I'm not £15 lighter of pocket.

As we hug and part ways, Reena seizes the opportunity to make fun of the fact that I'm on first name terms with the waiter. What can I say? I love pizza and pasta. Next time she's up I'll take her somewhere else.

I head to my car and call my boy. I didn't realise that all the fighting over the bill meant it's been about 40 minutes since he messaged me. I hope everything's okay.

He's a dead cert, and answers my call after two rings. "So I spoke to my mum, and I basically told her about us..."

That was quick.

"I didn't want to faff about any longer and since you've told your mum about me, it felt like the right thing to do."

"Wow, okay. And... how did she take it?"

"She took it well. In fact a bit too well, I think. She wants to know what you're doing next weekend?"

Shit.

20th January
I'm nervous

I'm nervous. It's so ironic that I've been waiting for this day... the day when a boy I like feels the same about me and, more to the point, he's marriage material. The right race, right religion, with a good job *and* his own space in London. It's all so... perfect. That's the scary thing. Is it *too* perfect? Am I being foolish filling my half empty glass up? Do I deserve such luck?

Things went from our own little secret, to a full-blown family affair within the space of a phone conversation. Just yesterday I spotted that he's shut down his online profile. I should be excited, relieved and glad things are moving forward. That fuzzy feeling should outweigh any nerves but I'm a worrywart and I can't help it.

The visit next weekend will be unlike any other. This time, there's no third party matchmaker involved. The boy isn't a stranger, our families won't be second guessing each other and there shouldn't be crossed-wires. However, though I set up this rishtaa visit myself, mum will treat it like a traditional arranged marriage introduction. Right down to the abundance of samosas she'll fry ahead of the meeting. All the trimmings, all the formalities. Yet the stakes are so much higher. The stakes involve the boy I think I'd like to marry.

Middle sis was the first person I called after he dropped his bombshell visit request. She was the obvious confidante.

"Awww, that's great news!" She was practically gushing down the phone. "See, I told you not all blokes off the internet are weirdoes or serial killers. After all, I lived to tell the tale!"

"True. But what if his mum doesn't like me? What if our mum doesn't like him? She was already a bit gutted when I told her he was bald. She keeps telling me about these hair transplants she's read about in the Bengali newspaper. Like he'd go for that!"

"Oh, you know what she's like, she wants a trophy groom as much as the next mum. But who cares? If he's as nice as you say, she'll be won over by him and not care about hair, or lack of. Let's just hope his mum's nice." Sis pauses before hastily adding: "Though I'm sure she will be."

Middle sis isn't entirely convincing, or reassuring. However, with her personal experience of finding a boy online and palming it off as a traditional introduction, her counsel is needed.

She continues: "The one thing I would say is this: don't act like you're already dating him. Keep up appearances and don't be over familiar. You don't want his mum thinking you're a flooze."

I didn't realise middle sis had such low expectations of me. What does she think I'd do? If funny business was off the cards during our dates, it wouldn't suddenly appear on the itinerary when we meet the parents.

As we say our goodbyes, middle sis has a parting warning: "And remember girl, nobody knows I met your brother-in-law online, so don't let the cat out of the bag with mum or your fella."

"Don't worry, your secret's safe with me. As mine is with you."

Naturally, mum is the next person I tell about this impending rishtaa visit. It's only polite, as it will be taking place at her house, with her acting as hostess.

She's unsurprisingly elated that this slow-moving vehicle is picking up the pace. "Masha Allah, that's great news. Good girl!"

I didn't get such applause when I graduated with a 2:1 degree in English and Marketing.

"So... when shall we have them round."

I'm tentative about this bit. "Well, they've asked if they can come next weekend."

"Next weekend?!"

ONE THING IS FOR SURE, us Bengali's can club together and make things happen when needs be. We simply get it sorted, like a brown mafia of sorts.

With less than a week's notice, mum has secured the attendance of both my big and middle sis to come from Bristol and Bradford respectively. It helps that my older sisters already know I've met someone. Perhaps they, like mum, were waiting for this day.

While middle sis and I bonded over our mutual secret online dating efforts (though her escapades were years before I entered unchartered digital territory - she really was a trailblazer), big sis was in the dark. She's 14 years older than me and had an arranged marriage back home in Bangladesh. I've always said it felt like there was a huge generational difference between us. She's much more prim and has that lovely

Bengali knack of giving out passive-aggressive criticism when it's both unnecessary and unfounded, so I was holding back on sharing my news with her.

When mum and dad were away at Hajj, big sis stayed over for a week with the kids. It was the half-term holiday so the kiddies got to spend time with their coolest auntie (me) and the most annoying one (little sis), while we came home to freshly cooked curry every evening. It was a win-win and I appreciated her presence. It was like having another mum around in lieu of our absent one.

One evening, little sis ditched us in favour of going to the cinema with her friends. She was clearly making the most of being free of parental curfews. I got in from a late shift at the office to find my two nieces and nephew asleep and big sis in full domestic goddess mode, cutting up a cucumber, onion and tomato salad as the rice cooker pinged to say it's done.

"Do you want some cake? I bought a Swiss roll on the way home." It was the least I could do as big sis had even hoovered mine and little sis' shared bedroom the day before.

She contemplated my offer before shaking her head. "Nah, I'll leave it. I'm supposed to be watching the sweet stuff. I want to drop a dress size by the summer."

Big sis would say this every year, despite rarely fluctuating from her size 16 frame. Her willpower is non-existent and she has the curse that inflicts all the women in our family. We're skinny fat. We breeze through our teens and twenties, eating whatever we want and never going to the gym, then age catches up and the metabolism slows. It hasn't happened to me yet but I suspect things will head that way once

I hit 30. Big sis was a petite size 10 throughout her 20s. Middle sis, who at 33 is six years older than me, was super skinny but is now hovering around a size 12. While that's by no means big, it's a reminder that nothing lasts forever and is perhaps nature's way of telling me to enjoy the Swiss roll while I can.

As I sliced into the chocolate sponge and spiralled cream, big sis had a change of heart. "Oh, go on then, I'll have a small slice."

Like I said, no willpower.

"What's happening this summer, anyway? Don't tell me you need to be burkini-ready?"

"Don't be silly. I don't even own a burkini, *or* bikini. I can't even swim. But I've got two weddings to go to on your brother-in-law's side, before he goes to Bangladesh. Without me for the first time." Big sis took comfort in her Swiss role.

"How come he's going without you this year?"

"Bangladesh stuff, to do with our house over there. It can't wait until the school holidays, apparently."

I don't know why I even ask. I never understand what's going on with my sister's other life back home. There seems to be a constant thing about land inheritance, making sure their house doesn't get encroached by squatters and who knows what else.

"Well, at least you've got two weddings to look forward to before he goes. Which means more shopping in Rusholme, no doubt."

"I was hoping it would be three but there doesn't seem to be any sign of *you* getting married."

Oh, and we were getting on *so* well.

"You need to get your skates on, little lady. Rashda's sister is getting married and she's a bit younger than you, isn't she? You're going to be 27 this summer. Isn't it time you sorted yourself out?"

And there it was. The passive-aggressive cow-bag.

"Well... if I *had* met someone, I wouldn't tell you anyway."

"Why, have you met someone?" Big sis threw me a knowing look and raised an over-plucked eyebrow. If she was doing some reverse psychology on me, it bloody worked.

"That's none of your business."

"So you have?"

I tried to stifle a smirk but I couldn't. As my best friend Julia would say, my poker face was terrible.

Seeing my smugness, big sis jumped on it. "So you *have* met someone!"

"Maybe I have."

"How exciting!" Big sis clasped her hands together in glee, just like she did after that first failed rishtaa came to visit me and we all thought it went well. "Gosh, little lady... you better tell me all about it!" She casually cut herself another slice of Swiss roll, throwing dietary caution to the wind.

"Well, I wasn't going to say anything as I wanted to tell mum first, once she got back from Hajj... but yes, I have met someone."

"So go on... who is he? What does he do? He's Bengali, right?"

"Yes, he's Bengali, don't worry. Well... he's from up north but he works in London, as an investment banker. He's a couple of years older than me and basically really nice. I'm not sure what else to say."

"It all sounds good. How did you meet?"

Big sis was the first family member to hear my fictional tale. "We were introduced through mutual friends. It was kind of like a blind date. Though we only met for coffee. And dinner, a few times."

"How exciting! Are you serious about this boy? Do you think I'll get my summer wedding?"

"Well, I'm not sure about that yet."

I said all the good stuff. All that was left was the filling in the shit sandwich, which I knew wouldn't be to big sis' taste. "So there's something else. He's really nice. A genuinely good guy and kind person... but he's bald."

Big sis clutched her head as though she was trying to stop her own hair from falling out in shock. "Oh no!"

"Don't say that!"

"I'm sorry! I just can't... oh no! I didn't see that coming! Like properly bald?"

"As bald as a baby."

"Receding?"

"No. Like really bald?"

"So does he have hair on the sides and none on top, like Mr Burns from The Simpsons?"

"What? No! Why do you think of this stuff? Actually, I don't know. If he did have side hair, I guess he shaves it off. I mean, who'd keep their hair like that, apart from dad? Anyway, when I tell mum, I need your full backing. Don't make out like the baldness is an issue."

"Oh lady, as if I would! I'm just happy you met someone. And if he lives on his own that's a bonus. At least you won't have to deal with in-laws."

"True. Plus he's exactly like me. He's outgoing, got a good social life and nice life in London."

"How lovely! If I got married in the UK, I'd have loved to have lived in London. There are so many saree shops there. Much better than Manchester. Anyway, I'm glad he's sociable. That's what I would have hoped for you. I've always said this, you're the most modern and career-driven of us girls. I envisioned you with a boy who was tall, dark-skinned and that would always be going out. Just like you."

I'm not sure where the skin tone came into it but big sis couldn't help but make a reference to my brown disposition.

She had almost devoured her second slice of cake when she stopped and put her spoon down to muse. "To be honest, I always thought that first rishtaa that came for you... you know, the tall and dark one, was your perfect match."

Why, oh why did she have to dig up the ghosts of rishtaas past? "I think you were more upset than I was that his family, or our shit matchmaker auntie Fatima, ghosted us. Anyway, can't you just be happy for me that I've met someone decent of my own accord? You said I should start looking."

"No, I am. I'm really happy for you. And of course I'll back you up when it comes to telling mum."

"Good. And no making a big thing of his baldness."

Big sis raised her hands up in surrender. "Okay... okay. One last question. Does his lack of hair make him look like an old man?"

WITH BOTH SISTERS PRIMED to attend the big event, there was one elder that was yet to be informed - dad. As always, he was the last to know, along with my teenage sis of course. Though her knowledge isn't paramount. She simply needs to show her face on the day, which would involve looking up from her phone for a millisecond.

Mum managed to have that delicate conversation with dad, where she explained how his precious daughter has eschewed the traditional arranged marriage in favour of a boy that she'd met through a friend of a friend.

Dad was surprisingly chilled about the whole thing. Perhaps he was more modern-minded than I thought. Or maybe he, like mum, was just glad I was possibly getting married. Either way, I was surprised and relieved that everyone was rolling with the situation. I also felt a bit silly about hiding in the bathroom while mum told dad the news. It wasn't as if my gentle pot-bellied father was suddenly going to rule with an iron fist and chase me round the house with a rolled up newspaper.

Now the formalities begin. This is where, as middle sis foreshadowed, the line between the online dating and arranged marriage world would become blurred.

To make it as legit as possible, I still have to submit my biodata to his family, and vice versa. Yep, I thought we were done with that crap, too. I figured that the whole point of meeting a guy through my own hunting efforts was that I could dodge some of the technicalities, with the biodata - or marital CV - being one of them. Alas, no.

Mum is taking this just as seriously as the first time I curated one, when I was genuinely single and relying on busybodies to find me a man. She corners me after work one evening when I'm hungry, therefore at my most vulnerable to go along with her whims. "We should check your biodata to see if it needs changing at all before we send it over."

I was about to tuck into my plate of rice and chicken curry. "What? Why? I already know this boy, so what's to change?"

"Oh, I *doh-no*. It's been a while since I looked at it. We might need to update."

"Nothing has happened between now and the last time we dusted it off." I lower my voice as dad comes into the room and switches on the Bangla channel to watch the news. "And again, I already know him, so I don't think anything on my CV will put him off."

I realise I'm sounding awfully cocky and glass half full. I hope this doesn't blow up in my face.

Mum mirrors my hushed tones, though her hoarse whisper is louder than her normal voice. "Yes, but it not only about boy. You need to impress mum too and you know how tricky *Bangali* mums can be? They be crafty and usually bossy. Except for me, of course."

Dad turns his attention briefly away from the news. "*Eh-heh*. I trying listen to election result. What you talking about now?"

"Nothing of your business. This women business. TV loud enough!" mum scowls before looking at my lukewarm plate. "Right, your rice needs to cool down, it's too *garam*. Get laptop in meanwhile..."

LIFE HAS A FUNNY WAY of coming full circle as I find myself adapting my biodata once again. It's a pointless exercise but I kind of get mum's logic. She wants to keep up appearances and shoehorn this very modern union into the arranged marriage mould. From what he's told me, his mum wants the same, in a bid to stop people gossiping and speculating about how we met. Given that I've also told a few fibs about our online introduction, I go along with this whole charade. However, I didn't expect mum to go *this* method with her acting. She's got me immersed in the role of my 25-year-old self, stressed over creating this make or break CV, while she's stepped back in time to be a pushy matchmaker. She relishes such exercises. It's the closest to an office job she'll ever get.

So once again, we run down my biodata basics:

- Name: nothing to change there.
- D.O.B: as above.
- Parents' village in Bangladesh (and that all important town address back home to show that we are prosperous urbanites, not backwater bumpkins): as above.
- UK address: as above.
- My vital stats: I still inwardly cringe at having to write this.

"Mum, this is pointless. It's all the same as before."

However, mum's all seeing eyes spot a fatal omission. "*Heh*, you didn't put in what you got for your degree. And you should underline the word 'masters'!"

I examine my education section. She's right. Not sure how I missed that out. I work in PR after all. Bragging is my main skill.

"It's fine. I doubt anyone noticed all the times before and it doesn't matter now. He knows I'm well educated so I'm sure that bit of info will filter down to his mum."

"It doesn't matter? Of course it matter! You should have checked better. We sent this out to Mr Choudhury without it saying you did well in your degree? Not making your masters look bigger? No wonder we -" mum stops herself mid-rant.

She was about to say something like no wonder we didn't get anywhere through the formal introductions route. I'm sure that's what she meant. Though I doubt that two numbers and a colon would have made the world of difference. I basically didn't have many options, it was as simple as that. In contrast to middle sis, who had eligible bachelors practically forming a queue for her hand in marriage, I wasn't so popular.

However, as mum is so concerned that not putting my pass grade will mean I'll fail to get past this first rishtaa meeting, I meet her halfway. I don't highlight my masters (that just seems silly and not something a girl with a masters degree would do) but I punch in 2:1 after my degree. Mum lets out a sigh of relief. Quietly and inwardly, so do I.

"Good girl. Glad that's sorted." Mum rubs her hands with satisfaction. "Now all we need is nice photo to send with the biodata."

My relief turns to resignation.

23rd January
What's in a name?

Given that this boy is coming round to my house in four days, I figure I best give him a name. Obviously he has a real name but as I've already left too many breadcrumbs which could reveal my identity, I don't want to out him.

I still haven't decided what to do with this diary. The more I write, the more I think it would make a great blog. Heck, it should be serialised in the Guardian or made into a comedy on Channel 4. Okay, maybe I'm getting ahead of myself but it *is* funny and I do think at some point, when I'm feeling brave, I shall share it with the world. So I really ought to protect my nearest and dearest by changing names and identities.

So what's in a name? What should I call this boy who might just be 'the one'? My previous naming format was admittedly childish. The first rishtaa that came through the door - Tall-boy, was, well... rather tall. At least for Bengali standards, that is. His 5ft 10in stats and sharp suit caught the eye of my mum and sisters, who were devastated when things didn't progress to a second meeting. As was I. We never found out what went wrong there. I guess it's irrelevant now as he's married and I'm kind of off the market, though I'm still pissed off with auntie Fatima. Anyway, I digress. The other two suitors weren't genuine contenders, so I nicknamed them accordingly. Small-boy was too small and Fedora hat-boy was a pompous prick.

As for my own hunting efforts, this only resulted in two dates, both equally unsuccessful. Shy-boy was too shy and Tight-git needs no further explanation. I'm still bitter about footing the bill on that occasion.

Naming this boy is harder. I can't call him Bald-boy. Well, technically I can, as this is factually accurate (thankfully, he wears it well) but it just feels wrong. I like him too much so attaching a label that highlights what most people see as a flaw is just mean. He doesn't really have any other quirks. Come to think of it, he says *to be honest with ya*, an awful lot. This proved slightly unnerving in the early days when I was figuring him out, as it suggested that every time he didn't end with that phrase he was being dishonest. I must bring that up with him sometime.

Anyway, I have to call him *something*, otherwise I'm confusing myself with the constant use of *him* and *boy*.

Oh sod it, I'm all for an easy life. His name begins with M, so that's what I'll call him: M. Yes, I'm a professional wordsmith so I should do better but, with my potential in-laws coming over this weekend, time is of the essence and I can't spend hours agonising over a moniker. There are bigger issues at large.

24th January
Déjà vu

My wardrobe is being picked apart by the most ruthless of stylists. Mum has decided that this rishtaa visit needs to be planned like a military operation. And first plan of action? Get an outfit together that WILL get me married.

This matriarch has folded and fried too many samosas for the families of boys I didn't end up marrying to risk this visit ending in anything *but* a wedding. No amount of insisting that M likes me and I like him and this is just a formality, will make mum ease up. She is determined to at least *feel* like she's project managing the whole affair.

It was bad enough having to go through the whole photo ordeal with her first time round. I still remember posing in the park in my pink salwar kameez, ignoring the advances of barking dogs and their intrigued owners, while trying to capture the following in one single shot:

I'm pretty, marry me.

I'm slim, marry me.

I'm modest, marry me.

I'm religious (but not overly so), marry me.

I'm a homemaker, marry me.

But I've got a degree (which I may or may not put to use after marriage), so marry me.

I might not be fair-skinned, but I'm not too dark either, marry me.

I can cook! So please, please marry me.

I have a newfound respect for the contestants of America's Next Top Model, who are constantly harangued by Tyra Banks to portray a million different emotions while smeyesing. In my life, mum is Tyra and there isn't a modelling contract at the end of it, there's (hopefully) a husband.

There is one saving grace. As the imminent rishtaa visit is just days away, M and I (or rather our mums) agreed that the biodata and photo exchange could take place after we've met. I question the point of this if both families will have met in the flesh but what do I know? Plus, M's mum seems as keen as mine to follow arranged marriage protocol and send my details to her oldest son, who isn't able to attend the grand occasion.

Mum takes this opportunity to do an inventory check on my saree collection.

"Why did you bother buying these cheap sarees online?"

"Well, if you remember mum, it was big sis who goaded me into getting them and £70 isn't cheap by most people's standards."

"It is for a saree that's covered in stonework! If you got something simple, it probably would have been fine, but no. You have to get *especial* sparkly-sparkly to get more bargain for money. So, of course, they cut corner with cheap quality. These stones... they're not even crystal, they be plastic!"

Mum tosses the emerald green saree onto my single bed, which is now covered in discarded clothing. Looking at it now, it is pretty hideous. The coloured stones are like sweets scattered all over the green polyester. That's the problem with online shopping, you really don't know what you're going to get until it arrives and if you don't like it, good luck trying to get a refund. That's why my Asian outfit collection is woeful. Forget ex-boyfriends, I have other skeletons in my closet, the clothing casualties of buyer's remorse.

I have a lightbulb moment. "How about using a photo from Iqbal's wedding last year? I think I looked pretty good that day, if I do say so myself."

I was wearing a blue saree with gold thread work on that occasion and impressed both standout beauties in our family, middle sis and Rashda, Iqbal's now-divorced sister.

"Yes, you looked lovely that day, Masha Allah."

That's the highest praise I'll get from mum.

Then she does her bottom lip stretching grimace thing. "But maybe you should send a photo with your hair covered. Otherwise you might look rude."

I should have known the compliment would be backhanded.

Mum gazes out of the window as if she's deep in thought. This won't be good. "Ah, I got idea. Why don't you wear that saree again? And we'll take nice picture at home."

I wonder if it's just my life that keeps coming back full circle or this is an affliction of every Bengali girl getting married? I've never known deja vu like it.

WHO KNEW SIX YARDS of material could cause such conflict? Mum and I clashed on how loose my saree should be draped, what jewellery to accessorize with and, crucially, how much of my hair should be showing in the photo.

I don't wear a hijab and mum doesn't expect me to, either. Living in a white area, we stood out enough as it is, so my parents never asked me or my sisters to cover our hair. The downside, however, of not being well-versed in hair covering means that on those rare occasions I've had to, I've not worn it well. My hair is a let-down at the best of times. So pair that with a loose covering of cloth and, well... it's not good.

As I get ready in the full-length mirror, I twist my hair up in a crocodile clip. Mum then pops behind me with a hair grip.

"Very nice," she declares after pinning the end of my saree over my head, leaving me hooded.

"No mum, lets pin it back a bit further." I loosen the grip, revealing an inch of hairline.

Mum's not impressed. "What's the point in covering your hair when most of it is showing?"

"Oh, come on mum, we know this is all for show anyway."

"*Dooro*! You always have answer for everything. Sometimes mum knows best."

Little sis walks into our room. This is my chance to enlist an ally. "What do you think of my hair like this? I still look modest, right?"

Sis examines my hairdressing efforts. "It's a bit messy on top. Here, let me fix it."

Little sis gives my crown a backcomb. I'm surprised at how quickly she can get to work. Someone's obviously been watching YouTube tutorials when they should be revising for their A-levels.

She then takes the grip out and reaches for a gold encrusted brooch of mum's that I borrowed once and never returned back to her room. She expertly feeds it through my hair and the saree achal. It holds my hair much better. I'm not sure why mum didn't try that. She should have known as *she's* the one who wears a headscarf outside the house.

"There. You're more presentable now." Little sis smooths down my side-parting. "I'd almost say marriage material. Until you open your mouth, that is."

I'll let that little dig slide as sis has done a pretty good job with my mane. I'm impressed by how much she has changed over the last year. She's morphed from moody, mono-syllabic teen, to someone who actually adds value to a conversation. Just a few months ago, I resented having to share a room with her. I lamented the lack of privacy. The fact that most girls my age had either moved out of home (well, my white friends anyway), or owned their own room at least, didn't help. Heck, Reena even owns her own house. Though she doesn't actually live in it, she bought it as an investment with her older sisters and she makes a pretty decent rental income. Though that's not the point. She has her own room *and* a bloody house. I, on the other hand, must make do with a solitary single bed next to a nearly 17-year-old. I have zero personal touches in my own room. It's all magnolia walls, cream carpet, and whichever bedding comes out of the wash. Even little sis has managed to make her mark with a giant world map on the wall, which is apparently for her studies. FYI, she's not chosen geography as a subject.

Happily, all of the stuff that used to really grate on me doesn't bother me in the slightest anymore. I think I've reached a good middle ground, both in my life and with my sister. She is no longer the little shit she used to be. In fact, I think my newfound sunny demeanour after meeting M, has made me easier to live with and, as a result, she is easier to live with, too.

So now that the youngster and I are getting on so well, I can drop her into one aspect of this onerous rishtaa preparation.

As she's about to head out of our room, clutching the mobile phone charger that she originally came in for before being distracted by my fashion failings, I harangue her for one more job.

"I don't suppose you want to take some photos of me, do you?"

IT TURNS OUT THAT ENLISTING an Instagram-obsessed teen to take my photo is possibly one of the best decisions I could have made. As she snaps away on her phone, that has a much better camera than mine, I look passably pretty and little sis introduces me to this great thing called the golden hour. She moves me towards the best lighting in our living room, giving me this natural glow. I'm oozing warmth, with the sun hitting all the right angles.

"You know, you could add a little filter. Just to make you look a little... prettier?"

"You're alright. Filters go against my very nature. I want to still look like me."

Sis rolls her eyes. "God... You're such a bra-burning feminist. Everyone uses filters. I bet the guy coming round is probably no stranger to a bit of retouching, so you should do a little something. First impressions and all that."

Bless her, she really has no clue.

"Even so, I think I look pretty good in these photos as it is."

"Okay, your potential husband, your choice. If you do change your mind, there is a great new filter that will chisel your cheekbones. It will make your face look less egg-shaped."

What is it with my family and sly digs? With that, sis leaves with phone and charger in hand.

Even Mum is impressed with her creative photography work. My only regret is that I didn't use her earlier instead of mum, when I first posed for those corny pictures in the park. I probably would've been married by now.

9th September
But I'm not hungry

I really ought to eat that samosa. I love samosas. Granted, the lettuce side salad looks a little limp and the chicken tikka is over-cooked but the seekh kebabs are on point.

"You should eat something," little sis verbalises my thoughts as she's sat next to me carving into her starters.

"I'm just not hungry," I reply.

"Are you sure? Or is sitting in front of 600 strangers who are watching your every move putting you off a bit?"

"Well, they're not all strangers but yeah, that might have something to do with it."

Why, oh why, am I on display for everyone to see me make a food-based faux pas? On my wedding day? Surely, given that I'm not exactly the most elegant of eaters, I should have been given a separate room to dine with dignity.

I glance down at my plate. The samosa is begging me, calling me to eat it. Then I look up. Every man, woman and dog has a bloody camera in their hand waiting to catch me in a compromising position, like talking with my mouth full.

The grand hall is packed with people. Its high, echoing ceiling, decorated with gold and green swirls as if it's some low rent Sistine Chapel (I haven't been but I've seen Sophia's pictures), only serves to make the muffled chatter of the many guests vibrate through the room. It's like white noise and it's giving me a headache.

I knew M said his family were well-connected and pillars of the community but come on. It seems like the entire Bangladeshi contingent of the North West is here. That's Bengalis for you. I'm pretty sure mum mentioned inviting the lady who used to teach me Bangla when I was five. I doubt she even still has Mrs Begum's number. Mum probably had to go to great lengths to dig it out.

I've never seen so many blingy sarees in my life. There's a sea of shimmering green, which reminds me that everyone thankfully adhered to the dress-code. Why did we choose green? Big sis must've been snorting something when she came up with that colour scheme. I mean, green? Why did I even agree to it? Every other wedding I've been to in the last five years has had a theme of peach, pink, or some version of purple. Never have I seen green. That's usually the reserve of the mehendi ceremony.

As I scan the room, I see that someone's flouted the dress code. As if that wasn't taking the piss enough, they've adopted *my* bridal colour scheme. The woman is wearing a deep, burgundy saree with a gold blouse. Just who is this cocky cow? The brave Mrs turns around. No way. No... bloody... way. It's auntie Fatima. She's got a nerve, lording it up in her dazzling saree on *my* wedding day! Oh my life, who is that I spot with her? Surely not? Surely that's not her niece that she tried to match make with Tall-boy, even though *she* introduced him to us in the first place. I can't believe she is still hawking this poor girl around. Clearly she's not married yet.

And clearly auntie Fatima is unrelenting in her mission to set her up with some willing British-born boy.

"Who the hell invited her?" I whisper to mum, nodding my rather heavy head, weighed down by my lehenga dupatta, in the direction of my very flaky fake auntie.

"Shush." Mum looks at me with bulging, angry eyes that are saying *don't cause a scene on your own wedding day.* "It be rude if you no invite these people. We've known them for years. They're from your dad's village."

Well, it's bloody rude when you play matchmaker and then ghost the family just after getting their hopes up. Not to mention getting *my* hopes up. Not that I'm bitter, or still pining after Tall-boy, but how dare she?

As always, formalities trump feelings. It's more important to mum to show face than face off with auntie Fatima. I've inherited that Bengali stiff upper lip, too, as while I think all this, I don't dare say it. Plus, with all these prying eyes (not to mention nosey ears), this probably isn't the conversation to have right now. I hope her chicken tikka is extra chargrilled, preferably inedible. Yeah, I'm petty like that.

"Anyway, you no worry about her. You just eat. You *dohno* when you get to eat next," says mum.

That's a little dramatic. Though mum always says you never know what you're going to get with the in-laws, I'd like to think I'll get fed. At some point at least. Plus, it's the one time that mum has actively encouraged me to eat in polite Bengali company.

I really should try to eat something, though. After all, if I can't eat now, I'm pretty sure I'll be a floundering bag of nerves when eating at my new mother-in-law's house.

Just as I'm about to dive into my samosa, I hear a familiar and comforting voice.

"You look beautiful," says Julia.

I doubt that anybody in the history of weddings has ever greeted a bride by saying she looks ugly but I'll take the compliment nonetheless.

Julia is decked out in a turquoise salwaar kameez. I'm touched by the effort.

"Check you out! You wear Asian outfits better than I do. Turquoise really is your colour."

"Awww, thanks. I wanted it to be a surprise for you. I got it from that place you always talk about. Is it *rush home*?" she asks, pronouncing it exactly how I'd expect her to.

"Well, I hope you haggled."

"Err... No I didn't actually. Should I have? It was only £150. So I figured I got a pretty good deal." Julia looks down at her salwar kameez with buyer's remorse.

Poor Julia. She should've paid half that price but hey, she's a lawyer. She can afford it.

"No, it's fine and well worth it."

Over Julia's shoulder I spot my cousin Rashda, who's dressed her hair with an emerald jewelled tikka, which is glistening beneath her loosely worn matching headscarf. I've yet to see her in any style she can't pull off. Even at her seemingly worst, when she was thinner, more fragile and dressed in muted colours at her brother Iqbal's wedding, she was still beautiful.

"How are you feeling?" she asks as she bends down next to my chair.

"I'm good, though I've strangely gone off samosas, which is most unlike me."

Rashda looks over at my barely touched plate. "It's not the samosas, you're nervous," she says, a voice of experience. "I was the same on my wedding day. Couldn't eat a thing."

That's strange, I think to myself. I don't feel nervous.

Despite bonding at Iqbal's nuptials over a mutual appreciation of my saree choice and a shared hatred of weddings (though I've since changed my tune on the latter now I'm no longer single), I'm still unsure of what to say to her. We never see each other outside of a family function. She's middle sis' age, has three kids and always had an air of detachment about her. Softly spoken, sophisticated and a little too perfect, Rashda was almost intimidating to be around. Plus the constant backbiting about her I was privy to growing up didn't help matters.

Still, I should make some effort as she's come over to see me. I just have to be sure to steer the topic away from her ill-fated marriage. In fact, I should take weddings in general off the table.

"So... do you have any words of wisdom to impart?"

Bloody hell. That's exactly what I *wasn't* going to ask her.

She laughs. "I'm not sure if I'm the best person to advise you on that."

I laugh nervously, too. I'm such a knob.

"I guess if I was to give you any advice, I would say be your own woman. Don't rely on your husband too much. Never quit your job, hold on to your money. It's important to keep something for yourself that defines you beyond being married. Otherwise, before you know it, he'll hold all the cards."

Rashda looks over to her table, where auntie Jusna is sat giving her daughter a narrow-eyed stare that screams *don't you dare*.

She continues on regardless: "And no matter what, if you and your hubby fall out, don't involve your parents, or his. Once you let your mum into your marriage, even if it's for advice, you'll open a can of worms that you won't be able to contain."

I'm not sure how to respond. I didn't expect such frank advice in this setting. People might hear her. Perhaps she no longer cares.

"Ha! I bet you wish you'd never asked!" says Rashda, no doubt sensing the awkwardness.

As she leaves me to my samosa, I wonder if it's Rashda's divorce and the subsequent community judgement that's humbled her, or whether she was always pretty down to earth. Maybe the perception of coldness was something that was put upon her, rather than a true reflection of who she is.

"Sorry, I forgot to get a picture," Julia interrupts my thoughts with her swinging selfie stick, which narrowly avoids yanking off my carefully pinned scarf.

She crouches down next to me in Rashda's place, stick now suspended in the air and tilts her head towards mine. "I need to get in there whilst I can, you're very popular today."

As Julia clicks away, I see what she means. Her initiative in approaching me for a photo has sparked a revolution. There's a line of people, mostly women, each more blingy than the last, inching their way through the makeshift pretend aisle towards me. It's like a scene from Braveheart or Game of Thrones, where all the angry soldiers run up the hill, seemingly out of nowhere, to the battleground. Except they're jostling to have their picture taken with me.

Well, I guess mum, little sis and Julia were right. I really should have eaten while I had the chance because I sure as hell won't be able to now.

27th January
Today's the day

Oh, bloody answer your phone, Julia. That girl is never free when I need her. I know she's a busy lawyer living in central London, helping divorced, wealthy couples mediate. However, it would be nice if she could be on standby just *sometimes*. Just for those moments when my potential future husband is due to arrive with his family, except they're running so late that my nerves are kicking in big time.

I know this one is in the bag. At least I *think* it's in the bag. M and I are sure of each other. We've been seeing each other since last April. By Bengali standards, that's like the equivalent of two years of dating. Even so, this will be the first time I see his family. And I really, really hope they like me. In fact, right now, I hope they actually turn up.

Meanwhile, my mum, from 2pm in the afternoon, has made a truckload of samosas, all freshly fried. She even diversified her standard starter plate for the first time ever. Instead of samosas, samosas, and more samosas, mum has thrown spring rolls into the mix. This was my middle sister's influence. She's just started making them herself and insisted that mum broaden her range.

She came over from Bradford early in the morning to give mum a dry run.

After examining the thin, crispy, tubular pastry, mum looked decidedly unimpressed. "Aren't they same thing? I mean, with same keema filling. So why not make more of my samosa?"

Middle sis had a brainwave, which was scary for all of us. "Well, if you like, we could make a different filling, like spicy vegetables? Or we've got time to defrost some chicken breast so we can make some chicken spring rolls instead."

Mum looked nervous and did her lip grimace thing. She should've seen it coming. Middle sis is known for making a mountain out of a molehill when it comes to cooking. What may start as a modest meal, suddenly turns into a five-course tasting menu. The problem is, we're the mugs left with the lion's share of the work and the washing up, as middle sis is more of a sous chef than a head chef. She's great with chopping, prepping and stirring. However, in terms of seeing something through, she's usually missing in action. Whether it's to tend to a crying child or a 'quick' call to hubby that lasts for 45 minutes, middle sis finds a way to walk away from the mess she created. Starter-finisher she is not.

However, she knows how to get to mum. She played on her weak spot, which is a deep-seated desire to get me married. "Look, first impressions and all that. You don't want her prospective in-laws to think we're stingy or we can't cook, do you?"

And with that beautifully executed money shot, the chicken breast was hastily defrosted. More onions were finely diced. Some sweetcorn was deployed. The whole thing was then bundled together in a spicy coating and sheathed tightly in a spring roll pastry.

Mid fold, middle sis got an urgent call from upstairs: "Mum! I tried to pooh in the toilet but I missed!"

Just like that, middle sis left mum and I to finish up the spring roll mess she started, while she tended to her daughter's mess upstairs.

MUM'S TETCHY. SHE was expecting an after lunch visit. Then 2pm became 3pm, which then became 4pm. Now the clock says 5.30pm. Mummy dearest is getting into a serious flap.

"They are coming, aren't they?" Mum inadvertently plants a seed of doubt in my mind.

"Of course they are, they wouldn't suddenly cancel. He messaged me this morning to say he's looking forward to meeting everyone."

"Okay *dooro*! You don't need to make obvious that he be your *especial* friend. Have some *shorom*. Show some shame! Your dad will hear."

Mum is a trailblazer in many ways. She encouraged me to go on a date with Shy-boy. Heck, she made me go to after work drinks because her Bangla paper said networking would advance my career. Yet she still feels uncomfortable about me talking openly about M.

She examines the fruits of her labour. "What will I do with all the samosas now? And those silly Billy spring rolls?"

"What do you mean?" I ask. "They won't be wasted. They're still coming. They're just running a bit late."

"A bit late! Bit late, you say? I know Bangla timing is bad but this is terrible. I heard that people who live in Asian area are always extra late. They have lunch at 4, dinner at midnight. No sense of time. Just like Rashda *maa*."

Mum can't help but make a sly dig. M's family used to live in an Asian area but have since moved to Droylsden and are as much the only brownies in the village as we are. However, as mum's already miffed that I'm talking openly about my special friend who's missing in action, I'll keep that bit of info to myself.

Instead, I head upstairs to examine my makeup. En route I bump into middle sis on our small square landing.

She puts her phone down. "Did you lay out the cushions I brought over?"

"Yes, we did."

"Good. Does it look better? We really need to break up the beige downstairs. Wooden laminate, beige sofa, brown rug. It's all so bland down there. I told mum ages ago to change the curtains. There was a sale at Dunelm, but it's too late now. Everything is back to full price. Anyway, while we're on the subject of beige, are you sure you want to wear that gold number? You might blend in with the walls."

"Well, I'm not getting changed now. I've matched my eyeshadow and everything. And you could've helped us tidy up downstairs. Mum's been doing my head in and she's been henpecking dad, even more so than usual. I've never seen him hoover so quickly. All while you've been on the phone to your fella."

"All right, all right. Well, I wasn't *only* on the phone to him. Big sis called, too. She wants to see how things are going as she's on her way. Do you know when they'll be coming?" Middle sis edges closer to mumble. "I think mum's being a nervous Purvis. That's probably why she's a nightmare."

The last thing I need is another reminder about my potential future husband's lateness.

Middle sis reads my anxious face. "Anyway, I'm sure they'll be here soon. You just top up your lipstick. It looks like most of it has gone on that samosa you had earlier."

The doorbell rings. Thank God. However, instead of hearing the polite salaams which would signify the arrival of M and his family, I hear the dulcet tones of my eldest sister. "Oh golly! Are they not here yet?"

I'M NOT SURE WHAT TO do with myself. I've reapplied my lipstick. I've written in my iPhone notes the places in the Far East I'd like to visit, based on what I see on my sister's world map. Little sis herself, who is normally a permanent fixture in our bedroom, is nowhere to be seen. Typical. Julia's still not got back to me, silly cow. I daren't bother Sophia. She was my constant go to for all things boy related. I confided in her when Tall-boy and his family went quiet. She gave her ruthlessly honest appraisal of Shy-boy and Tight-git. She's basically a cooler, more liberal, older sister. I could really do with her conversation at a time like this but she's got bigger fish to fry. Life with a new baby is probably pretty demanding given her lack of contact and she gets curt when she's stressed or out of patience.

Should I message him? You know, just to find out where he is? This morning he texted me saying he can't wait to see me and he's really looking forward to the next step. For once, he didn't add *to be honest with ya*. For once, I wish he did.

My phone pings. He must have read my mind: *We're just around the corner. Can't wait to see you :)*

M ARRIVES WITH A MODEST entourage of his mum, dad, younger brother and teenage sister. As I make my way downstairs and check my reflection in the hallway mirror, I can hear the muted conversation of my dad and M's in the front room. They're breaking one of the polite dinner party rules.

"I've always supported the BNP," says my potential future father-in-law.

Thankfully, he is referring to the Bangladeshi National Party, not the racist British equivalent. Though this presents another potential ticking time bomb... they're both on opposite sides of the political fence. This could get tasty.

After a long silence on my dad's part, he mutters: "We're an *Awa-Malik* family."

Another silence.

I can tell dad's trying to be restrained because if there's one thing that gets him riled up, it's politics. One time, when I was younger, I heard him shout *'bash-tard'* at the TV, at whom I came to realise was a politician from the BNP.

His declaration about our politics as a family is a bit strong. I know nothing about the Bangladeshi corridors of power. It took me years to realise that dad was actually saying Awami League, not *Awa-Malik*, who are currently in charge according to Wikipedia. Dad doesn't tell me anything.

It seems like M's brother is sitting this one out. Sensible.

"Hurry up!" hisses big sis as she breaks my internal stream of consciousness / earwigging, which I attempted to disguise by slowly adjusting my scarf in the mirror.

I do as I'm told and head to the dining room. The first family member I see is arguably the most important - the matriarch.

For a woman in her early 60s, his mum is very well put together. There is none of this muted tone that my mum often goes for. She is wearing a vivid silk sea green saree. Plus, she's got the bling to boot. The bangles are jingly, her earrings are dangly. However, despite the glamorous get-up, there are some hints of hard work and a life lived. Her hands are weathered and dry and underneath her black flowery scarf, I see a full head of grey hair. My mum reached for the bottle of dye years ago.

Overall, I'm rather impressed with M's mum. I just hope she feels the same about me. I really wish I'd changed from my gold salwar kameez in favour of something more festive. I'm hoping this hue doesn't make me look dark.

Middle sis and big sis are decked out in light blue tones. They didn't tell me they'd be matchy matchy. Little sis has opted for a chic white number with black beaded embellishments. It's like they're all trying to upstage me.

God, I need to stop being so paranoid. M has come to see *me*. His family has come to see *me*. Yet I can't help but feel that his mum has seen my elder sisters and expected the same. No matter how hard I try and regardless of the fact that I've met somebody of my own accord, I just can't shake off this deep-rooted belief that fair is beautiful and I am, therefore, not.

His mum is looking right at me. She's not quite smiling. Is that disappointment I detect? Or maybe, like me, when she's not smiling she has something of a scowl. I wouldn't quite call it a resting bitch face. That would be disrespectful, especially if she may go on to become my mother-in-law.

Her unsure face changes as the corners of her mouth curl up into a smile. "*Kitha khoro?*"

This roughly translates into '*what are you doing?*' in Bengali. Though what she really means is '*how are you?*' Don't ask me why.

"*Jee koontha nai,*" I reply, quite literally saying, *oh nothing much.*

M's mum reverts back to a confused face.

That was stupid. I think I was meant to say something like '*oh I'm well*,' or '*how are you?*' I am so very crap at this. The two-and-a-half decades of speaking in broken Bangla to my parents really hasn't paid dividends on this important occasion. Some people find it endearing. I know of many a Bengali immigrant mum who boasts about the fact that their child can't speak fluently. My family, however, are different. Mum has always been a little mortified about my poor command of Bengali. The tutor she employed when I was younger soon gave up, citing irreconcilable differences. What she meant was that I was a smart ass and questioned EVERYTHING. I wish I'd paid more attention during those lessons rather than giving attitude.

Mum rescues the situation by introducing two plates of samosas and spring rolls. I bet she's glad of the variety now.

Mum and M's mum exchange a few pleasantries, which are punctuated by a tonne of awkward silences.

"Have you always lived in Droylsden?" It's rhetorical, as mum knows the answer.

"No, we moved there three years ago. We used to live in Oldham."

"Oh. What made you move?" Mum is undoubtedly secretly wondering why M's family would move from an Asian area to a town that is possibly as white as ours. Like me, mum has always dreamt of living in a place where we're not the only ethnic minority.

Mummy M hesitates. "Oh... just, we thought good idea for getting bigger house."

Big sis, who's taken a back seat so far, assumes the role of umpire, darting looks from mum to mum during this most unnatural exchange.

I can see mum's face. She has a follow-up question.

"But bigger house when you have smaller family now?"

M's mum let's out a stifled, uncomfortable giggle. That's her answer.

The pleasantries continue on like this, awkward and stilted. I guess it's understandable as our two families are thrown together and may potentially be wedded together forever. Yet here we are, having to chat like casual acquaintances. The funny thing with meeting the in-laws is that everything is short and sweet. After a few polite words on my part and an exchange of nervous smiles, my briefing with the mother-in-law is over.

I've not seen M yet. I'm assuming he's the last item on the agenda, just like every other rishtaa meeting I've had. Instead, his younger brother and teenage sister come into the room. I'm guessing the brother was with M in the front room while the sister chatted in the kitchen with little sis. It's not that we're backward like that but on occasions like this, we do like to create a pretend gender divide of sorts.

His brother looks like a miniature version of M. A couple of inches shorter, slightly more rotund and also sans hair. There must be some male pattern baldness going on. He's dressed visitor casual, with dark jeans and a black hoodie. His face expresses pure bewilderment as he realises he's outnumbered in a room chock-full of women. Each dining chair has been utilised and our brown sofa is creaking under the weight of so many bums. Thankfully, I'm not adding to the pressure. As the delicate, prospective bride-to-be, I have my own seat further away from everybody else, near the safety of our curtain.

His brother flicks his head towards me. "A'right?"

"Yeah, I'm good. How are you?" I ask.

"Yeah a'right."

That's about the extent of it then.

His little sister smiles but doesn't say anything to me, though I'm not offended. From the sounds of things, she's bonded with my teenage sister, who has followed her into the living room to continue their conversation about whatever crap they were talking about.

M's little sis is quite the opposite of her brothers. She's small and petite, probably a size six and no taller than five foot. Like her mum, she seems to have made a real effort for the occasion. Her red-highlighted hair is curled and she's sporting a pair of rather obvious false eyelashes. Even I'm not wearing falsies and *I'm* the one on show. I wonder if I should have made more of an effort. Maybe it's something girls do when they're from Asian areas. She definitely looks more at ease in her maroon salwar kameez than my little sister is in her outfit. Her usual uniform is tracksuit bottoms and a hoodie.

Then big sis suggests something unorthodox. "Do you want to go to the other room?" She raises an eyebrow as if she's suggesting something scandalous. So instead of M coming to visit me in my living room chamber, I'm going to him like the independent woman I am.

She goes on ahead, my big sis leading the way in this big step in my life. Before she opens the door, she shoots me an enthusiastic grin. She is *so* excited about this.

Big sis pushes open the door to reveal M, my potential husband, sat looking rather fetching in a black suit and pale pink shirt. He threatened to wear something casual like his usual uniform of chinos or jeans, paired with a shirt and V-neck jumper. Thank God he dropped that idea. I love the pop of pink and I adore the fact that he wears colours. On our first date he wore a sky blue jumper under his brown leather bomber jacket. I'd grown tired of seeing navy, khaki, black and more black adorned by other boys I'd met or been introduced to. His clothing choice was as bright and hopeful then as it is today.

Big sis clasps her hands together, like a proud matchmaker. "Right, well... I'll leave you two to chat."

As I sit down on the very far corner of the opposite sofa to M, I suddenly feel a wave of awkwardness. This is like our first meeting in Caffe Nero. It's much more formal then our lunches at Nando's and far less fun than our bowling date. Without realising, I go into resting bitch face mode.

"You look nice," says M.

I stare at him with a furrowed brow. He knows what I mean. My eyebrows are ushering him to keep his voice down. I don't know what's wrong with me.

"Are you okay?" M now looks just as unsure as I do.

"Yeah, I'm fine."

Why am I being so frosty?

"What have you been up to today?"

Waiting for you guys to bloody arrive, I think.

My niece bursts into the room. "Can I have a samosa? There's no more left in the kitchen."

Middle sis isn't far behind her. "Hey you, I saved you one, come back here. Sorry, it's my daughter's favourite snack. Enough to make her overcome any shyness among strangers."

I actually don't mind the distraction of a little person. "It's fine. She can stay if she wants."

My niece comes in and perches herself next to me, pleased as punch that there is a plate of three samosas in front of us.

"Shall I put the TV on for you guys? It will give you something to... watch?"

It's a rhetorical question, as middle sis grabs the remote and furiously starts punching in some numbers. The first thing to come on is EastEnders and we find ourselves faced with a full-on kissing scene. I can see in the corner of my eye M is looking at me with an embarrassed smirk. My sister quickly changes the channel to a much more respectable episode of the Great British Bake Off.

"I want Tiny Pop!" My niece looks as though she's about to have a screaming tantrum.

"It's not on now. It's too late," says middle sis.

"It *is* mum! We always watch it at night time so you and dad can watch your programmes in the other room."

Middle sis lets out a nervous laugh. "That's not true! We only let you watch it on the weekends. Anyway, let me find the channel."

Unfortunately, the next channel middle sis finds is not Tiny Pop. In fact, it's not child friendly at all. Instead of the bright, colourful cartoon characters we were all expecting, there's a woman in a state of undress sat on the bed on the phone, staring into the camera while saying things I daren't repeat. I forgot to mention to middle sis that we recently ended our Sky subscription and changed internet service providers for a better deal. As a result all our channels are mixed up.

Middle sis is dying to laugh, while nervously trying to change the channel. Luckily, my niece didn't notice the dodgy channel we stumbled upon as she's busy tucking into a crispy golden samosa. I can't help but laugh and neither can M. If nothing else, it's broken the ice and thawed my frosty mood. I've said it before and I'll say it again, whether or not the meetings with rishtaas are successful, they always provide shit loads of comedy material.

29th January
Not the only brownie

Oh yeah, I've got a new job.

I forgot to mention this little titbit earlier because, you know, busy trying to get married and all that.

Before I met M, I was shortlisted for a regional PR role in a healthcare group. Obviously, my newly adopted positive glass half full streak didn't just come good on the man front. It bagged me a new role, too.

It's quite the departure from my previous role at the PR agency in the arse end of nowhere. I've gone from a busy, intrusive (in more ways than one) open plan office, to a small team who are largely missing in action due to endless site visits and remote working. However, the colleagues that are in the office most days are a really cool bunch. They're mostly my age, with a couple in their early 30s. We listen to the radio while we work and for once I'm not the only brownie in the room. As a result, I'm no longer on the receiving end of nosey questions about arranged marriages, Ramadan or what I ate at home last night (did the curry smell give it away?).

However, my fellow woman of colour, Bushra, isn't exactly a sister from another Mister. As Muslims go, we couldn't be more different. She's Pakistani, 28, and flat shares with two white girls. She frequents the bars of the city and often regales me with stories of what happened the night before at the Printworks, Manchester's clubland that I've only heard about. In the short time I've been working here, I've never known her to be hangover-free on a Monday morning. Naturally, all these shenanigans take place while her parents are blissfully unaware, living miles away in Leicester. They assumed their darling daughter moved cities for work.

If that sounds judge-y of me, let me add that Bushra and I have become good friends. She is constantly laughing at my sarcastic jokes and I just love her stories. She's single, more than ready to mingle and reminds me a little of myself when I was navigating this confusing dating world. Though her version sounds much more fun. It's nice to no longer be the single one. I actually have something to talk about on Mondays when we come back to work. As I tend to meet M every other weekend, I've at least got a lunch or coffee date to provide feedback on.

Though it's not to say that the awkwardness isn't still there.

Bushra predictably strolls into work at 9.45am (her unofficial start time). Her mascara is ever so slightly smudged. Luckily, our boss Bernadette, who tends to have a hands-off management style, is nowhere to be seen.

"What did you get up to on the weekend?" Bushra asks.

Do I mention the visit from my prospective in-laws? Bushra thinks we're still casually dating.

I decide that lying is the best option in this situation. "Err... nothing much."

Bushra shoots me a coy smile. "Did you meet your boy?"

"Oh yeah. We grabbed a coffee."

"I bet that's not the only thing you grabbed." With that witty remark, Bushra falls into a fit of giggles with her co-marketeer, Emma, who looks equally hung over. They go out together on the weekends, and Sunday night is like Friday to them.

"I'm saying nothing," I reply.

Emma gulps her extra strong black coffee. "At least one of us is getting some action."

They have no idea that my dates are more halal than Chicken Cottage. I still don't correct them, though. I'm finally fitting in somewhere.

Our office is deathly empty. Most of the marketing managers are out on site visits. The only other person in the small, basic room is James, the finance officer for our department. Thankfully, he is an unassuming grey-haired guy in his 40s who sits as far away from us as possible and generally keeps himself to himself. I think he's learnt to drown out our girly and sometimes inappropriate chats.

As Emma disappears into the kitchen to get her second strong coffee of the day, Bushra seizes the opportunity for a sisterly talk. "In all seriousness, is he being a gentleman?"

"Yeah, he really is."

"That's so good to hear. I never meet guys like that."

"Don't get me wrong, but going to Revolution every weekend isn't necessarily going to help you find your dream man."

Bushra looks at me, surprised at my response. I'm surprised she's surprised. We're always bantering with each other. Though maybe that was too close to the bone.

She sighs. "I know, I know. I keep saying to myself I'll start going out less. Especially as I've been broke since last month's Christmas parties. God, why do there have to be so many? Then again, bars and clubs are kind of my only social life. I don't always want to go drinking. It's the girls... they make me. We went to a beer garden last night. I was freezing my bum off. I'd much rather be at home with a nice man. It's just so hard. I mean, where should I go to find a decent guy?"

"You're not gonna like this suggestion but have you thought about trying to meet a nice Pakistani boy?"

Bushra does a lip grimace thing not dissimilar to my mum's awkward face. "I just don't think I'll have much in common with anyone from the community. I doubt many boys will want to take home a Muslim girl who drinks and is more familiar with the Davids of this world than the Dawoods."

"Well, you never know. One of my good friends is always saying there is someone for everyone. In fact, she's Pakistani. Should I ask her if she knows of anyone suitable?"

"Hmm... I think I'll leave it for now. I'd rather meet someone of my own accord then have it... you know, arranged."

Even Bushra, who from what I hear has been brought up in a typical Pakistani Muslim household, sees arranged marriages as a desperate last resort.

"There is, of course, another option," I say. "You could go online?"

"No, I'm not that desperate yet, but never say never."

As Bushra believes I've got the perfect Bollywood romance, I wonder whether to let her in on my little secret.

"I'll be honest with you, because you know that's how I am. You might want to consider changing your views on arranged marriages and going online. Neither are as bad as you think."

Bushra looks away from her laptop and focuses on me. "Do you know anyone who's been online?"

"Well... actually -"

Emma stomps back in, spilling half her coffee on the threadbare grey carpet en route to her desk. "Right, what did I miss? Actually, if it's you bragging about your love life, I'd rather not hear it."

"This one's trying to convince me to go online to find a man," says Bushra.

Emma slams her cup down, emptying what remained in it across her desk. "Oh shit! There go my meeting minutes. Bollocks! I'll see if I can salvage it with some kitchen wipes. Oh, and you're wasting your breath. I've been trying to get Bushra to go on MateMatch for the past year and she's having none of it. She thinks she'll only meet serial killers and rapists on there."

As Emma leaves again, Bushra leans over the office divider to talk in secret tones with the other brownie in the office. "You've probably guessed, I don't really talk about arranged marriages with Emma. She wouldn't really understand, so it's best not to confuse things."

"Oh, don't worry," I say. "I know all about keeping *that* world a secret."

11th February

Not again

Not again. Not this shit again. I can't take it.

Was I too cocky? Was I too presumptuous that me and M were a sure thing? Didn't I care enough? Did I take him for granted? Didn't his mum like me? Was I too much of a miserable cow when we had our obligatory one-to-one chat in my front room? I don't know why I was miserable. I don't know why I'm single-handedly messing up my chances of a happily ever after.

It's been a solid two weeks since M's family and mine congregated together over samosas, spring rolls and the prospect of our union. I expected - no, I assumed - there would be some sort of follow-up. A courtesy call which says we like your daughter, let's move things forward. I'd come to expect rejection with rishtaas of old. The boys I was introduced to through the formal route knew nothing of me and owed me nothing. This time it should be different, shouldn't it?

I vowed to myself I would never experience the same horrible feelings I did when we didn't hear back from Tallboy. Yet here I am.

M and I are still talking with the same frequency as always. We message about 10 times a day and even more so at night. Luckily, little sis is too busy on her own phone in her own single bed to notice my fervent typing. I see her phone brightly lit under her duvet, too. Who knows, maybe she's got a boy of her own. She better not, though. I need to be settled first. I am a decade older.

Anyway, while me and the boy are acting like everything is normal, deep down I'm wondering what the hell is going on. Unfortunately for me, so is mum. Every day we've been having the same conversation.

"You spoke to him today?"

"Yeah, we spoke at lunch."

"So what's going on? Is his mum saying anything?"

"Well, it's a bit harder, as he's in London, they're up north and they don't speak every day. I'm not sure if he's heard anything from them."

"What do you mean? Not heard anything? Surely they done some chatting?"

"Mum, that's all I know so far. I can't ask for much more. Remember, you're the one that's always warning me not to sound desperate."

"Okay but time be passing, no? If there be problem they need tell us now. How about he speaks to his dad?"

"There is no problem! Not everyone is in as much of a hurry to get their kids married as you are. And I already told you, his dad doesn't really get involved in these kind of things. Just like dad, really."

Mum can't argue on that front.

"Fine but remember, Mr Choudhury has his *especial* offer so we can meet other boys."

I need to talk to M. It's getting ridiculous. How do I approach the tender subject without sounding, as mum always says, desperate?

ON OUR NEXT LUNCHTIME check-in, from the confines of my car, I decide to grow a pair of balls.

"Have you spoken to your mum at all?"

"Err, I did a couple of days ago. Why? Is everything okay?"

"It's just that your mum hasn't called my mum yet. You know how these silly things go, with your side having to make the initial step."

"Oh yeah, I did ask her about that. She said she hasn't called your mum but she will get round to it soon."

Soon? When is soon? Is there no sense of urgency with this family? Of course, as always, my Bengali/PR politeness gets in the way of me saying this out loud.

Talk turns to our favourite topic, what we had for lunch. Though I've somewhat lost my appetite.

"I better go, I was only meant to pop out for a meal deal. I've got to write a press statement before 3 o'clock."

I wonder if M notices my hasty tone? It's unlikely. What I've learnt of him so far is that, like most men, he's tone deaf when it comes to passive-aggressive emotional females.

Naturally, the evening brings another line of questioning from mum. I know she means well and is just being a concerned mum. However, at the same time, she's not just planting a seed of doubt in my head. She's grown a bloody oak tree.

I have to get out for some fresh air. More importantly, I have to cut the crap with M and get to the root of the problem, if there is one.

As I put on my shoes, dad approaches me in the hallway.

"Are you going out? If you do, take coat. It looks like it going to be rain."

"Okay dad. That's the problem with Manchester. It always rains."

"Yes yes. *Eh*, since you out, get me phone card top up from shop. Lyca mobile please. And don't be long! It already dark. Actually, I come with you?"

"No, it's okay. I've got my phone on me."

As I leave the claustrophobia of our cul-de-sac, I can't quite escape Joe, the resident creepster.

I hear his wolf whistle before I even see him. It never gets old. Without fail, he does this every time he sees me, despite the fact that he's the same age as my eldest sister. I'm pretty sure he fancied her back in the day, too.

"You look nice!" he says, his all-perving eyes having a good gander.

If only there was a HR department for handymen neighbours. I'd have reported him years ago. And I look nice? Is he serious? I'm dressed in my very un-fetching work wear of black trousers, satin purple shirt and hounds tooth cardigan that sits just below the bum. Keeping it modest and all that.

"Thanks Joe. I just got back from work." I pick up the pace.

"Well, if that's your work outfit, I'd love to see your date night outfit."

"Nice try Joe."

"Always worth a try."

Joe's Ruddy cheeks, combined with his black curly hair, remind me of the Ronald McDonald clown. This only serves to add to the creepiness.

Luckily, my M is a dead cert. While he's rubbish at progressing things on the marriage front, he consistently answers his phone after the first ring. It's almost like he's waiting for my call, staring at the phone, willing it to buzz into action.

"Hey, how are you doing? Everything okay?" he asks.

Why does he always assume things are not okay?

"Yeah, I'm good. What are you up to?"

"I've just finished work and I'm at the gym."

"And you had your phone on you?" I tease, before launching my ambush. "Look, I don't want to harp on about this but I'm wondering where we stand with things."

"How do you mean?" he asks, as blissfully unaware as I thought.

"It's... It's just..." Oh God, I sound like a desperate bunny boiler. So shamefully keen to get off the shelf. I didn't want to be doing the chasing, or the asking, but it looks like I'll have to. Time to put on my big girl pants.

"Don't you think it's a bit weird that our families met a couple of weeks back and your family hasn't said anything to us. I'm beginning to wonder if they're even interested."

"Oh no, of course we're interested and obviously I'm interested! It's just my parents are a bit relaxed about these things."

"Isn't this the one thing they shouldn't be relaxed about? Getting married is a big deal."

"No, you're right, it is but -"

"I have to be honest," I cut him short as I'm running out of patience. "If your family met mine via the arranged marriage route and then there was tumbleweed for a few weeks, we'd move on to the next person."

M doesn't say anything. Did I go too far?

After a deep breath, he says: "I completely understand. I'm sorry if I've been a bit blasé about the whole thing. To be honest with ya, I assumed my parents were getting on with it. I guess I'm in a bit of a bubble being so far away, whereas you're in the thick of it and your mum is probably asking what's going on."

He's read her like a book.

"Leave it with me. I'll talk to my parents. Don't worry though, they really liked you."

"I'm glad to hear it. My mum will be too," I say.

You'd think with my determination to push things forward, mum would be happy. Instead, I get read the riot act when I get home.

"I hope you not talk to him rude! If you be pushy, you sound desperate. You no want to ruin this chance. Were you rude to him? What you say?"

I literally cannot win with this woman.

MY FIRM WORDS WITH M resulted in a phone call from his mum in the evening. I'd be lying if I said I wasn't crapping my pants. Is his mum going to tell my mum that I'm a forward, whore-ish floozie who has no place in her family? I swear, if this relationship goes tits up mum will have me on a plane to Bangladesh quicker than she hands out two slaps.

I try to earwig mum's end of the conversation.

"Oh salaam. Yes, good. How are you?... Oh, that what children be like these days!... No, no, not at all... Yes of course. She at home, my girls no go out at night. Unless it be wedding... Oh yes, most weddings are in day anyway."

Even when speaking in full Bengali to another mum, she throws in the odd word in English. It's like mum's showing off.

"You're quite right. So all the restaurant workers can get to work for the evening. Though last year I went to evening wedding... Yes, *Bangali*. Can you *buleev*? They trying so hard to be like Pakistani. Next they be dancing at wedding... One second, I call her."

Oh no! Is mum coming to get me? Will I have to talk to M's mum?

Mum comes over with a hand covering the speaker on the cordless phone.

"His mum wants to speak to you! It's okay, she being nice."

I grab the phone off mum and press mute. "You're so loud when you whisper! Why don't you just silence the call?"

Mum mutters something under her breath about not understanding technology, then I'm left to it. If ever there's a time to put my PR hat on *and* use my best Bengali, surely this is it.

After a tentative exchange of salaams, M's mum initiates the chat:

M's mum: "So...how are you?"

Me: "I am okay, Alhamdulillah. How are you?"

M's mum: "*Bala*, good. What you doing?"

Me: "Oh, nothing much. Just work tomorrow, so I'll watch the news shortly."

M's mum: "Oh yes, you work in the news?"

Me: "No, not quite. I work with private hospitals to get them in the media."

M's mum: "Oh okay. Do you write the stories? The ones in newspaper?"

Me: "No but... well, kind of. Sometimes my stories appear in the paper just as I'd written them."

M's mum: "Oh, so is your name in paper?"

Me: "No. The name will be of the journalist. But I wrote the story."

There's an uncomfortably long silence.

M's mum: "Why not your name? You should tell them to put your name if it's your work."

Me: "Well... It doesn't quite work like that. I'm paid to give them the stories -"

M's mum: "So is it your work?"

Me: "Yes, it is, but I'm not paid by the newspaper. So my name won't be printed."

More tumbleweed silence.

M's mum: "Okay, okay, very good. Stay well. Will speak again soon."

With that, I end the most awkward and nerve wracking conversation of my 26 years of life. My command of Bengali is broken beyond fixing. Add into the mix a straight-talking mother-in-law and I'm all tongue tied.

The good news is, I think that's her way of saying all is well so stop stressing, you desperate cow. Though I have to say, it's times like this that I wish I picked medicine, law or accounting. I've never met anyone who understands what PR entails and I've never been able to explain it clearly in Bengali.

No sooner have I hung up then mum is on my case about something new.

"Will you check your letters? I shouldn't have to always sort through them for you. I'm sick of seeing bank statements and payslips piled up next to the phone. You shouldn't keep them out like that. What if somebody comes in and sees your monies?"

"Okay mum, I'll check."

"You always say that. But check properly, don't open letters and leave there. If you do that when married, your in-laws no like it."

Luckily I won't be living with my in-laws, I think, but stop myself from saying to mum. Any show of self-assuredness seldom ends well for me.

I guess since I'm near the phone anyway, I should see what she's banging on about. I'm usually pretty efficient about putting my letters away in my little folder but I have been distracted of late.

As I sift through the anonymous looking white envelopes and the token brown one from work, I notice something different in the pile. A red envelope stands out. It's addressed to me. Intriguing. This is way more important than my bank and work stuff, so it gets opened first. Inside, there are two tickets to see Romeo and Juliet. They're dated the 14th of February next year. Underneath the tickets there's a small handwritten note:

I'm not really one for Valentine's Day or birthdays but I think it's time I change that. So I've taken the liberty to book Shakespeare's Globe, as you said you hadn't been. It's something for us to look forward to next Valentine's Day, when you're hopefully here with me x

This little gesture confirms two things:

M really is a keeper, as if I didn't already know that.

His handwriting is almost as bad as mine. If that's not proof we're meant for each other, then what is?

IT'S A GOOD THING I'M quick at typing. Conversations with M in the evening mostly take place via text. With a teenage sister in the next bed, I have to be discreet.

M: *Do you feel better now after speaking to my mum?*

Me: *Yeah, I do. Thanks for chasing things up on your end. I hope it wasn't too awkward. I know it's tricky for boys to have these conversations.*

M: *No, it's fine. To be honest with ya, it needed to happen. I think I deserved a kick up the arse as well. Mum really likes you though. She especially likes the fact that you seem to be pretty sensible and have a good job. You're not one of those girls that went to uni but now sits at home waiting to get married.*

Me? Waiting to get married? Never...

Me: *It's nice that your mum's not one of those mums that just wants a daughter-in-law with a degree for bragging rights, when all she really wants is someone to help in the kitchen.*

M: *No, not at all. She's never been like that, and we'll be in our own kitchen in London :). But seriously, she might not say so much and she's not really a soft mum type but she definitely likes you. I mean, who wouldn't?*

Who wouldn't? Who wouldn't indeed. That's actually the first time someone has ever said that to me. I've always been worried that I was never quite good enough. I was never the prettiest. I was never top of the class, despite being good academically. As for sports, forget it. I might be genetically blessed with a slim frame but I was piss poor at PE. I made up for my shortcomings by being funny and likeable and that carried me through life. But I never saw myself as anything special. So M's words are news to me.

Of course, I can't bring myself to say that. He is slowly breaking down my walls but there's still a few up. Just for me. Just for protection.

Me: *Exactly. You're lucky to have me.*

M: *I know xx*

Oh, does that double x signify that it's time to say goodbye? I wasn't done 'talking'. I see the typing icon coming up.

M: *How are you feeling now that it's getting real? You'll likely be moving to London by the end of the year.*

Would it be desperately keen if I said I'm fricking jumping for joy at the idea of moving to the capital? It's not that he's my vehicle out of this small white borough but I've always wanted to move to London.

M brought this up delicately on one of our earlier dates and was surprised at how nonchalant I was about the whole thing. I thought I'd struck brown gold. Not only did he live in London but his parents lived up north so we would be making frequent trips back to see my family, too. To me, that was a win-win. It's the kind of set up that Julia always said she wanted for me as it's such a norm for white people. I felt smug as a bug telling her that us Bengalis are not as backward as she thought.

Me: *I am happy. It's a bit surreal but it's exciting. I just hope we get to plan everything properly. I don't really want a rushed wedding. How about you?*

M: *I can't wait. You know me, I'm a bloke. I'm not bothered about all the details. I just can't wait for us to get married and for you to come over.*

Easy for him to say. I, however, don't want the Asian equivalent of a Vegas chapel wedding.

I think M's clocked my pause and lack of typing, as he's already jumping in with another message.

M: *Don't worry. We'll make it really nice. What I mean is, the wedding is just one day in all of our lives together. People get so hung up on trying to have the biggest, bestest party and miss the bigger picture.*

Me: *True. But as a girl, the wedding is still important.*

M: *I promise you'll have the wedding you want. But more importantly, have a think about where we should go on honeymoon...*

That's exciting. Then it suddenly dawns on me. Forget the honeymoon. If I'm potentially getting married this year, what the hell am I going to tell work?

12th March

Wax on, face off

"What are you doing today? You're not meeting your special friend, are you?"

"Wait, what?"

It still stops me in my tracks when my family talk openly about M. Especially when the family member is big sis, the poster girl for arranged marriages to boys from back home.

"No," I reply. "The only friend I'm meeting today is Sophia. Though I guess she's pretty special, as I rarely get to see her these days now she's got a baby."

Big sis furrows her brow.

"Don't worry," I say, reading her look of disappointment. "I'm not seeing her until later. I'll still have time to squeeze in most of the shops in Rusholme."

Big sis has come up for the weekend and she's very excited to see some sarees. This is on the agenda every time she visits regardless of whether she has any intention of buying or there's even an event that warrants such a purchase. She just loves the haggling.

However, on this rare occasion, big sis actually is in need of an outfit or two. As well as the summer weddings on her husband's side of the family, we've got a cini paan coming up at the end of the month. This Bengali engagement ceremony couldn't be more different to the English equivalent, where a couple host a fun, informal gathering with no intention of setting a wedding date (though there might be the vague mention of some point in the next two years). Our parties very much conform to the rules of getting engaged to be married. Usually a date is decided during the cini paan itself. Oh, and it's in the not-too-distant future. As in, less than six months away.

I once asked mum why our engagements are so short, leaving next to no time to plan a decent wedding. Her reply was surprisingly sensible: "Gives people less time to stir trouble."

In church weddings, the vicar will ask at the altar if anyone has a reason for the wedding not to go ahead, giving guests less than a minute to object. We, however, have the entire duration from the time we are engaged to the date of our wedding for someone to throw a spanner in the works. That's why we keep that time as brief as possible, thank you very much. It makes perfect sense.

The happy couple whose engagement we are attending is auntie Jusna's youngest daughter Hassna and... well, I don't know the groom. As if we'd get to meet him informally ahead of the wedding. All we've been told is that the marriage was of the arranged variety (wink wink, hello internet dating, marriage events and covert hunting). I shouldn't really speculate but I will anyway.

While we live in a white area, we have Asian shops galore just a short drive away. Sis however, has spent the last 12 years having to commute over an hour just to get halal meat. So saree shops are a real novelty, as are halal takeaways. Big sis loves a seekh kebab with all the sauces and salad.

I, on the other hand, am not very enthused for either. I guess I take them for granted. However, as a dutiful hostess (read: the only one in the household who can drive), I assume my usual role as a chauffeur and haggling wing woman. En route to Rusholme, we drive through Longsight, one of the most densely Bangladeshi-populated areas in Manchester. As I make my way through an aggressive stream of traffic (rather skilfully, if I do say so myself), I see big sis' eyes light up.

I know what's coming.

"Shall we check out the accessory shop?" she asks.

"You mean the one we always do? We never drive past this place without stopping off."

Big sis laughs. "Oh lady, you know me too well. Only if you can find parking. I know how hot and bothered you get on this busy road."

After conducting a rather undignified six-point-park to squeeze into a generously sized parking space, much to the annoyance of the aggressive drivers on the road, we indulge in a spot of my sister's favourite pastime – looking with her eyes with no real intention to purchase.

As soon as we enter the shop, which has wall-to-wall bangles in every colour imaginable, big sis makes a discovery. "Ooh lady, it says they do eyebrows here. For a fiver."

"Well, that's a bit more than I'm used to paying but then again, I don't have a regular threading lady after the last one," I say to big sis' raised, judgmental and only slightly untamed eyebrow.

"You and your fussy ways," says big sis. "You expect five-star service for £3.50."

"No, I just don't expect to be left waiting with one bushy eyebrow while the beautician goes and talks on the phone for half an hour."

Big sis rolls her eyes as she knows I'm exaggerating. "Anyway, shall we do it? Mine need a little tidy, and yours..."

There she goes again, judging.

"Yes, I know I'm long overdue. I'd tweeze them myself if I wasn't so cack-handed. Anyway, I still think £5 is way too much."

Big sis pats my arm. "I'll treat you, lady. What with me not working and you in a high-powered job, it's the right thing to do."

We head up the rickety wooden stairs of the accessory shop to be greeted with an assault on the senses. The heady smell of hairspray and nail polish is amplified by the constant hum of hairdryers. All the years of visiting this place and I never knew upstairs was a full-on beauty parlour.

As we lower ourselves into the slouchy, well sat-in faux leather sofa, I notice that we're in the company of a very mixed bag of clientele. The glamorous girl next to us doesn't look like she needs her eyebrows - or anything - done. Even her casual Saturday topknot doesn't have a hair out of place.

I, meanwhile, am sporting full brow regrowth and while I can boast of thick straight hair, I do precisely eff all with it. My go-to is an unintentionally low-slung ponytail. I really should get a chop before my next meeting with M. My layers need addressing.

However, it's not all glamour in this parlour. Salwar-kameez clad mums whose young children are running a-mock about the place, are getting their eyebrows done and upper lips waxed. There's even an old lady having a facial. All of us are bonded by the need to be groomed.

Big sis whispers terribly loudly in my ear: "Gosh, even the heifers get their eyebrows done," as if grooming should discriminate on size.

I say nothing.

The wait for eyebrows is long. I decide to peruse the bridal makeup portfolio to pass the time.

"You'll be needing that soon!" big sis elbows me in the ribs. "Mum said things have moved on a notch."

"Yeah, I think they're in the process of sorting out dates now. Which is easier said than done as we're having the wedding and walima together."

Big sis scrunches up her nose. "Hmmm, yes. That's the new way of doing things, I guess."

She's a stickler for tradition and harks back to the good old days when the bride and groom hosted individual parties, a wedding and walima respectively. My purist older sister had two big fat Bangladeshi wedding parties back home. However, families these days like to amalgamate. This is especially the case when the couple live within reasonable proximity to each other. With M's family just outside Manchester, we'll be going down that route.

I'm slightly disappointed about the two-in-one job, mainly because I wanted to be a princess for two days. When it comes to other people's weddings, I'm never the princess, so I want to milk my special occasion for all its worth. There's also this tricky matter of doing things together whilst ensuring that each side is happy with the arrangement - the venue, the catering, the decor... the budget. Just thinking about it is making me nervous. While Julia would say moving in with a boyfriend is the real litmus test for compatibility, for us, the test comes when we plan a wedding. This is where things can start to unravel.

A tall, broad-shouldered lady ambles towards us. "Are you waiting?"

There is no queue or appointment system so it's a bit of a lucky dip as to who will be seen first.

"Yes, just eyebrows please for both of us," I say.

The beautician does an exaggerated double eyebrow raise as she examines mine. Cheeky cow. Big sis doesn't get the same grooming-shaming. She plucks her eyebrows as threading isn't a thing where she lives, so she's slightly more on top of her follicular affairs than I am.

After appraising our faces, she asks in her deep South Asian accent: "Upper lip, too?"

"No thank you, just eyebrows." After visiting beauty parlours for nearly a decade, this question no longer offends me.

"Are you sure? It's only £2 extra and you both got a bit of moustache."

Okay, now I'm offended.

"No thank you!" says big sis. "We're saving them for an engagement party in two weeks. We'll sort out our 'taches then, once they're a bit... hairier."

Good save. Financially, I mean. Our dignity was sacrificed with her answer.

"Okay. Your choice. Just so you know we are running a special offer on full facial waxing for just £7."

That changes things.

Big sis looks at me. "What do you think, little lady? I bet that's what Rashda does. Her face always looks so peeled and smooth."

Well, if it's good enough for Rashda...

Before I know it, the burly beautician whisks me off into another private room, while big sis gets her eyebrows threaded before her turn with the wax.

I've had my arms waxed before but my face has never been touched. I've always wondered whether it would make me look lighter and brighter. My sideburns always sport a little peach fuzz, which I wouldn't mind losing. I've also noticed that when I get my eyebrows threaded and the beautician is feeling generous enough to take some forehead hair off, my whole face looks cleaner. Such is the power of facial hair removal.

Instead of having to recline backwards over a non-reclining chair with the rest of the mere mortals outside, I'm lying down like a queen on a chaise lounge. Well, it's actually a blue faux leather salon bed that's peeling at the creases and covered with a long sheet of what looks like toilet paper. Still, at least I get to lie down.

The beautician gets to work in her laboratory. As she warms a plastic pot of wax, there is no small talk. That's another thing with Asian beauticians. They never ask you about your holidays. Thankfully they never ask if you've got a boyfriend either. I remember one such incident at uni when the hapless trainee hairdresser was struggling for topics of conversation, so resorted to endlessly asking me whether I had a significant other. I didn't and didn't care for the reminder. Reena, meanwhile, was sat on the next chair chatting ad nauseam about her prick of a boyfriend Pritesh, while her hair was fashioned into a feathered style. She droned on about what he bought her for their first anniversary, where they planned to go on holiday after graduation and how they were totally, totally getting married.

It's ironic that now I have finally met someone and we're about to get married, I'm lumbered with a beautician that doesn't care to ask. That reminds me, I must book a hair appointment at Belinda's soon. We have much to discuss.

"Okay, while wax get hot, first I take off your eyebrows."

She doesn't give me a chance to think before shouting: "Hold!", the standard instruction deployed by all beauticians, which means stretch the skin on your brow bone with each hand to make it easier for them to grab those pesky hairs with the thread.

This beautician is swift and merciless. She seems to be digging into my brow bone with the thread more than necessary. Her nails are long talons that keep catching the delicate skin on my eyelid. I don't mind the odd bit of spit that flies out from her mouth as she's got thread clenched between her teeth. That's pretty standard procedure. I'm even ignoring the moment when some of her saliva lands on my lip. I must recount this to big sis so she can no longer say I expect a five-star service.

By some small mercy, the threading is over before the waterworks really get going. The scary beautician then dips a lollipop stick into the oozy wax before spreading it like butter across my forehead.

"Ooh! That's a bit hot!" I'm being polite. My skin feels like it's corroding.

"No worry. It take time to cool down." She proceeds to place her cloth, which may or may not have been washed between uses, firmly across my skin before pulling off with a snap.

It hurts like hell. And this is coming from a girl who regularly gets her eyebrows pulled out from the root with a piece of string.

I just want this to be done. Thankfully, the aggressive smoothing and pulling method is over in about three minutes. Clearly I'm not as hairy as she made out. Cheeky cow.

She doesn't ask me to check to see if I'm happy with the result. Nor does she hand me a mirror, as is customary. I have to check myself in the large mirror in front of me. After one look I wish I hadn't. My eyebrows don't look even and my face is red raw. I'm too scared to complain in the confines of this room where there aren't any witnesses.

I step back into the safety and coolness of the main area to see big sis having a blazing row with the poor beautician that threaded her eyebrows. Well, it's less of a row and more of a one-sided slanging match on my sister's part. The poor beautician, a petite looking thing, looks bewildered.

"You expect me to pay for this! Look what you've done!"

Sis interrupts her ranty monologue and turns to face me. Her brow bone is an angry shade of scarlet, her eyebrows are wonky like mine and the beautician has taken too much off the bottom, leaving my sister with a surprised look.

"Look what she's done to me, lady!" Then her expression changes as she realises it could've been a lot worse. "Oh dear. I might not bother getting my face waxed. I'm not that hairy anyway."

No sarees were bought that afternoon.

SOPHIA KEEPS LOOKING at my singed sideburns. Heck, I think her baby is even fixated by my over-peeled face. I must look like the skin of a pink grapefruit, all bumpy and textured.

Still, it's nice to see Sophia. It's been ages. The girl who was once my confidante in all things manhunt based, is busy in the throes of motherhood. I bet she's got new mum friends, too, but isn't telling me to spare my feelings. I'm sad to say we don't seem to have as much in common anymore.

"I'm so glad things are moving on with you and M. Really moving on! So you'll basically be getting married this year."

"It looks that way." I still can't quite believe it when I say it out loud. I'M GETTING MARRIED! I'M GETTING MARRIED! I'M GETTING FOOKIN' MARRIED!

"Do you have a date set?"

"No, it'll be decided near the time of the engagement."

"I'd like to take special credit, as I convinced you to give him a chance when you were being a shallow cow," Sophia smiles.

"Of course. I'd be harassing you for advice every other day. I miss those days a bit. I miss you, in fact."

I feel a bit cringe being such a needy friend, so I lower my gaze to my delectable plate of starters. I'm already on my second piece of chicken tikka and third samosa. Sophia has barely touched her food, just like the last time we had a lunch date here for my 26th birthday. It's like she doesn't know how a buffet works. Surely the constant queue of people at the counter lined with round silver food servers should be enough of a hint. Though this time she has another reason. Baby Imran is not playing ball. He's bobbing his head on and off her boob as she discreetly tries to feed him under her shawl. I'm impressed that she is brave enough to breastfeed in public. I don't think I could do it.

"Sorry hon, what were you saying?" she asks in between shushing a restless Imran, who's proceeded to kick the table with his deliciously chubby baby grow clad legs.

"Oh, don't worry, it's nothing," I say. "I'm just glad there's progress. For a second, I thought his mum didn't like me and I was worried I'd be back on the dating site again. Do you remember how I nearly resigned myself to a life of eternal singledom? Especially after mum suggested that pizza boy and -"

"Oh bubba! What's the matter? Do you need a nap? Shall we get home? Shall we go brum brum in the car?" Sophia clearly isn't saying this to me. She's bouncing Imran on her knee (after taking him off the boob, of course. I don't think anyone's *that* good at multitasking).

She finally turns her attention to me, unaware that she missed everything I just said. "He's been so restless these last few days. I don't know what it is. I can't tell if he's doing it for attention or he has a touch of reflux."

I've never heard of reflux so I'm guessing it's attention the little fella's after.

Sophia looks distracted and harassed. She's still beautiful. She snapped back to her pre-baby size just two months after giving birth. She still dresses immaculately with her moss-coloured nursing-friendly wrap dress. From what I hear from her sporadic text messages, she's got a packed schedule of baby club, baby massage and monkey music. She's even considering quitting work once her maternity leave is up, so she can be a stay-at-home mum and make time for everything and everyone. Well, almost everyone.

As she faffs about with Imran, I see a look I don't recognise from when my sisters were new mums. Kind of... vacant.

"Do you mind if we call it a day, hon? Oh God, sorry, you've not even finished your food. At least you've had one more plate than me. Let me get this and I promise I'll make it up to you next time. We'll have a proper catch up. I'll get Adnan to watch Imran. I really ought to start delegating more."

This is how most of our conversations go of late. I'm ignored and left hanging with the promise of a more meaningful conversation the next time. Sophia got pregnant after a long and painful journey, so I understand her not wanting to miss a moment of motherhood. That doesn't stop me missing her, though. She only came into my life last year. I'm not quite ready to lose her to her new mum life.

Sophia throws £20 on the table which doesn't even cover her half, let alone the entire bill. I let it pass.

Just before she leaves, she leans in. "Hon, I've been meaning to tell you something."

Oh, maybe she'll apologise for being so elusive.

"It's just I couldn't help but notice... I think you've burnt your skin. Have you tried a new cream or something? I'd get that checked out."

EN ROUTE HOME, I MAKE a pit stop to the salon that scarred me. I'm going to do it. I'm going to complain and demand a refund, or at least some kind of remedy. I cannot go to Hassna's engagement with third-degree burns.

"What can I do for... oh." The hapless teenage beautician that performed a terrible eyebrow job on my sister doesn't have the best poker face. "Did that happen here?"

"Yes. And you need to give me a refund. Plus, what can you do to fix it?"

"Oh, I don't know."

"Well, you need to do something. This is your fault and I have a wedding next week."

I'm feeling a bit braver as this girl is much more timid than the scary Mary that waxed me. Plus, changing the occasion and bringing the date forward gives a greater sense of urgency to my demand. They might offer me the luxury facial to make up for it.

"If you can't do anything for me, I want to see your manager." Ooh! I'm liking my attitude.

The teenager scuttles away before returning with her manager, who just happens to be the burly, heavy-handed beautician.

"What is it?" she barks.

Today is not my day.

27th March
An engagement (that's not mine)

My face is still smarting though I'm glad to say that, two weeks after the wax from hell, I'm only left with slight pigmentation where the beastly beautician burnt my skin. She did try to redeem herself by getting one of her minions to administer a facial. I was just glad she wasn't the one doing it with her big meat cleaver hands and sharp pointy claws.

Why do we women do this to ourselves? Men don't have to go to such great grooming lengths. Yet we have to pluck, wax, epilate and exfoliate using instruments of medieval torture, under the guise of self care. There is nothing caring about it. They say women are the fairer, gentler sex. Well, I'd like to see a man use an epilator to pull out his armpit hair. Then we'd see about that.

I wonder when all this extensive beautifying began. My mum's generation didn't do half the things we're expected to do now. Mum has never threaded her eyebrows, she doesn't wear any makeup, either. Whereas I reached for the tweezers aged 12. At the time, girls started wearing makeup to school and shaving their legs. Once we went down that road, there was no turning back. It's like HD TV. After you've watched one programme in high definition, anything else looks old, grainy, dated. However, it's not the non-HD stuff that's dated, it's our perception and view of the world that's changed. We've been conditioned.

It's even worse for my younger sister's generation. While I had to keep up with facial hair removal, she's growing up in a world where it's not what you take off your face, it's what you inject into it that counts. Fillers and filters have become the norm. At what point of distortion do we say enough is enough?

Anyway, I'm certainly not going to be the trailblazer for an anti-grooming revolution. After all, I'm hoping to get married. So it's a good thing my face is pretty hardy. If I suffered with sensitive skin, like middle sis, I'd probably have to skip the engagement party.

Though I wouldn't mind missing the cini paan of Hassna, who is six months younger than me (why did mum insist on having kids at the same time as auntie Jusna? It's like they were in competition or something). Just like her baby brother Iqbal, it looks like she'll be beating me to the marital post, too. Or at least she's getting a sparkly rock on her finger before me anyway.

What's worse is that, just like at the wedding of her brother, every nosey parker who comes into conversation with mum probes her on my single status. Though this is a small, intimate affair (I mean intimate by Bengali standards, there's still upwards of 60 people here), the guest list seems to be made up of the most meddling members of our extended family.

Annoyingly, I will be getting married - likely at the end of this year - but as nothing is formalised, we can't even talk about it. Typical. Just typical.

Still, they're serving samosas. Silver linings and all that.

Auntie Jusna has hired out the entire top floor of a restaurant in Rusholme. It must've cost a bomb. My poor uncle, I bet he didn't have a say in the matter. Like my dad, he's not one to get involved but as a simple pious man, I'm sure he would have preferred a more low-key affair. Especially as word has got out about their oldest daughter Rashda's divorce. Our lot can be terrible stirrers. Then again, maybe that's auntie Jusna's new strategy - show everyone that the show must go on. And what a show. There are black and gold his and hers thrones on the main stage. Fresh fuchsia flowers adorn each round table and they obviously couldn't settle for just a chocolate fountain (which is currently being massacred by my nieces and nephews), they've even got a cheese grazing table. Well, that's a complete waste of time. Bengalis don't care for cheese and we certainly don't graze. Those crackers will go damp before they touch anyone's lips.

What's more, there's no gender segregation, which means dad, dressed by mum for the occasion yet again, has to sit amongst us while we slate his side of the family. He looks small and resigned, like he'd rather be anywhere but here.

"Hmmph! Cheese! Who is here to eat cheese?" Mum obviously read my mind.

"Maybe they're trying something new?" Middle sis is surprisingly diplomatic.

"*Oh-ho!* If you think it's okay, why don't you go over there and have some cheesy grapes like strange lady?"

Middle sis winces. "You're alright, mum. I don't think I fancy eating anything right now."

Mum's still not done moaning. "Rashda *maa* is wasting her time. Who eat cheese when there be samosas on the table? Grapes? Still with the stems? I bet they're not even washed! Oh ho! I think I even see figs. But I don't have my glasses. Is that figs over there? Who having toilet trouble that they need so many figs? She must be going through funny lady change. Does she look red to you?" Mum attempts to elbow my big sis, who is the closest to menopause of all her daughters, but she's too late. Big sis is making a beeline for the cheese.

It's a far cry from engagement parties of yesteryear. Both my older sisters had their ceremonies at home. Big sister's engagement was held at our house in Bangladesh, which is pretty grand by UK standards. Middle sis' ceremony was a bit more modest as it took place in our three-bed semi. We made it nice though, with plastic flower garlands adorning the entire front room. We even erected a mini marquee in the garden, which was a nice touch (the only downside was that we were unlucky with the weather). Nowadays it's pretty unheard of to hold such ceremonies at home and I feel I have no choice but to roll with the times. I wouldn't mind hiring Hassna's venue out for my engagement. Or at least scope out the prices on the down low.

Mum is on form today. Not only has the cheese platter offended her no end, Hassna's grand entrance has only served to piss her off even further.

"Oh my *my*!" she mutters to nobody in particular. "Look at the shy bride! Or not so shy! I can't believe she sat on the stage talking on her phone! Who does she need to call on her own cini paan day!"

Little sis looks up from her phone for one second: "Mum, why do we call it *cini paan*? I guess it's cini as in sugar, and the paan is... well, paan?"

None of us know the English translation for paan. Is it an exclusively Bengali delicacy? I've never understood the appeal of chewing on a leaf and betel nut. Not to mention the nasty red stains you get on your teeth that even the strongest of whitening toothpastes can't get rid of. It's like a mark of honour for first generation Bengali immigrants.

Mum laughs at our inquisitive teenager like she's been caught off-guard. "Yes, that's right. Sugar and paan to you English kids."

Little sis isn't done yet. "But why though? What's that got to do with an engagement?"

"Well... I guess sugar is to sweeten your in-laws. Which is why the groom's family bring mishti sweets." Mum then reaches for some paan for herself, pulling a carefully folded leaf apart from its delicate display beneath the flower arrangement at the centre of our table. She never has paan. We don't even keep any in the house since dad kicked the habit years ago. I guess it's the equivalent of social smoking.

I'm as confused by the tradition as little sis. "I never cared for those syrupy sweets anyway. They're too sickly. Unless it's gulab jaman with ice cream. I just don't get the paan bit, though. If you're sweetening the in-laws with the mishti, what's the paan for?"

"Dooro! Why do you need to know everything? Not everything need to be life lesson! Something's we just say because we do. We always did! No need to make sense!" Mum has a hacking cough, no doubt brought on by the paan and being put on the spot.

I can't help but think that had little sis asked that question instead of me, she would've received a more considered response.

The mobile phone isn't the only thing covering Hassna's face. She's wearing a trowel of makeup. Her cheeks are illuminated with reflective highlighter to match her pearlescent saree. Her false eyelashes look spidery and she's sporting a dramatic sweep of mocha-coloured blush, providing a harsh contour. Even her real hair isn't detectable beneath the other person's mane she's wearing. Those extensions, a dirty blonde shade, are nothing like her natural black. And the crowning glory is a heavily jewelled headpiece fastened to the side of her fake, overly back-combed hair. She's become a caricature of herself for a day. I'm begrudged to say it but Hassna's naturally pretty. She didn't need all this.

Is this how I'm going to have to look on my engagement ceremony? Surely not. If I did, M wouldn't approve, he's all for minimal makeup. Then again, it wouldn't be for him, would it? Such exaggerated 'beauty' is not for men, it's for the female gaze. But then which woman thinks this looks good? Or is it less a question of good and more a question of appropriate? Should we be wearing our wealth? I think that's what it boils down to. Bling and bronzer equal prosperity.

While I'm deep in thought, Hassna's older sister, Rashda, sidles up next to us, wearing a loud look-at-me burnt orange gown. I notice that gowns are all the rage these days. Sarees are seen less and less at weddings and parties, which is kind of sad. Nothing quite matches the regal elegance of a saree so I hope it's not a tradition that completely dies down. I'd at least like some guests wearing it for my wedding.

That said, I'm glad for Rashda's bold choice of colour. At her brother Iqbal's wedding she wore the dullest of green outfits. It was as if it was an obvious attempt to dim her shine, downplay her beauty and fade into obscurity. She was in the midst of going through her divorce, so I wonder whether it was whispered in her ear that she shouldn't draw too much attention to herself to avoid unnecessary questions. Even though we've been bitterly jealous of her and her perfect family most of our lives, I didn't want to see her in such a resigned state.

"You look nice, missy," she tells me.

I notice I'm getting a lot more compliments these days. Could it be that secret bride-to-be glow? Usually it's middle sis that gets the lion's share of praise when it comes to beauty. Big and little sis get the leftovers and I usually get nothing as all reserves are depleted by that point.

"Thanks. I thought I'd make the effort." I sit up a little straighter from my slumped slouch, very aware that I am in rather attractive company.

"Well, I said it before and I'll say it again, blue really suits you."

Damn! I thought I'd get away with wearing the same saree that I wore at Iqbal's wedding but she obviously noticed, unless it was a genuine compliment.

"How are you getting on, Rashda, all things considered?" Big sis is as subtle as a brick, as always.

"I'm okay. Actually, I've never felt better. Why do you ask?"

Ooh, is she challenging my big sis to probe into her divorce? Maybe she wants to talk about it? Or she's just peed off with etiquette and wants to show the world that she isn't bothered at all about her single mother status.

"Oh, no reason, just asking." Big sis doesn't take the bait.

Auntie Jusna, no doubt terrified that her seemingly unruly divorcee daughter will spill the beans on her broken home, plants herself between us, shuffling her generous behind next to my poor niece, who is now nearly falling off her chair.

"Come on princess, there's room for both of us, you're only tiny."

My niece slides off the chair and makes a run for the chocolate fountain for seconds, with the used wooden skewer from her last visit in her hand.

"*Shundor oyse*?" auntie Jusna asks mum, before translating for us: "Nice?" as though we don't understand Bengali.

"Hmm, yes very nice. It's a lovely venue," says mum.

"Thank you. It wasn't cheap but we thought, let's spend on our last child to get married. Let me know if you need the details of this place when it's your one's turn." She nods in my direction.

"Insha Allah we'll need those details soon. Except we will have waiters. No one wants to get up and get their food. Especially not me with my bad knee," says mum.

"What you mean? Everyone has buffets these days," argues auntie Jusna. "You could do with exercise, too," she gestures towards mum's midriff. "Anyway, do you have news? Have you found someone for her?"

I love how auntie Jusna doesn't even use my name.

Mum realises she said too much and does her lip grimace thing. "No, but of course we are looking. So, Insha Allah, any time now. Make prayer for us."

"You know I will. I'm always praying for your lovely girls. I only hope you find someone as good as we did for Hassna." She rests her elbows on the table, giving us all a good view of her new shiny gold bangles. "We'll have two doctors in the family. Well, three if you count Hassna. He's a junior doctor you know, like my boy. Training to be a register."

I think she means registrar and Hassna is a pharmacist. So no, she doesn't count.

"The family are very good *Masha Allah*. Very respectable. They say they treat Hassna like their own daughter. The mum will do all the cooking as Hassna will be working. And did you see the gold they gifted? I tell them, why so much? Save some for wedding day! I never dreamed of finding such a good family."

I see Rashda give a wry smile, which doesn't go unnoticed by her mother.

"Anyway, I just came to collect my first born who keeps disappearing. We need to cut the cake."

"Do you really need me for that?" Rashda asks. "Can't the bride and groom get on with it?"

"Don't be silly. How will it look? Anyway, wouldn't you rather be on stage with your family for this *especial* occasion? Or would you rather just sit here and miss out again?"

"Okay, just start without me. You don't need all of us to cut one cake. My boy wants to go to the chocolate fountain. I'll come after that."

As she leaves, middle sis can't resist a bit of gossip. "Rashda seems a bit feisty these days? Do you think she's got another fella?"

"*Dooro!* As if! With three kids, it unlikely."

"Mum!" Middle sis, the more modern of my two older siblings, balks at mum's out-dated view.

"Don't mum me! I no make the rules. You know how hard it is for women to move on after divorce. It's hard enough without children but with three... Life is always worse for a woman. Husband on the other hand, will have no such trouble getting remarried."

"That much is true," big sis chimes in. "Hubby told me there's a rumour that he's getting remarried."

I know my sister is well connected with the Bengali community but even I'm surprised that she should be privy to this unofficial news all the way from Bristol.

"How does he know?" I ask.

"One of his partners in the restaurant has family from Manchester. He found out through them."

"Blimey," says middle sis. "Maybe that's what's got Rashda's back up."

"Okay stop talking about her business! Can't it wait until we get home?" mum whispers.

It's funny how Mum is now taking the moral high ground despite being the one that stirred the pot in the first place.

We finally get to the business end of the long, drawn out engagement party. Hassna's fiancé, a lanky fella whose pearl coloured tie matches that of his bride to be, takes to the stage to claim his prize. Or in Bengali terms, to sit quietly next to his fiancée and avoid eye contact. Though these two seem to be doing their own thing. Despite auntie Jusna strongly suggesting that they 'found' the groom and it was very much arranged, Hassna seems terribly familiar with her husband-to-be.

He slips a sparkly ring onto her delicate third finger and clasps her hand tightly. They hold the position for a photo call. He looks at her adoringly. If I wasn't so envious of this whole shindig, I'd find this all rather sweet. I hope M and I can have these kind of photos at our engagement ceremony. Though looking around me, I don't think that will happen.

I can sense the atmosphere heating up with the boiling blood of all the aunties who disapprove of this very public display of affection. They're already mightily put out by the fact that they had to get up for their own food at the buffet. And who's the most offended by all of this? My mum, of course.

I squint for a better look at Hassna's hand.

"Ooh, do you think that's a real diamond?" asks big sis.

Middle sis laughs. "It probably is, her fiancé *is* a cash register, as auntie Jusna says."

That was a good one.

"It makes a change though, from the Bangladeshi boat rings that we both had." Middle sis looks down at her ring finger, which is decorated with a 22-carat gold canoe shaped ring. Middle sis is perhaps the last generation of our women to be given the fabled ring. Nowadays, the boat ring is ditched in favour of the more western appropriate half-carat brilliant cut sparkler.

"What are you complaining about?" says mum. "That's what everybody got then, before girls become show offs and want to be white. You forget groom family spend thousands on gold necklaces and earrings and bangles. You no get that in English culture. So no wonder they give diamond ring. I mean, what else do British groom pay for?"

"The honeymoon?" I helpfully add.

"Oh yes. The honeymoon. While poor girl family pay for everything. If we were British, we would be beggars by now, with only four girls and no sons to marry."

Despite mum's protestations, I bet she'd be miffed if I didn't end up with a diamond engagement ring, especially now the daughter of her arch nemesis has one.

Just as were judging the old school way of doing things, Hassna spoons cream frosting in her fiancé's mouth. He laughs as some of it misses and it smears across his very thin lips. She wipes a bit off with her thumb. Ooh, salacious.

I'm waiting for a delicious rant from mum in 3... 2... 1...

"*Oh ho*! Feeding each other now, are we? And look at how they laugh! They think they Pakistani or something? Holding modern party like this! Next they be dancing at wedding! Jusna so two-faced. Remember when you dyed your hair?" she shouts at middle sis, who nearly jumps out of her seat. "When Rashda dye her hair, it no problem. '*Oh it fashion*', Jusna say. Hmmph!"

I'm not immune from this either: "She talked so much about us when you went to *uni-barsiry*, too. Everyone bad until her kids do the same. Then it be okay. Always got bad to say about other people's life but look at her house! If she lifts her arm, she think her armpits don't smell, too? She wrong!"

I do love a Bengali analogy.

"*Eh-heh*, so what if they eat cake?" Dad, who's been so quiet all this time that I almost forgot he's here, finally sticks up for his sister.

"You no talk! You always listen to her stirring and no see in front your own eyes. That's it! We're going home. I speak to this Droylsden mum tomorrow and get some dates sorted. Next time I see your auntie Jusna I'll have news to share… you're getting married! To banker boy with big job! And you be living in London all by yourselves. See how she likes that! Her cake-feeding princess move with in-laws in Bradistan!"

"Hey mum!" says middle sis. "Bradford isn't that bad!"

"Oh, you know it is! More Pakistani than English! Anyway, my girl done much better. Because I modest woman I don't talk these things. When things be official, I no be keeping quiet."

I can't resist asking: "Can I feed cake at my engagement then?"

"*Dooro* no! What will people say? People will know you were *especial* friends."

28th March

On a mission

When mum is on a mission, she ditches the unwritten rule book. The whole *'don't be too forward, let the boy's side initiate progress'* BS goes out of the window. I would like to remind her how she bollocked me for getting M to hurry his parents along after our official meeting. However, after nearly 27 years of living with this woman, I've learnt to accept her *do as I say, not as I do* mantra.

The funny thing is, you can take the mum out of Bangladesh but you absolutely cannot take the Bengali politeness out of the mum.

First, mum has to evacuate the scene. "What you doing now? Always reading newspaper! Take it to front room, I've got important business to deal with. Business you never help with."

Dad tumbles out, leaving mum to make her important phone call.

"Salaam... How are you?... Alhamdulillah we good... Have I caught you at a bad time?... Oh really? What are you cooking it with?... I haven't cooked *shutki* for long time. My kids don't really like the smell. But I did used to make many years ago..."

Mum darts a death stare at me. She's still bitter as she sees me as the reason she stopped cooking her beloved dried

99

fish, though it's technically not true. Yes, I might have implied that it smelt absolutely rank but I never explicitly said don't cook it ever again.

"You couldn't live without it?... Oh, I used to think same until I stop having it. I do miss it... Really?... Your kids never complained once?... Well, that's the right thing to do, show them you boss... You have more cultured children than me. Maybe because they were brought up in *Bangali* area. I wish I done same."

Another death stare. I can't take the blame for that one. It was dad's decision to live in the sticks. I was born the only brownie in the village.

Mum waves her hand rigorously, like she's trying to swat me away. I guess she's moving on to the business end of the conversation.

"WELL HELLO, STRANGER," I say down the phone to my missing in action friend.

Reception is patchy as hell on Julia's end. "I'm sorry! I'm on the tube but we're just going overground now so I can talk for a few minutes. I know I've been rubbish. Our firm is merging so work has been mental with late nights all over the shop. I even did a couple of all nighters, which is nothing like you see on TV. It's totally shit. They don't even order pizza here. They expect us to sustain ourselves by having a Pret sandwich. Anyway, how are you, my soon to be local friend?"

Julia was in the loop about my relationship with M from the very beginning. I didn't dare tell any of my other school friends. They'll think it's totally weird that I'm getting married to someone I've only known for a few months. They'd be even more weirded out by the fact that the exact details of the wedding, the when, where, how many people are coming and all that sort of stuff – is out of my hands. Now that I'm saying it out loud, it does sound a bit odd from a non-Bengali layman's perspective.

I've had to resort to updating Julia via text as she's been terrible at taking my calls. Thus far her slow replies to my major life updates have consisted of an obligatory thumbs up, smiley face or winky face emoji. Julia used to be my go-to for everything, my ride or die. But now, not so much.

There is another reason for her being so terrible at keeping in touch. She's seeing someone and I think this one might be for real. He's a departure from her usual preference of brown man. From what I've heard from snatch text messages here and there and a bit of Facebook stalking, Miles the auditor is pretty much the male version of Julia. Middle-class and prim. She's even changed her Facebook status from *single* to *it's complicated*. I'm not sure why she doesn't just got the whole hog and say *in a relationship*. It's not like she has to be on the down low until she's married, like me. Anyway, Julia has been terribly flaky. With her elusiveness and losing Sophia to mum life, I feel friendless at the time I need friends the most. Having been eternally single, I always thought that when I finally had a boy to talk of, I'd have friends to talk *to*.

"Yeah, yeah. I know the real reason you have not been free," I tease. "So how is Miles?"

"It's not that at all!" Julia goes into high-pitched defensive mode. "I've been really, really busy. I'm sorry, I just never knew being a solicitor in the city would take up so much of my time. Had I known I would've probably stayed in Manchester. Then again, there is a little bonus, as you're going to be joining me soon."

"Yeah, I guess I will be. I'm not quite sure when yet. But more importantly, tell me about Miles. Tell me everything."

Julia coughs and suddenly becomes very British. "Oh, you know, he's saying all the right things, doing all the right things. I've not needed to pay for anything at all and I'd say we're on our 20th date. However, you're not the only one that's scared of jinxing yourself. I'm still waiting for the catch."

"Maybe there isn't one. Maybe he's just genuinely a good guy. Or is that too crazy for you to comprehend? Besides, if he had a third nipple, I think you'd know about it by now."

I can almost hear Julia blushing through the phone. "Yes, no issues on that front. Anyway, how are things with you and M?"

I've trained Julia to call him M, too. It's like she's in on this covert journal / diary / potentially viral blog-in-the-making.

"Things are great. And, I too, am hoping there isn't a catch."

"So, when will you come to London to see me? I thought one of the main advantages of you dating a boy from down south is that I'd be getting to see you more, not less."

I love how Julia turns it round, like *I've* been the elusive one.

"I know but one of the advantages of dating a boy from London who is originally from Manchester is that *he* comes up quite often, so I don't need to go down. Unless it's for work. In which case I barely get to go beyond the office and Heathrow Airport, so I wouldn't expect you to trek to the very outer periphery of London to meet me for a hot chocolate at an airport terminal. Though I have to say, M always makes the journey to catch me before my flight back. Even if it's just for 20 minutes."

I can't help but smile with happiness/annoying smugness at the amount of effort M makes to sustain our long-distance relationship. Luckily, Julia can't see my cheesy grin.

"I love that," says Julia. "He's chivalrous, like all good men should be but sadly most aren't. Perhaps we bagged the last two old-fashioned gentleman."

"I see. So Miles is a gentleman? Well that's something. Who knows, maybe you'll be getting married before me."

"Oh no! We don't rush things as much as your..." Julia stops herself.

"My lot? Oh, come on, we've known each other since we were five. You're allowed to be a bit racist."

"Never! You know what I mean. Anyway yes, Miles is a gentleman. And to think, we can have some great double dates when you are down. What is the update on that front?"

"Well, that's why I called you. Mum is literally speaking to his mum at the moment. She's going to ask her when we should plan for our engagement and you know what that means. Our engagements aren't long, drawn out affairs like your lot. We'll be setting a date after that and trust me, it won't be in two years' time."

"Gosh! In which case, give me as much notice as you feasibly can. I need to check my weekend calendar so I can plan your hen do. And don't worry, it will be classy. There won't be an inflatable penis in sight."

I had no idea Julia was planning to take charge of my hen do. I had no idea I'd be even having a hen do. It's not necessarily a given in Bengali culture but I'm game for it. Though I'm slightly disappointed that she won't surprise me with a novelty inflatable. It would've made for a fun picture opportunity where I act all coy and mortified while I'm secretly loving it.

"Don't worry. You'll be the first to know. In fact, I can hear my mum coming upstairs now to update me. Gotta go."

Mum looks unsure as she comes into my room. "Okay, so we thinking of dates for engagement and she saying end of June could be good. It be hard planning as his big brother be going on holiday, and your sister still not tell me when her husband going Bangladesh."

Mum leans in to whisper to me but there's really no need. There is no one around to eavesdrop and M's mum is safely all the way in Droylsden, half an hour from our house.

"Truth is, from the talk we just had, his mum might be tricky customer."

"What do you mean?"

"She insist on dates that suit her family. Maybe it make life easy if we go with her idea for end of June."

Blimey. I'm always blown away how mum can be such a bad ass in the house, bossing dad around but she backs down so easily when it comes to other people. Then again, she is desperate for me to get married.

"That doesn't leave much time. I need to see what I'm doing as well," I say.

Mum scoffs. "Oh, you have nothing going on. It's not like you're going on holiday, is it? Hmmph!"

She's got me there.

"Anyway, it be worth having idea of wedding date, too. If engagement is hard to plan getting everyone in same room, wedding might be even harder. So your mother-in-law was thinking end July? It might be easier as it's school holidays."

"July, as in... four months away? And a month after we get engaged?"

Mum does her lip grimace thing.

When I said I couldn't wait to get married I didn't expect it to happen quite so soon.

9th September
The white table

Bernadette looks fab. She's decked out in a lime green lehenga. Or is it a gown? I can't really tell as she's sat behind a white plastic floral display. From what I see, I can deduce two things - her outfit is definitely from an Asian boutique (appreciate the effort), and I like it.

I'm impressed with my work colleagues past and present as they all attempted to look at least a little ethnic. There's my old boss Maggie with her purple pashmina that's got a smattering of sequins. I think it might be from Monsoon which is probably the closest she'll ever get to anything remotely Asian inspired. I doubt she even knows where Rusholme is.

Then there is Fiona. I really wasn't sure about inviting her but as we had a ginormous guest list at our disposal, she made the cut. Plus, she really made the effort to understand more about my culture during my last few months with the company, totally redeeming herself from that major faux pas of asking me in front of all and sundry, in our open-plan office, whether I'd have an arranged marriage.

Bushra, meanwhile, looks sublime in her peach salwar kameez, which highlights her fresh-from-Ibiza tan. However, I was expecting her to come clad in Asian clothes, so she doesn't get any extra brownie points (pun intended). I can totally see her ogling M's work colleague Ben.

My employee representation is disproportionately small compared to M's. When he told me he'd be inviting 21 co-workers past and present, it did seem a little generous. And to think my work quota would have been smaller still, as I only really invited Maggie in the hope that she'll gift gener-ously. Rumour has it she's wadded.

I'm slightly miffed that our families are splitting the bill on the hefty guest list, padded out even further by 65 of his friends. It also makes me look like a Billy No Mates as I only managed to bring a dozen pals to the party *and* that was in-cluding plus ones. He is a show off.

My wedding, keeping in tradition with every other Ben-gali wedding I've been to, has a clear separation of tables for... well... the white guests. As terribly segregated as that sounds, it's not really a designated white table per se. It be-comes that way by default, as said guests club together, even when they are perfect strangers. I don't know what it is but they just gravitate towards each other at weddings. It's like Morse code, or a secret language, where they're saying *we are the same, let's stick together and get through this weird shit show*.

I spy a cluster of un-melanated tables, with faces getting progressively redder as the mains are dished out. I hope they have extra jugs of water.

Back to Bernadette, I do have to applaud the lady. She's a great manager and is going through a horrible time. I only just found out through Bushra that she's been secretly fight-ing breast cancer. None of us had a clue. I didn't even notice the hair. Yes, the golden hue was lighter, but I assumed it was a dye job. She always kept herself to herself, so our general interactions were confined to our fortnightly one-to-one's. I didn't mind that, I quite liked the autonomy, though it did make me a little sad that Bernadette, a forty-something lone wolf (we all assumed she was single as she never talked about her love life - but then she never really spoke to us about anything beyond work) having to go through cancer treatment alone. With a big, interfering, yet loving family of my own, I couldn't imagine such a thing.

I wasn't actually expecting her to come to the wedding when I found out the news via text (a message that I now realise I hadn't replied to). So for Bernadette to buy a new outfit, which she will likely never wear again (I suspect she didn't haggle for it either), has made her go up in my estimations.

She notices me spying on her and gives me a thumbs up. I think she likes my outfit. I should bloody hope so too. Getting this lehenga was a whole other story.

1st April

The weird one at work

"Four months?" asks middle sis. "That's loads of time! How much longer do you want? I was married to your brother-in-law three months after meeting him! You've known this lad for how long?"

I feel sheepish. "Since last April. In between his parents went to Bangladesh for two months though, so naturally nothing was going to progress at that point." It's as though I have to justify our obscenely long relationship.

"It doesn't matter where his parents went! It's not like you stopped talking to each other in those two months, is it? So basically you've had a longer relationship than some English people before they get married. I think you've had long enough to figure out if you want to marry him."

"It's not that," I say. "Obviously I want to marry him. It's just that there's not much time to make it nice. Did you know, when most of my Indian friends get married, they get their outfits tailored back home and then get them shipped over. Some people even fly over for a shopping trip. Then there are all the other things I need to think about -"

"See, that's your problem right there. You're always comparing and never happy. Always looking at how your Indian or English friends do things. Newsflash – you're not Indian *or* English! You're bloody Bengali so accept it. This is how we roll. Stop trying to keep up with everyone else."

My sister is ever so feisty today.

"I'm not trying to keep up. It's just that I've worked all my life, so I wanted to have a nice wedding and I had a vision in mind. This wasn't it. There won't be enough time to do anything."

I can hear middle sis huffing and breathing heavily through the phone, as though she's run a mile to the nearest telephone box.

"What *exactly* do you want? Do you not know how we do things? You can't have it all ways. You want to get married. You moan when things are moving quickly. He must have the patience of a saint dealing with your dithering."

Ouch.

"What am I going to tell work? What will they think?" My voice becomes small.

"Who gives a toss pot? Once you're married you won't care. You're focusing on completely the wrong things. Do your colleagues tell you everything? Do you get a heads up if Jean or Tracy or someone is about to get divorced? Anyway, you'll be leaving the place soon enough, so who cares what they think?"

I don't work with a Jean or Tracy but middle sis has a point, even if her delivery is a bit aggressive. A lifetime of being the odd one out seems to be the way it'll always be for me. And for once I wanted it to be a little different.

A minute after sis abruptly hangs up, she pings me a message: *Sorry if I was harsh. Hormones x*

I've heard people say, I'd marry you tomorrow, when referring to the person of their dreams. It's a strong dramatic theme that runs in Bollywood movies, where the love-struck couple run away to a temple and have the equivalent of a shotgun wedding (minus the pregnancy – the Indian film industry might be progressive with its scantily clad actresses and kissing scenes but I think a child out of wedlock is still a stretch too far). The eloping couple often get married without any guests. The hero will cut his own finger to apply sindhoor on his bride. I never really understood what that red line signifies. I must bring it up with Reena next time we meet up.

It's a very romantic notion that love will conquer all else, including the need for a fancy wedding. However, that rarely translates into reality. I've seen enough episodes of Don't Tell the Bride, where said bride-to-be will forego having anything to do with the planning of her big day and leaves it all to the groom (incentivised by the fact that the BBC will pay for the whole sorry shindig), to know that when it comes to the big day, every girl has a vision.

Now I didn't picture a fairytale per se. I've been living in my own skin long enough to know that I'm not a princess that you read about in books but... I at least knew what I didn't want. I didn't want a rushed job where we'd cut corners, hire a crappy hall - or God forbid a school gymnasium. That was actually a thing back in the day. I've been to many a Bengali wedding where I've had tandoori roast chicken in an indoor basketball court. Sometimes they didn't even bother putting the equipment away. As though the waiters were going to shoot some hoops after a hard day serving

300+ guests. I never knew why weddings would take place in school halls. I guess it was cheaper? Or maybe in the olden days, before the emergence of banqueting halls catering specifically for weddings, they were the only venues that had capacity for so many hungry people.

I just wanted something better. Better than I've always had. My whole life, I've been second rate. At school, most of the kids had two working parents. The double income meant they had better trainers. Their phones were the latest version. Mine would always be a hand-me-down when middle sis was due an upgrade with her mobile contract. Even hers was outdated, so the one passed down would be ancient. Everyone noticed. They always noticed. I remember buying a pair of Adidas trainers for £20 in the sale. I was so in love with them and so proud to show them off on sports day at school. My new trainers, a long overdue replacement, certainly got attention, just not in the way I would have liked.

"You'll be wearing them for the next twenty years!" joked Carly, the only other ethnic minority in our year, who made it her business to make me stand out even more, so she'd fit in better.

I laughed along. After a lifetime of this, I want people to talk about my wedding for the right reasons. Though it seems that it's not finances that may jeopardise my dream day, it's the timescale.

If my life were a Bollywood movie, this would be the bit where I say:

'Yes, I'll marry him in four months. In fact, I'll marry him today, wearing this salwar kameez that big sis bought me from Bangladesh 12 years ago and I still haven't managed to part

with. I don't need the fancy lehenga, I don't need a big venue. I don't need the samosa starters. All I need is... love.'

And if we're going really Bollywood, I'd be the daughter of some aristocratic Asians living in London. My house would be a frigging castle and I'd have numerous outfit changes throughout the day and drive a Lamborghini where the door opens upwards. That's a mash up of a few movies I've seen in my time. It's not about subtlety.

Anyway, I digress.

I've said this before, and I'll say it until I'm even browner in the face, this isn't a Bollywood movie, it's my life. And that shit doesn't happen to me.

If I say to my mum *"all you need is love"*, I'd get two slaps, a *"dooro"* rebuke, or at the very least a nervous laugh. Love is not a word us Bengalis throw around easily. Or at all.

Second, I want to have a decent wedding. I think I deserve it. And you better believe I'll be getting a chocolate fountain.

BUSHRA AND EMMA DON'T know I'm about to get married. I really should've started planting that seed sooner. More to the point, my manager is none the wiser. Bernadette, who needs to sign off my annual leave, is responsible for my appraisals, or in this case has to accept my resignation, doesn't have a clue that I'm even seeing someone. She's never asked, so I've never offered up the information. Not that I wanted to keep it a secret. For the first time in my life I have a relationship. For the first time I can talk about dates (even if they're day dates, they still count). For the first time, I'm part of *that* conversation.

However, though Bernadette is incredibly amiable and enjoys a laugh, she's chalked a clear line between work and life. It's a line she doesn't seem willing to cross. In this over-sharing world in which we live, this makes her something of an anomaly, which has made her vulnerable to office gossip. There was a rumour swirling that she's a lesbian, based pure-ly on the fact that there's never talk of a man. When I think about it like that, I realise what a sad state of affairs we're in as a society. I wonder what fodder my single-and-living-with-parents status created back in the day. I imagine people just boxed me in with the traditional Muslim girl category. Which wasn't that far from the truth.

With Bernadette's disinterest in my personal life, I'm at risk of being the weird one at work, yet again. The funny Asian, as opposed to Bushra, the cool one. I'll be known as the one who is getting married to someone she barely knows. I bet they won't even believe it was a proper courtship to begin with and I made him up and I'm actually having an arranged marriage, to a stranger. It would all seem rather odd.

Truth is, I've managed to make an oddity of myself even when it's not been my relationship. When middle sis got married, I decided to leave it until four days before the big day to request that weekend off work. I remember the awk-ward phone call with Paula, my manager, like it was yester-day:

Paula: "I've received an annual leave request from you, to take this coming Saturday off. I just want to check I read that correctly?"

Me: "Yes, that's right..."

I was a teenager so I really didn't know how to make conversation and fill the void like I do now.

Paula: "Right, okay. It's just that normally we like a little more notice. Saturdays are our busiest days and when we're shortest staffed. Of course you can have it off for an emergency. So I have to ask, is there a real need?"

Me: "Well, yes. My sister is getting married on Saturday."

There was a long silence.

Paula: "Oh, right. I see... well (scoffs)... well of course I'm not going to stop you from attending your sister's wedding. It's just you never mentioned anything before so... right... not to worry though. I'll find some cover, or arrange something. Well, I guess I won't see you before then, so... I hope your sister has a lovely wedding. Oh, and in the future, if one of your family gets married again, just give me a bit of a heads up."

Short notice aside, you could argue that it wasn't really anybody's business about my sister's personal life. Yet it's so intrinsic in the working culture that you talk about your life outside the office – your weekend plans, your boyfriend, your family – that, like Bernadette, my silence spoke volumes. I didn't want to bring the topic of my sister getting married to the table. Honestly, I didn't want the questions. *How lovely, how did they meet? Are they living together? What's your brother-in-law like?*

The answers would've made me stick out even more – *"they met through my family, when he came to my house for samosas with his parents. No, of course not... we don't live to-gether before marriage. And honestly, I don't know what to tell you on that front. I've only met him twice and exchanged a few pleasantries, so I don't really know what he's like, though he seems nice."*

So I did what I usually do – avoid the issue. Don't offer up any information, so I need answer no questions. I put it off as long as I could, until I needed a day off for the wedding. I cringe looking back at this.

Now I think of it, if a white colleague had a quickie wedding, nobody would think anything of it. Nobody would question the girl's welfare or the authenticity of her feelings. Perhaps it's one rule for us and another for them. Or maybe it's all in my head. I don't know. What I *do* know is that there's a TV show called Married at First Sight and I hear it's pretty popular. If the same exact show featured only Bengali Muslims, would it get the same response?

Work weirdness aside, there's another niggle. I'm not mentally prepared to get married in less than four months. I'm beyond glad and embarrassingly grateful that my perfect guy has come into my life. There is no question that I want to marry M but, at the same time, this seismic change involves leaving my little world. I know I complain a lot about my life set up. When I was ostensibly single it felt like everyone around me was moving on with their lives. While I felt like I couldn't wait to start this next exciting chapter, in reality I can wait a little. Just long enough to tidy any loose ends and get myself in order.

Of course mum has no idea what I'm talking about.

"What is the problem? I thought you wanted to marry this boy? Is it so bad to get married this summer?" she asks, stirring a steaming pot of a very pungent and unmistakable substance. She hasn't even bothered to crank open a window in our very narrow kitchen that barely has space for both of us.

"I'm just worried we won't have much time to plan anything properly and make it nice," I say, trying not to scrunch up my nose.

"Oh, you no worry," says mum, continuing to stir her pot. "We make it nice. We no be stingy with your wedding. People get married in much shorter time and it be still nice. I got wed weeks after meeting your father just once. You lucky that way. So you can't say you no time to prepare. Anyway, if you no get married in July when you want to?"

Mum turns her attention to her coriander-topped chopping board. I don't know why she's bothering. No amount of herb-age could disguise the smell of dried fish.

"I don't know. Not much later. I just thought... I don't know," I say, stepping further away from the noxious-smelling pot.

I'm not usually one to procrastinate but it's all just come so suddenly. It's stupid really. I feel stupid.

"In life you not always meet a boy that's good, that you get to know, and most important likes you."

"Alright mum, I'm not that bad, am I?"

"No. That's not what I say. I mean, not everybody marriage end well. Many people make big compromise. No big compromise here, so I don't think we should delay too long. You don't want to upset in-laws before they your in-laws.

You know how our people are. When auntie Jusna hear, she be calling everybody she knows in Droylsden to see what stirring she can do about us. She no want to be only one with smelly armpit."

"Speaking of smelly, do you want to -"

I stop myself before I say any more. It's a test. Mum is forever saying I'm the reason she stopped cooking shutki. Maybe it's the conversation with M's mum that's inspired her to cook it again for the first time in years. She's deliberately kept the windows closed on this mild April day, trapping the smell inside the confines of the kitchen. It's like she's taunting me, willing me to complain, so she can take comfort in the fact that she was right all along and I was the one who got in the way of her and her precious dried fish delicacy. I won't take the bait.

"Our armpits aren't that bad either. What could they say about us?"

On that note, I really better do an audit on my Facebook account to ensure that there's nothing from my uni days that could be discovered, manipulated and misconstrued.

"Not just us. It take two people to get married. Who knows what that woman will find out about your in-laws. It not worth the trouble. Anyway, I think finding a date is getting tricky. We need someone else involved. Just think, if we can't even agree on a wedding date, what else will we disagree on?"

Having planted that massive seed of doubt, mum heads out into the garden to retrieve the washing as she's seen one dark cloud form. She has no idea how, with a single comment, she can throw my whole life into a calamity. Can disagreeing on the wedding date cause so much trouble?

I'M ON A MISSION. I've got my appraisal with Bernadette in ten minutes and my main aim is to segue a conversation about M into the mix. It won't be easy.

To make matters worse, our usual safe confines of the marketing office is out of bounds due to an office refurb, so we have to hold our appraisal in the smaller staff kitchen which offers zero discretion, with its packed in seating arrangement of round tables of four. Even more unfortunate is that we'll be in the company of Ahmed, one of the IT geeks.

Asian colleagues are like buses, you wait for ages for one to come along to make you feel less of an oddity and then you get two. Though Ahmed and I aren't in the same department, we share the same pokey kitchen, one of four located throughout the building. From what I've seen so far, there may be more kitchens than ethnic minorities in this company.

Ahmed is possibly the whitest brown person I have ever met. I don't mean Bushra's level of coconut, where she'll drink on the weekend with the other execs. Ahmed is another kind altogether. The specific breed of brown person that will act like every Tom, Dick or Harry at the work social, or basically any environment where he is a minority. He'll largely ignore me in such circumstances. However, when he catches me alone in the kitchen, he acts like a brother from another mother.

I've arrived ahead of Bernadette to find Ahmed chomping loudly on a burrito, which I can only assume is a second lunch as it's gone 3pm.

"Are you looking forward to Ramadan?"

I would bet the budget of my upcoming wedding that Ahmed would never ask me anything about Ramadan in front of anybody else. After all, that'd totally give the game away that he is Muslim.

"I haven't thought about it yet. Isn't it in September or October this year?" I ask.

Ahmed shrugs, no doubt realising that it's such a ridiculously desperate attempt to find common ground. He gets back to crunching his burrito, dripping salsa and shredded lettuce onto the table in the process.

"Anyway, I've got bigger fish to fry," I say.

"Oh really. Is everything okay?"

Well, I guess I must start making it common knowledge that I'm in a relationship so my impending marriage doesn't sound so weird. Ahmed can be my dry run.

"Actually yeah, I'm fine. I'm getting engaged so Ramadan hasn't been at the front of my mind."

Nice segue, if I do say so myself.

"That's brilliant! I'm made up for ya."

He barely knows me.

Ahmed stands up from his chair, leaking burrito still in one hand, as if he's about to give me a congratulatory hug. Then he stops short and instead pats me on the arm in a brotherly manner. Wise move.

"Do you know him?" he asks as he returns to his chair, stepping on his burrito juice en route.

"Who?"

"Err... your soon-to-be fiancé?"

I'm shocked at the line of questioning. Then I remember, despite his best efforts to act otherwise, Ahmed is in fact Pakistani so he knows my world well.

"Of course. We met through friends."

Yeah, that's my lie. And I'm sticking to it.

"Sorry. I didn't mean to pry. Nothing wrong with it if it was an arranged marriage. My parents are in Pakistan right now, looking for me."

I did not expect such an admission. He'd never 'fess up to that at one of our work socials.

"Oh. Well, good for you. I hope you find someone suitable. Or I hope *they* do."

Bernadette comes through the door, signifying the end of our conversation. She's accompanied by Amy, a business development manager who has just finished her appraisal. I don't know Amy very well as she's recently got back from maternity leave and she only pops into our office every couple of weeks or so. She's usually on the road, visiting the different hospitals under her remit.

"So sorry to have cut it short, Bernadette," says Amy. "It's such a nightmare having to work to a pumping schedule. If I don't express now, my boobs are going to explode."

"Of course love. You do what you gotta do. At the end of the day, baby comes first. We need more women like you balancing the mum and work thing and doing a great job of it. Anyway, we're all ladies here -"

Bernadette stops mid-sentence as she notices a small trail of salsa on the floor leading to a burrito besmirched Ahmed.

He looks sheepish. "Sorry Bernie, I'm nearly done. As soon as I'm finished eating I'll clear my mess. Then you women can get back to your gossiping."

Bernadette doesn't dignify him with a response. Rumour has it she hates being called Bernie.

"Anyway, it really is great to have you back, Amy," says Ahmed.

I doubt Amy even knows him, however Ahmed wants to make his presence felt.

Amy reaches in the fridge for her handheld breast pump and an empty baby bottle. "Thanks Ahmed. It's good to be back, even if I've got to do this every two hours."

Ahmed pushes his round Harry Potter-style glasses up against his brow. "More power to you, I say. And it's a win-win for all of us as we've just ran out of milk for our tea. Hehe."

Nobody else laughs. Amy's mouth gapes open in horror. She clutches her pump close to her chest and dashes out of the door. He really is the worst.

"Right, well, shall we crack on missy?" Bernadette opens up her folder as she settles down in the chair opposite me. "So, as you no doubt know, you're getting on six months here. It's crazy as it feels like you've been here forever."

"I know, it's been great being part of the team."

I think Bernadette picked up on my past tense, as her next question is: "So what would you like to achieve in the next six months? Are we doing everything we can for you here?"

I'd like to get married and move to London, goes my inner monologue. I figure I must say something more meaningful and relevant to the job though.

"I'm not sure really," says my outer monologue. "I guess, just more media outreach. Some more national campaigns. I've got some great stuff in the Daily Mail for the Scottish hospitals but I'd like some more of that and do something a bit more strategic."

I sound vague as hell, largely because I know that this job is coming to an end.

"Anything else?" she looks at me directly.

I know Bernadette doesn't suffer fools. Her eye contact, which she uses sparingly, is unnerving.

"Well, to be honest, I wasn't sure how much further I could go, as there isn't a PR person that's senior to me. I figured this is the peak in this role?"

"No, no. There is room for growth and there is definitely room for you to develop. In the time you've been here you've made yourself an invaluable member of the team. You're always bringing solutions instead of problems and speaking of which, while we're on that note, I just wanted to address the elephant in the room."

Huh? There's an elephant? Does she know I'm about to get married? Has Bushra already leaked news of our relationship? Am I office gossip fodder? It's a good thing if I am, actually, as it makes my segue into talking about M and my future plans all the easier.

It seems that Ahmed is equally as paranoid about her remark, as he proceeds to mop around us with a paper towel, wiping up the salsa remnants. "Alright Bernie, I know I've got a bit of timber but that's a bit harsh."

"Sorry Ahmed? What was that?" asks Bernadette.

"You said elephant in the room?"

Bernadette looks at him, bemused and unamused.

"I'm just playing with ya. Anyway... I think that's my cue. I'll leave you ladies to it."

Poor try-hard Ahmed. He was never with us to need to excuse himself in the first place.

"Okay, so now the one-man comedy tour has hit the road, I wanted to address the actual metaphoric elephant. You're probably aware that Mel is under review."

I'm clueless. As always, clueless. I love how Bernadette assumes that what she knows in management trickles down to us minions.

"Actually, I didn't know."

"Well, perhaps what you do know is that she's been missing vital events and then getting you to cover up by creating PR stories, which then impacts the rest of your work. I appreciate your initiative and willingness to help. One of your strengths is that you bring solutions instead of problems but don't feel like you have to cover anyone else's backside. I don't want people taking advantage of your conscientiousness."

"Sorry, Bernadette. I just didn't want the story to pass. So when she called me the day before the event saying she needed a press release, I had a window of time so I just wrote it."

"Look, I'm not blaming you at all. You're a true professional who ensures that the show goes on but, when your colleagues aren't pulling their weight, you shouldn't have to carry them."

I'm flattered by the high praise. That's something I've always received everywhere I've worked. Though the truth is, it's not just because I care about the show going on. I always oblige because I feel that's my only real offering. A lifetime of trying extra hard to fit in means I really struggle to say no when there's an opportunity to prove myself invaluable. It's not for more money. It's not for recognition. It's to make up for the fact that I'm different. Since I don't go to the piss-ups on the weekend, I can't bring gossip to the table, so my value is based on being wholly reliable. And a bit funny with it. Though not quite at Ahmed's level of being constantly switched on to the point of annoyance.

"Onto more exciting things," says Bernadette. "There are lots of opportunities for you that I hope will help achieve your objectives. This isn't hugely common knowledge yet, but as the company is expanding there will be a big PR campaign to go with it. Head office have already planned to make a song and dance about the office move from Kew to Liverpool Street and I reckon there's room for the regionals to tap into that momentum. It would be a great opportunity for you to get involved on a national level. I know that's what you want to get your teeth into."

I knew the office in London was moving but I didn't realise where they were moving to. This takes on a whole new significance.

This is my opportunity. I'm going to say it. Going to bring it up. I'm going to bring *him* up. Though I don't know how to refer to him. Boyfriend just doesn't feel right as I don't see him like that. Partner seems far too grown-up. Special friend is just ridiculous.

Bernadette taps the page on her notepad with the end of her pen. I need to jump on the subject before she moves onto the next point.

"Oh, are they moving to Liverpool Street? That's where my boyfriend's from."

Ooh, that sounded weird.

Bernadette looks up and smiles. "Lovely. Anyway, as I was saying, there's lots of room for development. Right, shall we talk about your targets for the next six months?"

"Okay, so... national campaigns sound good. Perhaps getting more strategic level project work under my belt rather than ad-hoc press releases would be great," I say, scrambling for something substantial to add.

"Yes, I agree. I think you would be really good at strategic stuff. Also, we do have a small budget if you need any external training. It doesn't have to necessarily be directly related to your role as we're really into professional development."

"That would be really good. I was just talking to my boyfriend as he works in finance and he often deals with company turnover and it sounds so interesting so maybe... something along those lines."

I have no idea what I'm talking about.

Bernadette scribbles ferociously. "Yeah, that could work. Brilliant! I'm going to be thinking about this."

"Oh, definitely. I don't wanna be in the same position for sure. In fact, I was having a conversation with my boyfriend -"

"Sorry, if you don't mind... it's just... I've got another appraisal straight after you, so if we could..." Bernadette winds her hand up, signalling for us to move things along. I've obviously taken M-planting too far. If I could dissolve into my chair, I really would.

"Oh yes, sorry," I say, running my hand along the binder of my notebook. It's like giving myself a scratchy hand massage.

"But I'd love to talk about your overall aims later, we just need to keep to the points on this rather long agenda."

At least I got to put in a few words about M. So hopefully when she finds out I'm getting married, it won't be such a shock.

I DECIDE TO USE THE commute home wisely and call M.

"So I had my appraisal today and I found out something pretty interesting. The London office is moving from Kew to somewhere more central," I tease.

"That's good. It will be easier for us to meet up when you're next in London for your meetings. Does that mean you'll be getting the train in from now on? Not that you'll have many more meetings, I guess."

"Well, here's the thing, it's pretty crazy really. Of all the places in London that they could move to, the office will be relocating to your neck of the woods. Liverpool Dock."

"Erm, do you mean Liverpool Street?"

I am such a dingbat. "Oh yeah, of course. Liverpool dock is in Liverpool I guess. Or is that Albert Dock? I never understand why London has other city names. Don't get me started on Scotland Yard. Anyway, yeah, they're moving to Liverpool Street."

M laughs in disbelief. "That's brilliant! What are the odds? Do you think you could get a transfer? I know you like your job."

We really are kindred spirits. "I was thinking the exact same thing. I'm not sure if they'll go for it. I don't know if, as a regional PR, I can be based remotely in the capital. But Bernadette loves me so I'm figuring it will be worth an ask. I don't wanna get excited though so let's see."

Glass half empty, glass half empty. This is too important to jinx with optimism. I'm as shocked as M at this latest development with work. Sophia would always say to me, if it's meant to be with a guy everything will fall into place. Surely this is another sign that we're right for each other?

"How do you feel about it all? You know, the potential wedding in July," I ask.

"You know me. If I could, I'd marry you tomorrow. I just want you here."

I knew he watched Bollywood movies but I didn't know he lived by their extra dramatic rules.

"What have you told your work?" I ask.

"Nothing much yet. I mean, I obviously told them about you. They knew about us from the beginning. Once we get engaged I'll obviously tell them but they don't need to know the ins and outs of our business."

"Don't you think they'll find it a bit weird how one minute you're seeing me and within the blink of an eye you're getting engaged and then married?"

"No," says M, rather confidently. "They're pretty open-minded so they understand that we might do things a bit differently. They've had enough conversations with me to not be surprised by a quick Bengali wedding."

"What about your flatmate? What does he make of all of it?"

"I mean, he thinks it's pretty quick. So I explained to him how things work and now he can't wait to meet you. Though he is a bit gutted that I'll be moving out. Which reminds me, I've been keeping an eye on the flat rental situation and I've seen some nice apartments near where I'm living. I'll send you some links. Would you be okay if we stayed around Liverpool Street? I think it might be easier as it's familiar."

Oh my God. Oh my God. Oh my God. We have to figure out where we're going to live, too! This is mental. There are so many details I haven't even thought of. I'm not sure why this surprises me. Of course we have to live *somewhere*.

"Yeah, Liverpool Street way will be fine," I say, like I know any different. Beyond the East End, I don't have much of an opinion on the boroughs of London.

"Anyway," M continues, "to be honest with ya, I don't really care what anyone thinks. The only thing that really matters in all of this is that you're happy. And you are happy, right?"

"Yeah, of course. I just worry that things will be rushed. It's basic things, like I won't be able to order customised outfits in advance for my sisters. I probably won't be able to order a lehenga that's custom made from India."

"Would you have expected to?" asks M. "I thought most people buy them from the UK?"

He's got my pretentious arse there. It's only my Indian and Pakistani friends that have outfits custom-made from their respective motherlands.

"I know you're a bit apprehensive," says M. "It's understandable, as you're the one that's going to be coming here having the big life change. For me, I guess, it's kind of business as usual, except I'll have you in my life every day. But I said it before, our wedding will be great. I'll make sure of it."

He really is a keeper. My Bollywood–esque hero.

"But I have to go," he says. "I'm heading to the gym just now. Better get my wedding bod in shape. Plus, I didn't wanna say, but I can barely hear you. The reception is really bad. Have you got me on hands-free?"

"No, sorry. I'm rubbish with technology. You're on speaker on the passenger seat. Full marks for persevering for this long, I had no idea it was bad on your end. I can hear you fine."

"Well, if you're happy to, I can coax you out of your technophobe ways. Only if you'd like to."

"Hmmm, not sure I'm ready to commit to learning a new skill like that but we'll see," I joke.

"Fair enough. Just commit to me for the rest of your life instead."

Every conversation with M helps me learn something new about him. This call has taught me that the difference between his upbringing in an Asian area, in contrast with mine being the only brownie in the village, is palpable. He's just so much more comfortable in his own skin. M's not bothered if our hastily arranged marriage seems weird to anybody outside of the community. He has those awkward conversations that I avoid like the plague. He's basically more at ease being Bengali in the UK than I have ever been. I applaud his confidence but it also makes me a little sad. I think I've been white washing my culture my entire life. Speaking to him just reminds me of that even more.

When did I became so desperate to be anything but Bengali? One memory sticks out. One time in school, when I must've been about four or five, we were all told to paint a picture of our mums as a Mother's Day gift. I proudly painted one long rectangle, the shape of a thin cupboard, in red. I dipped the brush in the red again and painted a diagonal sash across the top. Then, I took the brown paint and drew a circle for a face and long, strong arms.

There. My mum. Like no other.

"What's that?" asked a classmate whose name I no longer remember.

"It's a saree." I was pretty proud of my recreation of mum, my muse.

When I looked around me, I could see that everyone else's picture was different. Their mums didn't wear a saree. Some had painted two vertical stripes for the legs. Others had painted triangles, with two L-shapes underneath, pointing outwards for feet. Nobody used brown paint. Most used the palest pink for their circles. Others opted for white.

By the time the next Mother's Day came around I didn't use the brown paint. I drew a triangle skirt and did my best attempt at a T-shirt.

My mum, who has been used to a life of difference ever since she moved to the UK as a newlywed teenager, never said a thing. The new painting took pride of place on the fridge, replacing the old her.

I doubt M would have painted his mother in anything but a saree.

The second thing I've learnt about him is that his priorities are so different to mine. I'm being really anal and asking for the impossible of:

a) Getting married and progressing a relationship.

b) Taking enough time to ensure that I get to have all the little things I've dreamt about.

c) Beating Hassna to the marital post.

He doesn't care that we're getting married sooner, he doesn't care what our wedding day will look like. He just wants... me. I've learnt that, perhaps for the first time in my life, I am enough.

I should say the same thing about him, but who am I kidding? I still want a better wedding than Hassna's. Even if I have to run around like a mad bitch to execute it in record time.

AS I OPEN THE DOOR to my home, mum is already in the hallway waiting to greet me like an eager beaver.

"I spoke to his mum today..." she says.

We're at the stage now where we don't even need to explain who 'his mum' is. It saves a lot of preamble.

"And?" I'm hoping it's promising.

"We're going for an end of June engagement. I've checked with your sisters and that works out. Obviously you free as you never busy. You'll be happy as now there be more time for wedding. We'll go for after the school holiday and I think the best thing is..."

Mum does her lip grimace thing. Bloody hell, what's she going to come up with now?

"It's better if we get someone else involved in the wedding planning. You know, someone between boy family and ours. Just to avoid any tricky talk or argument."

As if our wedding wasn't convoluted enough. I guess in our culture, there is no such thing as too many cooks spoiling the broth. The more kitchen help the better.

10th April
The middleman

We love nothing more than muddying the water with a third party. In the case of my wedding planning, the appointed mediator is my uncle Tariq from London. He's mum's second cousin and closest relative in the UK. After a couple of tricky negotiations between my mum and M's, we narrowly avoided a wedding date for, basically, tomorrow (all they needed was a mosque in Vegas and an Elvis -impersonating Imam).

Uncle Tariq seems to be a reasonable mediator. If we employed one of my brother-in-laws, unconscious bias may have crept in. The same issue would have occurred if M's older brother was roped in. So my maternal uncle is the ideal fit, a distant relative in both blood and miles, yet mum will have his ear. Win-win.

Also, there's a sneaky little bonus. I get to hear the gossip about my cousin Naila, who got married last year to her white boyfriend. Mum is also relishing the opportunity to find out more. We're both nosey cows.

WHENEVER I TRY TO TALK to mum about getting things planned for the wedding, to understand what we need to do in some kind of chronological order, her answer is always the same - '*khe zanoo*'. Basically, *who knows*, said in a harsh way, like how dare I even ask.

Mum is not one for details and she firmly believes that everything will kind of figure itself out and that's what uncle Tariq is for. However, uncle Tariq will be operating at a macro level. He won't be in charge of things like getting flowers sorted, or my wedding makeup. All that will be on me and I want to know what else I'm missing. However, mum is even more glass half empty than I am and is scared of jinxing things by planning too early. There's the conundrum with Bengali weddings. I totally get that she doesn't want to jump the gun in fear of things going wrong. After all, I haven't even told all my friends yet. Yet, at the same time, there really isn't much time left for venues, custom outfits or much else. It's a Catch 22. Don't do things too soon then risk leaving it too late and having a crap wedding. Now I know why weddings used to take place at school halls. They obviously didn't have enough time to book anywhere decent.

So, with the grace of three months, I decided to compile a list. A wedding planning list. I'll probably share it with M, after all it's as much his day as it is mine, though I'll omit my personal grooming bullet points from the master list. He doesn't need to know about *that*. I'd like to retain some mystique.

Here we go... In no particular order, this is everything I *think* I must do ahead of my wedding. Oh crap, there's the engagement to plan, too. So I guess I need three lists, engagement planning, wedding planning, my MOT.

Cini Paan / Engagement

- Buy engagement saree. M's family is going to give me an outfit and hopefully some jewels to go with it but I need to arrive in something. That something must be bling-tastic and expensive. My tight purse strings are already straining.
- Book a venue. This one is very much the responsibility of my family. However, given mum's relaxed attitude, I better do some of my own research, lest I end up with a school gymnasium. First job is to scope out the cost of Hassna's engagement location. My poor purse again.
- Sort catering menu. Food is usually thrown in with the venue, so that's pretty straightforward.
- Try out hair and makeup artists. Probably the most important one for me. I can kill two birds with one stone here. If I find a good makeup artist, I'll book her for my wedding, too.
- Waxing. Not on the face this time, thankfully.
- Order a cake. My family and M's family will do a cake swapping kind of thing.

As I look at the list, I'm pretty sure I've missed a tonne of things out. I'm also glaringly aware of how easy boys have it when it comes to planning the engagement ceremony. As far as I know, M's (or his family's) job is to get me an outfit and ring, rock up to the venue with a truckload of mishti (fingers crossed there is some rasmallai and gulab jaman in there) and enjoy the ceremony.

Okay, onto the wedding:

- Find a venue.
- Book a hair and makeup artist.
- Get waxed.
- Other personal grooming that I don't even know about but I'm sure will be necessary.
- Create meaningful wedding favours.
- Hire pretentious crap like a chocolate fountain. I defy anyone who says that's a luxury, I'm having one.
- Get a bridal bouquet.
- Choose a wedding lehenga that M's family will pay for.
- Hire limo so I can arrive at the venue in style.
- Book a mehendi artist.

Oh crap! That reminds me... we have a mehendi to organise too, which is a whole other thing. The mehendi will be bigger than the engagement but smaller than the wedding. We'll need taals. I won't be making them, thankfully, but my family and other guests will have to pull their fingers out and bring some photogenic serving trays with carved fruit and other such delicacies to present to me at the ceremony. That'll need a list of its own.

I'm getting a headache. I shall take a break and look for a standard Bengali wedding list online or something that I can just cut and paste.

Without a brother in the family and a dad who likes to exclude himself from most responsibilities, I'll be carrying the can for most of this.

Big sis is miles away. I can't expect much from her and I shouldn't, really. She's been the parent/appointed adult for most of her grown-up life. With my parents' poor command of English, she was the one writing the sick notes for school, the one filling out the forms for everything we needed, whether it was grown-up financial things like sorting dad's life plan or the onerous form filling that came with the unfortunate yet brief spell that we had to sign on for benefits.

The only time she really got things taken care of for her was during her wedding. One of the advantages of getting married in Bangladesh is there are a whole host of busybodies to take care of every detail. From the uncles who don't give a toss about you ordinarily, to the domestic staff who can be called upon to do the leg work. One of the disadvantages, however, of getting married in Bangladesh is also that there are a whole host of busybodies to take care of every detail. Big sis didn't have a say at all. She didn't get to pick a makeup artist. There were no trials. She was driven to the most convenient beauty parlour and had to make do with whoever was working on her face. Luckily, because of her fairness, she didn't go far wrong with the makeup artist she got.

After marriage, the responsibilities came back two fold for her. She didn't have the luxury of relying on a man to take care of her affairs. My big brother-in-law came with his own poor command of English. He had his own needs, his own respective forms that needed filling out. Once again, she was the grown-up. Now, with her own kids, she might as well consign herself to a life of adulting. So I guess I shouldn't expect her to step up to my wedding planning.

Middle sis is busy with her own life. She just revealed that she is expecting again, which explains why she's been so short tempered recently. As a result, I can't expect much help from her either. She always said three was the magic number when it comes to kids so I'm delighted for her, even if the timing is off.

As for my teenage sister, she's a teenager. If it's nothing to do with her phone, she won't know what to do. I suppose she can help me with the online shopping part.

It's times like this I wish I had a big brother. You know, like a proper grown-up to take care of all the man's jobs rather than having to rely on uncle Tariq. In fact, there have been many occasions in my life when I would've liked a brother but none more so than now.

15th April
I'm getting engaged!

I'm getting engaged in six weeks. I'm getting engaged in six weeks. I'm getting engaged in six flipping weeks!

I'll just say it one more time, purely to get my point across – I'm getting engaged! In six weeks!

Now I'm over the panic at the speed of it all, and I've managed to pepper in conversations – albeit very un-subtly - at work, I'm allowing myself to enjoy the moment and revel in the fact that I'm actually, actually getting engaged. To a boy I like. Who would've thought it?

Also, bonus points for beating some of my closest friends down the aisle (even if it's a pretend makeshift aisle as we don't do churches). Not that it's a race but even so... I'm getting engaged!

OKAY, I SHOULD REIN it in a little. I don't want to jinx myself. As mum frequently reminds me, a lot can go wrong between now and the 4th of June.

"Have some *shorom*," mum says, begging me to adopt some modesty when I acknowledge the fact that I've done pretty well choosing a decent boy.

I can't help but be a smug git. At one point, I didn't expect to meet anyone at all. Or I figured it would be a serious compromise.

Julia and Reena, for all their past relationships and generally more progressive outlook on marriage, always worried about me. So it's nice to know that I, with my medieval background and arranged marriage process, have met a great guy before them. I'll be marrying him, too.

So for everyone who's been pooh-poohing the modern arranged marriage process where you get introduced and make your own intros, I just want to stick it to them. The system works. Surely I'm allowed to be self-satisfied about that?

Anyway, can't spend all day revelling in my own sense of accomplishment, I've got an engagement to plan.

20th April

The great gift exchange

N ew addition to engagement list:
- Buy a gift for M.

Gone are the simpler times when an engagement ceremony was a cup of tea job at your house. Now they're like
mini weddings. Some lucky girls, like Hassna, even get gifted
a small gold necklace and earrings set from their husband-to-
be. Another thing I noticed at Hassna's engagement was that
she wasn't the only one on the receiving end of such generosity. She had gifted her fiancé a watch. Not just any watch, an
Omega stainless steel watch. Bloody show off.

Given that gifting the groom is all the rage, I have no
choice but to conform. Plus, I think it helps balance things
out. After all, I'll be getting a ring, makeup, a saree and
other gifts. I won't quite spring for an Omega watch. A quick
Google search made me hastily retreat to my stingy ways.
Just where does Hassna get her money? Or maybe it's her
poor dad. Mum reckons they are pulling out all the stops to
ensure that this marriage goes more smoothly than her older
sister's. I'm inclined to agree with her theory.

Having said that, I do want to gift him something pretty
smart. After all, he is worth it. It will also be a nice project.
I'll be able to take care of this side of the engagement planning completely by myself. I'll screenshot a few watches for

him to choose from. I'm thinking if I show him what he's getting, it may go towards getting a better diamond ring and a more dazzling saree.

ONE EVENING AFTER WORK, M's sister-in-law rings my house, wanting to speak to me. I've no idea what she wants. Is she the appointed middle-woman from his side? I haven't had the chance to meet her, let alone speak to her, so my Bengali politeness and nervous formalities kick into play.

"Salaam, how are you?" a voice comes through the phone. She sounds like a young girl. M's big brother got married in Bangladesh, though you wouldn't know straight away that his sister-in-law is from back home. Speaking with a mixture of Bengali and clipped English, she seems at ease with the latter language, and her accent is barely traceable.

"Walaykum salaam. I'm good thank you, are you well?"

"Oh, very well. You know how it is, I'm just busy with my kids. Well, I guess you don't know yet but I'm sure you'll find out soon enough. Anyway, welcome to the family, I can't wait to meet you properly. Also, I need to check something... You know we've got to get you some makeup? So I want to make sure we get it right. Obviously your future husband doesn't really know anything about these things. Neither does your mother-in-law, so could you tell me what makeup you'd like? You know, if there's any brands you use, that sort of thing?"

This is tricky territory. I can't be too cheeky and task them with getting the makeup I need to replenish. So while my heart wants to do a big word vomit of: *Mac! Illamasqua! Bobbi Brown! Nars!* my head makes me say: "Oh, I'm not sure really. I'll be happy with whatever you get."

This will not do for my big sister-in-law. "Honestly. Tell me. Don't be shy. We'd rather get you something you like and actually use than just anything. If you could say, that would help."

As if I'm going to start dictating the makeup I want. Or... should I? No, I don't think any good will come of reeling off a list of my beauty must haves.

"Honestly, please just choose. I don't have a preference," I say.

"I know you're just saying that but you don't need to worry. You'll be doing me a favour if you tell me what you like as I'll be getting it for you," she tells me.

This is super awkward.

"I appreciate that but I don't want you to go to too much trouble or expense. Honestly, I'll love whatever you get. I'm sure it will be great."

She huffs.

Is she annoyed? I'm really not good at this.

"Okay, okay. I'll see what I can get. I just hope that you like it. I look forward to meeting you at the cini paan."

Mum shuffles towards me before I've even put the phone down.

"Is everything okay? What she ask you?"

"She wanted to know what engagement makeup I wanted."

"That be nice of her to ask. You didn't be greedy, did you?" Mum is so concerned that I'm going to blow this engagement.

"No! Of course not but she was really pushing it. She really, really wanted me to choose my own makeup."

Mum laughs. She's been down this road before. "Oh that be what they say all the time. She being polite and be shock if you tell her what you wanted. She not expect to buy £30 of makeup."

"£30!" I gasp. "More like £300! If I was to be honest, she'd be spending £30 on one foundation."

Now it's mum's turn to gasp. "What? I don't *buleev*. Good thing you kept quiet. She's only expecting to buy you a beauty box. Like those ones they sell in Debenhams. Anyway, you no buy a £30 foundation yourself. You too cheap."

She's got me there.

WHILE I SHOULD'VE BEEN working, I've instead been tackling my list of things to buy for this shindig. First, for some inspiration. The competitive world of social media tells me that you can buy cute little duck egg coloured boxes as wedding favours. Some people fill them with sweets, some people choose something more sentimental, like a sprig of lavender. I can say right now, without any hesitation, that a dried flower would *not* go down well with hundreds of hungry guests at a Bengali wedding. Often, the sweets that lie within the favour bag get gobbled up as appetisers as the food is always late to arrive. These cute boxes, at £1.50 a pop, are a little on the pricey side given the size of our guest list. I'll put them in the maybe box.

I'm also thinking about taals. I know I shouldn't really be concerned with this as it's for everyone else to make these for me. However, there's no harm in looking for ideas to send to my sisters. I screen shot a picture of a taal featuring a watermelon expertly carved into a basket. I doubt either of my older sisters could be that creative so I'll add it to the maybe pile.

One thing that's in the definite pile is a watch for M.

I've sent him a selection of watches to choose from. I ensured that the price points for each timepiece are in full view. It's a rather impressive range, too - there's Hugo Boss, Armani and some Scandinavian brand I'd never heard of but M had mentioned once. I hope he appreciates the thought. The prices range between £180 at the lower end, right up to the princely sum of £450. How dare mum call me stingy?

However, within this open basket of generosity lies a test. If he goes for the most expensive item, he'll go down in my estimations. I've heard horror stories of men picking the most elaborate watch or wedding suit *purely* because it was being paid for by their prospective in-laws. According to legend, one such guy kitted himself from head to toe in Gucci at the expense of his poor (quite literally after that) bride-to-be. He even bought the socks from Selfridge's, just because the opportunity was there. Now that's really taking the biscuit. I'm hoping M is much more modest and will just be grateful for the gesture.

My email pings with his reply: *They all look pretty good. You've obviously got good taste ;-). I think my favourite is the*

*Hugo Boss one but the Armani is nice too. Here's some others
I've seen as well.*

Oh no! He's going to milk me for all I'm worth. How
did I not see this coming?

As I open the attached screenshot with trepidation, my
anguish turns to relief when I notice that every single watch
in his screenshot falls nicely within the lower end of the price
range of the watches I sent. He passes the test and I failed
it by not giving him enough credit. I should really also stop
panicking before I've had a chance to open the email. I really
do assume the worst.

Another email from him. This time it's a one liner: *I like
them all but I'll let you choose :-)*

Just for that, I decide to buy the Armani one. It sits
just above the mid-range price point, at £323. It's the right
amount to show that I'm not stingy but I ain't no mug either.
Perfect.

"What do you think of this?" I ask Bushra.

She leans over the top of my screen. "Oh nice. He's a
lucky boy."

Bushra doesn't know I'm about to get engaged, though
I have strongly suggested that it's heading in that direction.
I'm hoping, through her, word of my progressing courtship
will filter through to my work colleagues so when I do an-
nounce my engagement I can palm it off as a romantic surprise. As opposed to the reality of it being a carefully curated
event, orchestrated by my uncle Tariq who I barely see.

"You do know that you can get that exact same watch for
a lot cheaper?" says Bushra.

"From where?" I'd only looked at the Goldman's website so far. What does Bushra know that I don't?

"Here, let me have a look for you."

She sidles over and perches herself on the end of my desk, offering a generous up-skirt view to Ahmed, who's fixing the hot desk computer behind us. Clambering about on all fours and fiddling with wiring, his head nearly snaps off as he attempts to get a better look. Then he retreats in disappointment upon realising that Bushra's thick tights preserve some modesty.

"Here you go," Bushra straightens up defiantly. "I've just saved you 100 quid."

"What *is* this site? Where did you find it? The dark web?"

Bushra laughs. "No, it's totally legit. You're just paying through the nose if you go through one of those retailers. This is cheaper because they don't have a shop front."

It's tempting. "Will he know though? Will it be obvious it's from a cheap shop?"

"No, it's fine. It will look exactly like the one you're about to buy."

"Oh... I don't know Bushra..."

"What's to know? You'll be saving a packet for the same product and he will be thanking you if he's any kind of bloke."

"I'm just nervous. What if it comes without the box? It wouldn't be a knock off, would it?"

Bushra laughs. "It's fine. Goldman's will be buying the same watches from the same supplier and marking it up to pay their staff. All the big shops do it."

"I've got a Skagen watch from them before." Ahmed emerges from under the desk. "Honestly mate, you'd never know where it's from."

That's the brand M mentioned. Am I the only one who's not heard of it?

"There you go. If it's good enough for Ahmed..." says Bushra.

I can't tell if she's being sarcastic, though her argument's compelling.

"It's up to you. If it were me, I'd save the hundred quid and put it towards the honeymoon fund. Think of all the burkinis you could get." She winks at me, obviously very proud of the Muslim in-joke she just cracked.

It's just occurred to me that this is the most densely brown office I've ever sat in. Poor James, it's bad enough when it's just us girls talking shop. With three Asian Muslims, he must think we're taking over.

With a bit of peer pressure and a lot of my own penny-pinching ways coming to the fore, I ditch Goldman's in favour of this online watch shop I've never heard of.

"I CAN'T WAIT FOR YOU to see your watch. I think you'll love it."

I'm so pleased with my generous (though not too generous) purchase, that I have to tell him on our evening call while my little sis is downstairs.

"Well, I hope you didn't spend too much. There is really no need," says M.

"It's fine. You can make it up to me with a diamond ring."

"Oh yeah. On that note, is that what you're expecting?"

Is he joking?

"I... I suppose? Isn't that the norm these days?" I can't quite believe I'm uttering these words to Mr Modern.

"I don't know really. I think when my brother got married, my mum just bought the ring," he says.

"Oh. Is it a diamond ring?"

"I think so. I wasn't too involved to be honest with ya, as they did it all in Bangladesh."

"Then I doubt it would be a diamond. Was it a boat ring?"

"What's a boat ring?"

Are we actually having this conversation? "It's a ring that's shaped like a canoe. People used to give it back in the day. Now I think most people give proper diamond engagement rings. At least that's what girls have come to expect."

"Ah, okay. I couldn't tell you what shape the ring was. I thought it was diamond but I wasn't paying that much attention. Would you mind if my mum got the ring for you?"

Oh dear.

"I'm not too sure... I think... it would be a bit weird. I know that was the done thing back then, especially in Bangladesh, but things have moved on a bit since those days of getting engaged to your mother-in-law."

I figure a bit of humour can cut the tension.

"Ha ha, yeah, that's true." He's trying to lighten the mood, too. "Okay, well I'll find out. I'm not trying to do you out of a ring. It's just that I genuinely don't really know. I'm a bloke so I'm not really sure what the norm is for any of this. I'm just going by what my brother did."

His lucky sister-in-law. Now I'm really glad I didn't give her an honest makeup request.

"When did your brother get married?" I ask.

"Over ten years ago," he pauses as the maths speak for itself. "I guess things have changed. Obviously, English people give diamond engagement rings but I never thought of what we did."

"Well, maybe you should." I don't mean to sound like a bitch, I just can't help it. "Anyway, I have to love you and leave you. My sister is going to come upstairs any minute now."

"Okay, well, I guess I'll speak to you tomorrow?"

"Yeah. Sure." I'm hoping he picks up on my lousy attitude.

"Well, you have a good night."

Is he serious? So I might not have a proper engagement ring? Instead of flashing a sparkly diamond ring I'll be sporting a fresh from Bangladesh banana boat ring? I'm glad he's getting a cheap watch now.

3rd May
Saree shopping

I'm still reeling from the bombshell that is ring-gate. However, I think I have to suck it up. Maybe this is the compromise mum keeps banging on about. The one thing that might not go my way. Funny though, I thought the compromise was that he's bald.

When I told mum about the lack of ring, she didn't want me to make a fuss.

"Yes, it be disappointing. Hassna had such a big and lovely diamond ring but remember, they be spending thousands on your gold so don't expect too much. You no want them think you greedy. Anyway, once married, you have whole life to make him buy you expensive things."

Mum does have a point. When someone at work gets engaged and flashes that lovely solitaire ring, I know that's all they'll be getting. Whereas I will be gifted more gold than Mr T, more outfits than a duchess and even some dubious makeup to boot.

While I'm accepting (kind of) of the fact that I might not get a ring like Hassna, I'm not letting M off that easily. I'm still going to be passive aggressive about it. Rather than a full-blown argument, I've resorted to my modus operandi. I'm being flaky with returning his calls. My messages are pretty short and bittersweet, too. Hopefully that will be enough of a hint to make him realise the error of his ways. Silly boy.

Given that there won't be a sparkly on my finger, I've decided I'll be sparkly everywhere else. So what could be more sparkly than a festive saree?

Off we head to Rusholme again on what, I suspect, will be the first of a few visits over the next few months.

As this trip is going to be an expensive one, I've enlisted some heavies to help, in the form of my two older sisters. Big sis has trekked up from Bristol on the train with her three kids. As she is the most cultured of all the siblings, she's best placed to advise me on the most appropriate, fashion forward saree for the occasion. Plus, she haggles like a pro. A penny pinching pro at that, which is the best kind.

Middle sis, no doubt feeling guilty about the ear-bashing she gave me when I was such a ditherer about wedding dates, got her hubby to trek her hormonal, nauseous arse across the M62 with her two kids to lend a hand with the shopping. She's also intent on being chief wedding planner and everything else.

"So, I was thinking, I could do your makeup if you like?" middle sis told me the night before she was due to arrive in Manchester.

I already had it sorted. I just decided not to tell anyone, as my sisters always like to have a say in beauty and sartorial matters. Too many cooks in this case really do spoil the broth and push my anxiety through the roof.

"Oh, I'm good, thanks. I've booked a makeup artist from the beautician above the bangle shop in Longsight."

"What, you mean the place that burnt your face?"

The story of my brush with danger has become the stuff of legend in my family.

"Well... yes but I'm not using the same beautician."

"Have you had a trial? You kept that quiet." Middle sis sounds most unimpressed.

"No, I haven't but I saw her portfolio and it looks pretty good." I say, hoping that puts matters to bed.

"You haven't had a trial?!"

Like I said, middle sister is not helping my anxiety.

"No... but there was no time. What with work, finding a venue, booking a cake, there's hardly been any days to do a dry run."

I didn't want to tell the truth. They didn't actually offer a trial. However, at £60, they were by far the cheapest and could also accommodate me at super short notice. It turns out most brides-to-be book their makeup artist well in advance. So once this engagement's out of the way I need to either book the girl again (if she's good) or find a new one AS-AP.

Middle sis tutts. "Well, I hope she's cheap."

"I did well on that front. It's only £60. Hair and make-up."

"Sixty! I could've done it for free!"

That's been my sister's answer to everything of late. So far, she's wanted to make my bridal bouquet, create all the wedding favours and apply my mehendi. I'm half expecting her to offer up her services for my body waxing.

"Between that and the cost of the engagement venue, I hope you - or mum - has some money left for your actual wedding. I still can't believe you're paying £13 a head just to secure the same venue as Hassna. Anyway, I'll try and save you a few quid with the shopping."

She wishes. Middle sis isn't the best haggler, though I appreciate her effort of being present nonetheless. I'm also thinking safety in numbers. It's always handy having more than one person with you so you can pull faces of disgust at each other when the price seems too high or mumble under your breath about wanting to leave. A bit of good cop, bad cop (or interested buyer/uninterested buyer) really comes in handy in this haggling game.

We head to the premier saree shop in Rusholme (there's not much competition as the entire street has a terrible selection. I always think if I had the funds to set up a saree business, I'd blow everyone else out of the water).

"You should've worn a tighter salwar kameez!" big sis groans at middle sis. "You don't look pregnant enough to get a seat. That family of 50 certainly aren't going to give up their chairs for you, with your tiny tummy."

Middle sis smirks at the unintended compliment and places a hand delicately on her non-existent bump.

"I'm still in my first trimester so no belly to show. We don't all pop when we're preggo."

"There's still time, lady. There's still time. I didn't balloon until my third one. So don't get too cocky," says big sis.

Annoyingly, big sis is only slightly exaggerating about the expansive family that are holding court in the shop. It looks like three generations of a household have come out. This can only mean one thing - they're wedding shopping. Not the modest engagement sort of buying that I'm going for but a full-on groom's side shopping for some lucky bride-to-be. The boy's side will have to pay through the nose for sarees that may never be worn as it's a total stab in the dark as to whether it'll be to the girl's taste. The groom's expected to give a number of sarees as well as the wedding outfit. Each saree is, rather originally, named numerically as 1,2,3... in ascending price. Legend has it that Rashda got up to 20 sarees. Though it didn't end well for her, at least she's got a bursting wardrobe to show for it.

Middle sis definitely won't get to sit on one of those dramatic black and gold throne-like seats. All six chairs are taken up by the elder members of this family, including what looks like the pensioner parents of the groom. The rest of the family have to make do with perching atop the bed style set up so familiar in such shops.

Whether it's the Curry Mile that is Rusholme, or the plazas in Bangladesh, every saree shop has a raised section, like a giant bed, covered in a white sheet. This is where the staff - mostly female in the UK, though it's the opposite back home - prance about barefoot. Their role is multi purpose. At the will and whim of customers, they pull at the sea of sarees, each one neatly folded to create a colourful tapestry on the vast shelf behind them. They do a try-on, folding swathes of material over their tunic and leggings (I'm always impressed at how their haphazard way of fashioning a saree is still neater and more elegant than my very careful and considered attempt). They get involved in some light haggling, establishing a baseline price before escalating the bartering process. They even engage in a little amateur dramatics, gasping in horror, shooting looks of disdain and other Oscar-worthy performances as the customer tries to get a bargain.

Then, at the end of it all, they're left to clean up the rubble, folding away the discarded sarees before placing them back on the shelf in a Tetris-like fashion. It must feel like Groundhog Day every day for them.

I think the manager's seen this family coming a mile off. He's usually missing in action during the browsing stage and only wades in when the haggling gets a bit tasty. On this occasion, he is sat among his staff, skinny legs folded under him, shoes off, revealing moss green socks.

"This be pure raw silk. You won't find any better in Manchester," the shop owner says, draping the baby pink number over his outstretched arm.

There is muffled chat amongst the family. They're speaking in Bangla in hushed tones, taking comfort in the fact that the Gujarati owners won't understand a word they are saying. We, of course, do, and it's delicious.

One grey-haired and feisty lady, likely to be the mother of the groom, whispers: "You really want to spend that much? It's only the number three saree! We need a bigger discount with all we're buying."

"What can you do? We been everywhere. How much more you shop?" says an old, weathered-looking man wearing a white prayer hat and grey duffle coat that's totally inappropriate for the weather.

"Shhh... they understand us!" the mum says as she clocks the shop owner smiling. "We'll go to Birmingham. There's time still."

"*Eh heh*, just get it, dear." The old man sounds like he's running out of patience and breath.

"That's enough from you!" the woman hisses. "Is this a wedding or what? We need some money left for the loft extension."

It's like seeing my parents in ten years' time.

Meanwhile, The smaller members of the family are groaning about being hungry and wanting a kebab and chips. The littlest one is kicking her feet on the array of sarees piled up on the bed.

The groom is nowhere to be seen. I guess this stuff is considered women's business. In which case, there's no point in me peppering M's mind with my favourite colours. I suspect he'll just get the bill at the end of it.

I love being a fly on the wall. I learn so much about life that way. Right now, I'm educating myself on the consumer power struggle between the sexes. Women, it seems, no matter how rich they are, want to get a bargain. Men, no matter how poor they are, want an easy life and to get the hell out of the shop.

I wonder what M is like on that front. I'm hoping I won't need to suppress my bargain-hunting ways in front of him. From what I've seen, he does like a designer item but he's not averse to a sale either. He called me one time asking if I wanted a Ralph Lauren rugby top as he was in Bicester Village. Out of politeness, I said no, though deep down I totally meant yes. He didn't pick up the hint. I guess with blokes, subtlety doesn't work. I'm wondering if he's noticed my passive aggressive-ness about the ring? I might just have to spell it out.

The manager shoots a knowing look at his charge. She's all to familiar with that face and dutifully starts folding away the saree, as if to put it away.

"Shall we just get it?" a woman wearing a golden yellow hijab who looks to be in her thirties, asks the mum. I'd bet she's the groom's sister. "The kids are hungry and we're not gonna find it any cheaper."

The mum nods, defeated.

The daughter (I'm assuming) comes into her own as she's the one who can speak English. "Okay, we will take it for £250 but we want a matching petticoat thrown in."

Shop - 1 : Customer - 0

I think we need to balance out the score.

The family shuffle out with armfuls of bags. I'm a bit gutted that we only got to witness the tail end of the haggle war, though we're about to embark on our own battle.

The manager ushers us to take a seat. I'm guessing my elder sister's matronly appearance, combined with my marriage appropriate age, has made him deduce that we're about to spend some money.

"Do you like to see some sarees? What occasion?"

"Oh, no occasion. We're just looking." Big sis knows the rules well. In fact she may have invented them – you never tell them the occasion unless you really, really have to. Otherwise they try and show you the most overpriced items.

I have to do my level best not to blurt out: "I'm getting engaged!" I'm excited and I want to tell everyone.

"Okay, do you have a budget? How much you spend." The manager is keen to establish whether we're window shopping or real shopping.

"No budget. Just looking." That's the second rule, delivered by middle sis, which she no doubt learnt from our eldest sibling. "Could you show us that one please?" She points to a blue and purple velvet saree with a pearl trim.

"Pearls are in now," big sis informs me.

The saree is stunning, but that specific shade of aubergine might not be very flattering for my complexion. Still, I play ball.

"Is it for you, dear?" The manager is totally onto us.

I'm not sure if I'm supposed to give the game away but I nod out of nervousness.

"Achana!" he shouts. "Could you pull out that one? And some more party wear sarees? And Nandini, bring the ones that were delivered today."

"Oh gosh, they're getting out all the expensive ones!" big sis says, in the loudest whisper ever.

I think the manager heard. "Don't worry dear, we give a good price."

I'm mortified.

I'm guessing the manager isn't sure how much he's going to get out of us, so he moves on, clamouring off the bed to make a beeline for the wall-to-wall salwar-kameez clad mannequins, which are being admired by three middle-aged women.

Though the sarees are all undoubtedly beautiful, it's very hard to make out what they look like from them being folded away on the shelves, though I daren't ask them to bring many out for a better inspection. It's a tricky conundrum. The more you pull out, the more mess you make, the more obliged you feel to buy something. There is nothing more heart wrenching then getting poor Achana or Nandini to disassemble a dozen sarees, only to have to fold them back, neatly and sadly, onto the shelf. They seem to execute the latter with the demotivated dejection of someone who's about to lose their job. It might all be part of the performance, but it works. I wonder if these ladies are on a large commission rather than a regular wage.

Nandini fans out an array of sarees in front of me. I was immediately drawn to a blood red number with circular mirrors and gold thread work. It's net material, which means it will be a bit midriff revealing.

Nandini notices my eye scan over the saree and opens it out so I can have a better look. "This will suit you. You got nice body."

Bless her. She doesn't know that us Bengali Muslims do not show our bellies.

Big sis has her own reservations. "I'm not sure if that colour is going to be the most flattering, lady."

She makes a good point but I can't help but dream of how I'd look like in such a number. I guess I'll be like a low rent Bollywood actress. "How much is that?"

"£300."

"Three hun-!" That's way too expensive. I've learnt the delicate art of haggling too.

"Let me go check," says Nandini, even though I didn't ask her to.

Nandini goes towards the till to ask the manager, who rather swiftly lured his three victims into a panic buy, for the best price.

"Okay, £130," is her answer.

How did they manage to discount £170? I'm so tempted but I know it's not going to suit me. I'd only end up with buyer's remorse.

I turn my attention to two pink numbers. One is of the on-trend ombré variety, with a baby pink subtly fading into a deep fuchsia. Its antique rustic gold work sets it off beautifully. I bet it's got a beautiful price tag, too. The second is more salmon coloured on closer inspection, with wiring and Swarovski like stones.

Both sisters approve. I suspect middle sis is just going along with what we say so we can quickly head to the kebab shop. She was practically salivating when she heard the other family talking about it and, well... cravings.

Nandini passes me on, like a parcel, to Achana, who dutifully pushes me into the cubicle. That's what I like about this saree shop in particular. They actually have cubicles. Others have makeshift rooms, which are in actual fact storage for the vast array of shoes and bangles that didn't quite make it to the shop floor. This one is a proper job, with a door instead of a precariously hung curtain. Even the shop floor is spacious, with enough walking space between the clothing racks for even the largest of families to browse in comfort.

However, the dignity is still left outside the changing room. Achana comes in with me and at the speed of lightning, wraps the saree around me and starts tucking in the pleats with a ruler-like contraption.

"What's that?" I ask.

"It's to keep them all neat and together." Achana doesn't look up when she speaks.

"That's genius. I can never get the pleats right. Neither can my mum. Do you sell them?"

"No."

Achana's not one for small talk.

"Here." She grabs me roughly by the shoulders and turns me towards the full length mirror. With her thin, bony fingers she pulls my hair away from my face into a makeshift updo, leaving my shortest layer to fall and frame my face.

I look... grown-up. Like a woman. Regal. Okay, the last statement's going a bit too far but I look pretty. Who wouldn't put a ring on it? M, it would seem, but that's beside the point.

We haven't discussed the price yet. Achana keeps saying, "don't worry if you like, we can talk and give good price."

That's her way of suckering me in and it's working.

I get a thumbs up from both my sisters, though I can tell middle sis is just going along with things to make a speedy exit. She looks more red-faced than usual. In the short time I was in the cubicle, the store has gone from roomy to heaving, with three clusters of customers now filling the gaps between the racks. Three teenage girls are taking a group selfie, flouting the no pictures rule (this saree shops is terribly paranoid about their exclusive clothing designs being copied). Meanwhile, what looks to be a newlywed couple are admiring a maroon and silver velvet saree on a mannequin.

"I'll never look like that," she tells her man. "That mannequin is nothing like a real body." She pulls her trench coat closer over her front.

"You'll look better," he replies.

How sweet.

My sisters barely have a chance to examine my polished look, before I am unravelled and re-wrapped in the second number. The salmon pink with gold wiring looks a lot more grown-up. A mother of adult children could wear it. I'm not sure if it's me, though I am totally into the stonework. It is so heavily decorated that it looks like it's worth hundreds. This kind of saree will more than make up for the many, many cheaper ones I've worn in the past.

"Lady, what about this one?" Big sis throws in a red herring. Well, it's actually a pink one. A pale pink delicate chiffon saree with only the lightest of diamanté work.

"Don't distract her with more things," says middle sis, who has now moved near the door, which is offering merciful gusts of wind with the arrival and departure of each customer. "She only needs one saree!"

"I know but she needs to make sure she chooses the right one." Big sis hands Achana the pale pink number.

I'm rigorously frisked for the third time before contemplating this one final saree. It really is a curve ball. This saree is definitely more flattering than the second salmon-pink alternative. The lighter material drapes elegantly, while the salmon number, with its coating of stonework, adds a bit of volume. Then again, I'm slim enough to be able to pull off a bit of extra layering. It's a tough call. The first one is my favourite, so in theory I could just get the one and be done with it.

Once I'm clothed in my now boring looking outfit of jeans and a black kaftan, big sis whispers: "You know, if we buy two they'd probably give you a good discount."

The manager comes over, smelling the money. "So, what do you think, dear?"

I get my haggling game face on. "They're pretty but it really depends how much they are."

"Tell me which one you like and I give you good price."

"Okay, how much for this one?" I point towards the first one I tried, the one that made me look surprisingly presentable.

The shop owner looks like he's trying to remember the price but we all know the score. It's a made up number based on how gullible we look. "This one go for £450."

As if.

With my army of two - big sis, game for a bartering battle and middle sis, weary from the war - we launch our attack.

Big sis: "That's much too much uncle-ji!"

Shop man: "This is the best I can do."

Big sis: Pauses and says nothing. It's all part of the strategy.

Big sis: "Surely you can go to... £275?"

Shop man: "There's just no way dear! These are the latest designs. They came in just yesterday. You won't find any better in Rusholme."

Big sis: "Well, we can go to Bradford then. It's much better there, that's where my sister lives."

Big sis gestures towards middle sis who is gasping for air in the doorway and holding a bottle of water to her forehead.

Shop man: "You're welcome to check there but we are the best. You know we ship from India every two weeks."

Big sis: "In Bradford, they do the same. Except they get it from Pakistan. We'll just look there I think."

She looks at me and nods.

Shop man: "You're very welcome dear."

Big sis: "We've got a big shop to do. This one is getting married. We were going to do it all here."

Shop man: "You're welcome. You're most welcome. We be happy to have you back."

Big sis: "We won't come back if you're not going to give good price."

Big sis, who should really know better, is starting to imitate the shop man's broken English. There is even the tiniest hint of an Indian accent. Good job nobody is politically correct here as it's a teeny bit racist.

Shop man: "Dear, this is the best I can do. Look at this print."

He holds up the cloth again against him and throws it over his shoulder to demonstrate how beautifully it drapes. Now he just needs to add a few pleats and a set of bangles and he'd be good to go.

Big sis: "We've been shopping here for years. We've given you so much business."

Shop man: "And you're very welcome. We happy for your business. We always will be, dear."

Big sis: "Okay, £300."

Shop man: "Right dear. Because we're feeling generous today, how about you give £375 for both?"

That was a pretty decent climb down. I figure I should bring something to the table as my middle sister is missing in action. I never knew that pregnancy could make you both nauseous and hungry at the same time.

Me: "Oh uncle. That's just too much. How about £350 for both? If we can do a deal now, we'll be back for more in a few weeks. There are a lot of us and we all need outfits for the wedding."

Shop man: "And you're welcome."

He's either not getting this or is playing a blinder.

Middle sis (shouting from the doorway, with one foot outside): "Oh, let's just go! If they're not going to give us a good discount we won't give them our business! We left our kids at home for this? Such a time waster! I'm walking out right now!"

She is deadly serious. Middle sis heads out of the door and into the street, standing outside the window with her arms folded up under her armpits like a petulant child, glaring at us between the mannequins with utter contempt. It works a charm as the shop man immediately retreats.

"Okay. £350 for both." Then he asks: "So which two do you want?"

Oh crap. We decided on the first one but I hadn't actually chosen between the delicate classy pale number or the still classy but much heavier salmon pink saree. I think the delicate one is beautiful but it's probably not worth as much as the salmon pink one. I just can't help myself, the Asian in me can't disassociate the link between the number of stones and the cost. It's a scary decision to make, as the shop offers no such thing as a refund. At best, they provide a hastily scribbled and illegible credit note they won't recognise on your next visit, or the chance to exchange on the spot for another item of the same value. Without tags, they usually try to shaft you the second time round by claiming a far inferior saree or salwar kameez is the same price. So I need to get this purchasing decision right.

"I think I'll take the salmon one. Oh, and we want petticoats thrown in for free!" I'm pleased with my last defiant bit of bartering.

I'm feeling lighter of pocket but totally smug about my bargain. To think they wanted to charge us £450 for one saree, when I ended up paying £350 for two!

I drive my sisters home, armed with a heaving bag of sarees (those stones weigh more than me) and another heavy bag of a dozen seekh kebabs for the kids, mum, dad and my little sister. Oh, and a container of samosa chaat for me. It feels wrong to leave Rusholme without it.

As we stop at the lights, big sis has a thought. "Do you know what, lady? I think the pale pink saree might have been better actually. The salmon one might be a bit... ageing?"

27th May
Countdown

I'm getting engaged in seven days. That's mental.

I feel like I'm pulling off a feat of unimaginable proportions. I know that reality stars often get married in a matter of days but they have a whole TV crew to help. I just have an un-merry band of sisters, an overbearing mum and a gentle yet vacant dad.

M's watch arrived a few days ago. I was bricking it on two points. First, I was worried it wouldn't even arrive as it was taking its sweet time. Then, when the brown jiffy bag finally made an appearance, I was terrified that it would be obvious that I'd cut corners on the price. Would it come without a branded box? Perhaps it'd be missing a manufacturer's guarantee? Or maybe, just maybe, it would be engraved on the back with the message: *Enjoy your knockoff timepiece from your cheap bitch wife, you sucker!*

Thankfully I could breathe a sigh of relief. There were no such tell-tale signs. It looks like, to all intents and purposes, a regular Armani watch.

Today is also the last day I'll see M before our engagement. On this rare occasion, he's not coming to Manchester, nor are we meeting at Heathrow Airport. My work seems to be rooting for us, as I've got a PR meeting in central London. Head office finally decided that it would be more equitable (and cost-effective) for us regionals to get a train into central London and meet at a nearby hired venue, rather than getting up at the crack of dawn, taking a flight from Manchester Airport (or a train, two tube trips and a taxi ride for Michael, my midlands-based equivalent), spending hours in security on either side, only to be at the head office for one hour.

Instead, we've got a day of internal training. I'll be meeting M after work and staying at uncle Tariq's that night. It's far too long a day not to stop in the capital. Plus, it'll be nice to stay with my family for the first time in years. We used to go there every summer and my cousin would regale me with her stories of debauchery with any Tom, Dick or Harry (there was never a Syed or Bilal in the mix). I wasn't sure whether to believe her stories but then she went and married a white guy. As she'll be stopping over too, I'm looking forward to catching up and hearing the gossip as her wedding was very hush-hush.

The funny thing is, I've not told my colleagues in HQ that I'm even seeing someone. So it'll come as a bit of a surprise when they find out I'm about to get engaged and I'm hoping to book a seat at the new head office.

I CAN'T WAIT FOR THE work day to be done. Delilah, the head of PR, has taken it upon herself to hire an external trainer to teach us how to deal with journalists (it's not like that's what we do every single day).

"The nationals love a good human interest story. Especially ones about hospital openings," says Damian, the trainer, as he reaches for an avocado and sun-dried tomato sand-wich, the last meat-free option. I guess that's me done for lunch, then.

Jamie, my south region equivalent, speaks for us all when he takes issue with this.

"In our experience, the only time the national media is interested in our stories is if there's a breakthrough treatment, which we hardly ever have."

"Or a bad news story like medical negligence, or gross misconduct, which we have quite a lot," I chip in.

Damian disagrees. "Anything can be a story. Context is everything. A big focus is on the BAME community. The number of times I've been approached to give comment from the perspective of a 'man of colour,'" he does a finger quotation wiggle, "I've lost count. If that's what the media want, I'm happy to oblige. So, if you have any medical voices that are black or Asian, and I suspect you have a few Indian doctors, you should use them."

He looks directly at me for his last point, as though I've been assigned every single ethnic minority medic in the business under my PR portfolio.

Jamie leans towards me and whispers: "Am I a minority? Being gay?"

"I don't think that counts. You're not brown enough. Sorry," is my educated response.

Damian's not done dishing his pearls of wisdom. "Oh, and blogs! I'd definitely look at blogs but choose them wisely. I write a technology blog and beauty PRs are always reaching out to me. It's great but there's only so many nail polishes my daughter needs."

If they're not his target market, why is he even accepting nail polishes? More to the point, you get free beauty stuff just from having a blog? Even if it's unrelated? I need to get on this pronto and publish my diary. Though I think I'll wait until after the wedding and still keep things anonymous. Just in case M divorces me out of sheer shame.

AT THE END OF THE SESSION, my colleagues head to the pub. I politely decline, not just because I've sipped enough cans of coke today. "I'll have to see you guys at dinner," I inform everyone.

"Why? Where you off too?" asks Jamie, the serial nosey parker.

"I'm going to meet my... this guy I'm seeing, for a bit." It still feels super awkward to say 'boyfriend'. I think I'll just graduate from boy I'm seeing/dating/getting-to-know-for-the-purposes-of-marriage, to husband.

"Ooh... say no more, lovey. Kept that quiet, you minx," says Jamie.

"Leave her alone," says Delilah. "Not everyone shares every detail about their personal life at work."

Jamie looks offended but he does share everything. Every single swipe right.

Having excused myself, I rush to the very small bathroom with my wheelie travel trolley to put some makeup on. There's barely any room to swing a cat inside there, as the building is basically an old townhouse. Like most properties in London, what was once a family home has been converted into office spaces or flats for rent. The peach tiled bathroom I'm in must've been the spare one back in the day, used by household staff.

There is precious little room for my wheelie suitcase as the toilet is so close to the door, so I abandon my plans of getting changed and just apply a quick slick of my trusty eyeliner and another smear of muted pink lipstick.

M's already outside, waiting for me in his Audi TT, parked on a double yellow line. I hope he doesn't incur a fine. The last thing I want is for our collective wedding expenses to rack up.

"Have you eaten?" he asks me as I climb into his car.

"Well, I had a sandwich lunch, if that counts. It was a shared platter." That's my code for saying *'I'm hungry, let's eat'*.

Luckily we're synced enough for M to say: "Okay, shall we grab something? I thought it's a nice evening so we can drive somewhere then walk a bit. I can give you a little tour en route."

The sun gradually sets as we drive through central London.

"So, this is the Tower of London. I know you said you've seen that, so I'll go down Embankment and head towards the London Eye. Are you okay, by the way? You're very quiet."

I'm letting him do the talking for once as I'm taking in the atmosphere while listening intently to my tour guide. We drove through the Tower of London as a family years ago when going to a wedding. I didn't drive, thankfully. I'd be far too nervous in such a busy place. That duty was bestowed upon my eldest brother-in-law. One of the responsibilities for any men who marry into my family is to become the designated driver by default. I'm looking forward to being more of a passenger after getting married. It's kind of part of the deal.

The traffic is busy but flowing, while Coldplay's *Fix You* plays on the radio. The window is wound down, just enough to let in the spring air. It feels warmer here than Manchester. I look up in awe at the imposing, grand tower that's above us. I'm not familiar with all the bridges in London but I doubt there'll be one more majestic than Tower Bridge.

Unlike me, M is at ease behind the wheel. Driving through perhaps the most congested street in the country doesn't faze him one bit. His relaxed demeanour bleeds into every aspect of him. From his chilled out attitude towards wedding planning, to the comfy attire he's wearing tonight. I like his navy Ralph Lauren Polo t-shirt, paired with tan chinos. I wonder if those are the chinos he was wearing in the first photo I saw of him. As I look down I see his Adidas sliders. I'm going to try and un-see that. I detest men's feet.

"I'm okay," I say. "I'm just exploring my soon-to-be home."

"Sooner than ever now. How do you feel about it all?" he asks.

"Good. I feel good. I know I've been a bit indecisive. That's been more to do with the timing rather than anything else. I've never really doubted us."

"Or maybe at the beginning you doubted me, right?"

He's got me there. I think he might be recalling our first coffee date, where I was a little hesitant. I'd gotten over my shallow concerns but it would be a bit of a stretch to say I was sure he was the one I was going to marry. "Yeah, at first I wasn't sure but then who is?"

"I was. I knew from the first time we met."

I laugh. More out of nervousness than anything else. The compliments are much easier to absorb over the phone than they are in person. "You watch far too many Bollywood movies."

"And you struggle to take any kind of praise. I'm surprised you're not used to it," says M.

He parks up on what he informs me is the south side of the river. We meander down a narrow street, which then opens out into a pedestrianised area, alive and bustling.

M points to an old round black and white building with Tudor-esque wooden beams. "And this is Shakespeare's Globe, where we'll be going next February. This way is the Millennium Bridge."

I'm hungry at this point and wondering when food will be coming. I'm hoping there is something on the other side of the bridge. This part of town doesn't look like it'll be up to much in terms of food offerings.

As we walk up the ramp of the footbridge, M stops me to point out yet another iconic structure. "So behind you is the Tate Modern and can you see on the other end?"

I look over to see a white domed building I've seen on TV countless times. "Oh yeah. What's it called? I can't for the life of me remember."

I turn around to find M on one bended knee, with the Shakespeare's Globe providing a suitable backdrop in the distance.

Oh my God, what's he doing? Is he serious? Is he proposing? With a Bangladeshi boat ring?

"That's St Paul's Cathedral. Now it's my turn to ask a question... will you marry me?"

He's holding open a small wooden ring box. Thankfully, the Millennium Bridge is well illuminated so I can see that inside is a ring, made of platinum or white gold, with a small, solitaire diamond. I can't believe it. This stuff doesn't happen to me. I never in a million years thought I'd get proposed to in this way. It's the kind of thing that happens in movies, not in my life. The wedding is in the bag. He didn't actually need to propose.

Before I can think up a rational response, these words start coming out of my mouth: "Oh, you'll do."

I'M PLEASED TO SAY after the rather magical, yet arguably somewhat pretentious proposal, M's got back to his northern England Bengali boy roots. We eschewed the many chain restaurants around the Southbank in favour of a kebab shop. I opted for a chicken tikka wrap for my pre-dinner dinner, while a donner kebab was his meal of choice. Though he was quick to inform me that this would be his only meal, unlike me. He's on a mission to get his wedding body in shape.

"So, you were winding me up when you said your mum will be choosing my ring?"

"No. That was the plan. Then, after speaking to you, it was pretty clear that it's not the done thing. So I told my mum I'll be getting you a ring."

"Did you really need me to tell you?" I ask, still in shock.

"The thing is, only a couple of my mates are married and we don't talk about that stuff, so I have no idea what they bought their wives, or if they even proposed."

I take a closer look at my ring. I can't quite believe I'm wearing it.

M catches me twisting it around on my finger. "Is it a bit loose? I had to take a guess at your size. The bloke at the jewellers laughed when the only measurement I could offer was 'slim fingers'. It took several trips to Hatton Garden with my poor colleague Jane to get the right ring for you."

He went to all this effort for me? I've heard of Hatton Garden. It seems to be the place to go for the man who wants to impress.

That's not the only length M went to in order to find the perfect ring. "You're gonna think I'm mad but I've actually bought you a second ring to compare. They're both really similar but the other one is more yellow in colour. You know, the things that you have to look for when it comes to diamond -"

He stops schooling me on precious gemstones when he sees the smirk on my face. "Yeah, I'm a bit of an expert now. I guess I could be a gemmologist if my finance career goes to pot."

"Well, hopefully that'll never happen but it's always good to have a backup. By the way, I'm sorry about my response to your proposal."

M laughs. "Don't be sorry. It was brilliant."

"It's just that... you know how I am. I don't mean to be." I look down. I really am no good at this.

His laugh turns to a genuine smile. "I know. And I know you. Don't change."

NOTHING CAN GET ME over the high of tonight. I was proposed to in a way I'd so often seen in movies and on TV. The one that colleagues gush about but I didn't ever think I'll experience.

I'm not sure if I've ever been this happy or content. My glass is definitely half full.

That's not the only thing that's full though. I've eaten three dinners. Three. I'm not even joking. I panic-ate at the work dinner because the food looked so good. M dropped me off in Soho at this incredibly cool dimly lit Vietnamese restaurant. I didn't tell work about the surprise proposal because I left the ring with M to resize. Plus, I didn't want to risk losing it on the train home or worse, leaving it at my uncle Tariq's.

I was only planning to nibble on something out of politeness and mention that I met with my boyfriend (now fiancé) for food, so wasn't overly hungry. Then I saw the summer rolls. I've only ever had the deep-fried spring alternative. After one bite of those cold rice paper rolls, dipped in rather pungent fish sauce, I was hooked. To make matters worse, the menu had a halal chicken option. It's rude not to eat when there's the coveted halal offering which can be few and far between in any cuisine other than Indian. Dinner was rounded off with banoffee pie, which was sensibly shared between the four of us. It was too tasty not to get involved, plus

I only ended up having a few spoons. Everything seemed to taste better at the restaurant. Maybe it was my positive demeanour rubbing off on my tastebuds.

Then I was force-fed at uncle Tariq's. Okay, force-fed is a bit much. I would say it was strongly insisted by auntie Rukhsana.

"You've gone so thin! That's not good with your wedding coming up. Men like meat on bones. Good thing you're getting married before *ruza*, otherwise you'd be a skinny bride!" she said as she laid down a bowl of water on the shiny mahogany table for me to wash my hands. There was no need for such formalities. The table was already creaking under the weight of multiple delectable curry dishes. I could wash my hands in the kitchen. I'm not a special guest.

She's right, I do lose weight to the point of being gaunt during Ramadan. Which is why I'm so glad that this year it falls just after our wedding.

Auntie Rukhsana plied me with roast chicken. It was Bangladeshi style, meaning drumsticks and thighs, pan-cooked in a thick, dry onion masala. It would be rude to refuse really. I haven't tasted my auntie's food for about eight years. It's still how I remember it. Heavily spiced, well seasoned and rich in oil. She does a mean roast chicken, possibly on a par with my mum's.

Us Bengalis are feeders. It's practically blasphemous for a host not to offer a full meal. It's equally offensive if guests refuse such a meal. It doesn't matter what time of the day or night you arrive, you'll be getting rice. My taxi got me from trendy Soho to up-and-coming Tower Hamlets at 10.30pm. I didn't even bother changing into a family-appropriate salwar kameez before arrival. I figured that given my cousin Naila's situation, they wouldn't be judging.

I don't dare ask uncle Tariq anything about the wedding mediation. Since we're not even engaged yet, I don't think there is actually anything to ask. He'll soon be getting in the thick of it though, being the go-between when we sort out the venue, decide on the menu, and arrange those finickity things like timing of mine and M's arrival. Plus, it would be rather bold and forward to ask my uncle about my forthcoming nuptials. I mean, what business is it of mine?

It's funny, this used to be such a familiar place growing up as it was an annual summer holiday destination. We stopped coming here as we got older. It didn't seem appropriate for us to sleep three in a bed and too many of us daughters started outgrowing the upper age limit of the child pass on the family railcard.

Yet, all these years on, it feels like nothing has changed. The pokey council flat in the high-rise tower block is still teeming with furniture. They don't have the luxury of a living room and separate dining room that we do. Canary Wharf still twinkles in the distance. My uncle, though slightly more weathered with time, still sits on the window ledge in his lunghi, smoking and polluting the already thick London air. I always wanted to swap our three-bed semi with their more modest living arrangement. I feel like I was born a city girl and something of a fish out of water being the only Asian in a white community. Here, you couldn't move for Bengalis. While my cousin complained about it, my uncle and auntie never had any desire to move.

So strong was Naila's dislike of brown-ness that she seemed to make it her business to date every white guy that she came across. And there weren't many, I imagine, in Tower Hamlets.

Naila married someone called Darren. We were never invited to the wedding. I never really heard much about it. Her brothers have also flown the nest, moving under the guise of work. I've not heard of them getting married but I couldn't comment on their domestic arrangement. Uncle Tariq just doesn't talk about it.

Despite their kids perhaps choosing a different path than they would have liked, they don't seem to mind. Or at least they don't show it. My mum would be going out of her mind if I married a white guy. She's always complaining about something, too. House is too small. Daughter still not married. My uncle and auntie couldn't be more different. They appear happy with their lot. Content. A permanent state of glass half full. That must be nice.

"OH MAN, YOU HAVEN'T changed!" says Naila. I'm not sure if she's saying that's a good thing or bad. My money is on bad.

"So, are you excited to be getting hitched? I hope you tried before you bought?"

She hasn't changed much either, it would seem. Even her grammar is as terrible as I remember.

Naila can still read my face like a book. "Oh you haven't? Oh bless ya, man. You're still a village bumpkin but I love you for it."

She's always had this way of making me feel inferior, innocent and a bit simple. I've always had a way of conforming to my environment. In front of my white friends and colleagues I talk a good talk, or at least I go along with the assumptions about my relationship. Yet with family I'm always treading carefully. Cautious of who will say what, how things will get exaggerated beyond recognition. Even so, I'm still the odd one out. Sometimes it feels like I'm leading a double life and not fitting into either.

"Without properly getting to know him, how did you know he was the one?"

I didn't anticipate such a deep question. "It wasn't one specific thing. It was just the more I thought about it and the more I got to know him, the idea of not having him in my life was worse than having him. I remember one time, quite early on, he didn't return my messages for hours. It sounds like nothing and we had only just started dating. My head filled with irrational thoughts about how maybe something bad had happened. I know that's really melodramatic but as our relationship was a secret then, I didn't even have anybody to share it with, which made things worse. Anyway, it turned out he was just playing football and he always keeps his phone on silent, which is actually very annoying. I didn't tell him how worried I was, he might think I'm a bunny boiler. At that point I think I knew. That probably sounds really sad." I look down, waiting for a patronising response.

"No, that's not sad at all. It's really sweet. And your reasoning is way more romantic than mine."

"Why, what's yours?"

Naila blinks her full, thick lashes for a long second. It almost looks like her hazel eyes are going to well up. "Don't you know? It's old news around here. I'm the Brick Lane bike, innit? Everyone knows my shit. I've always told you, that's the bad side of living in Bangla town. Yeah, I went out with a few white lads as a teenager but I always figured I'd settle down with a Bengali boy. No chance. In east London, everyone knows everything. People I don't even know started chatting shit to my dad. Dad was annoyed enough that I hadn't gone to uni and I decided to be a makeup artist. From that point, he'd kind of written me off. So with parents not looking for a rishtaa, what choice did I have? I met Darren, he didn't care about my past. So that was it. I married him. Do you wanna know the saddest bit of all? Nobody even stopped me."

"That's better though, isn't it? I figured half the issue with marrying a white guy is all the crap you get from your family."

"Yeah, you get crap, if they give a crap. That's my point. They stopped caring. Dad called a few people, I guess your mum was one of them, telling them that I'm getting married. I didn't even have a proper wedding. It was a cup of tea job at home, to make things halal. The thing is, I act like a coconut but I'd have loved to have worn a lehenga and all that. Doesn't every girl?"

I think she's expecting more sympathy from me. That would be the natural reaction. It would feed the narrative

I've seen on the news, in countless soap operas and TV shows. Naila the damsel in distress and her parents the pantomime villains. It fits in nicely with the western view that us brownies are a backward bunch. However, in so many stories like this, the other side rarely get to say their piece. Uncle Tariq and auntie Rukhsana came to the UK as adults. They spent their lives in a country where there was *only* their own community *to* marry. The only world they knew was one where boys and girls are expected to be good and get married to someone suitable. It's how everyone did things for centuries. So to find that their kids have taken a different path must have been hard for them to reconcile. I'm not taking their side, I'm not justifying their position, but I can understand their conflict.

Naila's staring right at me, waiting for a response. It's unnerving. I'm trying to do my best non-judge-y poker face but I can't stop thinking how much my uncle and auntie have aged. I saw a picture of them at a family wedding from about three years ago. He wasn't anywhere near as leather-faced back then and she didn't have a single grey hair.

Street-smart Naila sees straight through me, with my naive, village bumpkin ways. "Still, I made my bed I guess," she says. "Anyway, it's all good. The thing with marrying a white guy is they don't judge my past. Boyfriends are expected. It'd be weird if I hadn't dated anyone. His family are lovely. I feel like I've wiped the slate clean. It's a fresh start. I didn't get my lehenga. So instead I wore the whitest fucking dress I could find to look pure and innocent for my wedding day."

She turns to her dressing table mirror to adjust a false eyelash. Funny, I thought it was real. I must ask her what brand it is. Perhaps tomorrow morning though, now doesn't seem like a good time.

"You know what, none of that really matters. It's not like you were disowned from the family," I reason. "I mean, you still come and stay over."

"This is the first time I stayed over since I got married last year and I only live down the road in Dagenham. It's not that they stop me coming, it's just that they never ask. I've come home now because I want my mum's cooking. It's been too long and Darren and I eat like students. After a bit, spaghetti Bolognese made with Dolmio sauce gets boring. So yeah, I'm not disowned. There wasn't a big argument. I just didn't live up to expectations. Funny, dad was always telling me how brilliant you are."

"Me?" I didn't think uncle Tariq even gave me a second thought.

"Yeah, you went to uni. Got a proper job. Now you're marrying a proper decent Bengali boy. I know I give you shit, calling you a village bumpkin and all that but you actually turned out okay."

Naila hugs me goodnight, before retiring to her brothers' old room. I get to stay in her bed. Now it looks like it's a guest bedroom, devoid of all her personal touches.

4th June

An engagement (this time it's mine)

I must be a proper mug. Like seriously, why do I never learn?

Here I am at the scene of the crime... where half my face was nearly burnt off, on THE DAY OF MY ENGAGEMENT.

"Don't worry sister," they said. "We do good makeup for you," they said. "You will be very fashion, too," they said. "All for a good price," they said. That's the bit that got me. Damn my penny-pinching ways.

So, I didn't get the burly beautician. Instead, I got the poor, fragile looking teenage one, to whom I gave an ear bashing on my last visit. To be fair, her makeup application is better than anything I would've had at a department store. My previous experiences in such establishments haven't been very encouraging. The makeup artist usually takes one look at my brown face and finds the deepest shade of chocolate foundation assuming that, like white people, I want to go darker with my makeup. I do not.

The kid makeup artist's efforts have been bolstered by the clean canvass I've been prepping prior to the day itself. I did my favourite home-made Ayurvedic face mask of yoghurt, turmeric, gram flour and a drop of honey. I learnt this at uni from one of my Gujarati friends, and it's a revelation. It peels away any dry patches and blackheads and I swear my skin is two shades brighter after application. That's probably the turmeric.

My eyebrows are freshly threaded, courtesy of the beauty parlour I discovered behind my work. You can get away with a multitude of makeup sins when you've got a clean brow.

Nonetheless, credit where it's due. She's applied some nice eyeshadow, matching the colour of the saree blouse I brought with me for context. I've decided I'm going to wear the ombre pink and gold number, my first choice from the saree shop.

However, the teenage beautician has committed a few beauty faux pas. She finished my face with a dusting of what looks like talcum powder. According to the YouTube tutorials I've been studying, that is a no no. I just hope she has set my face properly. The last thing I need is a makeup meltdown at my own engagement party.

Also, while I'm whingeing, the lipstick selection is a bit poor. There were some brand names I recognised but they were few and far between in a sea of generic, non-descript shades. I suspect the rest of them were bought in bulk from a market.

I'm not happy with the hair efforts either. It turns out that she can only do one style. That is tight ringlets piled on top of my head in a ponytail situation. I dreamt of a chignon or at least something that my own teenage sister wouldn't be able to have done for me for free. I asked for big curls, she didn't understand what I was saying as she is new to the UK.

So, to my dread, she called on the burly beautician to translate.

"We no do curls. This is very nice though, it suit you," she tells me.

I don't dare challenge her.

My ringlets are set with what looks like gel. Isn't that for boys? As a result, if I was to sustain a mild head injury, my hair would smash into a thousand pieces like the snake-haired mane of Medusa.

I drive extremely carefully on the way home, much to the annoyance of the aggressively hurried drivers in Longsight. I do not want to crack my curls. Again, another small whinge - I would've loved to have had someone come to my house and do my makeup. For sixty quid though, I couldn't really argue (side note: I was shit scared to argue anyway with the big beautician).

When I get home, I'm greeted by my super punctual older sisters. It's only 11.30am and they managed to commute from their respective homes to get here in good time. I'm especially impressed with big sis, who must've got up at the crack of dawn and ferried her kids into the car. As it's my engagement, it's a worthy enough occasion for my brother-in-law to also come, so sis was spared the packed-out train.

However, middle sis is determined not to be outdone in the best sister stakes. Not content with my rebuttals of her offers of basically doing everything for my wedding, she arrives with gold scarves for all of us to wear. She sewed them herself from leftover salwar kameez material.

"Oh, thanks but... I was just planning to cover my hair with the saree," I say.

"This is much nicer though. It'll really set off the gold stonework and we'll be all matchy-matchy." She says this as she's already securing the scarf on top of my ponytailed head with kirby grips. I guess I'm wearing it then.

"I won't have to cover my hair, will I?" Little sis is clearly concerned that her efforts to wake up early (well, 10am, which is early for her) to carefully curl out some loose waves will have been futile.

"No," replies middle sis. "The style is just reserved for us married ladies and the soon to be married one. But is there a way you can work it into your outfit? You've got some gold detailing on your salwar kameez."

"Speaking of gold, you really need to buy some decent jewellery, you know," big sis informs me. "You can't be getting married with a simple chain necklace to your name."

Big sis got married in the golden days when you could buy ingot bars like bars of chocolate. So she pretty much had a set of wedding gold before she even got married. It's a different climate now, plus 22 carat gold is not really my aesthetic. Girls my age don't even really wear it now. It seems pointless for the groom's family to have to spend thousands on the wedding gold that will be worn for one day and put away for eternity. It seems even more pointless that the bride, just to show that she's not peasant-poor, comes with some gold of her own. That said, I don't really want to be done out of gold by M and his family. I'm a conformist in some ways. So I suppose I will need to get myself some bling. I must add that to the wedding list.

"Where's mum?" I ask.

"She's now in the kitchen, doing everyone's nut in," says middle sis. "She obviously doesn't get that it's the groom's side that have to make all the taals and get the gifts. She is frying samosas and kebabs like she's marrying off a son. I'd steer clear."

Mum, with her all-hearing ears, bursts into the hallway, where I am being manhandled by my older sisters.

"I didn't hear you come back. Let me see... oh." She examines the artistic efforts of the teenage beautician. "Ya Allah! What has she done?"

"Mum, don't start now," I warn.

"But... but it's the eyes. They're so... pink. let's try and make it less."

Of all the times. "Mum, I'm not gonna take it off now."

"But it looks scary terrible."

"It's too late! Don't start trying to touch my face now." I swat off my mum's hand as she tries to pull some strands of hair out of my rock solid ponytail to create an eye covering fringe.

"*Dooro*, it's not too late! You can't go like that."

"What am I going to do now mum? What am I gonna do?"

"You got makeup upstairs! We got baby wipes downstairs. I always use them to clean table. Hold on, let me get some and wipe your eyes little bit."

"You can't. You'll ruin all of it. Leave it. It's not that bad, is it?" I look in the square hallway mirror before turning to my sisters for support and validation.

Big sis looks away. "Well, little lady, it is a *bit* much. Maybe in the pictures it will look okay?"

"She needs to look okay in person! Or shall we tell all our guests and our new family not to come and we'll just send picture! Hmmph!" Mum is determined to do a haphazard makeover on me. I don't trust her with a barge pole though, she doesn't even wear any makeup herself.

Middle sis sees this as her golden opportunity to get involved. "Why don't you come upstairs with me, I can try and tone it down for you. Then I'll do a little gold smokey eye," she says.

"No, you're not doing smokey anything! You're always trying to do my makeup and it always goes pear-shaped because you do colours that would suit you. And everything bloody suits you! I've paid 60 quid for this face. I'm not messing with it now!"

"What about you?" Mum turns to my teenage sister, who's busy fussing with her wavy curls in the mirror, jostling me out of the way in the process.

"I can't do it. I don't wanna get grief if she doesn't like it," she says, tossing an elegant loose wave over her shoulder.

She is still in the hallway. They'll be referring to me as M's wife next.

"You'll be fine," says mum. "Your makeup is always good. You quickly do something for her. Maybe nice baby pink on eyes." She is really getting desperate now.

"Mum, I'm not doing it," says little sis defiantly. "What if her fiancé doesn't like it and decides not to marry her? I'll be blamed for ever."

"*Dooro!* Then why bother watching YouTube videos if you can't help your sister! Hmmph! Four daughters and none of you can do makeup!"

"So, you want me to not bother going to uni and just be a makeup artist instead, mum? Like everybody else?" asks little sis.

"*Dooro* no! You do it as side job. On weekend, in summer. That's when everybody getting married."

Mum reaches for my hair again to try and pull out a side-fringe but pokes me in the eye in the process.

"Right that's it! Get off! Just get off!" I shout at mum, who jumps back in shock. "You always say something when it's too late. So leave it! You're all pissing me off now! Nobody touch me or my hair!"

Dad comes into the hallway. "*Eh-heh*, what's going on here? Getting late." He's wearing the most olive of olive greens. He looks cute though, in his embroidered Panjabi. I bet mum dressed him.

"You no worry! This lady business!" mum shouts back.

Dad shuffles away, knowing his place. "*Eh-heh*. Everything lady business in this house," he mumbles.

I DIDN'T GET A THRONE. Why is there no throne?

When Hassna got engaged at this very same venue, she sat on her own throne, looking damn regal. What do I get? A bloody chaise lounge. Yes it's gold, with a shiny nail-head trim, but really? It's still a chaise lounge. The kind of thing you'd get in a grand house. It's not fancy enough for an engagement. Not a £13 a head engagement! With their his and her thrones, Hassna and her fiancée got to stand out from the guests in all the wedding photos. Me? I'll be sitting among the rest of the riffraff, fading into anonymity.

Bloody Hassna's lot. It's always a competition. They always have to do better.

Annoyingly, we had to invite them to the party. Reciprocity and all that. So not only do they get to see me in my lower rent seating arrangement, Hassna will be there lording it up, flashing her sparkler around for all to see.

"Masha Allah beautiful!" Auntie Rukhsana cups my face, her eyes creasing up with a smile.

"Oh, thank you. I'm so glad you could make it. Is Naila here?" I ask.

Auntie Rukhsana let's out a high-pitched nervous giggle. "Ah, she couldn't come. She busy with work. As you now know this time of year is start of wedding season. So brides need makeup!"

She excuses herself under the guise of needing some paan. She really must stop with that habit. Her teeth are stained a deep burgundy brown.

M and his family haven't arrived yet. This gives me plenty of opportunity to take some solo shots on my chaise lounge. Except solo shots are a bit tricky when there is ample space on either side of you. I'm joined by various distant cousins, nephews, nieces and a couple of randoms whom I have never met and I can't really imagine why they made the engagement party list, given that we're limited with numbers.

It's annoying enough that my photo opportunities are being sabotaged, I'm also paying for the destruction. Well, at the moment mum and dad are paying for it. Whenever I ask about settling the bill, she just replies with "we'll sort it later," or "we'll talk about it after the wedding". I'm not sure if she's expecting to foot the bill for my wedding. I earn enough myself. However, I think the tradition of parents paying for the wedding is something that mum and dad just can't shake off, out of pride more than anything. I don't want them to be out of pocket though, after all I've been stingy all my life so I might as well spend a bit now.

Mum comes onto the stage. "You eat now. You won't have time when his lot come."

I've been given a nice long table at the side of the stage, just for me and my immediate family. The samosas are disappointing, laden with grease and the thick, doughy pastry so synonymous with restaurants. I much prefer the crispy, thin variety made by mum. I guess it's a good thing that the food is pants, as it gives me less chance of ruining my lipstick. Of course, I forgot to bring a lipstick to top up with me. I'm so rubbish like that.

The mains of chicken and vegetable curry are better, though I barely get a chance to enjoy it. I hate eating curry and rice with a fork. Especially restaurant rice, with their loose, fluffy grains. I'm scooping, gathering and piling on my fork, which takes twice as long to eat than if I'd just got stuck in with my hands. Still, it's not for nothing that I've been growing my nails for the last fortnight. Little sis gave me a French manicure last night and I'll be dammed if I stain the white tips yellow. I want to flaunt these talons at work next week, along with my brand new ring from my 'surprise' proposal.

About five mouthfuls in, I hear a bit of a commotion. There are whispers that the groom's side is arriving. I'm ushered off the table to the other side of the venue, which is handily sectioned off with ugly room dividers. They're the kind you'd get in an office. They didn't even bother trying to decorate them. A little bow stapled to the wall wouldn't have gone unappreciated.

Heading to my family's side of the venue, I get to see the rest of the guest list, which, of course, I had no say in. Auntie Jusna is back with Rashda and the kids as well as her son Iqbal and his new wife. It's nice to see the new addition to the family without a shit-tonne of makeup on. I've only seen her twice before. Once at her wedding, where I almost couldn't detect any human features under the mountain of bling. The second time we'd invited her round for the obligatory dawat lunch, where we fed them roast chicken and samosas and a cup of warm, sugary milk as a welcome to the family. It's always a fun occasion, Iqbal's wife Rehana played her part well, feigning shock when we presented her with the also obligatory gift of a saree. There was a fuss with her not wanting to accept it (though she obviously wanted it - I helped mum choose well) and after playing a fake tug of war with a shopping bag, she relented. Today she looks fresh faced with her fashionably black saree finished off with silver work. I notice Iqbal is wearing a black tie to coordinate. Cute.

Next thing, M's mum and his older sister-in-law have come through the barrier. Okay, that sounds a little dramatic. It's not like they bound their way through like a couple of boulders. They walked through the very easily accessible opening at the front.

I don't make eye contact with his mum, not for any reason beyond the fact that I think I should be shy. However, when mum turns to me and says "say salaam," I realise I made the wrong call.

M's mum greets me back and then continues talking to my mum. I'm still scared of her. I guess it comes with the territory to have a healthy amount of fear of your mother-in-law.

All my siblings have stood to attention, so seizing the opportunity, M's sister-in-law comes and sits next to me. "You look so pretty," she says. "How are you feeling?"

"I'm okay. A little nervous though."

"Don't be." She leans in. "They're really nice people. And everybody likes you."

She clasps my hand, interlocking her fingers with mine. I like her. I think she'll be on my side.

Uncle Tariq makes an appearance, with an entourage of M's older and younger brother. The siblings are wearing matching black suits. I'm not sure if that was intentional or black is just the easiest colour and it was a happy accident. All three wise men are laden with gift baskets and bags of mishti, which they promptly settle on my table, right in front of me.

"There you go. Gifts for bride. Go on, I know you want to look." Uncle Tariq was always a big tease. He said the exact same thing, minus the bride, when he used to come to our house when we were little, weighed down with bags of sweets and multipack crisps. Except this time it's a little more embarrassing as my future mother-in-law is stood right there, smiling nervously. She doesn't know his humour so she perhaps thinks I'm just desperate to see the spoils of my man-hunting efforts.

I try to look anywhere but at the gifts in front of me, though I'm very intrigued. All this for me? Well, not all the mishti sweets obviously. It's still flattering nonetheless. I don't think I've ever had so many gifts since my 21st birthday.

There is a little fuss about where I'm going to get changed. Sometimes the groom's side heads back to the bride's house and she wears the saree that they've bought to do a little fashion show for them. However, uncle Tariq, the appointed mediator, comes back with some crucial intel.

"They won't be coming round. So... she'll have to wear the saree here," he says, looking mortified at having to discuss the idea of me getting changed. "I've looked at the bathroom and it is completely unsuitable. It's barely a bathroom." His dark leathered skin takes on a slight blush. I'm embarrassed for him.

Mum looks ever so slightly relieved that she won't have to host my in-laws at home. That means her beloved freezer stash of samosas will live to see another day. Though this new development does present its own challenges. Namely, where the hell, and how the hell, will I get changed in an open-plan restaurant?

Middle sis, who still doesn't look remotely pregnant, hatches a plan. "You know they've got those screens over there, you could get changed behind there. It's totally discreet."

Behind the anonymity of the screen, I get to examine the precious booty that has been curated for me. A baby pink satin effect saree, with a diamanté stone trim border, is delicately wrapped in a cellophane basket. I imagine that was my sister-in-law's handiwork.

There is another gift basket. This one contains a diamante necklace and earrings set, bought to match my outfit. There's also, rather hilariously, one of those metal suitcase type thingies you get in department stores that contain terrible makeup that you'll never wear. It probably cost about twenty quid, so it's a good thing I didn't give my real request to my sister-in-law. It would've been terribly ill judged. Luckily, I'm not expected to wear the makeup, though I imagine mum would have loved to use some to mute out my pink eyeshadow.

Big sis, the saree aficionado among us, is in charge of doing the Superman-quick outfit change.

"You could do a bit better with the pleat job," I tell her, as she hurriedly gathers the material and stuffs it down my petticoat.

"Lady, this is the best I can do. I'm feeling the pressure. God, didn't they even give pins? I need safety pins!" she shouts like a fashion designer backstage at London Fashion Week.

Suddenly, there is another pair of hands as mum starts tugging the saree border further over my head.

"We need to cover more hair!" says mum as she manages to almost crack my brittle overly-gelled hair style. "Stop pleating the front, you'll see boob! It looks rude!" she shouts at middle sis who has now got involved and is daring to make the saree look remotely chic.

"Don't worry, it's not like she has anything to show!" cackles auntie Jusna, who has taken it upon herself to pop round the screen and get in on the action.

I've never been so violated in my life. Plus, I'm wearing a high neck saree blouse so there really isn't any boob on display. There isn't a full length mirror in sight, which is perhaps a blessing as I won't get to see how much of a hot mess I am. I emerge from the screen as a vision (of sorts) to make my way to the stage once more.

Now I can get a full view of M's side of the venue. I can't see him, as there's a group of blokes around him. Then, they seem to part like the Red Sea, no doubt giving him the chance to have a better look at his bride-to-be, who's now sat on the stage. M's smartly dressed in a navy suit and his baby pink tie isn't lost on me. We're already coordinating. A guy I have not seen before, who is perhaps one of his friends, smiles and whispers something in M's ear. M smiles too, looking at me. It's nice that he invited a friend to share the day with him. I didn't think to ask Sophia or Julia. Now though, I think it would've been nice to have them enjoy it with me, as it's a day we talked about so often.

My sisters, mum and dad come and sit next to me on the stage for the standard family photos. There's no professional photographer. So it seems like that responsibility has been unofficially bestowed on several people, including uncle Tariq, Iqbal and his wife. I'm not hopeful for how this photo will turn out. Between a man in his late fifties and a loved up young couple, I'm expecting lots of heads cut off and unflattering angles. Still, beggars can't be choosers. I did consider hiring a professional but given that it was more expensive than my monthly salary, it just didn't seem worth it. I'll save that for the wedding and mehendi.

Big sis, who has taken pride of place next to me, whispers: "Don't make too much eye contact with him! Try and be a bit coy and look down. Right! Let's get the kids in as well for a group shot."

My mum, who's sat on my other side, has her own advice to impart. "Don't smile too much. Okay, smile a bit. Just *lit-ool* smile. Don't want to look too happy, like you're desperate to get married."

Oh, how I wish I had my own throne so I could avoid these matrons in such ear-bending proximity that they can give me a complex. I revert to a non-smile, which unfortunately for me is a resting bitch face. I don't really have anything in between.

Speaking of thrones, I don't see Hassna here. Perhaps she's busy trialling the top makeup artists for her own big day, the ones with over a million Instagram followers and a price tag to match. Not that I'm bitter or anything.

Now it's the turn of M's family to take to the stage for some photo opps. There is an unspoken order of appearance, a bit like the Oscars red carpet. First the big brother, who shuffles awkwardly and fusses with his tie as he sits down on the one seater gold chair, as far away from me as possible. His wife, however, sidles up next to me.

"Just leave it," she hisses to my soon-to-be brother-in-law. He then straightens out his tie one final time, before lifting his jacket by the collar, as if to make himself appear taller. Or maybe broader. I don't really know.

"Come on, say hello to your new auntie," M's sister-in-law tells her children, an adorable boy and girl.

The boy looks terribly shy and doesn't say a word. Instead, he sits on his mum's knee and plays with the toy car he's got in his hand. The little lady seems a lot more confident, greeting me with a cute: "Hi! My name's Sameera!"

"Nice to meet you, Sameera. I love your dress," I reply.

"Thank you. It's my birthday dress."

"Oh, and how old are you?" I ask.

"I'm seven," she replies, obviously very proud of her advancing years. "This is Ibrahim. He is five." She points towards her brother, who has now buried his face in his mum's sequinned shoulder. "And he's a little bit shy."

My brother-in-law scarpers as the first unofficial photographer, Iqbal, puts down his mobile phone. His wife hangs back. "Oh, just so you know, after the photos, your in-laws are going to come and present you with the ring. They're a bit old-fashioned like that. They're not into the whole couple sitting together exchanging rings kind of thing. Is that okay? I think you'll like the ring. He showed me earlier. It's very pretty."

I smile to avoid telling an outright lie. I guess M wasn't fibbing when he said his mum normally does the ring shopping. I notice his sister-in-law is wearing a Bangladeshi boat ring. Poor thing.

It's hardly likely that I'm going to be able to object to the ring request. So I guess I'm getting engaged to his mum. I assume someone from my family will slap M's watch around his wrist. I'm glad Hassna is not here to see this.

As they exit the stage, the family arrangement goes a bit rogue. Next thing, my little sister and M's equivalent join me, one teenager on each side.

"You look boot-ful," says M's sis.

"You scrub up well yourself," I say, genuinely. She looks really nice in her blue and green ombré effect saree. Her streaked hair has taken on a purple tone. What a cool kid she is.

Along with the amateur paparazzi, both teenagers proceed to take a bunch of selfies with me.

"Shall I send you the pics?" M's sister asks mine.

"Yeah, that would be great. Your phone camera's way better than mine."

"Okay, I'll take your number."

Though this digit swapping could have taken place off stage, I also find it rather sweet. They've reached the next phase of their friendship. M and I better go through with this wedding to preserve this blossoming relationship.

M's mum and dad finally come to the stage. My face reddens. I've had basically zero interaction with his dad, and a few stilted conversations with his mum. As a PR person communication is my forte but that's communication in English. When it comes to my raw hand-me-down basic Bengali, I get tongue-tied.

As M's mum places the delicate diamond ring on my right hand (I don't dare correct her), she asks: "Is it a bit loose?"

"Erm, a little bit," I say before immediately regretting my response. Should I say that? Does it sound like I'm complaining? Or ungrateful?

"Don't worry. You gain weight after wedding so it will fit just fine."

M's mum looks at her husband as if to prompt him to say something, anything.

"*Bala nee?*" he finally asks, whilst looking down at his functional Velcro-fastened leather shoes. It looks like his wife also dressed him. I'm sure that like my dad, if he had it his way, he'd like to fade into obscurity.

"*Jee bala*," I reply, assuming that "*yes, I'm good*", is the right response. Or have I got that wrong, too?

With that obligatory pleasantry out of the way, I lift my gaze into the crowd that has now gathered. Some are there to take photos on their respective phones, others just to have a good old nosey.

The only person I can't spot in the crowd is Rashda. She's instead still sat on the other side of the partition, tucking into the desert of gulab jamun, while every other place setting has an uneaten bowl. A dessert I'll be missing out on as I have to sit on stage as the main prop in everyone's photo call.

She must feel my eyes on her as she looks up and gives me a thumbs up, then grabs a second round of the sticky sweet dessert, nabbed from her mum's place setting. Divorce has turned her rebellious, nonconformist, and camera shy. She's like a whole different person to the cousin I grew up admiring. Though I think I like this new badass version more.

I CAN'T STOP STARING at it. I can't stop staring at the ring in the shiny wooden box on my shared bedside cabinet. It's not big and flashy. It's understated. Simple. Mine.

"Can you turn the light off now?" Little sis is obviously exhausted from the long day of work she didn't do.

Still, it's 11.35pm on a school night. I don't think I'll get a comfortable night's sleep as I'm still rocking my rock-hard Medusa hair. It doesn't matter though, it's a small casualty for a perfect day. Even if M and I spent it with a minimum distance of three metres apart, it was our day.

I do my ritualistic phone check before bed. There are several consecutive messages from M:

I'm just driving back to London but wanted to stop off to message you.

Today was amazing. You looked stunning and my sister-in-law was saying how nice you are.

Thanks for my watch. I love it! You chose really well. And not just the watch ;)

Did you have a good day? I know our families didn't manage to talk about setting a wedding date. I think my mum is going to call your mum this week to finalise. You can bet I'm just counting down the days until you're here with me.

8th June
Sisters and Misters

I miss Sophia. I miss Julia. It totally sucks that I'm the happiest I've ever been but my friends, who were there with me in pursuit of happiness, are now missing in action. I don't want to be one of those girls that ditch their mates as soon as they get a man. I've been on the receiving end of that one too many times so I know it's not nice. Yet, inadvertently, that's what's happened. Except I've not ditched them. They've forgotten about me.

This time last year I relished my weekend meet-ups with Sophia and I lived for my pizza dates with Julia. Now I live for the ping on my phone that signifies a message from M. It's always him. Rarely anyone else. My sisters and scam telemarketing calls don't count.

Is that how it's going to be for me? Does it have to be one or the other? Why can't I have both friends and a fiancé?

One of the things that made me feel so different from the rest of my girlfriends was the lack of a man to talk about. Growing up, all my friends had boyfriends at some point or another, with the exception of bookish Helen. I always assumed that it's something my white friends did, not the reserve of a good Muslim girl. Then I went away to university and found that lots of the Asian girls dated, too. That was an eye opener. I never quite fit but now I do. Now I have commonality, I just have no one to share this with.

MUM BARGES INTO MY room looking delighted. She doesn't bother knocking and is blissfully unaffected by my towel-wearing, leg-epilating self.

"Ninth of September. We have a date! Masha Allah, we have a wedding date! 9th September. We got bit more time now."

Mum can't hide her glee at finally palming off her third daughter. "Hoo! I breathe now. I was getting worried that we never agree on anything - me and your mother-in-law. She just called now though, to make things firm."

"Oh, that's good. I might start telling people at work now. And my friends."

Mum does her upside down lip grimace thing. "Are you sure you want to start telling everyone? I understand work but friends? Isn't it bit soon? Maybe wait till we're closer to wedding date?"

Only a Bengali mum could think telling your closest friends you're getting married three months before the actual wedding is a little premature.

"That's ridiculous! Can I not just be happy and share my news like everyone else? Most girls share their ring on Instagram the moment they wear it."

"They be silly girls," says mum.

"No mum, they're not silly. They're normal. We're not. We never do anything properly. We always have to be weird. Can't I be normal, for once?"

"Okay, maybe your English friend Julia and that Pakistani girl you made friends with last year. Don't get too ahead though. There is still plenty of time -"

She was about to say there is still plenty of time for things to go wrong. I love her confidence in this union.

Given that I've got the room to myself (little sis affords me a pinch of discretion when I've just had a shower), I decide to call Sophia. After one ring, it diverts to voicemail. She must have seen my number and pressed decline.

Maybe I'll have better luck with Julia. Her phone rings terminally, before transferring to her clipped voicemail message.

As I don't see Reena that often these days, I'll save my message for a bit later. Yes, I am my superstitious mum's daughter.

I text both prodigal friends with the click bait message of: *I'm engaged!* Just in case there's any ambiguity, I follow this up with a sparkly engagement ring emoji. I'm tempted to send them a close-up shot of me wearing my ring but I decided against it as it may seem a bit too eager. Plus, the diamond might look small on screen. I can't believe that I have to think twice about sending happy news to my friends.

As I continue to de-fuzz my neglected legs, I anxiously wait for a response from either of my friends. It shouldn't be like this. Don't friends share everything? Or is it more fun or interesting for them when I'm sharing bad news? Do they live for my disastrous dates?

I've always thought that, as women, we can sometimes be our own worst enemies. We struggle to be happy for each other, unless we are fully happy ourselves. I found this out first-hand in the early days of my man hunting. A girl recommended someone but decided not to follow it through. Maybe it was a sport? Is there a little bit of a Machiavellian in all of us? A primal instinct of survival of the fittest or most worthy of marriage? I could almost, almost understand if that's the case with Julia, as she is forever in and out of relationships. But Sophia? Happily married and now a mum. Surely this should be the happiest time of her life. Could she not extend that happiness to me on my happy occasion?

Sod it, I'm sending a picture to Naila. I snap a close up of my ring and hit send. As soon as I put the phone down it pings with her reply:

Nice! How many carats is that? Is it a real diamond? I can't tell.

Cheeky cow. I knew I shouldn't have sent a picture. Like I say, women are bitches. My phone pings again and I'm a little too keen to get to it. It's M:

Have you heard the news? Mum just called to let me know. I was going to ring you but I'm a bit busy at work. Are you free tonight? It'd be good to catch up. And I'm going to start annoying you with a countdown to our wedding day now. I can't wait.

I'd normally be beyond giddy, like a schoolgirl, to receive a message from him. It's just not who I expected.

I head downstairs to be greeted by the smell of samosas frying. Someone's excited.

"Our freezer be full! So I better fry to make space. I thought we'd finish them off on your engagement but your in-laws no come here, so more for us! Maybe I finally have one! Come! Sit!"

I grab the ketchup and help mum take the plate of samosas into the living room. I get another message. Much to my relief, it's Sophia:

Hon, you know I love you, so don't take this the wrong way when I say it. It's just that I get Imran to nap between 12 and two, so that window is pretty precious for me. So, could you not call me within those hours? I don't mean to sound difficult, but I can't even put my phone on silent in case Adnan needs to call me. He gets panicky when I don't answer my phone. I hope you understand, hon.

I can't believe it. It's like she's a different person to who I met last year. The one that would have me round to hers for dinner the moment she noticed I'm feeling down. The one who, crucially, pushed me to go online as she was convinced that I needed to expand my options. She was right but this feels so wrong. Did she even see my message?

If I'd have known that would be her response, I wouldn't have even bothered messaging. I think back at our relationship, did it suit her when I was single? Was it convenient as a friend being always available, always entertaining with my stories, always in need of her crumbs of wisdom? Does it not sit right with her now our dynamic has changed? And also, how hard is it to nap a baby? Don't they just... sleep?

I RECEIVE ANOTHER MESSAGE from Sophia at the end of the day: *OMG! I've just seen your message. Congrats hon! I'm over the moon for you! Here's wishing you an amazing future with your lovely man.*

Wishing me... an amazing future? Does she not want to be part of that future? It sounds like a Bon voyage message.

No response yet from Julia.

11th June

Another countdown

Text message from M: *So it's happening. 90 days until we get married. There's no getting rid of me now :)*
Me: *Ditto. You're stuck with me, too.*
We are cornballs.

"OH, IT'S GORGEOUSSSS!" Bushra squeals upon seeing my sparkly new ring. "How did he propose? Tell me everything."

She's gathered around my desk with Emma and Amy, who has made a rare appearance in the office. There have been whispers that she's been skiving since coming back from mat leave. It looks like she's trying to put those rumours to bed by having a full, productive day with us.

I choose to begin my tale with the most western-appropriate element of the engagement, the actual proposal that he surprised me with on Millennium Bridge. I don't even need to exaggerate my surprise. The fact that I wasn't going to say no, as our engagement was planned well in advance with a date agreed upon by our parents with the conduit of uncle Tariq, is just a minor detail that can be left out. It'll only muddy the water.

"That's so romantic! Now I get why you didn't bother booking a hotel for your stay, you dirty girl," Emma winks.

They all laugh and I giggle along with them. Me and my double life.

Do I mention the actual engagement party? Before I have a chance to gather my thoughts as to how I'll explain pulling off such an elaborate event (at a top restaurant in Rusholme that needs to be booked weeks in advance) with a few days notice, I'm already pulling up the pictures on my desktop. Yes, I insisted on getting the photos from the camera phones of everybody that attended, then saved them into a folder on my work laptop so I could share at this very moment. I don't care who judges. This is *my* moment, *my* engagement. I *will* milk this.

As I browse the various versions of myself sat with different members of mine and M's family for the photos, Amy has a question.

"Why are you looking down in the photos?" Her voice is careful and measured, like she's scared of offending.

"Oh... I was trying to be demure. You know, play the part. I think I overdid it."

"Ah, okay. So sorry, I hope you don't think I was ignorant for asking. I just wasn't sure. It looks like you've been shouted at." She bites her lip, realising that her comment was indeed slightly ignorant.

Bushra interjects: "I see what you're doing. Playing the innocent coy bride. Ha ha. Only we know different."

Do they though?

Emma would also like to poke holes in my fantasy. "Are there any pictures of you and your boy?"

"Yeah... Oh, actually... I don't even think I've got them saved here."

I realise the only photos anyone managed to get of M are of him stuffing his face with cake and being presented with his brand spanking new watch by my big brother-in-law. I am obviously nowhere to be seen in the photos. I decide to end the slideshow to avoid further questions.

"You look amazing though," says Amy. "Absolutely stunning. And it's great that you managed to get something organised at such short notice. When I booked my engagement party I couldn't find anywhere decent. I had to wait four months to book the upstairs of Wetherspoons on the weekend."

I say nothing.

I'm hoping word of my engagement filters up to Bernadette. If not, I'll have to drop that bombshell at my next one-to-one. It'll be a bit of a triple whammy. I'm engaged, getting married in three months and I'm moving to London. Oh, and if there is space for me to pull up a pew at the head office and do my northern role from there, well... that would be just grand.

"SO, WHAT'S FOR LUNCH today?" M asks during our regular call.

"Salad on this front. The carb-y kind, with lots of potato and pasta," I reply between mouthfuls.

"Is that the hospital discount one?"

He knows me too well. "Yeah. The perks of having our office next to one of our biggest hospital sites. Honestly, I might miss the 70% staff discount more than my own family when I leave."

"You never know, you might get it here if you manage to get a transfer. What do you think the chances are?"

"I'm not sure really. On one hand, Bernadette loves me. Not bragging, just facts. Then, on the other hand, expecting to do a northern role from head office might be a stretch. Nobody else has done it. I figure that I can only ask as I've got nothing to lose. In the worst case she'll say no and I'll start job-hunting."

"Don't worry about that, though. There is no major rush," says M.

"But I've never been out of work since I graduated! I'm not expecting to be a kept woman." I'm sounding more defensive than I intended.

"I know. I just don't want you to feel pressured to work. Get used to the place first. It's gonna be a big change for you so don't add any more to your load."

The subject of working, or not working, isn't the easiest for me to tackle. Thankfully, I spy my two cronies heading towards me through the sea of hospital visitors in the canteen.

"Well, it's something we can discuss anyway but, I'm going to change the subject in a minute as Bushra and Emma are coming over. I've not told them I'm going to request a transfer."

They both head over to the sofa area I saved for us. Bushra has a salad that mirrors mine, though I've got more beetroot. Emma is obviously feeling flush as she eschewed the heavily discounted salad for a hot dinner of roast beef, which comes with a measly 20% discount for staff. Still, it's payday and all.

"I'll leave you to it but, just quickly, I'm coming up again this weekend," he says.

"Oh, you can't keep away. At least your mum won't be so suspect now as to why you're making such frequent visits."

"Yeah, that cat's pretty much out of the bag now. Anyway, are you free?"

Of course I am, I think to myself. "I... should be. Meet up?"

"Yeah, sure. The other thing is, my watch is a bit loose. So I'm just thinking, while I'm up, shall we get it adjusted together at the jewellers?"

Oh fuck. Fuck. Fuck-ity fuck.

I can't think. Why can't my brain process quickly? How is it that I can bash out a reactive statement for a major crisis in 30 minutes yet I can't even concoct a simple lie (or perhaps preserve a secret, that sounds much more PR-friendly)?

"Yeah, maybe. I'll let you know what I'm doing. Speak later?" That response might save me a couple of hours.

"Cool. I'll catch you after work."

Bless M, my easy-going, unassuming fiancé.

I WAIT UNTIL EMMA AND Amy bugger off to the kitchen to do a tea run. They always seem to do that in twos around here. Not that making tea is that hard. It's hardly a big order either, what with just five of us in the office, including finance officer James, who we ask out of politeness.

"So you know that watch that I got... the Armani one?" I remind Bushra.

"The one I helped you save a packet on? Did he like it? Can I get a finder's fee?"

"He loved it. Though that's not the point. He wants to get it adjusted!"

"So..."

"So? So I'm buggered! He thinks I bought it from Goldman's. A proper shop. Bloody hell! I knew I should've got a leather strap watch."

"Hey, Watches Galore is a proper shop. that's where I bought this from." Bushra shoves her wrist in my face, which is dressed with a rose gold Michael Kors watch. At least I *think* it's Michael Kors.

"Why don't you just tell him where you got it from? He'll be impressed with your savvy money-saving ways."

"Stingy penny-pinching ways more like. It doesn't bode well, considering he's just got me a half-carat diamond ring."

"I thought you said it was a third of a carat."

"Oh, whatever. It's just easier to say half a carat," I tell her. Plus it sounds better, I tell myself. "Why did you show me that stupid website? You know how much I'm a sucker for a bargain."

"Yes, I've spent enough lunch breaks with you covertly scanning the reduced aisle in Morrison's. Don't forget, though, that stupid website saved you over 100 quid. So... You're welcome."

Bushra returns to her work. I say returns but it would be more accurate to say starting for the first time at 11.30am.

Clearly she's going to be no help in getting me out of this hole she helped me dig. I bet she's even enjoying seeing me squirm. I thought I detected a hint of jealousy when she saw my ring.

I need to get out for some air. And I really, really need to speak to someone about this. A problem shared and all that. Sophia is no help these days and Julia is busy being a legal eagle. I need the counsel of my sisters.

"Oh, I don't know lady." I can almost hear big sis shaking her head in disapproval through the phone. "It's just that you're starting your marriage out on a lie."

"That's a bit dramatic! It's not like I've had an affair or anything."

Perhaps she wasn't the best person to call.

"No, but you have told a little porky when you didn't need to. Was it really worth it to save £100?"

This coming from the woman who will haggle until she is red-faced and hyperventilating to shave £10 off the asking price of a £300 saree.

She's not done. "It's just that, well, you only get engaged once. And if he's bought you a diamond ring, not to mention all the other gifts, you should have just splashed out. I mean, is the watch even genuine. Or is it a knock-off?"

"It's not a knock-off! That much I know. It had a proper guarantee book and everything. The girl at my work buys from there all the time."

"Well, then you should've told him from the beginning that you bought it from so and so. Actually, that would've made you sound stingy. Oh, I don't know. I just don't know. Like I say, you'll only get engaged once. Or at least you hope that will be the case."

She *cannot* be serious. "Oh, you are the worst! Right, I'm hanging up okay, bye."

Could this watch cost me my marriage before I'm even married? Maybe middle sis will offer a more reasonable voice.

"What a tosspot! Palming it off to you and putting you on the spot like that. Isn't it enough that you've bought him a watch? Now it's up to you to fix it, too? Why can't he do it himself in London? It's not like it's going to cost him that much, is it?" middle sis huffs.

"It's not the cost. I think he's probably just assuming it will be a nice thing to do together and asking quite innocent-ly." I'm already on defensive wife-bear mode.

"Nice thing to do together. Yeah right?"

Hormones are making my sister slightly aggressive. And a little scary.

"I just think I made a mistake to save a few pounds. I should've got it from the bloody proper jewellers."

"No, don't feel guilty. You've made a massive saving. It shows that you're sensible and you're not gonna spend loads of his money in the future. If he has a problem with that then he's a bloody mug!"

Are my two sisters even related to each other? They couldn't be more different in their reaction. Sadly, neither is helpful right now.

14th June

I can't get no sleep

Message from M: *Just 87 days until we get married. I've been busy thinking about ideas for the honeymoon. Don't worry, I won't throw any spoilers your way. Except to say, I think you'll love it!*

Me:...

I couldn't respond. I didn't know what to say. I've not slept for the last two nights. Last night was exceptionally hideous. I tossed and turned. Tossed and turned. To make things worse, my annoying little sister was snoring. Snoring! I never noticed that before. Unless it's a new skill she's acquired. It's not like a full on foghorn snore. It's more nasally, like a baby rhino.

The main issue occupying my mind is, can I really rock up to Goldman's with M, only for the jeweller to say: *"Sorry love, this watch isn't from here."*

Or

"Do you have the receipt?"

Or

"Do you have proof of purchase? A bank statement?"

Or worst case...

"I'm very sorry... but this looks to be a counterfeit. I mean, it's not even Armani and it's certainly not from our shop. Where did you get it from? A market stall?"

Not that I'm saying market stalls sell counterfeit watch brands. What I am saying is that I've managed to buy 'cashmere' jumpers from market stalls for the princely sum of £4. You do the maths.

I worked through all the scenarios in my head over a sweaty night of no sleep. Every option that I played out ended badly. I could vividly picture M's face. The look of shock, surprise, disbelief. I lied. I duped him. He'd think, *she's lied about this, what else has she lied about? Do I really know who I'm marrying?*

Yeah, it was a bit much. I'm a creative though, my mind goes to the extremes.

Not that our relationship is quid pro quo but if it were I hadn't kept my end of the bargain. I received a diamond ring from Hatton Garden. He received a watch but I'm not 100% sure it's a genuine article.

I even called Sophia, something I'd not done for a long time out of principle. She's never available so I didn't want to come across as desperate. It's so bloody ironic, I spent all of last year worrying about appearing desperate to prospective boys. Now I've landed a fella, my concern has shifted to my missing in action friends.

This time, however, Sophia answered after a mere five rings. When I explained my predicament, she giggled. No, she cackled. Maybe I was wrong. Maybe she wasn't the best person to speak to. Silly me, I just assumed as she's only one of three people in on my online secret, I thought I could confide in her with this.

"Sorry hon. I don't mean to laugh. It's just, how do you get yourself into these situations?"

"Hey, I did my due diligence. My friend Bushra buys from them all the time, they've got good reviews, too. It felt like a fool-proof plan."

"Are you sure the watch is legitimate? Or is there a slim chance you've got a fake?"

Sophia has managed to hone in on my deepest fear. What if it isn't really Armani? I would die.

"I'm pretty sure it's real."

"Pretty sure? That doesn't sound convincing."

"Okay, I'm really sure."

"Look hon, if the watch is the genuine article, then tell him. Otherwise you risk making it a bigger lie than it needs to be. You never know, he might appreciate your thriftiness."

"That's what I'm hoping. I just wish I'd told him from the beginning. Now I'll be backtracking so I have to admit that I kind of lied in the first place."

"There is no kind of about it. It's a straight up lie."

I thought motherhood may have mellowed Sophia but she's as cuttingly blunt as ever.

She's not done yet, either. "In the grand scheme of things, it's not a big lie. It's more like you tried to impress him with a nice gift and still bought the exact same gift but managed to find it somewhere else at a better price. So just 'fess up and be done with it."

When she puts it like that, it doesn't sound so bad.

"Thanks hon, I've been stressing out of my head. And thanks for listening. I know it's hard for you as you don't have as much time these days."

Sophia sighs. "Yeah, I know I've not always been available. Motherhood is... well, it's not how people tell you."

"Planning a wedding isn't how people tell you either! I thought the hard bit was finding the man!"

"Hmm... yes. Just remember though, when it comes to weddings, if you've not upset or offended someone, then there is something very wrong. So hopefully this might be the only faux pas you make. Anyway, for my part, I'll try and make more time to help you navigate these premarital dilemmas."

I appreciate the gesture, though I know I can't rely upon her like I used to. She's in a different phase in her life.

As we say our goodbyes, I realise that I hadn't asked her how she was. What did she mean about motherhood? I'm sure she'll fill me in next time. Plus, I can't think beyond watch-gate right now.

SO I DID SOMETHING rubbish. I copped out. I told M that I'm not free this weekend to avoid a watch-shaming of epic proportions. It's not that I won't tell him, it's just that I don't have the balls to tell him *yet*. I just need to buy my time, keep this secret for a little longer. The downside is that this means I won't see him for at least another two or three weeks.

What choice did I have?

18th June

Russian foxes

Message from M: *83 days and counting. Does it feel like a long wait for you? Or is it flying by?*

Me: *A bit of both, really. On one hand 83 days is a lot of days, but then there's still loads to do.*

M: *Don't worry. You're not doing it by yourself. I'm here to help remember, as it's my day as much as yours. So you can offload stuff onto me.*

Well, it's not quite as much your day as it is mine, I think but don't say. And secondly, do you want to trial the makeup artists for me? You do have lovely long lashes.

"I PROMISE I HAVEN'T been elusive on purpose," says Julia as she sips on her latte.

"Well, it started to feel that way. How did you forget to tell me that you were going on holiday with Miles?" I ask, chugging down my now room temperature hot chocolate.

Yep, I'm the classy one in this relationship.

"Honestly, I've pulled that many all nighters with work that I actually thought I told you." Julia leans over the table. "I'm not supposed to say this but we're handling the divorce of a Premier League footballer. I can't tell you his name though."

223

Julia's just dying for me to press her on the subject. I won't, as I know bugger all about football and footballers. Unless it's involving the Beckhams, it'll be totally over my head. I doubt it will be anyone properly famous though. I've known Julia long enough to learn that she's the biggest tease. It's probably a Premier League footballer that isn't a household name and spends most of his time on the bench.

Realising I'm not taking the bait, Julia moves onto more important matters. "The holiday was a bit of a surprise. He basically told me he'd booked an AirBnB cottage in Cornwall for my birthday..."

Oh no! I forgot her birthday. I've never forgotten her birthday in the last 20 years. I'm hoping I can pull out my getting married card as an excuse for everything I'm forgetting and will continue to forget moving forward.

"So anyway. I was a bit deflated about the Cornwall bit but hey ho, a holiday is a holiday."

"You are *so* middle-class!"

"Shut up! I said hey ho, didn't I? Albeit reluctantly. The point is, I was game. Packed my bags, met him at Kings Cross. So imagine my surprise when we weren't getting the train to Cornwall, we were getting the bloody Eurostar to Paris! So in the blur of it all I didn't even congratulate you about your engagement! How are you feeling?"

"Whoa whoa whoa! Let's rewind it back a second. First, sorry I forgot about your birthday."

"Oh, don't worry about that, you've got much bigger things going on."

Phew, my impending marriage card is working itself.

"Second, he surprised you with Paris! Isn't that amazing? How did you even know to bring your passport?"

Julia slowly and carefully takes another sip of her latte before placing it down and cupping it with her delicate, French manicured fingers.

"That's the thing. I didn't pack my passport. He sneakily took it from my room."

"Wow, that's pretty..." I can't find the words.

Julia attempts to fill the gaps. "Obsessive? Weird? OTT?"

"No! I was going to say super romantic. I mean, the guy went to great lengths to surprise you, Miss Can-never-be-pleased, with an amazing all-expenses paid trip. Isn't that what you always wanted? The old-fashioned chivalry? Or is he not brown enough?"

Julia stares at me open mouthed, before bursting into a giggle. We both know she's got a type and blonde haired, blue-eyed Miles isn't it.

"Oh shush. I've had plenty of... English boyfriends."

"Yeah, but that was out of circumstance more than choice. As soon as you went to uni and there were Asian boys to pick from, you never looked back. Anyway, this one sounds like a keeper. I would love it if M did all that for me."

"I'm sure he will, after you're married." Julia knows our halal modus operandi all too well. I've always said she is the brownest white girl I have ever met.

"Anyway, before marriage comes your birthday. So... lunch here?" she asks. "I'll come up for the weekend. Unless of course you've got plans with your man. I suppose I have to share you now."

If only. I'm currently avoiding him, though I hope to have figured something out by the time I turn 27. I don't think I could cope with a whole month of lying.

"I reckon I'll be free," I say.

"Perfect. Second and arguably more important - the hen do. I would like to personally take it upon myself, as your oldest friend, to organise the shebang. It's my way of making up for being so shit recently. So, what would you like to do? A spa weeke -"

Julia stops in her tracks. "Or a spa day? Or a night at the Palace Theatre?"

Like I say, she is a sister from another Mister. She knows that weekends away are only acceptable when it's work-related.

I'm so relieved that Julia is stepping up. Truth be told, I don't think there's anyone else that would organise it for me. My sisters are too busy with their own lives. Though they made a valiant effort to be available before my engagement, they've not been so forthcoming recently and have so far ignored the pictures I've sent them of taals and wedding favour inspiration. Plus, hen dos aren't really how we roll. Even middle sis, who's probably the more modern of us all, didn't have a hen do. Or at least not one I was aware of. Who knows with that one?

I'm not sure about her suggestions, though. With my dad being a constantly silent but looming presence, I don't think a late night will be in order. I also doubt Sophia would want to leave baby Imran for a whole evening. Then again, she probably couldn't commit to a spa afternoon either as she seems to be a hostage to nap times and breastfeeds. She'd probably be more comfortable somewhere she can duck in and out depending on her bubba's needs. That doesn't leave many options.

"I was thinking something... maybe more low key? I mean it's not what you do, it's who you do it with, right? So how about lunch or dinner at this place?"

Julia looks around at the exposed brickwork of the Italian restaurant we've been dining at for the last seven years as though she's appraising it for the first time. "Here?"

"Yeah. Why not? It's easy, we know the food is good. It's pretty cosy. I don't want to have one of those hen dos that gets out of hand and starts growing arms and legs. Then it becomes a logistical nightmare for anyone to get to."

"Okay, I can look into that." Julia doesn't sound too sure. "Speaking of logistics, do let me know who you're thinking of inviting, as I don't know many of your other friends."

She is being polite. She doesn't know *any* of my other friends that aren't from our school. I've segregated them. The brown friends from uni with whom I talk about the endless quest for a man. The friends from school with whom, up until now, I avoided boy talk like the plague because I never had a love life to speak of. Then there are the new work friends, with whom I talk a good talk.

Also, there is the small fact that I don't have too many other friends. I've never been the one with the big group, though I'd have loved that. I've always been a cluster kind of girl, with small pockets of friends here and there from different facets of my life. I'm not sure if I want to piece these fragments together, even for one night.

"Obviously I'll liaise with your sisters too," says Julia. "Would your mum want to -"

She stops herself as she remembers that:

a) Mum is Bengali

and

b) Bengali mums do not attend hen dos however halal they are.

Julia remembers all too well the few lunches she had at my house when we were younger. We dined on beige oven food but the smell of curry mum was eating secretly in the kitchen, was unmistakable. From there I think she made the educated guess that mum wouldn't be into pizza or pasta. She was also a witness to the domestic mum and dad had when my usually genteel father stormed out of the house with a 20kg bag of Tolly Boy long grain rice, grumbling how he wishes he had sons. I never knew what the argument was about, though I suspect it had something to do with dad getting lumbered with all the heavy lifting. Julia saw it all and was savvy enough, even at the age of eight, to deduce that mum and dad weren't exchanging pleasantries in Bengali.

I'm glad she brushed over the sisters bit, too. We're just not that kind of family. My friend Reena and her sisters are more like mates. Their friends all know each other. Heck, even their boyfriends past and present know each other. Whereas me, with my double, sometimes triple, life has to draw a firm line between friends and siblings. In fact, I even cut the mates into three different pieces. I've got one limb in all the different worlds. Sometimes it's hard. Usually it's lonely.

"I guess I'll just stick to friends," she decides. "Right, so lunch here for your hen do. Brill. Leave it with me."

I'm embarrassed for both of us.

"Cool. Just keep me in the loop, that's all I ask. Plus, as I missed your birthday, let me get this. It's the least I can do."

I grab the receipt from Sergio, who's probably relieved that Julia and I won't have a bill-fight like I did during my last visit with Reena. I bet he can smell the awkwardness as we try to plan what would essentially be a glorified pizza for my hen do. Annoyingly the cost of this lunch is £38. Julia had two coffees, one with her meal and another afterwards. Oh well. It's not like I'm saving for a wedding or anything.

WITH UNCOMFORTABLE hen do planning out of the way, I've got more exciting things to look forward to this evening. I found a makeup artist on Instagram and she's coming to mine to trial some wedding makeup. She's not hugely well known. I did initially enquire into the work of Aisha Khan, a top MUA influencer type person who boasts 500k followers. However, I made a hasty retreat upon realising that she charges £1,000 for wedding and mehendi makeup. One... thousand... pounds. Four figures. For that price, I'd want them to create a prosthetic makeup mask that I can wear on any occasion at will. Not some face paint that can be smeared off with a wet wipe.

The lady that's coming round today, Rania, is more modestly priced at £300 for bridal makeup and hair. After stalking her profile, I was glad to find that her makeup was pretty on point, which is always a comforting testimonial. Though I suspect, like everyone else on social media with the exception of myself, the photos have probably been touched by the magic filter.

RANIA, A PETITE WOMAN with a childlike frame, arrived with a disappointingly small silver makeup box. It's not dissimilar to the metal cosmetic briefcase I was gifted by M's family for my engagement. I'm paying 30 quid for this trial. So, if that trinket doesn't spout products like Mary Poppins' bag, I'm going to be miffed.

"Have you thought about your hair?" asks Rania as she starts laying out some eyeshadow pallets on our dining room table.

"Erm, well I was thinking maybe some kind of updo..."

"Do you want pieces?"

"Pieces? Of what?" Should I know this?

"Hair. Hair extensions. That way you won't just look good for your wedding day, you'll have great hair for your honeymoon, too."

"Oh yeah, that sounds nice. Is that something you do?" I ask.

"Yeah. I'm big on Russian hair extensions. Real hair."

I'm not sure how I feel about having a Russian head of hair on top of my Bengali mane. "Is this included in the price?"

Rania looks at me with flared nostrils and a raised eyebrow, as though I'd just farted.

"No love. It's extra. What about your lashes? Have you thought about those?"

"I didn't know I should be thinking about my... eyelashes."

Clearly this makeup business is some seriously deep shit.

"Well..." Rania claps her knees, "I would recommend... rather than going for a strip lash, you use individual lashes. They'll stay in much longer. So even after the wedding, when you're taking photos you want to look your best, right? You won't even need that much makeup as your lashes will do the job for you. Where are you going on your honeymoon?"

"Oh, I don't know yet. It'll be a surprise."

"Well wherever you go, odds are there'll be a beach. So just imagine, going makeup free but having these insane lashes."

"Are they from Russian women too?" I ask.

"No love. Fox hair."

Nasty. I'm not even going to ask if that costs extra. My stingy-sense tells me that the fox won't be cheap.

Rania holds up a paltry three lip liners for me to choose from. "So... shall we go for a brown, red, or pink lip?"

Is that it? Is that her range? Three lip liners? No shades in between? I've got more lip liners than that, and I hardly wear makeup.

"Maybe red," I reluctantly reply.

She lines out my lips and then begins taking out the rest of her lip products. It doesn't take long. There aren't many. I also notice that there is an absence of the big name brands I'm familiar with. That's disappointing. When I'm forking out hundreds of pounds for a makeup artist, I expect them to have premium makeup.

"Did you know your husband?"

Oh... I see. She is doing the hairdresser thing, making small talk.

"I did, yes," I reply like I've won some kind of marriage lottery.

"Oh, that's lovely, love. I knew my man, too. Met him when I was 18. We're still going strong 20 years later."

She looks a lot younger than her age. It must be the fox lashes and Russian hair.

"Awww, that's great. How did you meet? College?" I ask.

"No love. I didn't bother with college. Neither did he. Not that we've done too bad. Right, what colour do you want for your eyes?"

"I think I'd like to go traditional. You know, like a maroon or deep red."

Rania hunts through her limited product range. "Oh, I don't actually have either of those colours."

An Asian makeup artist without the traditional red bridal eye colour? Surely that's blasphemous?

"Let me see... let me see. Okay, I'll do a workaround. I'll just mix a few shades together. I'm sure I have maroon but I've just not packed it with me."

Sure, Rania. Sure.

This makeup mixing and making do goes on for another 30 minutes. She largely works in silence, with the odd punctuation of a prompt for me to start having facials as my skin is rather dull. Apparently every bride-to-be needs a good buffing before their big day.

I have zero patience for these makeovers. I'm anxious to see what she's doing but I'm under strict instructions not to look in the mirror. She says I'll be scared if I look midway through her work, as though I'll be painted like Pennywise - just for her amusement - before she does a proper job.

I busy my mind hatching a plan for M's watch. He hasn't mentioned it again and neither have I. However, it's only a matter of time before he brings it up, likely coordinated with his next visit. There's only so much I can avoid meeting him before he thinks I'm having second thoughts about marriage. I wonder if I could pay an Asian jeweller beforehand and get them to fix the links? Nah, that'd look proper dodgy. That bribe could get lost in translation and I'd be rumbled. Maybe I could just take the watch off him and get it done? But then I won't know how many links to remove. Why, oh why didn't I buy a leather strap watch? Bloody Bushra and her iffy recommendation. Bloody me and my bargain-hungry ways.

"All done!" Rania interrupts my thoughts with a final sweep of blush.

She holds up a round mirror for me to see her handiwork. The makeup looks very pretty. Though the look is a little gothic for my liking. It's not quite the bridal look I want and I think that's more to do with her missing a few vital shades of red.

I really need a second opinion. I arranged for Rania to visit when there'd be an empty house. After mum gave me a huge complex on the day of my engagement because she didn't like my makeup, I decided she wouldn't be the best person to have as a wing woman when trying artists. More fool me.

As Rania fiddles with her three lip liners, I send a sneaky selfie to Naila. She's a makeup artist, after all.

She texts me straight away: *Nice but a no-no for your wedding. Dark, vampy makeup = slutty. Save it for your honeymoon ;).*

I see her point. I've seen enough of mum's Indian dramas on Star Plus to know that the darker hues are the reserve of the wanton harlot, or the evil stepmother. The heroine is always painted in the lightest, brightest shades to symbolise innocence and purity.

Mum, dad and my little sis come through the door. I don't think I'll be using Rania so I'm happy for mum to interject with her specific blend of sass.

Mum takes one look at my made up face and does her lip grimace thing. "It's a bit dark," she says in Bengali, safe in the knowledge that Rania, being Pakistani, won't understand. For once, mum's not talking about my complexion but is referring to the overall dark aesthetic created by the eyes and lips.

"Salaam auntie, what do you think?" asks Rania.

This is dangerous territory.

"Pretty but maybe *litool* bit dark on eyes. But pretty. Yes, pretty." Mum perfected the art of delivering a shit sandwich before it became a thing.

Rania looks unperturbed by mum's critique. "We were just talking about the lashes. I've put full strip ones on for now. I think the way to go on the day would be to have lash inserts that last for up to two weeks. *He na,* auntie?" She's looking for support in the wrong place.

Mum furrows her brow. "Won't that stop *namaz*?"

Ooh, good call mum.

Rania's eyes dart from side to side as she searches for her comeback. We might be the first potential clients that use the need to be makeup free and clean of soul for prayer, as a reason not to buy her fox hair eyelashes.

"Oh... well... it's just that's what the customers want. Girls demand long-lasting lashes these days, so what can I do?" Rania looks at me, pleading with her eyes for help.

"Well, thank you so much for coming over. I love what you've done. It's pretty autumnal. And I'll definitely think about my hair and lashes."

Rania folds in her metal case, deflated. We both know this is the end of the road on our fledging relationship.

The search for a makeup artist continues.

30th June

Meet the parents (without me)

M essage from M: *Just to let you know, your family are on their way back home now. It was nice having them round. I think they liked my beef massomam too.*

Me: *I'm so jealous that they got to try your cooking before me!*

M: *Not long now until I'm cooking for the both of us! P.S. 71 days until we get married. I bet you thought I'd forgot!*

Me: *No, I knew you wouldn't forget. Your maths is much better than mine. Then again, I'm words and your numbers.*

IT'S CUSTOMARY FOR the bride's family to pay a visit to the house of the groom ahead of the wedding, without the bride. It's really just to check they're not living in abject squalor. Kind of like a recce of sorts. I'm guessing it would be too forward if I was to rock up and critique the place myself, so my parents do it for me.

"Yes, the house be okay," says mum, as she puts the kettle on for a de-brief. "Bigger than ours but still three bedrooms. The area be as English as where we live. I still don't understand why they left Oldham."

Oh, my mum. If she's not digging to see if there's a monster-in-law, she's bitching about the neighbourhood.

"How is everyone? Did the daughter-in-law do all the cooking?" I ask.

"No, well she did lot of serving and things but they always do for show. His mum look quite hands on."

Phew.

"I think he be quite nice," mum declares. It's so cute how she still can't bring herself to say his name. "He even made curry. It was a bit dry but at least he tried."

"Oh, that's coz it's not a Bengali curry. It's from Indonesia or somewhere and it's meant to be dry."

Mum puts the kettle down and looks at me. "How you know what he make?" Then with a raised eyebrow, she says: "*Oh ho*, okay," like she's in on some naughty secret. "What else you talk about?"

This is dicey territory.

"Nothing much. He's sent me some pictures of flats, though. He keeps saying that we'll pick something together once we're married but I'd rather it got sorted before I came."

"Maybe he can't afford rent by himself. You need to do it together," says my modern-minded mum.

"I don't think it's that. He probably just wants to look together, so I feel involved."

I'm in denial that M might have any financial constraints. In my mind he is a wealthy investment banker and that's the story I'm sticking to.

"London rent be expensive. It might be hard for him to get something before you come. Maybe he be shy to ask you to share rent. You should ask him. Now it different to when I got married. Back then, man paid for everything. You had to be grateful. Now it be better. You get choice. And you got your own money. Money make world go round."

Mum dunks her Rich-Tea biscuit into her black, piping hot tea. "Oh, and while we talk money, your uncle Tariq speak to them about how much money to gift you. I'll tell you what they say."

Oh, the dowry. It seems so irrelevant these days.

"Mum, I don't really need to know what they want to give."

"What you mean, you no need to know? It be about you! It be your money. You don't want them to be stingy."

"What's the most they're going to give, anyway? £5,000? £10,000? It's hardly going to change my life. I have my own money."

"Yes, but it not be about you having money. They have to give *something*. It has to be good. Otherwise it looks like you've gone for cheap."

I forgot I was a cow in a cattle market.

"Mum... please, really, I'd rather not know. So many families argue because of the dowry. It breaks relationships. I don't want to be one of them."

"Who tell you people argue over money?"

"*You* do! You're always telling me about other people's business. I won't be so petty. I understand why people used to give a dowry. It was a woman's insurance policy when they didn't work and came to the marriage with nothing. It doesn't matter now. They'll give what they give."

Mum's nose wrinkles. "You'll go for anything will you? Hmmph! What will people think? We look desperate!"

"I don't care. I don't want to know." I head upstairs away from the conversation.

I'm surprising myself by how un-shallow I'm being. However, I can't claim credit for this very modern mindset. It was actually Sophia who, back in the day, told me how she refused to engage in any conversation about money exchanging before she married Adnan. The first time round, young and naïve, she went headlong into a conversation with her then fiancé. This built up resentment and was duly thrown back in her face when they were on the verge of splitting up. Her advice to me was, under no circumstances, get involved in such delicate debates. "Leave it to the grown-ups," she said. "Let them argue amongst themselves but don't let it tarnish your relationship with your man."

Oh, how I long for her wise words now.

Having walked away from mum, I am now wondering what princely sum will be paid for my hand in marriage. Damn mum and her seed planting ways.

However, mum isn't done. "Don't go yet!" she shouts as I'm at the top of the stairs. "One more thing. His family no mention wedding shopping yet. Has he said anything to you?"

"No, not yet."

"Okay, maybe you ask. As we no sure how they want to do things. We can go shopping for your outfit to get ideas."

On it goes to the list.

"IT WAS REALLY NICE seeing your family today. Especially your dad. Him and my dad are very similar. Both are pretty quiet but they came out of their shells together," says M.

I decide to have *that* awkward conversation. Not the watch-based one, I'm still operating on the basis of he asks me no questions, I tell him no lies. This one is hopefully an easier conversation, though no less awkward.

"So, what do you want to do about our living arrangement? When I move down?" I ask.

"Well, I've sent you pictures of flats and I'll keep looking, so hopefully we'll sort something. If not before, then when you're here. Would that be okay?"

It would be a little bit weird, living with his friend. "Erm... I think so but obviously it'd be better if we had our own space from the beginning. So I want to check..."

Gosh, this is a tricky one.

"Is there an issue with – not an issue... but would it be easier if we rented together?"

"To be honest with ya..."

Oh, here we go.

M continues: "It probably would be a bit easier if we could share – or you could contribute something to the rent. Because at the moment I'm paying half with my flatmate. If you couldn't initially, don't worry. We might just have to live a bit further out. Which is okay."

Bless him. Money is an issue. Of course it is, he lives in London. I'm sheltered from all of it being at home rent-free.

As we say our goodbyes and I retire to bed, I can't sleep. It's just... the unknown. Where will I work? What will I do?

I've not been out of work since I finished uni five years ago. Not only have I grown to like structure, I've gotten a taste for money, too. I'm not lavish in any sense but I'm independent. I don't need to ask anyone for anything.

I've always thought of money to be a fleeting thing. It's here today but might be gone tomorrow. There was a time in our lives when I think we were pretty comfortable as a family. Dad had started his own restaurant business. We got an extension at the front of the house and there was talk of a loft conversion. When I started high school, I was charged with having my own money. Every morning I'd wake up to find a row of coins waiting for me. All shiny and silver. There were 50 and 20 pence pieces and sometimes I'd even find a £2 coin. I never spent that one and put it in my money box.

Then the chatter about the loft conversion died down. Mum, who always had ideas above her station and just loved buying the full fat Greek style yoghurt from M&S, reigned in her dairy habit. She did her best to hide this seismic change. We've never been flash, we always shopped in the sale and spent within our means, so the transition wasn't terrible. Though it did feel like just as we got used to something better, it was taken away.

Poor mum had had her whole life governed by the actions of others. The fate of her marriage was in the hands of her parents, who chose my dad. The fate of her fortune was in the hands of my dad, who set up a business I always thought was doing well and then for reasons I'll never know, decided to retire early. Mum didn't have a say in so many things in her own life. I guess that's why she bosses the hell out of him at home. It's her only grab for power.

One morning there wasn't much tuck shop money. I spotted some copper coins within the 5p and 20p pieces. Then came the forms. Big sis, lucky her, always tasked with the household admin, gave me the forms to hand in to school that would let the teachers know that I'd be getting free dinners.

Even at such a young age, I knew of the stigma attached to benefits. All the free dinners kids ate together at lunchtime. Some of the cool kids, a.k.a. the school bullies, would call these children 'gyppos'. They weren't gypsies though, they were just kids who needed to have their dinner paid for. It wasn't their fault.

The system didn't help either. There was a different line at lunchtime for the kids that had free meals, segregated from the ones who parted with cold, hard cash. I hated joining that line. Julia knew I hated it, too. So she'd always stay and chat with me as long as she could, until we got to the lunch lady who'd separate us with a ticking off.

This whole mortifying experience shaped me in several ways. I didn't ask for much at home. I learnt not to ask much of anyone, for that matter. I realised that in this life, if I want to live well, I really needed to make something for myself. It was so important. And I did. I make a good living. I save much more than I spend. I've only allowed myself the smallest of luxuries. While M rolls around in an Audi TT, I swapped my shitty Ford Fiesta for a slightly less shitty Ford Fiesta. I don't own swathes of gold jewellery like my sisters did before marriage. Even when I dropped a few hundred pounds on my engagement sarees, I felt a mix of adrenaline and unfamiliarity. I've never spent so much. Certainly not on myself.

I didn't really care for the loft conversion. I thought it was embarrassing. We were the only Asians in the street and the only ones that had a UPVC front porch. I hated having free dinners though. So I learnt then to never rely on a man because you never know how much, or how little, they can provide.

1st July

Trying my luck

Message from M: *Hello you. Just 70 days until we get married :).*

Me: I know. *I can't wait :)*

Crap! 70 days? There's still so much to do. Why isn't anyone else feeling time pressed like me?

Another message from M: *You're probably gonna get sick of these messages but you're stuck with me now! What's the plan today? What media crisis are you conquering?*

Me: *No crisis, I hope. But I've got my fortnightly 1:1 with Bernadette. I'm currently in her good books as I just PR'd a new hospital wing opening on a shoestring budget and all the big regionals covered it. Which is even more impressive given that I spent more time browsing Pinterest for wedding favour ideas than I did actually planning the event!*

M: *That's amazing! You're my little star. x*

M doesn't quite realise the enormity of this meeting. It's not just a regular one-to-one. Well it is, as far as Bernadette's concerned. For me, however, it's a sweaty palm moment. I'm going to do it. I'm going to bite the bullet and tell Bernadette my big news and see if there's even a smidgen of a chance that I could transfer my role to London.

"I JUST READ THE PAPER this morning. Fantastic!" Bernadette declares. "It's not every day we get a double page spread in the biggest newspaper in Manchester."

"I know. To be fair though, it was a great story, I just pitched it."

I am so full of insincere crap.

"Plus, the media love anything to do with children. Throw in a WAG and you've got the perfect PR opportunity right there. I couldn't believe it when I saw the mention on the front page," I add, just in case Bernadette missed those additional few column inches. I work in PR after all. If I don't blow my own trumpet, who will?

"Oh, I didn't see that. We were on the front page, too?" she asks.

I actually have the folded up paper in my folder but decide not to take it out. It might scream swotty schoolgirl rather than grown-ass, kick-ass PR woman.

It's probably better to tell, not show, in this case. "Yes, we were."

Ever the no-nonsense businesswoman, Bernadette starts thumbing her way down her handwritten agenda.

I better strike while we're on a good note. "I did have some news, though."

"O-kay... go on?" Bernadette sounds unsure as to where this is going. So am I.

"Well, I've been meaning to say... I'm getting married!"

"Amazing!"

"Yeah... and my fiancé's from London. Well, he's from up north originally, but he lives in London."

"Ah. Lovely." She really doesn't know what to expect. Again, neither do I. I'm totally ad-libbing.

"So, I'll be moving too. And I was wondering... as my role is largely remote, I could do it from anywhere, really. So, I don't know if there's any... You know with the office move into central London... If there would be an opportunity that I could... work from there?"

"You mean base yourself in the central London office but continue with your Northern region role?"

When she puts it like that, it sounds silly.

Bernadette exhales a little deeper than she needs to. "Well, the thing is, I don't want to see you go. You've made such an impact on the region even in the short time you've been here. You've put PR on the map, when our focus has been so heavily on the sales side of things. I'm just thinking... leave it with me, I'll have a word with Richard at HQ. If I pitch it right, maybe we could show them that you'll be able to loop into the national campaigns more effectively. I always thought you're a bit wasted with 80% of your time pitching to the really small local papers. You've proven that you can deliver to big regionals as well as some national case studies. Hmm, it's definitely a conversation I can have. Obviously, I can't promise anything and I'll also need to have some careful conversations with the bods here, so they don't grumble that they're not going to get support."

I feel I should add some reassurance from my end. "I'll come back regularly. One of the great things is with my parents here, I can head up north whenever needed and I don't need to stay in a hotel."

That's the money shot. Or should I say the money-saving shot?

"Yeah. That all makes sense." Bernadette consults her notes again, though I don't know what she's looking at exactly. This conversation has completely thrown off the agenda. You could call it an ambush.

"So, I just need to lay out exactly what you need. When will you be getting married?"

This is a teeny bit awkward. "September."

"Sep-! Oh, okay. Wow! Not long at all." She laughs nervously. "So when do you think you'll be moving there?"

This is the part I hadn't thought through. "Okay, so I'll probably go on honeymoon for two weeks, after Ramadan. So I reckon October-ish?"

"Right, okay, that gives us a bit of time." Bernadette exhales, this time with relief rather than shock.

However, I'm not done yet. "So, as I'm in the throes of wedding planning, I was hoping maybe I could have a couple of weeks off before the wedding..."

"Right. That's reasonable."

"And then... just because there's so much to do... I was wondering if I could go part-time from next month in the run-up."

"How part-time?"

"Maybe two..."

Bernadette shoots me a cutting stare. I think I'm pushing my luck.

"...Or three days a week?"

Bernadette sighs. "Okay... right. Let me just make sure I've got this straight," she scribbles ferociously while she's talking. "So... you want to go part-time effectively a couple of weeks from now, then have about a month's annual leave."

Again, when she puts it like that...

"Yes."

Bernadette exhales heavily. "Okay. I'll see what I can do."

I feel like doing a big exhalation of my own.

"I'd love to know, how did you meet him?"

That's an easy one to answer. "We met through friends last year." That makes it sound like less of a shotgun wedding. I must keep track of the different stories I'm telling different people to avoid cross-contamination.

"Oh, brilliant. Well, I'm really happy for you."

I think Bernadette is just relieved that I'm not forced into a quickie marriage. It actually works out quite well that she's not one for small talk. That way she's not really aware of the blistering breakneck speed at which my wedding is taking place. Small mercies.

M IS BEYOND PLEASED with my potential work development.

"That would be great if you get a transfer. Especially as the office is so close to where I am now. We could rent somewhere near," he says.

"Well, let's not get too excited yet. Bernadette might come back with a no. She can't promise anything."

Glass half empty and all that. I'm beginning to realise just how optimistic M is. We're like the opposite ends of a battery.

"Okay, I won't jinx it but I have to say, I've got a good feeling about this. My mum's been saying that we're meant for each other since she met you."

"Your mum?" I never realised she harboured such thoughts. I figured we had a totally formal mother and daughter-in-law-to-be dynamic, in that we think nothing and hope for the best.

"Yeah. She's always saying it sounds like you're really hardworking and we're well matched. How everything else has fallen into place so far... well, it's a really good sign," he says. "Anyway, what you up to tonight?"

"What I've been doing most nights. Wedding planning. Tonight I'll be looking at invitations."

"Ah, okay," M replies.

That's all he can say, really. Wedding invites isn't an area he can help with as his family send out their own set of invites to their guests. It's like two separate weddings in many ways. I bet he'll be doing something social and fun tonight. I'd rather not hear about it.

"Have you sorted your wedding invites yet?" I ask.

I can almost hear him shrugging through the phone. "I'm not sure to be honest with ya. I don't think so, anyway. Mum's dealing with all of that."

"Really? How will she order the cards? Can she speak English?" Not that I'm judging but M's mum looks older and seems more old-school than my mum, who's grasp of English doesn't get her very far.

"No, she can't speak English but my sister or brother will sort the cards. She'll oversee it. Like a project manager. I dunno, it'll get done anyway."

"It must be nice being you, just rocking up to your wedding after having everything taken care of by your family," I laugh but I'm slightly bitter.

"You should be palming off stuff, too. Get your sisters involved with the things I can't help with," says M.

"Hmm, yeah maybe," I reply rather unconvincingly. Truth be told, I'm not sure how much my sisters will help. Nobody's recently piped up with offers of support.

"Anyway, there is one job you can tick off your list," he says.

"Oh? What's that?"

"Well, I've got my watch fixed here. I was in Westfield so I just popped into Goldman's. I didn't think they'd fix it without a receipt but they did it there and then. Must have been a quiet day for them. I hope you don't mind, I know I said we'd do it together, it's just that I had it with me, as I'd taken it to work to show my colleagues..."

I don't have the words but my silence must be audible.

"Is that okay?" he asks.

"Oh... yeah... No, don't worry about it. You've got it done, that's the main thing. To be honest with ya, I completely forgot about it."

Biggest fucking lie ever.

16th July
All the trimmings

Message from M: *55 days and counting.*
Me: *I know!*

I'm running out of original, funny or affectionate things to say in response.

I DON'T MEAN TO SOUND like a pretentious twat but I'm going for all the frills for my wedding. I managed to bag the same venue for my engagement as Hassna, so mum and I are going to try our luck again, to see if we can book our mehendi ceremony there at a discount. Yes, there are other restaurants in Rusholme that have their upstairs available for hire. However, after a lifetime of eating there, I've learnt that not all venues are created equal. So, if it ain't broke...

CHEEKY BASTARDS.

I can't believe it. I dropped the best part of a grand on that venue for my engagement party and they couldn't even give a discount. They're not even shaving off the £1 per head for soft drinks. You'd think they want the repeat custom. Especially when I told them that small fib about having a sis-

ter one year younger who is getting married next year. Hint
hint, lots of business to come their way. They didn't take the
bait.

"You should not just walk away like that. That be rude,"
says mum, breaking the silence on the drive home.

"He was rude! He's taking the piss. I told him we'd go
elsewhere and he kept saying 'you're welcome, welcome'. I
didn't thank him! There's nothing to be welcome for! He's
just like the bloke in the saree shop, who also wasn't welcome! They're all the same. It's like they're not even bothered
to have our money. Well, I'm not bothered for them, then."

"Yes but you shouldn't be all *gusha* and *garam* with the
man. Your hot temper is trouble. How will you manage with
in-laws?"

"Well, lucky I won't be living with the in-laws, with my
grumpy hot temper!"

I got her there.

There's a moment of precious silence.

"*Yalla!* Watch out for the bumps, you kill us both!"

"Mum it's okay! There are potholes everywhere around
here."

"You need to be more careful driving! I saw on news
once a car fell through a hole. It was in Manchester."

"Yeah alright, mum."

"*Hassa!* Believe me when I tell you."

I don't have a response. Luckily, my mum is great at filling silences when I'm trying to focus on the road.

"Shall we go back to the restaurant? Time is going. You
only have two months before the wedding and you know
nowhere else is good."

"No! I'll find somewhere else."

"You and your big head! Hmmph! Where? Where will you find? Not that horrible buffet that's cheap and nasty with mouldy jelly and skanky carpet."

I can't believe mum knows the word skanky.

"There'll be other places. What about the one in Longsight that's just opened?"

"No no! They have wooden laminate floor and service is slow."

"What's wrong with wooden laminate?" I ask.

"My feet get cold."

"Mum, you're not going to be dancing barefoot! Shit, I've taken the wrong turn!"

I slam the breaks, narrowly avoiding a collision with a green Range Rover that is going the right way down this one-way street. With mum in my ear, I didn't even notice the 'No Entry' sign.

As the driver slowly manoeuvres around me, he rolls his window down and says: "Just take it easy, yeah?"

He should be in a car with my mum for half an hour. Then we'll see how easy he takes it.

"That be scary!" says mum. "Anyway, now we stop, shall we drive back to restaurant?"

"No! No we shouldn't! I don't even know why I bothered bringing you, you're no help! You can't speak bloody English or Urdu so you just sit there, pecking at my head but you don't even help. You just make things worse. Bloody useless."

We drive back home in silence. I feel crap for having a go at mum but she makes my blood boil. Not only is she a backseat driver, she's a backseat negotiator, too. She always has an opinion but never brings anything to the table when it matters. That bit's always left to me.

Annoyingly, mum is right about the other restaurants. Every time I've been out for dinner at an Indian restaurant in the last year, I've scoped out venues for their potential to host a wedding or mehendi party. Yes, that's a little obsessive but I figured that one way or another, whether I marry M or some other poor sucker, I'd be getting married. Sadly, this restaurant is the best of a bad bunch. And I think I've just burnt my bridges with them.

THIS IS A JOB FOR ONE of the English-speaking elders.

"Can you just call them for me?" I plead.

"Lady, what would I be asking for?" Big sis is clearly looking for any excuse not to help a sister out.

"I've already told you. I want to book the venue for 60 people on Friday the 7th of September. In the evening."

Honestly. It's not rocket science.

"Okay. What should I ask about the food? I don't know what you want for your mehendi party. I don't see why you can't just call them and say you've changed your mind."

She's still trying to wiggle her way out of this. It should be her comfort zone. Her husband is a restaurant owner.

"I can't possibly call them after I stormed off. They definitely won't offer a discount if I come back, cap in hand. Anyway, it's not like they have lots of food options. It'll be one meat, one chicken and then a side. Maybe vegetable."

"Are you sure you don't want daal as a side?" asks big sis, over-complicating things.

"I'd rather have veg to be honest. I don't really like daal and I guess I should enjoy what I'm eating, given that it's my mehendi."

"I've ordered daal from there before and it was good, when I ate at the restaurant downstairs. I think they had it at Hassna's engagement do, didn't they? It was nice then, too. Your guests might prefer daal. I think that's what most people go for."

"Well, the guests aren't paying for it." I'm getting annoyed now.

"Right. Right... Okay. Just give me their number and I'll try and call them later, lady. I'm just making a fish curry."

Big sis resumes her domestic duties, leaving me hanging. The sad thing is she's my best option right now. I tried to see if middle sis would call the restaurant but whenever I call her she is usually about to nap, just got up from a nap, or busy with the kids. Pregnant and with a family of her own, she is next to useless. My teenage sister is too young to bestow with such responsibility. And dad is, well... dad.

I wonder how M is getting on with his mehendi planning. I guess that will be the subject of our next call.

"I'M NOT SURE TO BE honest with ya. I'm a bloke so I guess it will be something chilled out at home. My mum and sister-in-law will probably organise something. I'll just turn up."

He laughs. I don't. It's not funny. It's so much easier for boys. Not fair.

19th July

If you want something doing...

"Did you call the wedding venue?"

"What? Lady, I'm still in bed. What time is it?"

"It's half eight. Aren't you getting the kids ready for school?"

"It's the summer holidays, silly. Hold on."

There is a rumbling and rustling sound on the phone. No doubt big sis is attempting to get her brain in order.

"You mean for your mehendi. I haven't called yet. I forgot, to be honest. Since your brother-in-law's been in Bangladesh, I've been overrun with the house stuff. Everything is on me."

I forgot that he's been in Bangladesh for the last week but that's beside the point. Everything is on *her*? She doesn't know the half of it.

"I'll call them tonight, lady. If you still want me to." That's my big sister's way of saying she'd rather I just did it.

"Just forget it. I'll do it myself."

"Oh, don't say that, lady. I told you I'm sorry. I'll do it later."

"Don't bother. You've had long enough. If it's something you needed, I'd be on it. I always am."

"Gosh lady, there's still time. I'll call them now then. Actually, they won't be open yet. I'll call them around 1ish."

"No, leave it. I'll be quicker doing it myself. All the things I do for you and you can't do one thing for me. I'll remember this the next time you need a favour."

"Don't be like that," says big sis.

"Like what? Honest? Annoyed? I can be how I like!"

I hang up without saying goodbye. Of all the times I've gone out of my way for her. For both my sisters. Carpooling when they stay over. Cancelling catch-ups with Julia last minute because they're visiting last minute. When I need something, everyone is busy. They haven't had the time. I'm sure when it's one of her kids' turns to get married, she'll find the time.

"Who are you talking to so early in the morning?" asks mum as she comes down the stairs.

Dad is fast asleep. As is my little sis as I now realise it's the summer holidays. Mum still gets up for me to ensure that I have breakfast before I go to work. Even though I'm going to be 27 in three days and I'm totally capable of pouring milk into my own cereal.

"Oh, it's big sis. She's being a right lazy cow. I told her to call the restaurant for me to book the mehendi venue and she still hasn't done it. She's had loads of time! Worst thing is, she forgot. So if I hadn't called her and assumed she'd done it, I'd be without a venue. I'd have to hold the ceremony in our bloody front room."

"You mean like your other sister did," mum reminds me.

"You know it was different back then. You said yourself you want me to have a good wedding. Nobody holds their mehendi ceremonies in the house anymore."

"Well, if you just agreed the price with restaurant and no be so stubborn, you would have no problem. Always have to make things long and be difficult."

I'm not in the mood for an *I told you so*. I head to the hallway to put my shoes on.

Mum is not done. "Have you had breakfast?"

Should I lie? No, it probably wouldn't work. Mum will deduce that I haven't eaten by how much milk is left in the fridge.

"No, I haven't had time. I was too busy calling my useless sister."

"*Dooro*! Don't be rude. You shouldn't call her so early. The restaurant wouldn't be open now anyway. Not everything about your wedding."

If I wasn't pissed off enough, mum has to lay it on thicker. I need to leave the house before I say something I'll regret, again.

I open the door before mum shouts back. "Hold on, let me get you something. You can't go to work hungry. You'll have headache. And you're getting so skinny."

"Mum! There's no time. You always make me late."

"*Dooro!* It will take a second. Just wait."

"I don't have a second!"

"Don't be silly. You can tell your work that you haven't had breakfast. They no mind you being bit late."

"Of course they'll mind! Just because you've never worked a day in your life... I can't just rock up when it suits me." I rush outside and climb into my car, desperate to escape.

As I'm about to start the engine, mum runs out, still wearing her cotton maxi nightie, having hastily wrapped a scarf around her head. There is no need for the latter addition as there is literally nobody around to see her this morning. Most of our OAP neighbours are still asleep.

"Here, take this." She shoves a blue plastic bag through my half open car window. "Stubborn girl."

I pull into my work car park five minutes late and grateful for the fact that Bernadette rarely sits in our office. It dawns on me that I am really going to have to call back the restaurant myself. Oh the shame! I blundered out of there all high and mighty and principled. Now I've got to blunder my way back into their good books, quite literally, their booking book. I'm still going to try for some kind of discount, though. It should be their obligation as I've already booked with them previously. If nothing else, they better offer everyone one free soft drink.

I bundle together my work laptop, handbag and the stupid plastic bag mum burdened me with. Then I notice the contents. Mum's curated for me an orange juice carton, a brioche bun and a small yoghurt. She's thought of everything to see me through the day. Even though I have a work canteen that offers copious amounts of food options at a reduced rate. Even though I'm a grown ass woman on the wrong side of 25. I actually don't like brioche but that's not her fault. She shuffled it together in a rush. I don't think anybody else would ever do that for me. Probably not even M.

Bushra pulls up in the parking space next to me. Predictably, she's late too. I have to hide my face, as I don't want her to see me crying ugly tears, triggered by a juice carton.

I'VE NEVER DONE PRETTY sobbing. Mine are always full-on injured animal whimpering. My face and eyes will be swollen and puffy for hours afterwards. Luckily, there's only Bushra in the office today, as Emma and Amy are out on site visits. Though she keeps darting the odd nervous stare in my direction. She probably thinks I've been dumped by M or something.

Anyway, there's no time to explain my moment of emotion, I'm too busy for that. I've spent the last 25 minutes sourcing three quotes from printers for personalised chocolate favour wrappers. Now it's time for some real work. Beautifying work.

It seems like finding a makeup artist to paint me beautiful for my wedding is harder to come by than a man. I mean, my hunt for a husband was easier, wasn't it? I forget now.

After Rania and her dismally minimal makeup palette, I found one bridal makeup artist via Facebook. She had a flashy website and impressive portfolio and claimed to initially offer a phone consultation. Only this never happened. I was promised a call, which was rescheduled twice. I finally gave up. I mean, how could she tell I'm stingy before we'd even had a phone chat? We hadn't even got to the stage of talking money. Or talking at all.

The great thing about having autonomy at work thanks to a missing in action manager means I've got plenty of time to scope out makeup artists online. In between doing actual work, like writing press releases and covering the arses of half-arsed business development managers and such like.

Thanks to the exhibitionist social media world in which we live, I managed to track down the makeup artist Hassna used for her engagement party. I know that makes me sound like a desperate copycat but it wasn't that hard to find, really. I just had to set up a fake account and send Hassna a follow request, which she'd accepted. Silly girl. Of course, she had multiple photos of her engagement ceremony, including close ups of her big rock, which I'm happy to report was bought in an anonymous sounding jewellers in Manchester. Hardly the prestige of Hatton Garden. That aside, in one of the pictures she tagged her makeup artist and a host of other people she called her glam squad, posting the equivalent of an Oscar's acceptance speech. Yes, I'll probably post the exact same fake-gushing thank you on social media after my wedding. They say if you don't document something online it didn't happen. There is no way I'm letting the fact I'm marrying a boy I like ever be questioned.

Anyway, I messaged Hassna's makeup artist, Shazna, and we've now taken our courtship to the next level - messaging on Facebook.

Me: *Hi, I'm getting married on the 9th September, are you free to do bridal hair and makeup?*

Shazna: *I am.*

Me: *Great. Do you offer a trial? And if so, how much do you charge?*

Shazna: *Yes.*

Okay, looks like we've got ourselves a woman of few words here and possibly a confused one at that. That's okay, she must be very busy and in demand.

Me: *Would you be able to come to my house for a trial? Or do I need to come to you?*

Shazna: *No, I can't come to your house, you come to me.*

Me: *Okay. What about on the day itself? Would you come to my house then?*

Shazna: *No. You come to me, as I have other clients that day, before and after you.*

Me: *Okay, how much is it for a trial?*

Shazna: *Yes.*

Erm... maybe English isn't her first language. Her makeup skills are good, though, so I'll soldier on with this.

Me: *No. Sorry, how much do you charge?*

Shazna: *Come have trial and then we talk prices.*

"Oh, this is just ridiculous," I say, a little too loud.

"What's that?" Bushra looks up from her screen.

In my previous company I'd be worried about being seen to skive. Not here though. Bushra and Emma have clocked up many work hours cyber stalking men they met from the weekend before. It's a good thing we all work in-house rather than at an agency. I'm not sure how we'd bill all the client time spent on personal admin.

"I'm having a nightmare looking for a makeup artist. They're basic at best, or bloody elusive. I should've got it sorted by now."

"I know someone. Well, actually, it's my cousin. She's really good."

I'm wondering why she never mentioned this before, then she answers my question: "She's just arrived from Pakistan and she worked for a big beauty parlour in Lahore," Bushra adds, rather proudly.

She can stop right there. At the risk of sounding like a self-hating Asian (yet again) beauticians from back home (or in this case, Bushra's homeland), don't fill me with confidence. I've seen their handiwork first hand when I went to Bangladesh for my sister's wedding. They painted her ghostly white. They even used talcum powder on her arms. Luckily big sis is naturally fair, so could just about carry it off, though she did have a hint of Queen Elizabeth II about her. Darker complexioned brides didn't fare very well at beauty parlours. Indians, Pakistanis and Bangladeshis all bond over the belief that fair is beautiful and are willing to attain this at any cost. In this case, the cost is a chalked-up face. No thanks.

"Do you want her number?"

"Erm… I'm okay at the moment as I've got a couple of others lined up. I'll bear her in mind though, thanks for suggesting."

"You're alright. The offer is there if you need it. Anyway, are you all set for your one-to-one on location?"

Oh crap! I totally forgot it's one-to-one day today. I've got to drive to Rochdale to meet Bernadette at a hospital site. Why she can't just meet me here, our actual office base, I'll never know. I hate driving to new territory and the stress of finding a makeup artist and looking for a mehendi venue combined with predictable hunger from skipping breakfast, has left me with a stinking headache. I'm also worried that Bernadette hasn't mentioned any feedback from HQ regarding my request for a transfer. I knew it was a long shot but I started to get my hopes up, especially with M's talk about us meant to be together and fate working in our favour and blah blah blah. Bernadette's silence is deafening so I'm not so sure.

AFTER A MISSION DRIVING to Rochdale (which is just a bit too north of Manchester for my liking) and a scary parking situation (why is Lancashire so hilly?), I tried my best to compose my out of puff, dishevelled self in front of Bernadette. There was simply no time for a bathroom stop to mop my brow, or my sweaty upper lip. I must fix that air con in my car.

Bernadette manages to go through everything pertaining to my job - my PR calendar, upcoming potential crises in the hospitals, even the key points raised in my appraisal. She is thorough, though sadly not thorough enough. She's not mentioned anything about my transfer request. Not a peep.

Just as I'm about to pluck up the courage to ask her outright, Alistair, the hospital's executive director, pops his head round the door.

"Don't mind me Bernie, just a quick one to say hello. Ooh, 'ello you!" says Alastair upon spotting me. "To what do we owe the pleasure of you visiting our little old hospital. Is there a photocall I don't know about?"

I think Alistair's being a bit bitchy about me visiting rarely. In my defence, I do have 17 hospitals to get around. Plus, it's not like I need to be on site for the sake of it. At least that's what I'm banking on, as it's my main ammunition to get Bernadette to agree to me working remotely from London.

"No, don't worry. No photographs today," I reply.

"Ooh, that's a relief." Alistair clutches his chest, fake gasping for air. He is so theatrical. "And what's that I see there? Is that a special ring on your special finger?"

How did he even spot my engagement ring? It's hardly big or flashy. I'm not sure what to say. Thankfully, Bernadette rescues the situation.

"Oh yes, this one is getting married. A handsome man is making an honest woman of her," she says. Not that she knows if he's handsome or not. She's never asked to see a photo.

"Amazing love!" With that, Alistair's quick hello turns into him parking himself down on the chair next to me for a good old gossip. He's very familiar for a man that I've met about four times since working here. "I didn't even know you were seeing anyone."

"Well, I don't really talk about my private life," I say, which was true up until about a year ago.

"Well, I best fix that. 'Ooh is he? What does he do? How long have you been seeing him?"

I start with the thing that will make it sound the least like a forced marriage. "We've been seeing each other a few months now."

"A few months! Well, are you sure about him? Sounds quick!"

"Come on Al, leave the girl alone," says Bernadette, keen to get back to the agenda.

"Ooh, I've gotta ask these things, Bernie."

Bernie purses her lips at being called by her much-loathed nickname, again.

"It's just living in these parts, you hear all the stories." Alistair's not mincing his words. "Is it arranged?"

Aaannd we're back to that. I thought I'd left such nosiness in my previous role. I've had such a good run at this workplace that I forgot people are still wary of the dreaded A-word.

"Erm, no, it's not. We met through friends."

"Ooh, thank God for that," another fake gasp and chest clutch from Alistair. "I wouldn't be doing my civic duty if I didn't check. My courtship took a lot longer. I was with Mike for eight years before we made honest men of each other. To be fair though, four of those years were trying to get his old man on board with the whole thing. Thankfully he died before the wedding. God rest his soul."

Bernadette stares intently at her silver Gucci watch. Not only is this eating into our protected one-to-one time, it's also put her completely out of her comfort zone discussing life outside work.

Despite her eagerness to continue, Alastair isn't done. "Do you love him?"

My face turns a flash of red I haven't experienced for a long while.

"Oh, leave her alone Alistair! That's not really any of our business."

Alistair ignores her and continues trying to delve into my soul with his piercing blue eyes. "Do you though?"

"Yes... I do." I'm not sure why I feel so awkward to say it out loud. It occurs to me I have not said the L word to M at all. Even when he said it to me that night he proposed, I didn't say it back. It just feels too awkward.

Alistair looks at me, still unsatisfied with my response. Then I do something even worse, something that should never be uttered. "Whatever love is."

Why did I say that? What does it mean? It's the words from the world-famous engagement interview of Prince Charles and Diana. That didn't turn out well and he was panned for his comment forever. Heck, we even used it as a PR case study on how not to answer personal questions. That must be where I got it from, it crept into my sub-consciousness. The worst kind of subliminal message.

Of course, that gives Alistair all the ammunition he needs. "Whatever love is? What does that mean?"

"Right Alistair, I'm really sorry but I have to push on. I've still got my three o'clock with you, so can I grab you then?" Bernadette's clearly as eager to end this interrogation as I am.

"All right boss. I've been told." Alastair throws his hands in the air, rolls his eyes and heads out.

As soon as he closes the door behind him, she mumbles to me: "He's a bloody nosey so and so."

"He's just curious," I say, rather diplomatically as my thoughts are exactly the same as hers, albeit a little more sweary.

"There's curious and there's bloomin' invasive. Just because he's an open book with his life, doesn't mean everybody else is."

Why do I feel like this is more to do with Bernadette rather than my personal life?

"Anyway, I'm sorry to cut the conversation short, though I imagine you are delighted. It's just that I didn't want him to delve into your future plans before we finalised them. For your role here, that is. At least not before I've had written confirmation from HQ."

"Right, okay." I'm desperate to know more but don't want to push my luck. Thankfully, Bernadette reads my mind.

"Just so you're in the loop, HQ are fine with you being there in principle. They're just working out the logistics. I'm pushing for you to be sat in the thick of it with the PR team. I don't want them to pull a fast one and just shove you in a broom cupboard."

I'd probably go for a broom cupboard if it means I can move to London with a job in hand.

"That's so good to know. I'm glad they're okay with me going there. I think I can really make it work."

"Oh, I know you can. I've always said to all the exec directors, you're one to watch. You'll be going places. We just have to be a bit careful politically, just so that the likes of Alistair don't get twitchy about the fact that you won't be able to offer hands-on support. It's more of a perception thing, really."

There was me thinking she'd forgotten about my request, when in fact she's been working some serious logistics behind the scenes.

"Thank you Bernadette. You've always had my back."

"And I always will," she says.

I bloody love Bernadette.

23rd July

Location location location

M essage from M: *I would do a wedding countdown, but since we saw each other yesterday there doesn't seem a need!*

Me: *I honestly don't know how you keep count! My math-lete!*

M: *Oh by the way, my wordsmith, which one was your favourite gift?*

Me: *The desk fan for sure.*

M: *I knew you were a keeper :). P.S. There is still one very important thing. I want the honeymoon to be a surprise but just so it's not a total shock I wanted to share a couple of ideas, can we speak tonight?*

Me: *Yeah of course, catch up later.*

Finally, a wedding-based project that doesn't involve my management.

To be fair to M, he is really trying to be spontaneous, though by his very nature he's a planner. He surprised me yesterday by calling to say he's waiting for me in the petrol station around the corner from my house. Who said romance is dead?

I had no idea he was planning to come down but he wanted to surprise me for my birthday. And it was a surprise. A tricky one at that. Thinking I was dateless on my birthday (and not for the first time) I had planned to have lunch with Julia at our beloved Italian. So I had a super quick catch up with M in the petrol station forecourt, where he presented me with a very functional desk fan for a birthday gift.

I thought that was it so I ran back to my car to drive to our Italian, running late yet again, to find Julia waiting patiently at our pizzeria with a pink gift bag on the table. Just as I was having the mildest of bitches about my desk fan, I got a text from M, asking if I could meet him after my lunch date to give me my real gift. I had a sudden rush of adrenaline, combined with panic that I haven't actually ever bought him anything besides the cheap watch, so on the way home I ducked into the supermarket to peruse the men's fragrance section. I was expecting there to be a piss-poor choice so was relieved to find YSL among the more entry-level brand names.

I went to meet M at a coffee place and this time I was the one surprising him, with a gift exchange! He was touched with his present, as was I when I opened my second gift of a necklace with three cubic zirconia crystals. M mentioned between mouthfuls of cherry bakewell that he seldom wears perfume but will make an extra effort to wear this. I meanwhile kept my feelings to myself on the necklace, as it's the thought that counts. Once we're married I'm sure we'll be much more forthcoming about gift choices. At least I intend to be.

SO I'VE SORTED THE mehendi venue - praise be. I even tried my luck to get free drinks thrown in and it worked! Everybody will get to enjoy one fizzy drink at the meal. And to think my dear mother was trying to talk me out of even asking for it. If you don't ask, you don't get.

Now onto more pressing matters. Personal maintenance.

I need a facial, apparently. Not just one but a series of facials, starting at least six months before my wedding. Every beautician and makeup artist I met pointed this out to me. Apparently, I've also got dehydrated under-eyes. How do I get dry *there*? Especially with the amount of water I'm swigging at work in between looking at wedding outfits, favour bags and anything else in my seemingly never ending list of things to do to have a wedding that can at least be up there with Hassna's shindig.

Since the beautician planted the seed about my peepers, I'm now noticing dark circles. I think that's M's fault. I mean, it was watch-gate that gave me a few sleepless nights, no doubt adding to my brown panda aesthetic.

Anyway, I digress. As there's not much of a run up to my wedding and I'm supposed to have a facial every six weeks, I conclude that I need to book at least one in between now and September. However, upon whom I bestow this privilege is the big question.

There's also the small matter of body hair. I'm loyal to my trusty epilator but even I know that for my wedding, a quick going over on my arms and half of each leg won't do. I need a proper MOT.

Julia knows nothing of this as she's blessed with blonde body hair. However, my more hairy-Mary friends such as

Reena (OMG - I must tell her I'm getting married soon!) have said that for a special occasion, only waxing will do. Full body waxing.

For our Asian ball at uni, I opted for a rather demure orange-ombré saree (I was rocking ombré before it became a thing, or dare I say, even fashionable. I'm an accidentally ironic trendsetter). Meanwhile, Reena went for a daring teal lehenga with a low-backed blouse. In preparation for the ball, she underwent a gruelling body wax and gave her boyfriend at the time grief about it for the entire final year of uni.

"God! The things we have to do to look presentable! Not just for the ball, for our bloody men. And all he does is brush his teeth! Sometimes not even that by the smell of things," she moaned to me at the time. I guess the warning signs were there that they wouldn't go the distance.

However, as with all things in my life, attempting to make myself wedding-ready is anything but straightforward. There's a sea of Asian beauticians in Manchester. You can't move for them. However, a simple booking for a waxing in four weeks time seems to throw them into disarray.

"Just call on the day you're ready," says the hoarse-voiced lady on the end of the phone between coughing and retching.

"Will there be appointments on the day? I'm scared of leaving it to the last minute."

Another cough followed by a gag. I think something's stuck. "Yes, usually okay."

"Usually?" She's not filling me with confidence.

"Yes. Just don't book err... Saturday. Monday and Tuesday be fine."

Yeah, because it's not like I work or anything. Speaking of which, I must confirm with Bernadette when my marital sabbatical starts.

"Can I just book now? To secure a slot?"

"No because we might not have that slot then," Coughy McCoughface replies.

"What do you mean? Do you not take bookings?"

"Yes we do dear."

"Erm... so can you take *my* booking?"

"Not now?" Another cough. "Sorry, got terrible cough."

She really didn't need to explain that, she'd been doing a great job of show not tell thus far.

"Okay. Should I call later?" I'm tempted to ask to speak to the manager but I had a dreaded feeling I might already be speaking to her. You just never know.

"No. No point. We don't know what girls we'll have working in four weeks. That's why I be saying, call near time."

Oh... now I get it! It's a staffing issue. That's the problem when you don't have contractual obligations, or basic worker rights in place.

"Just call in four weeks and say you need eyebrow threading."

"But I don't need eyebrow threading!" Well, I probably will do nearer the time but that's not what this conversation is about. "I'm calling about booking waxing."

"Upper lip waxing?"

"No! Full body." I lower my voice at the last two words as the Bengali in me feels terribly embarrassed at my request.

"Oh. We no do body waxing, my dear."

Well, I guess that's that then.

So with waxing to be confirmed, I must turn my attention to other more pressing issues - getting this facial everyone tells me I need.

NOW IT'S MY TURN TO do a countdown.

I'm getting married in 48 days and I HAVE NOTHING TO WEAR. Truthfully, I've been browsing lehengas on the down low since I got engaged. Even more truthfully, I've been looking since the day M and I met. I also may or may not have kept a Pinterest board entitled *'desi wedding inspo'* since last year. That, however, was more out of boredom than anything else.

I've got a rough vision of what I want to go for. I think I'll forego the current trend of piling as much sparkle on as you can so that you look like a Swarovski Christmas tree. Instead, I'm thinking a more classic bridal aesthetic with deep red and gold will be more me.

I know that with Bengali weddings it's customary for the groom to pay for the lehenga. However, as every family does things slightly different, I'm not quite sure yet how M will do things.

When big sis got married in Bangladesh, I went wedding shopping with middle sis, some members of my brother-in-law-to-be's family and, bizarrely, without my actual sister who was getting married. I guess it was seen as too forward for her to come out and pick the outfit she wants in full view of her future in-laws. Instead, middle sis and I were left with the awkward task of having to decipher what saree she'd like, based on very vague instructions from the bride-to-be. We also had to be very careful not to appear too pushy or go for an outfit that was too expensive. It was like walking a tightrope.

Further compounding the awkwardness of the whole situation, my sister and I were also to be gifted outfits of our choosing. Said choosing also took place during the shopping trip in front of the eyes of the buyers. Oh, and it was our first proper interaction with them, which would stay in their minds as an indicator of us as a family. That was a lot of pressure for my pre-teen self. I ended up choosing a purple and pink embossed salwar kameez. It wasn't the most expensive, nor the cheapest, so it played into the safe middle ground.

Thankfully, when middle sis was getting married, we were spared such a cringe worthy shopping ordeal. Most of it was done without our involvement. Or middle sis for that matter. At least that's what I was led to believe. As she and her hubby were special friends, I'm pretty sure she sent him some very detailed descriptions of the outfit she wanted for her wedding.

Which reminds me, I must start dropping hints soon.

DURING MY RITUALISTIC call with M, there's a lot to talk about. For once, it's him bringing the first item on the agenda to the table.

"I know you've been pretty stressed with the wedding planning and I was going to make the honeymoon a surprise, but I thought I could run some options past you. Have you had any thoughts about where you'd like to go?" asks M.

Is this another thing that's going to be delegated to me? Also, should I really have a say? We're not going halves on this, are we? I might be a newbie to this getting married business but even I know that the guy pays for the honeymoon in all cultures. Or so I thought.

I'm going to use his line and see how he likes it. "To be honest with ya, I haven't had a chance to think about it, what with looking at wedding outfits, favours, decorations and all the rest of the stuff." I hope my subtle mention of the lehenga is a big enough hint for M to bring up the wedding shopping whilst we're brainstorming ideas.

"Well, I was thinking, how about something like the Far East?"

"That would be amazing!" I was thinking he'd choose something closer to home. Somewhere in Europe, which would be a lot cheaper. This has surpassed the low expectations drilled into me by mum. "Whereabouts were you thinking?"

"Maybe Malaysia? Or what we could do, since we've got a couple of weeks, is visit a few places. So Malaysia, then Singapore or something like that?"

Again, still not 100% sure that he's footing the entire bill, but I'm hoping so.

"Yeah. That sounds good. But I don't want you to be spending too much either."

Another hint. Nicely played, if I do say so myself.

"Don't worry about that. It's a honeymoon, we might as well splash out."

We?

"Okay," says M, "I'll have a look at a few ideas and I might email you at work. I figure I ought to give you at least enough of an inkling, so you'll know what to pack."

"Great. I can scope out some destinations, too, if you'd like."

That's a lie. As a complete novice when it comes to travel, and with only trips to Bangladesh organised by the family under my belt, I ain't got nothing for this one. "But remember, don't feel like you have to splash out. I'll like you just the same wherever we go."

Okay, that was a bit of a heavy-handed hint-edy hint-hint.

"It's okay. You deserve it."

I think that's confirmed things in my mind. I'm having a pinch-me moment. I can't wait to tell Julia about this.

"I've got one more bit of news, too. You know how I've been looking at flats? Well, it turns out that one of my work colleagues is going on a sabbatical in September so he's looking to let out his flat for a few months. It's a two-bed right near Liverpool Street and he'll do mates rates. It might just sort us out while we look properly together when you're here. Shall I send you some pics?"

He had me at mates rates. M really is a guy after my bargain-loving heart.

"That sounds good," I say, happy in the knowledge that things do fall into place when you meet the one.

"Oh, and another thing," says M. "We need to talk about your wedding outfit."

Finally.

"So, my mum knows a place in Green Street in London. She was going to speak to your mum about this anyway, but maybe you could go and choose something from there?"

And... back down to earth with a thud.

"WHAT YOU MEAN, WE BUY from shop in London?" is mum's rather predictable reaction as she rifles through a rack of lehengas protected by plastic dress bags. "That make no sense! They don't even live in London! Why we need to go there? Is it their family-owned shop? Or just really, really cheap?"

With precious few weeks now until the actual wedding, mum and I are having to browse for lehenga inspiration after work. I sense that my already long day is going to be a lot longer after mum is done.

"I don't know, mum, but they're the ones buying, how fussy can we be? Mum! You can't lift up the plastic covers! They're there to protect the lehengas. Can't you see the big sign that says no touching?"

Mum has precious little regard for the stores attempt to keep their more premium outfits unsullied by the hands of shoppers.

"Stupid idea! How can we see outfit when they be hidden! They want us to buy or no?" Mum whispers in extra loud broken English, just so the shop assistant picks up the hint.

It works. A very short saleswoman, whose simple dress code doesn't quite fit in with the elaborate outfits she is surrounded by, makes her way towards us. "Can I help you, Madam?"

Mum shimmies the plastic cover back down over the lehenga which she was trying to get an up skirt view of. "Can we see your bridal lehengas?"

"Oh yes. What price range?"

That's always the opener. Yet we never know the answer.

After delivering the usual line of *"we don't know, we're just looking"*, the lady makes a mental note that we are not serious buyers and directs us towards a young girl who is undoubtedly her subordinate.

The girl proceeds to ask us the same question, so mum and I resort to a more primal method to deliver a brief - pointing.

Mum raises a weather-beaten finger to a mannequin dressed in a green and pink outfit. What is she thinking? It's beautiful but something you'd expect to see at a Pakistani wedding, where the blouse of a lehenga is more of the long variety. I'll probably only be this slim for a short while so I'm not going to be drowned in a giant tunic on my wedding day.

"How much is that one?" asks mum.

"£2,400."

Mum raises enough eyebrow to indicate that it's out of our – or should I say my future husband's family's - price range.

"Do you want to try it?" asks the shop girl.

I tell her I'll leave it. There's no point trying on something so ridiculously expensive.

It's my turn to point. I spy a beautiful blood red silk lehenga with diamante embroidery. Yes, it goes against my initial choice of being classic gold and bright but, oh my, it's stunning. In that outfit, I'd be the blingiest of blingy brides and surely put Hassna in the shade.

I don't ask how much it is. I'd like to just try it on and hold onto the fantasy for a little while.

The nice thing about this slightly more upmarket boutique is that they've got a whole floor dedicated to bridal wear. I even see them offering another family glasses of water as they sit down going through numerous outfits. They don't offer us a glass of water but that's okay. I'm just happy to be in the room.

The replenished and hydrated family seem to be finalising a big order. There are five girls ranging from teens to what looks to be early 20s, all decked out in matching navy gowns. There's a bit of swishing, posturing in the mirror and predictably, one unhappy sibling.

"I don't like it!" says the grumpy one. "It makes me look fat!"

"It doesn't!" claims a sibling that looks like she's lying through her teeth. "You look *fiine*. We'll do some alterations to make it a bit looser around the front. Is there enough time to do that, sister?" she asks, addressing the more senior sales lady.

"Yes, yes. There will be plenty of time. No worry."

"How long does it take to get the custom outfits made?" I ask my subordinate shop girl.

"When is the wedding? How many you need?" she asks.

"Three outfits for my three sisters. The wedding is in September?"

"Okay, maybe... let me think. We need six weeks at least. It has to go to India to be stitched. So maybe end of September could be ready but we can't be sure, sister."

"Oh, I need it for the beginning of September. Is there any chance of that?" I'm not sure why I'm asking, I already know the answer.

"No, no sister. Not enough time to even design, let alone alterations."

Another thing I can't do. I just wish we'd spent less time faffing around with wedding dates and second guessing M's family and instead had a longer engagement. It seems that everybody else can get this bit right apart from me and my family.

Still, being glass half full and all that, I look pretty damn good in this lehenga. It's funny, that specific shade of red, bordering on bold, is usually one I steer well clear of. Yet this is working for me.

I send a sneaky shot to M, being sure to take an aerial view and not include my face. After all, if our relationship doesn't get to the wedding, I don't want him doing some kind of very modest revenge-porn of me in a lehenga without a scarf.

I show mum, who is sitting on the crushed velvet sofa outside the changing room like a queen.

"That's really pretty. You look nice," she says, before turning towards the girl shopkeeper. "How much?"

"Uh... let me check," she says as she reaches for the tag inside the back of the blouse. This place seems to be unusual in that they actually label the prices, rather than making it up on the spot. If only I knew, I would've just checked myself and saved having to create a poker face when I'm horrified at the price.

"£1,600," she declares.

That's actually not bad. Mum comes closer to me to examine the intricate embellishments.

"You know... if you like it, we could get it," she says.

"Huh? How?" I think mum is having a funny turn, like she's completely forgotten the whole conversation about the shop in London.

"Well, we could say you like this one and if it's too expensive for your in-laws, we pay towards it."

Oh, my trailblazer. I'm touched that mum is trying her best to help me have my princess moment. At the same time, I really don't want to rock the boat with M's family. "Would it not be offensive? I mean, how would you even broach the subject of money?"

"We'll find a way. Just let me know, do you like it?"

I examine the net scarf the shop assistant has placed over my crocodile-clipped hair. It's exquisite but is it exquisite enough to risk causing any potential conflict with my soon-to-be in-laws?

"You know what, mum? This is the first one I've seen. So let's not do anything rash."

Mum does a small smile, the one she reserves for pity. She thinks I'm selling myself short.

"It be up to you. Your day. But... I will not have you being forced to choose a cheap outfit for your wedding. You only get married once and everybody will see. We don't want Rashda *maa* thinking you've gone for cheap dress and cheap money."

Money? Do she mean the dowry? Now she's got me thinking. How low *is* my asking price? For the second time today, I don't dare ask.

I don't bother trying any more outfits on. There's no point even teasing myself. Perhaps it wasn't the best idea coming here with mum. On the plus side, I have learnt that red is my colour, despite a lifetime of thinking to the contrary.

As we make our way downstairs, I bid farewell to the red lehenga that wasn't meant to be. I leave it behind, along with the gaggle of navy-gown wearing girls giggling whilst the bride-to-be tries on her dress of dreams.

27th July
Wedding invitations

What should be a simple note to tell people where and when to turn up becomes a posturing game of one-upmanship. Big sis had a simple cream shiny card with some kind of gold filigree detail. A few years later, Rashda upped the stakes by going for a slightly more elaborate card with three layers inside - one for each ceremony and each in a different colour. Middle sis had no choice but to follow suit. She didn't go for all the inserts (the poorer cousins as always) but she did go for a colourful card in bridal red.

Fast forward nearly a decade and I find myself facing off with Rashda's younger sister, Hassna.

Her wedding card has just arrived. Only it's not a card, it's a blooming box. As in 3D. I'm surprised it even got through the letterbox.

As mum opens the thick envelope, small jewels adhering to the colour scheme of the card sprinkle out onto the table. The card is devoid of the usual details such as a groom on horseback or a bride that's in her doli carriage and being carried to her prince by four strong men (I wish the doli tradition still existed, that would have been awesome). Hassna's card doesn't have any pictures but instead boasts a technicolour design, kind of like a peacock. There's also a single peacock feather hanging loose, like it's a bookmark. The card opens up to fan out into a 3D peacock (I get it, she likes peacocks). It doesn't actually look like a wedding card for a Bengali ceremony. It looks like something you'd get custom-made from Harrods. Pretentious cow.

"*Oh ho*, poor Rashda's daddy, having to pay for all this nonsense," mum huffs, while running a finger across the textured inside of the card in admiration. Yep, the card is textured. On the inside.

"Where all the details?" Mum is looking for the three inserts for the mehendi, wedding and walima party respectively. Except there aren't any inserts. The details are underneath the peacock:

Shahin Uddin, BSc (medical doctor). Only son of Barik Uddin BA (Hon) and Meher Khanum
Weds
Hassna Zubeida Mahmood Bsc.

And the most important detail:
No boxed gifts please. Your duas are most welcome.

This roughly translates to *this wedding is expensive so no crockery or tea sets please, give us the money. Prayers are appreciated though not mandatory. But the dough is.*

They're having a separate wedding and walima as the groom's side is from Bradford. She'll have two princess moments. The wedding is due to take place on the 5th October. So she got engaged before me but is getting hitched after. She's got loads of time to plan and I bet she's getting her outfits custom-made.

I'm hoping mum's slight envy and my sheer, unadulterated jealousy will inspire some movement on our card shopping front. Not to mention all the other bits like the show stopping wedding favour I'm planning.

"Shall we sort out our cards?"

"Yes yes. You should." Mum nods her head vigorously.

"Why does it always have to take me to prompt these very obvious things?" I say to mum. I thought one of the advantages, as well as a distinct disadvantage of being Bengali, is that your wedding is done for you. I thought I was just meant to rock up on the day.

"Why you no do something?" mum barks at my unassuming dad, who nearly jumps out of his seat, newspaper still tightly gripped. "What about the man that used to print cards? You know, the one who printed the menus for the takeout?"

No, no. Oh God no. Dad only ever printed his takeaway menu once. When he first opened the joint. A *long* time ago.

"You mean Abdul Miah? I've not spoken to him in maybe 10 or 12 years," dad shrugs, before straightening out his newspaper.

I guess that's his contribution for the day.

"Useless," mum hisses. "Everything on my head, like always."

"No. Everything's on my head! Nobody is doing anything to help. You couldn't wait to get rid of me. Now you finally are, you can't be bothered to do anything."

Mum looks at me as though I've questioned her parenting. Or cooking. "Okay, okay. Go get computer. I go fry some samosas. We sort this now."

TWO HOURS, ONE AND a half cups of tea and seven samosas later (three for me, one each for mum and dad and two for my little sister who suddenly became interested in what we were doing after getting a waft of fried pastry) and we're no further forward on the wedding invitation front. Obviously, the first place we looked is where Hassna got hers from. The name of the design was handily printed on the back of the invite. I guess they're not fancy enough to pay extra to not have a marketing label.

Anyway, it turns out that their invite is not quite from Liberty in London but a very chic looking Asian event planning agency. Each card is £3 a pop. Is she only going to have 100 guests or something?

"We could look at the same place where Lily got her wedding cards from," mum suggests. "Wait. Let me go find it."

Lily is a distant relative of ours who got married two years ago. Mum still has her wedding invitation in her sideboard, like it's some kind of souvenir. Maybe weddings are the Bengali mum equivalent of going to a gig. You keep the invite as a memento of the special occasion.

Lily's card also has the company name on the back. A bit of internet research reveals that their invites are much more reasonable, at around 50p for one. However, they're also very generic. They're like the million other invites I've seen over the years. Plus, they come top on Google, confirming that Desi Dulhan is indeed the go-to for cheap and cheerful wedding invitations. I don't need to spend mega bucks but I would like there to be *something* unique about my wedding.

There's no time to make such rash decisions as I've got my facial at 6:30pm. Mum's unimpressed.

"You always do this. You moan that nobody is helping you and when we sit down to look at things you always have to go away!"

"Because I've got things to do, mum. I'm getting married in less than two months and I don't want to look ugly. So I've got to get a facial."

"Well, when do you want to sort this out?" mum asks.

"We'll look again tonight. When I'm back. I need to look online anyway to sort out the wedding favours and the chocolate fountain."

"What? Are you still going on about chocolate fountain?"

I may have brought it up once or twice after going to a certain someone's engagement party.

"I already told you, it will be a waste of time. Cost a lot of money. All the kids will make a big mess, then you end up with bigger cleaning charge. I tell you, all these things won't matter on the day," says mum.

"I'd like a chocolate fountain. It'd be cool," is little sis' input.

"*Dooro*! You be quiet and no encourage her!" says mum. "We can instead spend that money better on lehenga." Mum is not letting that one go.

"I'm not telling him we're going to buy our own. You always tell me not to say too much, and to compromise. Well, this is my compromise. The bit I'm not compromising on is what *is* in my power and what I can afford. Which is a chocolate fountain."

"Hmmph! Next thing you be wanting cheese cracker."
I had thought about that.

I WANTED TO GO TO SOME nice spa in town for my facial. However, an hour of ringing around various beauty salons in Manchester city centre when I was supposed to be working, sent me reeling. £60 to scrub my face? No thank you. So I ended up in Longsight.

I'm not ashamed that my facial decision was mainly a fiscal one. If I'm going to be dropping money on invites and favours and a chocolate fountain and all that, I need to be frugal in other areas. Ultimately, I'm blessed with good, hardy skin so I don't have to be so choosy about the products that are applied to my face. It's a bonus that this facial I booked uses rather renowned products. The kind that are on the shelf at Harvey Nichols and Selfridges. So it's all good.

I'm hoping looks are deceiving as I enter the salon through its dubious and domestic looking front door and up its steep, narrow stairs. Why are so many Asian beauticians on top of some other establishment? This one takes pride of place above a pound shop. I'm expecting it to open out like the tardis. It doesn't. It's a pokey little environment. However, if the facial is good, who cares?

"I'm here for the deluxe facial," I tell the lady at reception, interrupting her tea and biscuit break.

"Okay. Good timing. She's just waiting for you inside." She ushers me through a dimly lit room emanating soothing sea sounds. Fancy. Maybe it's not so bad after all.

"*Okee!* Take your shoes off," says a deep, familiar sounding voice.

The beautician turns around. She looks at me. I look at her. We both have a stare-off. She's the same beautician that gave me the wax job from hell.

What *are* the chances?

"SO... HAVE YOU MOVED jobs?" I ask, knowing that clearly she has. Maybe she burnt the face off someone else?

She ignores my question. "You want bleaching?"

Cheeky cow. I say no and explain how facial hair lightening isn't on my agenda today.

"A whitening facial?"

Again, cheeky cow.

"No thank you," I say, lying back on the paper towel covered bed.

"Why you no want bleach?"

"I don't need to bleach my hair. I'll do threading later."

"No. Not bleach your hair. Bleach your *skin*."

Oh wow. Can I call her a cow again or is it getting repetitive? And also... what? Is that a thing? It sounds like an iffy business to me. However, Miss Pushy is insisting that it's something I should definitely go for as all Asian women do this, which is a pretty big claim.

"If I bleach my face, my neck and body will look darker. It won't match up."

She leans over me, daal breath and all. "If you trust me. If... you trust me..."

Clearly I don't. You burnt my face, you mad bitch, I'm tempted to say but still too scared after our last interaction.

She goes on: "Bleach your body, too."

This is getting out of hand.

I ask the beautician if she bleaches her skin. She says yes. She's darker than me so either she's a liar or a bad advertisement for what she's pedalling.

On the shelf above, I see all the dodgy-looking whitening products, all of which should probably be banned by trading standards. I'd like to make a run for it but I've already taken off my shoes so it feels like I've committed to the procedure.

I stick to my guns and stay strong. Even if I did want to beach my skin, which I don't (adoration from M has made me more comfortable with my brown-ness), I certainly wouldn't task this burly beautician with the job.

The facial itself is pretty standard – lots of massaging – sometimes nice, other times uncomfortable – cleansing and exfoliating, and a steam session. The steam is dispensed through a nifty device which is essentially like a kettle boiling on my face. I wonder if I'd get the same effect at home. Must hover over the kettle next time we brew up.

With my pores all open and exposed, the beautician uses a fine pointed metal tool to manually remove blackheads. It hurts to the point of tears. I think I see a faint smile as she does this. Sadist.

As I leave the salon, all red raw and tingly of face, I spy Hassna across the street. What's she doing in these parts? Thankfully she looks engrossed in a phone conversation so she doesn't get to see me looking like an angry beetroot. I dive in the car and head home to tick one more job off my lengthy wedding planning list.

1st August
Barter like a boss

M essage from M: *Hey, are you on the train now?*
Me: *Yeah, we just boarded.*

M: *Cool. Can't wait to see you tomorrow. Also, if you're free for a cheeky coffee (or kebab!) let me know.*

I appreciate M's offer, though I highly doubt I'll be able to sneak out on this occasion...

I'M GETTING MY CARDS from Desi Dulhan, I'm not happy about it but it is what it is.

What's the reason for this change of heart? I hear no one ask. Well, it's the reason I reckon most people have for shopping with them. A reason they're no.1 on Google - the guest list.

Six... hundred... people. I'll let that sink in.

Annoyingly, only about 250 of the guests are ours. Exactly how does M's family know that many people? He says it's mostly made up of guests from the town where he grew up... Oldham. This place, I've come to learn, is more Bengali than Brick Lane in London. Heck, it's even more Bengali than Bangladesh. On the plus side (as always, I try to remain glass half full), it kind of pokes holes in mum's theory that his family have left behind some scandal in their hometown or something. She's always determined to see the worst in people, negative Nancy.

Anyway, I'll be aiming to bring the positivity today, as we are currently en route to London. Me, mum, dad and little sis are enjoying the nauseating delights of a high-speed train that tilts ever so slightly, not enough to make you fall about but enough to make you not want to look at books, magazines or your mobile phone. This means we've got two hours of talking to each other. Even little sis and dad are without their trusty tools of choice. My teenage sis has been forced to put her phone away and keeps adjusting her anti-sickness bracelet. Meanwhile, dad's rolled up his newspaper and is resorting to looking straight ahead, over my shoulder, between little sis and my seats, into the distance. I'm not sure why he doesn't just admire the rolling British countryside.

"Now remember mum, when we go to the shop, don't be too fussy. It's only going to be him there and all of us, so I don't want to make him feel pressured into buying something expensive." I feel like the grown-up having to brief the child. I'm pretty sure mum gave middle sis and I the exact same order when big sis got married in Bangladesh.

"Me? What I say? You choose what you want. Maybe his mum make surprise visit to choose outfit for you," says mum as she fiddles with her brown and gold shawl.

"No, I'll tell you once and tell you a thousand times, it'll just be him." At least that's what M's told me.

"I bet there be only cheap clothes anyway," mum whispers under her breath.

"See? You see?" I say to nobody and everybody on our table despite having a rather uninterested audience. "That's exactly what I mean. No negative or snarky comments."

"Okay, okay. I no be sneaky or snake-y or whatever you saying. Hmmph! Get married in cheap clothes and look desperate."

"You both bad as each other," dad chimes in, though barely audibly.

Mum and I both stare at him, aghast. He turns to face the window. "Oh look. Lots of cows. Just like Bangladesh."

I'm not sure if he's referring to the cattle outside or the ones in the carriage.

UNCLE TARIQ PICKS US up from Euston Station, just like he used to all those years ago when we'd make our annual trips to London. Our stays were always pretty formulaic. We'd never stray further than the East End but I still loved it all the same. I can't quite believe this city is going to be my home in a matter of weeks.

My uncle used to be a man of great stature. He'd pace towards us through the stream of commuters on the concourse like some Amitabh Bachchan impersonator. Now he makes his way towards us with a slower stride. His steps are more careful, his back more hunched, his shape more sinewy. He even appear smaller, more frail. I believe he is younger than mum but you wouldn't know by looking at the two of them. One thing that hasn't changed is his warm, welcoming smile.

AUNTIE RUKHSANA HAS cooked a feast for the thousands as always and I'm glad to report that within the range of dishes is her roast chicken that never fails.

While dad becomes a social smoker in the company of uncle Tariq (he's such a bad influence), us women finish up eating. My nosey parker mum can't resist asking about the Prodigal daughter.

"Will Naila come round?"

"Who knows with that one. I'm always telling her to visit with her husband. So what if she married white man? He converted. I don't care," says auntie Rukhsana.

It's funny how my auntie would always discuss supposedly grown-up issues in front of us and think we won't really pay attention as we are children. Even now, I'm closer to 30 than 20 and she still sees me this way. Lumped in with the kids. It's quite endearing really. Mum, however, is more cautious and darts a look at my teenage sis and laughs nervously. She's worried about her getting ideas.

Unperturbed, auntie Rukhsana continues: "She keeps saying that everybody look at him in the community. She doesn't like Tower Hamlets anymore. She thinks that we have problem too. And why? Because we no roll out red carpet, make roast chicken every time they come? She think I treat my boys better but that's not true. All these things, they in her head. If I could have her round every day, I would." Her voice trembles and she breaks off, putting her head into her hand, thin sparkly bangles glistening like her tears.

It's funny how mother and daughter have such a different view of the same situation. As I thought, in the mix of it all, there'll be the truth.

UNCLE TARIQ INSISTS on driving us to Green Street ahead of his shift, despite my insistence that we can get the tube or pay for another taxi driver that's not a blood relative. It's bad enough that we'll be eating them out of house and home this weekend, I don't want to totally take the mick. One saving grace is that this visit, and my last, didn't involve them camping out on the downstairs floor to make space for us like they used to. I guess that's the plus side of being empty nesters, you can entertain in comfort.

M offered to pick us up in the morning, before realising that his snug Audi TT won't house all of us. Instead, he is meeting us at this fabled shop.

I'm nervous as we roll up Green Street. I have no idea which shop we'll end up in. Mum's cynical theory that my future mother-in-law is karting us 240 miles down the road for me to choose a lehenga because the shop has special mates rates is playing on my mind.

Block after block of saree shops, punctuated with the odd eatery, this place makes Rusholme seem like a village High Street. We pass a few of the more upmarket boutiques that I've read about in Asian Bride magazine. As we are heading towards what seems like downtown Green Street, my heart sinks a little. I can't speak for M's mum but would *he* send me to a shit shop? Then again, as he's constantly reminding me that he's a bloke, therefore doesn't know girl's stuff, would he even know if it's shit? If it is indeed a cheap shop, I'd rather just be dropped off right now and make our way there on foot, rather than have our uncle see where we're heading.

"Here we go, Laila's Boutique," announces uncle Tariq in full cabbie mode. He must be preparing for the next 12-hour stretch. "I can't stop here so I'll just drop you off around the corner and go."

Hmmm... Not too shabby. Not too shabby at all. I look at mum with my best *I told you so* face but she's too busy exhaling a sigh of relief to notice.

M's already in there. He's wearing cream chinos I've not seen before and while his navy long-sleeved Polo top isn't quite weather appropriate, it does enhance his shoulders. He did say he's been upping his gym game.

My poor dad. He had no choice but to come with us as uncle Tariq's got work and he feels too awkward around auntie Rukhsana while she does women's things like cooking. He's the first to sit himself down at the front of the shop, where the standard bed thingy lies.

"*Bala asoyn nee?*" M opens up with the usual *how are you?* after the obligatory salaams. It's funny, I've only heard him speak Bengali a handful of times. Like most of us second-generation immigrants that speak second-hand mother tongue, his pronunciation is a bit off.

Dad duly responds and they fall into conversation about goodness knows what, leaving mum, little sis and I to engage in some women's business of our own - shopping.

I'm immediately drawn to this maroon and gold lehenga, which is sparkling under the shop lights. It goes against my original vision of classic gold and red but oh my, it's quite spectacular. The skirt must have something in the region of 1,000 crystals, with delicate gold wire threading it's way around each one, like a sandy beach dusted with diamond pebbles.

"Do you like it?" M appears next to me, interrupting my trance.

"It's nice but it's probably way too expensive," I reply.

"If you like it, try it on," he urges.

"No, it's... actually, shall I? Just to see?"

M laughs. "Well, yeah, that's why you're here. To be honest mum and I had a recce a few weeks back on Green Street and of all the shops and all the outfits, this one stood out for me, too. I'm glad it's still here."

"So am I," I say.

I head to the changing room, which thankfully is a proper one, to try on my outfit. Yep, I'm already calling it mine. Of course, it's a sample size so is huge on me. Thankfully, the shop assistant makes her way over and starts pegging the blouse to tighten it around my back and clips the skirt. Finally, she places the maroon net and diamond-dusted dupatta over my head. It doesn't sit properly because I've worn my hair long and loose. On the day, however, I'll have some kind of chic updo. As I look in the mirror, the memory of the first lehenga I tried in Manchester, the blood red number I fell a little bit in love with, slowly slips away.

"How much is it?" I ask the lady.

"You no worry about that. If it's for your special day, we'll give you a special price. Most important thing is, you like it."

Yes, that's the usual trick they try but there will be no fighting from me or my family for a change.

As I pull back the changing room curtain, which leads straight into the shop floor (rather undignified but now's not the time to argue), mum is the first one I see. I'm expecting some kind of negative feedback. She doesn't say anything and instead just looks at me, smiles and mouths *Masha Allah* under her breath. My mum, like me, is not a woman that's often lost for words.

Even little sis makes the effort to peel her eyes away from her phone to say to me: "Wow. That is *so* nice."

High praise indeed.

What about the man who is paying for it all? We don't have such customs as bad luck for the groom to see the bride in her dress. M is back in his seat at the other end of the shop bed thingy, in deep conversation with dad. My father is more animated than I've ever seen him, with lots of hand gestures. He's like a statesman holding court. M is listening intently, like he's genuinely interested. I can't spot a single eye roll. It's all rather sweet. In a house full of women, dad is often dismissed. We always assume he doesn't have much to say. In truth, however, we don't really ask or involve him in anything. I decide not to make eye contact with them to let them have their moment but M spots me anyway. It's hard not to with my megawatt sparkly dress.

He looks for a second, before doing a raised eyebrow, head nodding kind of gesture of approval, before returning to talk to my dad, very aware of being respectful around my family. My mum catches the little exchange and smiles to herself. I think every parent has a bout of anxiety when their daughter gets married. There is a Bengali saying that it's only when you sit down to eat rice with someone in their house (or something like that) that you know what they're really like. We don't get to live together, and any pre-wedding exchanges are terribly formal, with each party putting their best foot forward. So what do you go by? It's the little exchanges. The small gestures. The eye contact and the effort. These glimpses reveal so much. Right now, I can see that both mum and dad feel reassured by M. It makes my heart swell.

"Do you want to try any more?" mum asks.

"No, I don't think so," I reply. Anything else would be wasting the shopkeeper's time.

M leaves dad for a moment to check in. Dad turns around for the first time to see me in my lehenga (I know I shouldn't keep calling it mine, but still). He coughs a little and nods his head before looking away. I think he approves.

"What do you think?" M asks.

"I like it but I'm not sure how much it is."

"Don't worry about that, let me ask them."

Now I'm really hoping he has in fact got a friends and family discount.

WHILE I'M SAT WAITING as M talks to the manager, Julia keeps texting me about the hen party, eager to secure numbers. I can understand her sense of urgency. I've already messed her around having changed the venue from our trusty Italian restaurant to the less trusty Indian buffet. I figured that this would be easier on Sophia, as she can duck in and out if she needs to. As she's told me she wouldn't miss my hen do for the world, I think I ought to make it worth her missing her son for. Bushra and Emma are still 'checking their diaries' and my old school friend, Helen, seems to be getting revenge for the many times I've bailed on her by simply not replying to my message. Rude.

Julia has also been hinting that it would be easier for her to organise if I could bring one of my other friends into the planning stage. However, there is the small issue that the friend that is the most reliable, Reena, doesn't even know I'm getting married yet. That aside, there is an even greater issue at large. Friend mixing. It's a tricky business at the best of times for most people, I imagine. My particular situation is even more delicate. When you share different versions of how you met your future husband to various friends, it's hard to keep track of who's been told what.

M and the manager seem to be having what looks like a heated debate. I've never really seen men barter.

"Oh dear, maybe the shop man isn't his relative," whispers mum, revising her earlier theory.

"That's what I said all along, mum. You shouldn't always assume the worst."

"*Oh-ho*! Say you!"

So we're back to normal after that lehenga-based love in.

"Shall I go and help? Maybe say something?" I ask mum.

"I think you should. Maybe shop man bully him because he alone. They'll think he's forced to buy it because you want it."

I head over to interrupt the haggle. "Is everything okay?"

M looks hot and bothered. "Yeah, yeah, it's fine."

I knew he wouldn't want to trouble me. I look at the manager. "Is there a problem?"

"No, no. We just sorting. You don't worry sister."

He's fobbing me off.

"Can you go down to £1,200?" asks M.

"Brother, believe me. The original price is £2,500. Of course we can't go that low. It's for her wedding day."

M looks down. The shopkeeper is shaming him. However, this guy doesn't know me. If he did, he'd know that I am one stingy customer. Even when it comes to my own wedding outfit.

"Let's leave it," I say, shocked by my own words and unsure where this strategy is headed.

"It's fine. You sit down with your family. I'll sort it," says M.

"No, I'll stay here." He'll soon come to learn that behind every strong man is a woman determined to get a bargain.

The manager is surprised at my steely determination. M looks a little shocked too. I think he figured he'd have to fight this battle alone.

"Look, it's your wedding, so I'll go to £1,600," says the manager.

They're almost about to agree and the shopkeeper reaches out for a handshake. I discreetly put my hand over M's fingers. We're not done yet.

"£1,200 please. And also, we'll be living in London after our wedding and I've got my brother's wedding coming up. So I need new outfits for that, too.

A lie is but a lie is but a lie is but a necessity to secure a good deal.

The shopkeeper clutches my diamond encrusted skirt as if to take it away. I know this game. I've been training my whole life for this moment.

"Come on, let's go," I say to a bemused and confused M. "Mum, everyone, we're going."

Mum and my teenage sister stare at me blankly. Dad's face just looks the same, ever so slightly vacant.

Nobody really knows what's going on, except mum, my haggling ally.

"You heard her... *ooto*," she gestures with her hands up in the air, ushering my confused family to their feet. They're not sure how this will end. Neither am I, really.

We all start walking out of the shop. We keep walking and walking. Finally, the door buzzes and we see ourselves out onto the now rained on street.

"Are you sure about this? We can go back in," says M.

We both know that's not true. Once you leave the shop you can't come back, unless you want to pay double what you suggested. It's the ultimate sign of defeat. I blew it. I bloody blew it. The worst part of all is we don't have an umbrella between us to provide shelter from the rain and shame.

Mum looks at me, dejected and slightly unsure of our next move.

"Can we get some food?" asks little sis.

I guess a kebab might soften the blow.

"Hold on!" shouts a voice from behind us. "Come back inside. Please."

"No brother. If you can't give good price, there's no need," I say, resorting to a full-on broken English accent. Big sis would be proud.

"Okay, okay. Come in and we talk."

I don't move. Everybody's looking at me like I've lost my mind. I think I partly have.

"Oh, you tricky girl. £1,300!"

"Deal!" I say, though I really should consult with M. After all, he's paying for the damn thing.

I look at him. He mutters under his breath: "Nice work!"

There is one last bit of work to be done at the shop. I asked for a small customisation, obviously thrown in at the same price we agreed. I decide to change the shade of my blouse. I might as well make it a unique one-off piece. Then the female shop assistant frisks me as she takes my vital measurements. M and dad spare my blushes by looking out of the window and continuing whatever conversation they were having.

"Okay. This will be ready in three weeks."

Gosh, that's cutting it fine.

M says goodbye as uncle Tariq, who insisted we call him once we're done, picks us up on the corner of Green Street.

We've barely driven away before I get a text from M: *Were you really going to give up that lehenga to get a good price?*

I reply: *Yeah. Of course. I don't want you getting ripped off. Was I a bit too much though?*

I'm worried about the answer. Then he gets back with: *You were brilliant. Stingy cow ;)*

Uncle Tariq has Bollywood music blaring from his car stereo playing a suitable wedding song *Dulhe ka sehra*, about a bride being given away by her father.

Muffled within the music, I hear dad say to uncle Tariq: "He's good. He's a good boy."

"I DON'T THINK THE ROYAL Raja will be big enough for so many people," says uncle Tariq between inhalations of tobacco on his window ledge. "The groom's family say they went to a wedding there a few years ago and they only had space for about 300 people."

Dad, emboldened by his man-to-man conversation with M, chimes in. "Yes, yes. I think that be right. Remember, we been there too, few years ago? Very nice venue. Not big enough for 600."

Mum doesn't reply and instead shoots him a death stare for having his second roll-up of the day. Dad avoids eye contact, instead focusing on his Rizla, ensuring the tobacco is in a neat line before encasing it in the white paper.

It's a shame about the Royal Raja. Granted, the name is tacky as hell. However, it's a pretty nice venue, with a grand marble lobby, several water fountains and an Instagram-friendly flower wall. It's a Bengali girl's wedding goals. It won't be my goals though, thanks to our bloated guest list.

"There is another place. The Palace," says uncle Tariq.

"You mean the Palace Hotel in Manchester city centre?" I ask. That's surpassing even my expectations.

"Heh?" he says, pouring cold water on my dream. "No, this Palace between Droylsden and Manchester, so it works quite well. Big, big building. It will look good in photos."

Then I remember, wedding videography and photography! I need a wedding planner for all this crap as nobody in my family is stepping up.

"I know one of the owners. From our village in 'desh. You know. Jahangir's son." Uncle Tariq nods at mum, expecting her to remember this Jahangir fella.

Mum nods in agreement though her face spells confusion.

"They could give a good price," he adds.

It seems that despite my own research into venues, the place where I get married will be decided by the usual criteria - the headcount and price per head. I loves me a bargain but I was hoping that for one day in my life things could be a bit special. So much for having a wedding that will be different.

I bring this up with mum when we retire to bed in Naila's old room.

"So, I've actually been doing some research into venues and I've seen some nice ones in Manchester," I say.

"What have you seen?" asks mum as she gently pulls the gold clip out of her bun and begins detangling her hair with her fingers.

"Well, there's one place my friend at work mentioned. She's Pakistani and her cousin got married there and she showed me the pictures. It literally looks like the Houses of Parliament. It's only in Chorlton too, so not too far away from us."

"Really? Like Parliament?"

Now I've got her attention.

"We should look. We don't want cheap place. You only marry once," says mum, in full blown M&S Greek-style yoghurt buying mode. "Is it proper wedding venue? Do they do catering? Have staff?"

That's where I fall short. I only really ogled the venue in the pictures on Bushra's Facebook feed. "Let me check."

A quick Google search is futile. They basically only have rooms for hire. The rest of it is on you.

"It be too risky. If you have to find everything separate - waiters, knife and forks, food, too much chance to go wrong. Especially so late."

"Okay. Well, I hope this Palace uncle Tariq knows of at least has a chocolate fountain for hire. Otherwise I'll have to look separately."

"You and your chocolate fountain! Nobody cares for those things. I told you it's going to be so expensive. It going to cause a mess. What's the point?"

"The point is I want there to be something, just *something* special about my wedding. Everybody has these things now. It's so annoying! I knew I wanted to marry him since last year but we couldn't plan anything. Now everything is a crazy rush and it's going to be rubbish. We can never do anything different. We can never make it special."

"Why are you complaining? Think of good things. You're marrying nice boy. You've got a nice dress. Insha Allah, everything else will be okay."

"You can't just say that mum! You can't just say everything will be okay. We need to plan. Can't we just do things properly? You're always waiting. Always telling me *'don't say too much yet. Don't jinx it. Don't tell too many people.'* Now we've left things so damn late because of your worrywart ways!"

Mum turns away from me in bed. "You can't blame me for everything. I'm doing my best. I always do my best."

"Well your best isn't good enough," I say, more out of frustration than anything.

Mum says nothing.

Sod this. I'm telling Reena. I've got my hen do coming up and she is a busy lady. I can't drop it on her last minute. Especially as I might have to rope her into some of the organising with Julia.

Me: *Hey, I know it's late and I really wanted to tell you over the phone, or even better in person. But... I've met someone. And I'm getting married!*

Reena (replies straight away): *Awww... no way!*

6th August

In search of the one

This isn't happening. It's not going well. Not one bit. You'd think that money can buy anything these days. With so many options at our disposal - the web, social media, the old faithful family and friend recommendations. This search seems even harder than finding a husband - finding a half-decent, punctual and professional makeup artist.

Despite days of accumulated research, I have yet to find one of the most crucial components of the wedding planning puzzle.

I had a trial on Saturday, with the lady who does my eyebrows in the salon near work. I quite liked her on the threading front. On my first visit she offered me a glass of water, which is a rarity amongst Asian beauticians where it's a bit of a quick and dirty process. Her parlour seems busy with a mix of Asian and non-Asian clients. She offers a wealth of services from makeup, hair, nails and I think she even does bridal henna. Basically, it was all looking good and in my semi-desperate state I was already thinking she might be the one.

She wasn't. A tight-arse bullshit merchant is what she was.

I barely sat in the makeup chair, before she started harping on about facials. Yeah, that old chestnut. Given that my face was still suffering the after effects of the rather brutal facial administered by the burly beautician a mere two weeks back, I wasn't planning on doing one again.

After several failed attempts at pushing me to book a facial with her, she took the hint and got to work.

Now, I've had enough makeup trials in my time to know that a basic best practice is they apply fake lashes. No makeup look is complete without a set of falsies as it's the difference between a so-so look, and a transformation. I never use the lashes again, so would happily peel them off and give them back post-trial, but I need them applied initially.

However, lady BS was shocked at the suggestion, so she dug out a pair of purple novelty lashes (I'm assuming she didn't want to part with a more in-demand black pair) and made a sneaky comment about how I'm ready for my wedding now! Cheeky cow.

The rest of the trial followed suit. Her and her assistant exchanged catty remarks in Urdu or Punjabi or whatever the language was. I couldn't understand what they were saying but the eye rolls and side eye game was strong.

Annoyingly, I really liked her makeup. Not too heavy but with enough vibrancy in my cheeks to look a bit more special than daywear.

However, once I told her I liked the makeup, she went back on her original quote and bumped up her price by 50%. All this within the space of a few days between my initial enquiry call and the trial itself. You can't blame that on inflation. I still don't know whether she was lying or 'chose to forget' but I'm certainly not booking with her. Now officially not her friend, I'm going to have to find someone else to do my eyebrows. It's a good thing I'm moving to a new city, as I've depleted the talent pool of Asian beauticians in Manchester.

I could continue searching but it feels futile. Between this beautician and the previous one that had a limited range and the girl I used for my engagement that sprayed my hair rock hard, I've also had about a dozen email and social media exchanges which have been so disappointingly pointless it wasn't even worth noting.

Maybe, just possibly, I'll have to... do my own wedding makeup.

I can't believe it's come to this.

I NEED TO UP MY GAME. If... and it's a big if... I'm going to do my own makeup, I need to get the hours of practice in now.

Baby steps though. I decide to start by having a go at creating a mehendi makeup look, as the stakes aren't quite so high on this occasion. I mean, Sophia barely wore any makeup on her mehendi, telling me that in her culture they opt for minimal makeup for this event to be fresh-faced ahead of the wedding. She shared this titbit after spotting my very unsubtle poker face gaping at her barefaced photos.

I log onto the fountain of all beauty knowledge – YouTube – to see if I can copy their techniques. I find a video tutorial of green eye makeup, which would be great for a mehendi look.

One good thing about the trial and (mainly) error of my beautician hunt is that I've picked up a few handy hints along the way. The first of which is that you always need a primer of some sort to prep your face for makeup. That must be where I've been going wrong with my makeup meltdowns of yesteryear. As I glide on the primer I bought from a previous makeup trial in a department store (and never used since), I see it really does create a smooth base. What are these thoughts popping into my head? Gliding? Smooth base? I think I've been watching too many tutorials.

Now for the main feature of any Asian bridal look. The second thing I've learnt is to start a makeover with the eyes first. This is because any eyeshadow pigments that fall on your face can be easily wiped away without ruining the rest of your makeup. Again - what? Just *who* do I think I am?

This is where I get brave. Mehendi rules dictate green or even, dare I say, a yellow eye look. I'm doing both. I start with a yellow shadow on the inside of my eyelid, just as the photogenic makeup artist demonstrates in her video. Some of these colours are a bit tricky to get hold of as they are hues I would never, I repeat, never wear. However, the tacky metal case of makeup gifted to me on my engagement by M's family has its starring moment as it contains all of these garish colours.

Within the kaleidoscope of eyeshadow quads, I find the necessary green shade, hilariously called *Love and Money*. Was someone employed to think up these names? Anyway, that goes onto the centre of my eyelid. I need to be quick as I have approximately 30 minutes before my teenage sister comes upstairs to do whatever it is she has to do on her phone at 8pm precisely every night. I could do without the audience. I also don't have the tiny fluffy makeup brush that's used in the video with a handy affiliate link for the makeup artist to make a quick buck from my purchase. I just use my finger instead, employing a dabbing motion. At the risk of sounding cocky or jumping the gun, I think I'm pretty good at this.

To add further intensity (again, who *is* this makeup aficionado who's taken over my being?), I apply a fern shade (also from the handy metal case I'd been judging ever so harshly).

Dutifully following the tutorial, I blend the three shades together to, as the makeup artist says, 'reduce any harsh lines'.

To finish the eye painting, I'm advised to sweep an orange-yellow tone just under the brow bone. After a rustle through my makeup bag I resort to using a gold glittery shade from a palette I purchased during my early twenties when I went through a phase of buying lots of makeup and never using it. Second problem, I don't have the pointy nibbed makeup brush used by the online beauty guru. Her affiliate link tells me it will cost £26. For that *one* brush. That I will use *once*. Well, I am nothing if not versatile, so I dip a long neglected lip brush into the gold sparkly shade. A quick swish under my eyes results in more on my cheekbones than where it should be. I think now is the time to examine the fruits of my labour.

I take a few selfies on my phone, both up close and at a distance, looking straight at the camera and with a lowered gaze. I try with the flash and without. I look in the mirror, both using the regular view and flipping over the round mirror to reveal the magnified side. After observing from all angles, I can conclude that the result is... fucking terrible.

I mean, what was I thinking? I know I'm desperate, I know time is marching on but there is no way I can do that gorgeous beautiful bedazzling lehenga justice by doing my own makeup. Forget finishing my face, I'm stopping right here. Ain't got time for this rubbish.

Like clockwork, little sis bundles into the room cradling her phone like it's a newborn baby.

She struggles to stifle a laugh. "What are you doing? That looks so weird!"

I sigh with resignation. I just have to stick to my strengths. I grab my phone to text Bushra: *Hey, would you be able to give me the details of your cousin the makeup artist?*

9th August
Finally...

I think I've found the one...
   No, not M. The makeup artist of my dreams. It makes me giddy just thinking about it.

By the time I trialled Bushra's cousin, Kulsum, my expectations were pretty low, what with my inbuilt, slightly racist broad-sweep judgment of all beauticians from back home. Our text exchange was hard work, as she's getting used to English as a second language.

When we met, my seeds of doubt began to really take root. My unconscious bias assumed she was a girl my age and Bushra hadn't mentioned otherwise. However, I was greeted by a middle-aged woman at her house in Longsight, which I later learned was the home of her second husband. None of this was of any odds to me, had it not been for the fact that she had herself what I would describe as a dated look. She's naturally fair-skinned and powdered up to appear even fairer, with rainbow arched black pencilled-in eyebrows. I was contemplating cancelling on the spot. However, like that time I took my shoes off for my last facial, I'd already committed by stepping over the threshold of her coarse welcome mat and into her front porch. There was no going back.

My second pair of eyes, mum, and I were led to the basement of her new marital home which was converted into a studio, with an agreement that she would come to my house to do my makeup on the wedding day itself.

Unlike the other artists I've tried, which were all a bit wham bam thank you ma'am, Kulsum spent hours (yes, hours) applying my makeup. At a minimal cost of £25, she practically created my wedding look. She boasted a myriad of makeup, with an impressive array of premium brands. Granted, the lipsticks looked a bit manky, and I suspect some of the eyeshadows might be older than my 17-year-old sister, but beggars can't be choosers.

Plus, she worked with me to discuss colours, textures and also what would work under the harsh photographers light. In fact, after applying some primer, her exact words were: "How do you like your skin to be? *V-hite*, yellow, golden?"

That was the first time I've ever been asked, or even offered, the option of changing my actual skin colour, discounting the previous bleaching conversation of course. I ignored the blatant colourism (she's only just arrived in the UK and has yet to learn the art of political correctness) and suggested she paint me golden and glowing. There is no need for whiteface.

I felt like I was having a masterclass in makeup. Oh, and she didn't mention the need for me to get a facial. Not once. She even praised my youthful combination skin and patted away at my new pimples with concealer, without even the subtlest of catty comments.

"I like to take my time with makeup," she informed me between graceful brushstrokes. "I only book one client a day, as I need to lie down afterwards."

I was thankful for her dedication to each bride, as well as her possible low blood pressure that warrants the need to be horizontal after an afternoon of making up.

I was about to secure her time there and then but she wasn't done. She spent the last hour of the trial doing my hair. Not a single previous beautician had done this before. They'd all merely discussed my hair options and hoped for me to book based on their word. I did that once in the past for another family wedding and the beautician turned up with her assistant, who was also her 16-year-old sister. Said sister presented us with a straightening iron and offered us a choice of hairstyles, ranging from straight to curls and more curls. Kulsum, however, backcombed, added a fake hairpiece and even finished with a scarf and headpiece so I got a real feel for how I would look on the big day. The bitchy beautician from my last trial was wrong, I wasn't ready to get married with her stupid purple lashes, I was ready to get married after Kulsum's handiwork!

At this point, only a kick to the groin from the beautician herself would discourage me from booking Kulsum. She surpassed all my expectations with her level of service. She was polite, friendly and made my poor mum, who sat with me for hours while she worried about the chicken she'd left defrosting on the counter top, a cup of tea and biscuits. As mum began looking more fraught as this trial was taking much longer than expected, Kulsum even offered her a lie down on her bed. Very nice, though mum declined, feeling mildly offended. She's anxious, not infirm.

Before I left, I carefully picked the pins out of my hair to release the dupatta and fake headpiece. I was about to pull out the hairpiece, too, before Kulsum said: "Keep it in. You can take pictures at home. Maybe send to your husband."

I became girlish and so did mum. That's totally what I was planning to do.

I took some photos whilst at her studio - she has better lighting - and sent a sneaky shot to M.

He replied as I climbed into the car. Of course I could wait until we got home, especially given mum's nervous nature about leaving dad and my sister to their own devices without any food for so long, but I just had to see what he said.

You look nice. But you always look nice, was his reply.

Bloody men. All this effort and they barely notice.

THAT NIGHT, MUM DROPS a humdinger of a bombshell after receiving a call from auntie Jusna. Hassna's engagement has been broken off.

"What? Why?" I ask, hardly believing the revelation.

"I think they got too greedy," says mum as we sit down to eat chicken curry at 10.30pm. Dad and little sis made the most of mum's absence by ordering a KFC. "Jusna always do everything for show! Always bigger and better. You saw their cini paan? So pricey! And that diamond ring! I bet his family had enough of their showing-off ways."

"What makes you think that?" I ask, knowing that this is more of a conspiracy theory than actual fact. "What did auntie Jusna say?"

"Oh, you know them. Always other side fault. Just like Rashda divorce. They blamed in-laws. Maybe some truth there. But they not blameless. This time, they saying family were being stingy with gold and how much money to give. They also say they found out bad things about boy. Everything was fine with the register before. Now they got problem because it's no working. Problem is they wanted register to be cash register!" Mum laughs at her own joke. It was a good one, to be fair.

"What are they saying about the boy?" I ask.

"All usual nonsense. He had girlfriends. So what?"

"Poor Hassna," I say.

Mum searches my face as though she's not 100% convinced by my response. "You need to be careful, too."

"What do you mean? How has it got anything to do with me?"

"Don't be too greedy. Don't be too showy. Have some *shorom*. Small shame make big difference."

I think she means humility but that's beside the point.

Mum has yet more pearls of wisdom. "Be good person! Never judge. Never! Your big sis always talk bad of people. This person this, this person that. Now look at her, she chunky monkey."

I don't see what that's got to do with anything but I don't dare argue.

"How embarrassing it be for them!" says mum, continuing her ranting rampage. "They printed all those invitations, so fancy and expensive. Now everybody knows about their wedding. The wedding that's not happening. You know our parties, we invite every *Bangali* in UK. So now everyone knows their business."

"Is that why you're putting off telling people?"

Mum looks at me as though I'd asked if the sky is blue. "Obviously. Yes!"

"So that's why you're not rushing to get peoples addresses for invites?"

"How many time I say... yes!"

"But... but... how long will you keep putting it off? We're running out of time!"

"*Dooro!* There be plenty of time. Our people don't need lots of time. They decide the day before if they attend wedding. And they decide on the day if two people go or whole family of six! You send too early and then what? Look at Hassna, sending her stupid peacock feathers months early. Now look how embarrassing for them." She spoons herself some more rice.

Mum always uses the bad news of the Mahmood's as a life lesson for us. When Rashda got divorced, mum went into a blind panic and entertained the idea of me marrying the pizza boy from back home. Now Hassna's engagement has broken off, this will be used as ammunition to keep me in check.

Mum is always saying don't be too proud. Stay in your lane. Don't be too boastful. She might as well say don't be too happy.

18th August
A most halal hen do

In the vein of trying not to be too much of a bridezilla, I'm reining in my apparently lofty ambitions. I booked the videographer that I found on page two of Google and, as luck would have it, he'll do the photography as well. Of course he will. The truth is, I don't know if he's qualified for either. Still, his portfolio looked decent.

So, with that sorted, I'm taking my eyes away from my seemingly never ending and frankly rather stress-inducing list, to have a day of fun. Tonight is my hen do and, to make things feel a bit more normal and less chaotic, I'm having a brunch with my sisters beforehand. I'm glad to report that my two older ones, who have been missing in action, have graced me with their presence.

I've seen it happen on trashy reality TV shows all too often. Brides-to-be have a lovely family meal in the day, followed by a swanky event later, all of course captured on their expansive social media platforms. I don't possess much of a social media following, however I am going to post some sweet family photos and some bullshit captions about being best friends with my siblings or something along those lines. You know, just to show that I'm enjoying some of the basic pre-wedding rituals that most girls take for granted.

And then I remember that most families aren't like mine.

Brunch quickly becomes lunch as both sisters and their respective kids don't roll out of bed until 11am. This means I'll have to either have a light meal (not happening, I'll never do it), or have two proper meals within very close succession (obviously that's the option I'm going for).

"Hmm... not sure what I should have," says big sis as she examines the well-handled laminate menu. "Maybe the carrot halwa?"

"I don't think I can stomach that," grumbles middle sis, simultaneously wincing and rubbing her now blossoming belly.

"Well, why did you eat so much? You knew we were coming for brunch," I say.

"I had cereal. What was I supposed to eat? Tea on its own? In my condition?" she continues rubbing her bump like she's using it as her get out of brunch card.

"You could've had a smaller bowl of cereal. Or here's a thought, maybe you could've woken up earlier."

"We got to mum's after 11 last night. The kids didn't settle until midnight. How early did you expect me to wake up? Plus I had to sort the kids out before I left. Or did you want me to lumber mum with feeding and sorting out their wees and poohs?" middle sis asks.

"Yeah lady," big sis chimes in. "And I spent hours on the train to get here yesterday. In this heat! Only to do it again in a few weeks! Can't you just be glad we're here?"

I huff. "Yes, thank you for being here. You know it's pretty normal for the sisters of the bride to want to do something like this before the wedding. Usually they organise it for them!"

"Gosh, if you're that bothered, we can split the bill," says big sis.

"I can't," says little sis. "I didn't bring my bag. I only had enough room for my phone." She puts her hands in her unusually high cardigan pockets to reinforce her point.

"You never bring your bag!" I say, louder than expected.

"Alright, calm down lady," says big sis. "Is this because I didn't call the mehendi venue?"

"That, and not offering to help with *any* of the planning. Not asking me how I'm doing... If there's anything you can do to help."

"What can I do all the way from Bristol?"

"You've got a phone! You've got internet access! Don't make out like you're in the village in Bangladesh."

"That's a bit below the belt," says big sis. "Anyway, we never stay in the village. You know we're in the town. I need air conditioning."

"That's not even the point!" I shriek. "God... I wish I had a brother to help out with all this."

"We all wish we had a brother!" says middle sis.

"Ladies, sorry to interrupt. Can I take your order," says the waiter / unwitting referee.

"Could we have a bit more time?" asks middle sis.

How much longer do they need? "Okay, hurry up and decide! I need to go to my actual hen do, organised by someone that isn't me, in three hours. To think we'd sit and have a nice, leisurely meal and discuss a colour theme for the mehendi. I knew it was too big an ask."

"We can discuss it now," says middle sis.

"Oh, what's the point. I've been trying to get you to commit for ages. Every time I call either of you, the answer is '*oh, but I don't have that colour*', or, 'I don't like that shade'. Or, my personal favourite - '*oh no, everybody wears that shade*'. Well, newsflash, there are only so many bloody colours in the rainbow! We have to just pick one. So forget it! I'm picking. Buttery yellow."

"Oh, but everybody wears -" big sis stops in her tracks after seeing my angry face.

"Yellow will make me look dark," says little sis, whose skin is still lighter than mine.

"Well tough shit! It's my wedding so I'm calling it. You're all wearing yellow."

There's a moment of silence as all four of us look down at our menus.

"This isn't very fun," mumbles big sis.

"Don't worry, we'll take a fake smiling photo for Instagram. Nobody needs to know," quips little sis.

MESSAGE FROM M: *Do you like my new threads?*

He sends a picture of himself holding the skirt of my bridal lehenga up against himself, grinning from ear to ear.

Me: *Oh! It's arrived!*

M: *It has! So I'll be making a special delivery on my next trip up. By the way, how was your brunch with your sisters?*

Me: *Really good.*

I'm so glad this is in text message form so he can't see me lying through my teeth.

M: *You got your hen do today too, right? Hope you have a good one!*

Me: *Thanks. What about you? What have your boys got in store for you?*

M: *Well, there's talk of us going on a road trip somewhere, but they're not telling me. The only clue they've given is that I'll need my passport! So I'm guessing a hop on the ferry!*

Now *that's* a proper do. I'm jealous.

I'm still bloated from the paratha and curried chickpeas I had for the brunch that turned into lunch. I knew I should have opted for something lighter but you can't go out for an Asian brunch and have tea and toast. It's just rude.

As I'm changing into a red polka dot dress, my second outfit of the day to emphasis the fact that (lucky me) I'm popular enough to have two very different parties, Kulsum, the makeup artist of my dreams, calls. Will she be a nightmare and cancel on me? This isn't a day for messing me about.

"Hello dear," she purrs.

"Oh hi, Kulsum."

"Are you okay?"

"Yes. You?"

"Yes dear."

I don't have time for this. If she's cancelling, she needs to put me out of my misery now. "Sorry I'm just about to head out, so can't really talk. Was there a reason you called?" My hands are trembling.

"I just wanted to check in how you are. I know it's a busy time but just make sure you drink plenty of water and get lots of rest so you look well on the day and don't stress! This is time for everyone to take care of you."

"Oh... okay. Well... thank you. I'll try to relax."

"No worries. You take care dear and I'll speak to you soon."

Weird.

Thankfully my entire clan have decided to take the unprecedented step of going for a walk. No doubt my sisters want to cool off after the tense brunch lunch. I bet they're bitching about me. I can just picture them. That's A LOT of brown faces for our street. If there weren't any racists in our neighbourhood, the sight of three generations of Bengalis in a saree, salwar kameezes and a panjabi might be enough to make them turn.

At least having the house to myself means I can exit without an interrogation from mum. I'm already running late and fielding anxious messages from Julia.

However, I'm set to get later as I get a call from Sophia.

"Hey, are you running late, too?" I ask while wiggling one thick denier tights clad foot into a ballet pump.

"No hon. I'm not," says Sophia.

Her voice sounds small and weak. Not the usual shrill, confident and rather bossy tone.

"I'm so sorry to do this to you on the day but... I can't make your hen do."

I sit back on the stairs and take Sophia off speaker phone. "Why not?"

"I really wanted to come so I didn't let you down but it's just too difficult to leave Imran for any longer than about 40 minutes because I'm still breastfeeding. He won't settle with Adnan. Sorry hon. I would have loved to have been there."

"Oh no, could you just pop over for half an hour?"

"I can't, hon. The thing is, by the time I get everything set for Imran, make myself presentable, then head up to see you, it'll be time to come back and give him his next feed."

I'm tempted to ask why she doesn't just express like Amy from work. Looks like a bloody genius idea. However, as I'm without child, I can't really comment.

"Anyway, you won't even notice me not being there, you'll be too busy having fun with your baby-free mates and your sisters."

She knows my sisters aren't coming. I've told her this before. Wasn't she paying attention? Or is she just rubbing my small guest list in my face?

Sophia resorts to filling in the silence, which is usually my job. "Anyway, it's not like the hen do is the place for a nursing mum with raging hormones. I'm hardly gonna be drinking through a plastic penis straw?"

I don't have the words. I organised the whole bloody thing around her. She knew it was at the buffet where we first met. I figured it would be poignant as well as convenient. What will I tell Julia?

"Hon, please say something," urges Sophia.

"Well, it's just... I planned it around you," I say. This time my voice is small.

"What did you do that for? I didn't ask you to." Her shrill tone returns, with a smidgen of aggression.

She's always had this way of answering back, putting me in my place like she knows better, with her years of life experience and two bites of the marital cherry. Not this time.

"I know you didn't ask me. Obviously I was telling you all the things that I was planning! Why do you think I booked that buffet?"

"Because you love samosas and seekh kebabs?"

"Yes, well, that too, but the main reason was that it would be easy for you to get to. I planned it to accommodate you! Plus, it's where we met at that charity event." I feel pathetic for uttering my last statement. Clearly she doesn't care.

"It's just as easy for you to get there as well."

"No it bloody isn't!" I almost yell down the phone. "You've see me struggle to merge onto the A57. You've seen my crappy parallel parking. If it was down to me I would have booked my Italian -"

"Hey hon, don't put this on me."

"I'm not... but I just... I wanted you there. You were there when I was single and thinking I'd never get married. You were with me on this whole journey and now I know you're on your own journey but... anyway... look I've gotta go. Chat later."

That was metaphorical. I don't plan on calling her again in a hurry.

I'm mentally counting how many people are going to be at what is possibly the crappiest hen do of all time. Julia, Helen, Reena, Bushra, Emma and me. Oh my God, I have to count myself to make it look like there's more people. This is turning into a joke. It's not a hen do. It's just friends going to dinner. I won't be posting any pictures on social media of this shit show.

I'M LATE AS ALWAYS but why change the habit of a lifetime? What's scary about being one of the last to arrive to this particular gathering is that it's a meeting of minds that have never previously gathered and it breaks one of my unwritten rules - don't mix your friends.

As I get to the buffet, which I booked to work around Sophia, I see that everyone - all five of my guests - have already arrived. However my mood is immediately lifted as not only have they waited for me to arrive before plating up (I admire their willpower), they've also made the effort of decorating our table. Julia booked what looks like the best spot in the restaurant. A large round table where the centre circle spins so dishes can be passed around. We're also sectioned off from the rest of the room with Chinese blinds. Admittedly our private dining spot is a little empty, so my gang of girls have ensured that it looks less windy by putting their handbags on the spare chairs and sitting spaced out. There's sprinkled confetti on the table and a flower arrangement, which I can tell is Julia's expensive, elegant touch. This is contrasted with some penis shaped balloons and a similarly rude set of straws, which I suspect was a collective effort from Reena, Emma and Bushra. I appreciate the gesture.

Julia greets me with a hug. "Hello you. Fashionably late as always. Your throne awaits."

She ushers me towards a slightly elevated, regal looking chair. I can't help but smile. Sophia may have bailed but this might not be so bad after all.

"So what did I miss?" I ask as I get myself comfortable on my throne.

"We've been discussing you, mainly," says Helen, one of the few school friends, along with Julia, that I've kept in touch with.

I laugh nervously.

"Don't embarrass her," says Julia, sipping through a penis shaped straw, which goes against all of her prim sensibilities. "Though we did agree on one thing. You have to promise not to become one of those girls that puts Misters before sisters, okay?"

"Of course!" I say, taking a sip from my own appendage straw. I'm so glad our section is private, I'd hate for any distant relatives or nosey fake aunties spotting me in such a compromising position.

"Look at you, taking to it like an expert!" laughs Reena. She sounds tipsy even though this place has a dry bar.

Julia looks on nervously, Bushra and Emma look confused and Helen's already left the table to join the queue at the buffet. Thankfully everyone else decides that she's got the right idea and follow her lead.

Two plates of food in and with some introductory conversations having taken place, talk turns to how M and I met. I was dreading this bit.

Julia starts: "Now I'm not sure if you all know this..."

Oh crap, what's she gonna say?

"...but our girl's biggest concern was about his baldness!"

Phew.

"However," she continues, "he must be something special as he won her over regardless and I couldn't be happier for you. It seems like just the other day we were both single and I was worried about you... you know I was."

I nod in agreement.

"Yet you've gone and met the man of your dreams on your terms," she lifts her glass to cheers.

"Yeah, you beat us all to it!" says Reena. "You were the most Bollywood of us all at uni. Do you remember we said you were like Charlotte from Sex and the City, without the sex?"

Bushra and Emma shoot a look at each other and stifle giggles.

Mortified.

Helen looks suitably unimpressed by Reena's crassness. "Well, you might be the first to get married but you're late for everything else!"

Oh, we're doing stories about me, I take it?

Helen continues: "I remember calling for you in the morning to go to school. Remember, Julia? She'd have us waiting for ten minutes and on the way home we'd always smell your house before we saw it because of the curry -"

Helen stops her slightly racist tribute to me upon realising that there are three offended brownies in her company. There's a moment of tumbleweed as nobody sees the funny side of her terrible story.

"Oh, I've got one!" Bushra puts down her glass and holds up her hand like she's in school. "This one time, she was buying a watch for M, and -"

"Oh look over there!" I yell. "Is that cake for me?"

Thankfully, the waiter makes his way towards us with a cream cake with a single sparkler on top. I jumped the gun a little, leaving the girls to shout surprise, albeit not in unison, with Emma a full syllable behind everyone else. However, I had to intervene as the less people that know about my cheap and dirty watch secret the better.

As I admire my cake, which has mine and M's initials in icing, the sound of a bread knife being tapped against a glass echoes across the table.

"Speech! Speech! Speech!" shouts Reena.

I was hoping to avoid this. Despite my work lending itself to public speaking and my natural ability to talk for England, I'm lost for words. However, I feel compelled to say something about the effort they made. The day didn't start how I would have liked but I appreciated how it's ending. This group of girls, all from different backgrounds and walks of life, were thrown together by me and it wasn't altogether a disaster.

"Well I'm not sure what to say," I begin.

This is followed by jokes such as: "That's a first!"

"Okay... well, thank you so much for doing all this. Julia, I know it wasn't easy for you, bringing us all together. Reena, thanks for making the journey from Birmingham and Bushra, Emma and Helen, you only went round the corner so no big thanks to you! Seriously though, thanks all of you. And the penis straws are the best!"

Funny is all I have.

As I cut the cake, I look around at my random gathering of friends. My perfectly imperfect lady gang.

26th August
The most beautiful outfit I'll ever wear

M's brothers and some relative of his that I've never met deliver a huge briefcase to my house. The latter guest makes his presence felt by sending a strong whiff of tobacco through my open bedroom window. At least he's smoking outside. My lungs are then cleansed by the spicy smell of samosas, teasing me while I wait like a coy bride-to-be for them to leave. Finally, I hear the door slam, another waft of smoke (he must be a 20-a-day kind of guy) and I'm free to go downstairs in my maxi dress nightie.

I can hear dad chatting outside to his soon-to-be relatives. This is a bit of a first, dad taking the lead. Maybe holding an audience with an all-ears M at the saree shop has brought out a more confident side to him.

"You shouldn't have," he says. "You could have brought the lehenga over nearer to the wedding day, like we said. There was no rush. I hope it wasn't too much trouble."

"Nah nah, not at all," says a rather hoarse smoker's voice, who I'm guessing is the other relative. "The other clothes and gold will be coming soon."

Ooh, presents.

I come downstairs to see that mum's left three samosas for me, carefully wrapped in an oil-soaked kitchen tissue to stay warm.

I dare not open the briefcase with my now greasy hands, so mum does the honours.

"It's so heavy," says mum as she lifts up the skirt with gripped hands, jewels upon jewels unfolding and sparking under the dim yellow light of our dining room. It's still as beautiful as I remember it. Simply stunning. I can't believe it's mine. All mine. Mum only manages to reveal the top third before carefully resting it down again. It makes me wonder how I'm going to wear this for a whole day.

"Do you want to try it on?" mum asks.

I look at the time. It's 11.20pm. "No, I'll try it tomorrow. It's late."

I want to savour this moment and take my time, as it might possibly be the most stunning outfit I will ever wear.

27th August

Nazar

"So, you're on countdown now," says Bernadette. "How do you feel?"

"Good," I say, in complete honesty. "These last few weeks have flown by. Thank you so much for being so accommodating."

"Not at all. It's my pleasure. Like I've always said, you're one of our shining stars and though we'll miss you in the office, we're so glad that we're not quite saying goodbye and you'll still be part of our team."

Bernadette then gets back to business. "Right, so, as it's your last day, I need to check, is there anything you need to hand over?" She runs hers fingers through her freshly dyed hair.

"No, I think I'm done. The PR team at HQ have been fantastic, agreeing to take on some of the press release distribution. Bushra and Emma have been amazing too, offering to field any media queries. So I'm all set. If there's anything at all though, I've got a handover which I'll email to basically... everyone."

Bernadette looks on in surprise as I pull a four-page word document out from my folder.

"Gosh, you have covered all bases. Like I knew you would. So there's just one small thing..."

Oh dear.

"I hate to put this on you so close to your wedding but, as you'll be missing our quarterly meeting, there's a webinar I'd like you to attend. It's one of those HR things that offer minimal value in the real world but you have to be seen to be doing it."

Bernadette sees my face and quickly adds: "The good news is you don't have to attend live as there's a replay that will be available for a week. So all I ask is that at some point between 2nd and 9th September, if you could just log on so it'll track that you watched the webinar. And honestly, even if you just log on and get on with your wedding planning stuff or whatever else you need to do, that's fine. It's just a tick box but it'd be a big help if you could."

"No worries Bernadette, I'll make the time," I say, though I'm already terrified I'll forget.

"Good. Like I say, don't stress about it. I'll be watching the replay myself as and when I can fit it in," she says.

I've never known Bernadette to miss our quarterly meeting. Since we're kind of friends now, I dare to probe.

"Are you off anywhere nice?" I ask.

Bernadette smiles, running her fingers through her hair again. "Nowhere special."

As I get back to my desk, I see a card waiting for me, along with a smiling Bushra and Emma.

"Oh, you shouldn't have!" I exclaim as I pull open the envelope expecting to see a card and some gift vouchers, as is customary in this company when someone leaves.

Oh, they *didn't*.

There's a card, signed by Bushra, Emma and Bernadette and nothing else.

Emma quickly says: "As we're going to your wedding, we'll be giving you money then, so, erm, we can't gift twice."

"And I'm skint since I'm off to Ibiza next weekend," adds Bushra. "And it's not like you're really leaving. You're just moving offices."

"Of course," I say, more than a pinch disappointed. I mean, I'm *sort of* leaving.

WHEN I GET HOME, I eat my dinner (I always have to eat as soon as I get in, even though it's only 5.30pm) and have a cup of tea before heading upstairs to examine my lehenga. As I bust open the tight metal briefcase clasp to lift and reveal its contents, the outfit is just as beautiful as I saw it last night under the dining room lights. It's like uncovering treasure.

I climb into it, still wearing my black work leggings and pull it up over my hips. There's lots of material weighing heavily around my feet so I pull it up a little higher around the thinnest dip of my waist, the heavy stone and wire work now digging into my straining hands. That's random, it's still too long. How do brides wear these things? Do they fasten it to their chest? I guess I'll need extra high heels. I'm hoping M's family have bought some stilettos. I'll find out when they send over the rest of the wedding gifts. I grab the hook and eye fastener and join the two together, then pull up the side zip. When I let go the skirt immediately falls lower than my hips.

Hmmm.

I sit down on my sister's bed to stop it slipping further, then reach with an extended hand and pull the top out of the briefcase. The silk top, the colour of golden syrup goes perfectly with the deep, dark maroon skirt. It slips over my body with ease. It's good to know I haven't piled on any timber since my one and only fitting. It's almost too roomy, like a t-shirt. Still, that's what the corset-style back drawstring is for. I tug at each string as hard as I can and as far as it'll let me. Hmmm, still loose. I get up to examine myself from behind in the mirror, at which point the skirt starts sliding, slowly and heavily down my legs. Without grace, I climb out of it, leaving it like an elaborately decorated open sack on the floor. I notice that there's no room to make the top any tighter. All the loops of the corset back have met in the middle, yet the top is still hanging off me, shapeless. I've probably lost a couple of pounds with all the wedding stress though not quite *this* much.

Something's not right.

"JUST WHOSE MEASUREMENTS did you send exactly?" I shout down the phone, my voice trembling in anger. "In fact, did you even use anyone's measurements or just send us the outfit straight off the mannequin?"

"No sister, we wouldn't do that. We send it all to special tailor and they make the piece from scratch to your exact specifications. Did you get the free clutch bag?"

"Yes I did! Thank you for that," I say in response to the small bag they fashioned with the leftover material from my top. Nice touch but precisely bugger all use when my outfit's like a tent. "What are you gonna do about the lehenga being massive? I'm getting married in less than a fortnight!"

"Okay sister. Let me go check with my tailor to find out exactly what's happened. I'll call you back."

"When?"

"In an hour, sister. Bear with me."

An hour and a half later and nothing. I've been more than generous. Meanwhile mum is freaking out.

"I knew it be a bad idea to go all the way to London to get outfit. What you do now? What if you can't get it fixed in time?"

This isn't helping at all. I call the saree shop but, after six rings, there's no answer.

"I got idea! We buy the lehenga you liked from that other place? The red one? I'll pay for it. We don't even need to trouble your in-laws."

I ponder the idea. It was a beautiful lehenga but... no. "We'll have the same problem, mum. It'll still need to be re-sized and adjusted to fit and that will take however many weeks."

"Right. Call them again! They have to fix this." Mum means business.

Finally, an answer. "Okay sister, I've been speaking to my tailor and there might be some mix-up with the alterations.

So here's what we can do... my tailor comes in on Fridays. If you come in then, we can fit you in, take the measurements and get the lehenga adjusted for you to take away that day."

"So how long will it take?"

"You'd have to leave it with us for the whole afternoon. So, do you want to do that?"

I need to think. "Erm, could you give me an appointment slot or some kind of receipt or something I can show on the day?" I'm totally thinking on the spot here but, given that they made such a mess in the first place, I'm not sure if I trust them to even know who I am if I turn up on the day without any proof of purchase.

"No sister. No need. I'll be there to take care of you."

What choice do I really have? "Okay. See you Friday."

"I'VE BEEN THINKING about this all day," says mum.

Nothing good can come of mum thinking.

"Well... it be not possible for you to go all way to London with huge suitcase to get alteration."

"What else can I do? We don't know any tailors in Manchester!"

"You find someone. Otherwise you'll have to get train to London carrying that thing weighing more than you, then get tubes or taxi. Then do all of it, all the way back. You no be able to do that."

"I have to! I have no choice!"

"*Dooro!* It's a stupid idea! It was stupid in the first place for your in-laws making you choose from one shop in London. Most girls get to choose themselves from where they want. Hmmph!"

"How is this helping me now! You always have to find fault! Any excuse to say something bad about them!"

"What do you mean?" Mum looks at me, surprised.

"You have to be negative about everything! Moaning about how much money they'll give. Not wanting to send out the wedding invites until last week or something bad will happen. Leaving everything to me so you can say *I told you so*' or moan when it's not good enough. And you don't even help! You telling his family not to rush bringing the lehenga over! This is exactly why they needed to rush it over! Now I'm stuck!"

"I thought it would be fine. They took all your measures," says mum, her voice trailing off.

"*Eh-heh*. What's going on?" asks dad, coming in from the other room, newspaper still in hand.

"And you don't help! Why did you tell them they didn't have to hurry bringing the outfit over?" I shout.

Dad looks like a rabbit in headlights.

"I don't know what you say," his voice is quiet, like a chastised child.

"Don't be rude to your father! He was just saying what we are supposed to say. Anyway, you no worry, we make calls and find new tailor," mum comes to dad's defence for the first time ever.

"These stupid traditions! These formalities! Look where it's got me now! Useless! You're both useless! Saying we'll call tailors, who'll call tailors? It'll be all on me, like everything is. Because all these years here and you don't bother to learn English!"

"We never had the chance," mumbles mum.

"Yeah right! More like you couldn't be arsed. Figured your kids would sort everything out."

I rush out of the door leaving two parents, open mouthed, hurt, offended and unsure of a response.

Frustratingly, I know mum's right. It would be impossible for me to make the journey with that hefty suitcase. In my stressed out state, I don't even trust myself. I'd probably leave it on the train.

I need to cool my head. However, I look down and realise that I'm wearing my home uniform of a cheetah print salwar kameez. What was middle sis even thinking, buying this from the open cloth shop that was closing down in Bradford? And why oh why do they make the comfiest clothes in the most hideous designs? I can't go for a walk in this get up. I just can't.

I retreat to my car, where I realise that I am literally and metaphorically alone on this. I can't call Sophia as I'm still annoyed with her for crying off on my hen do and generally being flaky this whole year. I'm still annoyed with my sisters too as they've been no help throughout all this wedding planning. Julia and Reena are never available when I call them and, despite inviting them to my hen do, I'm just not close enough to Bushra and Emma. Plus, after getting Bushra involved in watch-gate, I don't think she's gonna be much help on this. She'll probably suggest some other kind of dodgy shortcut.

There's only one thing for it.

M: "Hey, you okay?"

Me: "Well, not really. I didn't want to burden you with this... but I've been having a bit of a nightmare."

M: "Oh no. Why?"

Me: "So it turns out that my lehenga is massive! I don't even think they customised anything. Or at least they didn't use my measurements. So I'm really stuck. I've called them and they say they can fix it but I'll have to go there with the eff-off suitcase, get measured again and... it's too short notice and..."

I break off as I can hear my voice trembling as tears come running down my face. This is a first, crying on the phone to my fiancé.

M: "Awww, don't cry. We'll figure something out. Even if that means me picking you and the lehenga up and driving to the shop to get it fixed."

Me: "No... I couldn't get you to come all the way from London just for this. It's on a workday, too."

M: "Don't worry about it. If there's no other way, that's what we'll do."

Me: "Well, let's see. I just need to think it through and -"

M: "What is it?"

I can't help but let out a pained cry. I'm embarrassed for myself.

Me: "It's just... it's the favours! I've not even had a chance to sort them."

I'm so thankful he can't see me ugly crying right now.

M: "Let me take care of them."

I pause mid wail.

Me: "How? I mean, do you know what to do?"

M (laughing): "I've seen a fair few wedding favours in my time so I'll figure something out. I can't promise Tiffany's boxes, that'll be pretty expensive for 600 people. Plus, what would I do with all the jewellery inside? Actually, don't answer that but yeah, leave it with me to work something out. I'll make it happen. And as for anything else, I've said this before, lean on me. I know traditionally the bride and groom's family do their own thing but sod all that. We're a team. Let's do our own thing together. You're not alone on this."

My cries of anguish suddenly turn to tears of relief and even a little joy. Things might be going pear shaped for my wedding but at least I've picked a good groom.

NAZAR, OR THE EVIL eye, is a big thing in our culture. It's one of the reasons we don't have long engagements. It's also why we don't brag about anything. Ever.

As humans we can't always be happy for each other unless we are completely happy ourselves. Yet we're never completely happy, are we? There's always something missing. Before I started the world of work, I thought £30,000 a year was a huge salary. That would surely mean I made it, right? Then I got promoted and got that salary earlier than I'd anticipated. Did I feel happy? Did I feel content? No, I moaned about having to pay a higher rate of tax and a bigger contribution towards my student loan debt. Beyond that, I didn't feel any different. Another girl, who started out as my friend, had a bee in her bonnet when she got wind of my quick promotion. That was the end of our friendship.

I couldn't be happy for Hassna. To me, she was having the bigger wedding, she had the more functional family. If I was to dig deep (heck, I don't even need to dig that much - these were surface feelings), maybe a part of me wanted something to go wrong. Her wedding plans, her fancy engagement party and her bigger diamond ring brought out the envy in me. Maybe I contributed to this thing we believe in. The nazar that threatens to destroy a girl's happiness.

I CAN'T SLEEP SO I decide to text Hassna, just to say sorry for what she's going through. I'm actually surprised I even have her number as I never ring it. We used to always play together growing up. We used to look forward to the annual sleepover at our respective houses, camping out on the floor or sleeping three in a bed. When did that change? When did we go from being innocent girls playing hide and seek to never speaking? I think I have a hunch. It's when we grew up and our inevitable comparisons and competition crept in.

It started with Rashda, who was often compared with middle sis. Hassna and I got off lightly in comparison, with the odd one-upmanship when it came to exam results and first jobs. However, the damage was done. The foundations for future dislike had already been laid. My sisters would love a good old gossip about her entire family. Mum would flit between telling them off and joining in with the bitching. It felt like harmless gossip. I mean, who doesn't do it?

I look at the time on my phone. It's 12.10am. I doubt Hassna will still be awake. I'm not even sure what to say.

What do you text somebody who's engagement has broken off?

Me: *Hey, mum told me what happened. I'm so sorry. I can't even begin to imagine how you're feeling. Sending hugs X*

My phone vibrates a minute later. I guess I'm not the only one who can't sleep.

Hassna: *Hey, thanks for reaching out and don't worry, nobody really knows what to say.*

Me: *I'm sure. I know we don't talk much, but I'm here if you do want to vent.*

Hassna: *Thank you. It's appreciated. Maybe we should stay in touch more. It's been ages. I hope your wedding planning is running a little smoother.*

Me: *You know, these things are always a bit frantic towards the end.*

Hassna: *Oh, why?*

I don't think I should get into this. Before I have a chance to think, my fingers are already typing.

Me: *Well, you know you have in your head this perfect wedding. Mine might be anything but.*

Hassna: *Why? What's happened?*

Me: *Sorry, I shouldn't bore you with it all... It's not about me I just called to check on you.*

Hassna: *No, try me. After all, it'd be nice to hear that someone else hasn't got it all figured out.*

It's funny, that's what I always thought about them. The perfect cousins. Maybe that's a false narrative that we were fed, on purpose or by mistake, by our respective parents. I tell Hassna about the lehenga. Maybe she could use the comic relief.

Hassna: *Well, I could help you with that. I can give you the number of a local tailor. She's an Indian lady that used to work for Panache.*

Panache? That's where I tried my other dream Lehenga the first time. If she used to work there she must be good.

Me: *Thanks so much. That would be amazing. And also, I'd love to see you on the 9th but I totally understand if... anyway, I'd love to see you at some point.*

Hassna: *I'll try and be there but I'll see how it goes. You know how these weddings are, there will be a million questions from everyone there and I'm not quite ready to talk about it.*

I don't blame her. I know *exactly* how these weddings are.

1st September

Not all heroes wear capes, some sew them

So it turns out that Mrs Singh is blooming amazing. As she examined the giant lehenga, which was drowning my frame, she used her hands to measure how much length would need to be taken off. Proper old school. She then double checked with her measuring tape. Less old school but, after the boob made by the shop it came from, I appreciated her being thorough.

"So, I will have to take this much off," she gestures with her tiny, bangle-laden hands spread apart the width of a ruler. I've never seen someone pair gold wedding bangles with a flowery shirt and beige tailored trousers but more power to her for blending east and west with such aplomb.

Part of me is crying inside at the prospect of cutting so much off my beloved outfit. Another part of me is wondering what she'll do with the leftover material and, more to the point, the leftover stonework. I reckon she'd get about 100 crystals from the bit she is taking off. However, I don't think I can really ask her to keep them for me in a doggy bag.

"So, is it quite straightforward, then?" I ask, rather optimistically getting into haggling mode. I've only got my teenage sister with me for support and I know she won't be any help. I must head into this battle alone.

Mrs Singh shakes her low ponytail slung head, letting some of her grey hair fall loose. "No, it's not straightforward. Not easy. Not at all. I've got to re-cut the blouse, and individually pick apart all the stones for the skirt. It will be very difficult. Take long time."

I hear my purse crying at the bottom of my bag. This wedding is already costing my side of the family upwards of £20,000, though to be fair mum and dad have absorbed the bulk of the cost thus far (they keep insisting we'll sort it later). Mrs Singh has got me over a barrel. She's doing this for me at such short notice, getting it ready literally the day before my nuptials. She can name her price and she knows it. I don't want to ask her but I have to.

"It will be £30," she says.

"O-kay, that's fine." I try to hide the sheer relief in my voice.

Honestly, she should charge more. Though obviously I won't tell her that.

"Will you definitely have it done in time?"

I'm a bit nervous about it not being ready until the day before. What if it still doesn't fit? Or it's too small? The thought is making me hot and I don't want to sweat through my lehenga blouse.

She looks straight at me and I can see the deep lines etched under her eyes, as though she's absorbed the stress of every flapping bride-to-be. As she rests one hand on my shoulder and raises the other, she says: "You see these fingers? They got permanent needle marks. I hand stitched stones on lehengas for 20 years for the top boutiques in

Manchester. I don't make mistakes. I don't make false promises. I don't let people down."

She can keep those damn crystals.

ON THE WAY HOME I GET predictably lost and my phone redirects me, at which point I realise how close Mrs Singh lives to Sophia. In a normal scenario I'd have dropped her a text before swinging by for a cup of tea and a chat. There is nothing normal about this, so off I head to my next appointment of the day.

"I STILL CAN'T BELIEVE you have to do this," says little sis, who has put her phone down in favour of a five-year-old copy of Asiana magazine that's on the coffee table at the beauticians.

"Well, I don't technically have to do it but you know, I don't want to be a hairy-Mary bride," I say.

"I get that but are you going to wax *everything*?" She winces.

"Well, I'm paying thirty quid for full body so it bloody well better be!"

"So gross."

WE DRIVE BACK IN SILENCE. I can tell by my little sister's face that she totally wants to know the intimate details of my wax but is also too repulsed to ask. It's kind of like watching the scary scene of a horror movie. You might cover your eyes but you peep between your fingers as you totally want to know what's going on.

Honestly though, I don't want to traumatise her or relive the ordeal. I'm not sure what was worse. The fact that she waxed bits that I didn't even think had any hair (I mean, why bother with the barely visible downy hair on my chest? I'm only going to get heat bumps there now), or that she found a (small, thank you very much) blackhead on my back which she decided not to ignore and instead pointed out to me by mumbling *"disgusting"* as she squeezed. Come on now, customer service much? Oh, and then there was the bit when she said *"ithni* hairy," while aggressively swiping the strip of cloth from my legs and examining the spoils. Of course I'd be *so* hairy. Why would I remove my hair ahead of getting it professionally removed?

Actually, I know the worst part. The claim of a full body wax was false advertising. She didn't go anywhere near the nether region, which means it's going to be yet another slap-dash swipe with a Bic razor. So really, it was 40 minutes wasted. The only reason I booked there in the first place is so they'd do a proper job. Had I known that the beautician thinks a Brazilian is someone's ethnicity, I wouldn't have bothered. I could have skipped the whole trauma, as neither my stomach or back is *that* hairy to warrant the unspeakable torture I was put through.

"So... did it hurt?" asks little sis, finally breaking the silence.

"Like a bitch," I say. "Like... a... bitch."

AS PREDICTED, THE BACK of my shoulders are covered in red raw bumps. Bloody beauticians. They're like dentists. Total butchers but you kind of need them.

As I change into my pyjamas I feel hot and uncomfortable so I swap my faux silk two piece for a cotton t-shirt and cropped trousers.

During my nightly check-in with M an interloper interrupts our text exchange.

It's Sophia. About time.

So there's no easy way of telling you this and I know it's going to upset you, but I won't be able to come to your mehendi party. Before you send an angry knee-jerk message I want you to know why. Since Imran's been born, I've felt different. Funny but not in a ha ha way. My head feels heavy, I'm not sleeping, and basically, I don't enjoy doing anything. It's something I've been trying to shake off and put down to a lack of sleep, but it's been like this for a year. The health visitor thinks I might have post-natal depression. I really, really didn't want to burden you with this so close to your wedding and I'm sorry I'm having to send this in a text message. It's not how I would have liked but I just want you to understand why I've been so crap at keeping in touch and doing things.

I respond straight away: *I'm so sorry to hear this. Why didn't you tell me?*

She replies: *Because you never asked.*

7th September
It's my mehendi and I'll cry if I want to

"I'm sorry I was so abrupt on the phone yesterday," I tell Kulsum.

It's my second apology of the day. My first was for being late to my appointment at her house. Though it wasn't my fault as driving through Longsight is a nightmare after 12.30pm, when the shops and takeaways start to wake up. She must be the only beautician that's a stickler for timekeeping. I only hope she practices what she preaches when she comes to mine on Sunday morning at 7.30am. "I'm just not used to beauticians calling me with suggestions in advance. Anytime they've mentioned something extra it's come at a cost."

"It's okay dear. I *under-shtand*. It's a stressful time but I'm not like the others. If I tell you one price, I stick to it. No surprises," says Kulsum, embalming my face with primer.

This time, I'm at my appointment alone. Mum and all my sisters are at home doing who knows what. I'm actually pretty pissed off about not having anyone come with me. What if Kulsum's makeup turns out to be terrible? What if she showed me her best work for the trial but her artistry on the day falls short? Just like when you're shopping for a saree, I firmly believe you need an ally when having your makeup applied. Instead, I'm alone, like I have been much of this whole journey of wedding planning. I feel vulnerable. My sisters said they better stay at home just in case mum has a panic attack. What's to panic about exactly? We told all our guests to meet us at the mehendi venue so she doesn't even have to fry a single samosa. I'll remember this when it's little sis' turn to get married.

A text from Bushra interrupts my bitter thoughts: *Hey, hope you have a fantastic day today and I can't wait to see you on Sunday. And I hope Kulsum's looking after you, she's a good egg.*

I don't bother replying. I guess I'm not... supposed to? Shouldn't I be busy on the day of my mehendi? Surely too busy to reply instantly to a text message? I ought to be fawned over by my nearest and dearest. I don't want to let Bushra know for a second that I'm not busy at all and instead I'm feeling a bit sorry for myself and I can't stop looking at my phone. Sophia's message still weighs heavy on my mind. I feel bad that she couldn't confide in me sooner. I feel upset that she couldn't tell me how she was feeling and left it so late. More than anything, I'm just lost for words. I don't know what to do. I don't know what to say.

"What do you think?" Kulsum finally lets me look in her dressing table mirror.

She's created a golden-yellow look to match my buttery golden saree. The lashes are long and voluptuous. My cheeks are rosy and my face has a glow that I could never create myself. Yet something seems... off. I don't know what it is. This is where I need a second opinion. What is the point of coming from a family of girls if not a single sister bothers to come with me on this appointment? Bloody half-arsed the lot of them.

"What is it, dear? What are you thinking?" Kulsum reads my mind. "Is it the blush? The foundation? Do you want to be more *V-hite*?"

"No, I'm happy with my colour as it is," I say for the first time ever. "It's just..."

"Is it the lips?" asks Kulsum, searching for an answer.

"Oh yes, that's it! The lips. They look a bit too... neon?"

Kulsum looks at me blankly. I think that word isn't in her vocabulary yet.

"Maybe make the lips a bit darker," is my second attempt at explaining.

I'm not sure what it is with me lately but my words are all over the place.

After fixing my lips, Kulsum teases my hair into a tight bun, leaving two inches of the front section for a side parting. This is just the beginning of her hair styling. She then attaches a ridiculously long over the top fake plait to the bun. It has silver tassels on the end and grazes the bottom of my bum. Nobody in the history of mankind would ever believe that it's my real hair but I don't care. That's not what today is about. Today is about being extra. Today is about being dramatic. Long lashes that nobody would believe are real. Hair so long that nobody would question its inauthenticity. Today is about being a princess for the first time in my 27 years of life.

I COME HOME TO A SCENE that's like something out of a movie. Lots of people hurrying around, not all of whom are direct members of my family. Unfortunately, auntie Jusna's here, though I don't see any of my cousins. While I usually don't relish seeing them on such occasions as they always have better outfits, or better hair and makeup, their absence does make me nervous. Given that we've booked the entire floor of the venue, I'm really hoping the guests fill the seats. Otherwise it could get very awkward.

"Oh good, you're back. Do you want me to help you with your saree?" asks big sis, impressively clad in a rich buttery yellow saree with a pink border. She adhered to the dress code perfectly.

As I thank her for her offer and take off my hoodie (I must've looked a right sight sat in traffic on the way home, with a fully made up face and mermaid length hair, teamed with a grey zipped top), middle sis comes out of the kitchen, balancing a silver tray on her now huge belly. More to the point, she is wearing the exact same saree as big sis.

Hold on a second.

As I follow her into the living room the scene is even more frantic, with all three of my sisters, dressed identically, fussing about the various silver trays, arranging an array of treats from ornately carved watermelon, to mountains of Quality Street chocolate.

"Did you coordinate for me?" I ask in shock.

"Yes. Surprise!" says little sis, the only one of my three sisters who appears to have had time to brush her hair.

Both my older sisters look flustered to the extreme. Redfaced, hair scraped back with kirby grips, the look of women on a mission. That's why they didn't come with me to get my makeup done. They've been slogging away, working tirelessly to make all this happen. Even little sis, who is slightly more groomed, is focusing her attention on adding the last few Ferrero Rocher chocolates to a bouquet shaped dome. And there was me bitching about them all this time.

I see a saucer of samosas come into my line of vision, before seeing the person it's attached to. My mum, of course.

"See... I told you everything come together in the end. You never believe," she says, brandishing a piping hot samosa, ready dipped in ketchup, just how I like it.

"It's just you never mentioned anything when I asked. I thought you wouldn't make any taals. There was no plan."

"Who say there no plan? Just because we no on Google all day no mean we no have plan. Mum's always know what to do."

"Thanks mum," I say. For everything, I think to myself. Just as I wonder why I don't just say this to her, mum's swept away on another job and the moment's gone.

THANKFULLY, PEOPLE are arriving. Uncle Tariq, who drove down today, has finally arrived and is sat with auntie Rukhsana and my cousin Shuhel, who I haven't seen in years. I was hoping Naila might make it but then that's wishful thinking.

I also wish Sophia was here but I'm not expecting her tonight or on Sunday. She's made it pretty clear that she needs her space. After the wedding malarkey is over, I'll reach out and I hope she'll reply.

I did invite Reena and Julia but neither could make it and both grumbled about it being on a Friday night and how they live too far away to come down on the Friday and the Sunday. I'm not too perturbed by their absence though as they'd probably feel like fish out of water due to our un-apologetic Bengali-ness.

However, one thing I'm not sorry for on this occasion is one of the real advantages of Bengali families - they're usually really big. So my worry about the event looking decidedly dead is unfounded. With the arrival of a few more cousins who are so distant they're barely cousins, some family friends, plus another pretend auntie that thankfully isn't auntie Fatima, we have ourselves a part-ey.

I'm glad to see that almost everyone adhered to the butter yellow I added at the last minute on the wedding invites. I didn't want to be a total bridezilla so I added a bit at the end of the dress code, saying '...*or whatever you're comfortable with.*' I decided to exclude the further caveat of *'however, if you decide that you're not comfortable with yellow, you won't make the cut for the wedding album.'* I like to think that goes without saying.

I FEEL LIKE A QUEEN at a banquet. I was so worried that there wouldn't be any taals at my mehendi, however, every cohort of guests came with an offering.

There's a giant fruit basket (a favourite at Bengali affairs), some confectionary based silver trays and a rather impressive plate featuring a horse and carriage made purely out of sugar cubes. I will NOT be eating that, however I will likely be posting about it on social media. It is *very* photogenic.

The gifting won't stop here though, as someone from M's family will be dropping off a mehendi saree, bangles and jewellery for me to change into.

"Okay, could you rest your hand on your necklace, like so?" My photographer Rashid seems like he is living out his own Cinderella moment through me, as he gestures animatedly with his hands, stroking it across his collar rather wantonly. I can't say I'm hating it. As I preen and pose, recline on the chaise lounge, hold out my bangles, look down to highlight my false lashes and follow every other direction of this very over-the-top photographer, I'm coming into my own. Though I'm not sure who this person is. I'm doing and being all the things I derided. Yet, for this one moment in my life, I'm milking the spotlight for all it's worth. After all, this is the best I've ever looked, or likely ever will. Yes, a small part of me feels like a knob but a much bigger part is loving every second.

Meanwhile, I'm getting dirty looks from all the prim aunties, both real and fake, who are already offended by the Bhahgra tunes blasting from the speakers. Big sis mentioned that she will go and speak to the waiters to see if someone can put on some more melodious mehendi appropriate Bollywood music. Suddenly I remember, Sophia told me that whenever I get married, she wants to be in charge of the music at my mehendi, no questions asked. I guess I didn't ask enough questions, or any, which is why she's not here now. I feel a pang of pain in my stomach.

As each family takes turns to join me on stage and feed me fruit, we exchange the usual niceties.

"Oh, I didn't see you earlier," I tell Rashda, who is resplendent in her lemon sherbet coloured saree. Only she could pull off such a pop of colour. Anyone else would look like a giant sweet.

"I just arrived. I drove myself and my three kids. At least that way I didn't get to hear more whingeing about un-marriageable daughters all the way here."

Gosh, she really is catty these days. It's fantastic.

"I'm guessing you heard about Hassna," she adds.

"Yeah, I heard. It's such a shame," I say, though I don't want to really get into it. My mehendi stage isn't the place for such talk. There's a photographer at large and any face I pull that isn't a smile pretty much falls into resting bitch territory.

"So, do you have a new car?" I ask, in a desperate attempt to switch gears. Though this disguises my true question, as I don't remember her old car, or indeed her ever driving at all.

"It's my new, first and only car. I passed my driving test last month," Rashda replies. "I decided I need the independence. Remember to hold onto yours, too. Take it from someone who found out the hard way."

While I ponder this wisdom, auntie Rukhsana sits her warm self next to me. She's gone for a more rustic golden, which narrowly fits the brief. "Your mum will lose a daughter but I'll gain one as you'll be coming near me," she says.

"Well, she's not really losing me," I say, her comment harder to swallow than the big cut of gulab jamun she just force-fed me. "I'll only be in London."

"I know dear but she wanted you here. She never wanted you to leave Manchester," auntie Rukhsana adds.

That pain in my stomach returns, quicker and sharper this time. It takes longer to pass.

"Look, that must be for you," auntie Rukhsana gestures towards the hampers and cellophane-wrapper baskets being brought in by my sisters and, to my surprise, M's sister-in-law. I had no idea she was coming. We'd sent an obligatory card to M's family (an absurd tradition in itself, swapping invites for your own wedding, but that's a rant for another day) but I didn't expect anyone to actually attend. This is my day, for my family.

More guests come for the feeding-me frenzy. Meanwhile, M's sister-in-law, who has brought along her kids for company, watches on.

"I better quickly put on the saree they bought," I tell middle sis when she sits on stage.

"Don't worry, you can put it on in a bit. What you're wearing is so nice, you might as well get some more shots in it," she replies.

More families join me on stage. Then more. At this point I'm full to bursting with fruit and syrupy sweets. I don't know how I'll sleep tonight with all this sugar running through my system.

Auntie Jusna comes next to me and, for the first time in recent living memory, acknowledges me directly.

"Is that the sister-in-law?" she asks, making it rather obvious who she's talking about as she points in her direction.

"Yes, it is."

"And where she live?" she asks.

"London."

"Ah, okay. Near your husband?"

"No," I reply, hoping that my curt responses will shut down the conversation.

"So what does your husband do?"

"He um... works in banking."

"Like cashier?"

"No. More like finance."

"Accountant?"

"No." There is literally no point asking, clearly she hasn't a clue what I'm talking about. Plus, this really is not the forum for 20 questions.

"Have you seen your mehendi saree from your in-laws?"

"No, not yet." I'm internally begging her to get the hint that her time on the stage is up.

"Oh, but you should!" she says, reminding me yet again that nosey aunties refuse to take hints. "Has your *maa* not told you to change? How will that look? If you spend most the mehendi in the outfit you bought and all the photos are of you in that, they'll think you no like what they've given!"

Massive stirrer though she is, auntie Jusna annoyingly makes a really good point.

It's time for yet another immediate family shot. With both my older sisters sat either side of me and mum on the next chair, I'll bring up this saree situation.

"Should I change into the saree they've given now?"

"Let's take some more photos first. Since we are all matchy-matchy," says big sis.

More photos, to the point that I'm getting camera shy and we haven't even started the mehendi application yet.

My mehendi artist, aptly named Henna, is waiting patiently on a table with my distant cousins from Ashton. Poor girl, she looks bored to death.

Finally, I'm summoned off the stage to eat. "Shall I change before dinner?" I ask mum.

"Don't worry, there's time," she replies.

I do not understand what the hold up is. Surely I should be decked out in what they've gifted for most of the evening, right?

I bring this up one more time whilst I'm sat on the table surrounded by my siblings. I'm beginning to sound desperate now.

"Shall I go and say hello to his sister-in-law?" I ask anyone who will listen.

"It's okay, lady," says big sis. "We're going to bring her over. Mum's already said hello. You shouldn't be seen to be walking freely."

Hearing that out loud sounds so bizarre.

"Maybe you should go over now then so it doesn't look rude. They're on the table by themselves," I say.

"Bloody hell, you really are keen not to put a foot wrong," laughs middle sis. "Don't worry. This isn't our first wedding rodeo."

As I'm carefully tucking into my chicken tikka and rice, desperately trying to avoid spillage on my beautiful saree, my sisters finally go over, as promised, to M's sister-in-law. However, auntie Jusna beats them to it.

"See! I knew they should've gone over," I hiss to mum. "Who knows what that stirring old bat is saying?"

"*Dooro!* You can't say that!" says mum. "Though I wondering what she say, too," she unhelpfully adds.

Bloody typical.

After what seems like an eternity, my older siblings manage to prize M's big sister-in-law away from the clutches of my pot-stirring nosey auntie, to bring her over to our table.

"You look beautiful!" she says. "I love that saree. Such a lovely yellow! I'm worried now, I don't think we've got you anything half as nice." She smiles.

"Oh, I'm sure it's lovely," I say, as it only seems polite.

"On that note, shall we get you changed?" middle sis asks.

Finally.

Big sis uses an excuse that she can't help as she's feeding her kids but as middle sis is blessed with fussy eaters that turn their nose up at curry, she is free to help me change.

I feel a huge sense of déjà vu as I head behind the same screen we used when doing a Superman-style change at my engagement party.

"What was auntie Jusna talking to her about?" I ask middle sis.

"I'm not sure really. Just niceties, I suppose," she replies as she unfolds the emerald green saree they gifted me.

My sister-in-law-to-be was right, my yellow saree of choice is a lot prettier.

"It's never just niceties with her. She's always got something to say. I told you to go over sooner. Instead you gave her a chance to get in with her shit-stirring. It's like I have to organise everything around here."

Middle sis says nothing as she gathers the saree into uneven pleats.

"You're doing them all wrong! Where's mum? She'd be better at this!"

"Right! Stop your whingeing!" Middle sis aggressively shoves the pleats down my petticoat. "Mum's finally getting to sit down after being on her feet cooking and making taals all day. She's been running around like mad for you! We've all been working like dogs! Do you think this is what I want to be doing at seven months pregnant? I didn't have any of this stuff when I got married. Did you hear me complain? No, so just shut up and be grateful!"

I'm stunned into silence. I've been the one shouting all this time, for so many months, but I really didn't expect anyone to answer me back.

Middle sis returns to silence as she drapes the end of the saree over my shoulder. Up close, I see that she has dark circles under her eyes and only a smidge of concealer to cover it. She didn't have time to get ready. It looks like she didn't have much time to even look after herself. All this for ungrateful me.

Now I'm dressed in the gifted saree, I take to the stage once more, for more photos, more feeding and for the mehendi artist, who's been sat patiently for nearly two hours, to finally have her star turn.

As Henna starts applying my henna (ha ha indeed), my sister-in-law joins me on stage.

"I'm so looking forward to having you as part of our family," she says, putting her arm around my shoulders to give me a squeeze. Her cute kids look adorable in their yellow outfits. Their efforts to coordinate, along with the burnt orange saree worn by their mum, doesn't go unnoticed.

Uncle Tariq, the unofficial stage director, signifies to everyone that there needs to be a break from any more group photos while my mehendi is applied.

After expressing dismay at my un-manicured nails (I forgot and nobody reminded me), Henna tentatively draws dots, swirls and flowers with precision. She's well worth the £50 investment, even if she didn't ask me once what kind of design I'd like or show me some ideas. Beggars, choosers and all that.

"That's really nice," I say, in a somewhat desperate attempt to make small talk and clear the thoughts of what a nightmare I've been these past few months from my head. "Have you been doing mehendi art for long?"

"On and off for seven years," Henna replies, without raising her gaze from my hands. "I mostly do this on weekends in the summer, when I'm not working at the cash-and-carry."

Well a girl's got to eat.

"Which cash-and-carry do you work at?" I ask.

"Halal Groceries."

"I shop there. I've never seen you before."

"Mm-hmm," she replies, obviously not caring less for my talking shop.

Henna then moves onto my feet, making me grateful for my leg wax as she begins spiralling with the mehendi cone up my calf. Still no chat from her end. Things go on like this for about an hour, which unfortunately gives me plenty of time to be alone with my thoughts and look around.

Mum looks like she's haranguing middle sis, getting her to pull her saree further over her protruding belly. In between poking and prodding to the point of nearly sending my sister into early labour, mum mops her brow with a napkin. She looks hot and bothered in her yellow cheetah print shawl (I wish she'd made a better sartorial choice). As she adjusts her scarf, several grey hairs escape. Mum is normally on top of her personal grooming, finding time to dye her hair a very inauthentic shade of black, in between all the chores she does like cooking for us, cleaning the house from top to bottom and worrying about my wedding. I guess she's not had time to do it recently.

Big sis is force-feeding gulab jamun dessert to my nephew, though he clearly seems more interested in the vanilla ice cream accompaniment. Dad, who's largely been missing in action the last few months, seems to be listening intently to his brother-in-law, while his sister, Auntie Jusna, seems to be wading in all hands flailing. I'd love to be a fly on the wall for *that* conversation. Little sis, meanwhile, is on her phone.

It seems like nothing has changed, yet everything is changing. Life goes on for them and it moves on for me.

"There. All done," says Henna triumphantly.

"So how long do I have to keep this on for?" It's already gone 10pm.

"Overnight."

"Oh. So how will I sleep?"

"You tie your hands and feet in plastic bags," she says, like it's nothing at all.

Suddenly things seem to come together like clockwork. I think uncle Tariq bursting into action, rather than relying on the photographer who is desperate to get the right shot no matter how many takes it requires, has made things move along. Just as Henna exits the stage, a personalised cream cake, gifted from M and his family, is placed before me.

There is a change in the music from the upbeat dance-y happy mehendi tunes, to a more emotional song. It's one I've heard at many mehendis gone by. While I don't understand much Hindi, I know the basic premise of this song is a girl sitting at her mehendi while her mum cries at the thought of an empty nest.

Mum and dad, rightly so, are the first to sit next to me. There is no sea of siblings this time. It's just me and them.

Mum and dad place their hands gently on mine as we cut the cake together. They each take turns to feed me a slice. The cream is thick and sickly sweet, the familiar flavour of an Asian shop's celebration cake. Out of nowhere, I get a kiss on my forehead from mum, who then abruptly leaves the stage. She is in tears. Not pretty tears. The hysterical cry that I do. Maybe life won't go on for her as I'm assuming. She is losing me just as much as I'm losing her.

I watch on as she leaves the stage and is comforted by middle sis, who looks at me through tears of her own. Even my teenage sister, who I'm convinced hates me on the down low, is no longer looking at her phone and is joining the chorus of tears. I thought she'd be happy to have the room to herself.

Everyone suddenly swarms around the stage to take pictures. When did this happen? I didn't even notice while I was having that last moment with my parents. Then I look for dad. He's no longer next to me. Where is he? I look beyond the crowd, squinting my eyes. He's sat right at the back, all by himself, rubbing his eyes with one of the rough paper napkins. It'll scratch his eyes out. They're for mopping up food, not tears. My hands start to tremble, as the song reaches its high-pitched chorus. I feel my heartbeat quicken, while my lovely false eyelashes seem to take on a personality of their own and I'm blinking uncontrollably. Oh no, oh no, oh no. I'm going to cry. I can feel it... but I can't! My makeup!

"Oh, stop pretending you!" says big sis, no-nonsense as ever as she sidles up next to me. "You don't want to ruin your makeup now. In front of all these people. You'll look terrible."

Granted, she's a blunt bugger but, right now, I wouldn't have her any other way. Her harsh nature is just what's needed to stop tears from running down my cheeks.

IT'S GONE PAST 1AM. Little sis is doing her baby rhino wheezy snore but I'm wide awake. It's been quite a night. It's the first time I've really seen my dad cry. It's the first time, as an adult, that my mum has had to help me go for a wee as I can't pull down my own underwear with my henna-decorated hands. Another grown-up first, mum undoing my fake plait and taking the grips out of my bun while middle sis wipes off my makeup. Perhaps the most poignant thing of all, mum feeding me water before bed, for the first time since I was a little girl. She even fed me rice and curry by hand, as she knew I was too nervous to eat properly at the venue.

As I lie in bed, a Tesco carrier bag on each limb and dried henna crumbs all over the bed sheet, I think to myself... there has to be a better system than this.

8th September
Oh, the irony

My sisters and nieces are all gathered round the table, making little bridesmaid bouquets by hand. Middle sis might be tired and hormonal but she is still the creative head of the family. She bought bunches of flowers from the petrol station en route to our house yesterday. I was too busy swishing around my fake plait to notice them sitting in buckets of water in the bathroom. As she instructs her team to wrap twine around the small, delicate bunches, before securing with thin, green masking tape, she spots me leaving with my bag.

"Are you going to the tailors to pick up your lehenga? I'll come with you, too. You know, just in case she tries to pull a fast one or has made a cock up. You might need some back-up."

I'm not sure how much back up she can offer in her current condition but I take her along for the ride nonetheless.

We drive in silence, both acutely aware of the words said the night before.

Finally, I can't take the awkwardness. "Sorry for being a cow yesterday."

"It's okay," she replies. "Sorry if I haven't been able to help that much."

More silence.

"Did you really mean what you said about your wedding?"

Middle sis stops stroking her belly. "About it being shit? Not really. I think I moaned at the time but I could have got married in a castle and I still would have found something to whinge about. That's what us brides do. We want it to be perfect but perfect doesn't exist."

I know exactly what she means. "I think for me I just wanted some control. My life is going to change beyond all control very soon."

"I was the same," says middle sis. "But, like you, I took it out on the wrong people. I gave mum so much grief. Which is sad really, I was the hardest on the person that loved me the most."

Suddenly, the tears I stopped in their tracks from last night pour out with a vengeance. I'm talking buckets. It ain't pretty and it certainly ain't safe. I pull over off the main road onto a side street.

"Bloody hell. Are you okay? You almost gave me a heart attack," says middle sis catching her breath.

"I'm fine," I reply between ugly sobs. "I just... I just... need a... m-minute."

We sit in silence again before I compose myself enough to drive on.

MRS SINGH KEEPS LOOKING at my puffy face. I try not to notice and instead focus on the fitting.

"Shall we take a bit more in here? Is it possible?" I ask, trying to act as though I wasn't crying hysterically just 15 minutes earlier.

"Yeah, maybe we could cinch the waist a bit," middle sis basically repeats what I said in a different way.

Mrs Singh nods and expertly unpicks her stitching and pulls the top over my head to take to her sewing machine, which is one of those old fashioned metal ones that are stuck to the table. The kind I've seen on documentaries about factory workers. The machine does a little hum as she presses the pedal with her dainty foot. She does some funny over lock thing to release the outfit and holds it up to me.

"There. Try now."

And to think those stupid boutiques say they need 6-8 weeks for stitching.

I try the lehenga on again. I notice that the skirt is a bit short when I wear my heels. You can see my gold sandals when I stand. I'm sure it's supposed to be floor skimming. However, while it's easy to take material away, Mrs Singh can't well add to something she's over trimmed. Even she's not *that* good. Anyway, at this late stage, and in the grand scheme of things, it doesn't matter. So I'll be an imperfect bride. I'm an imperfect girl.

I feel bad giving her just £30 for literally saving my wedding day, however it seems patronising offering her a tip. Instead I say goodbye with a promise of shouting about her handiwork all over social media, to all of my 62 followers. Mrs Singh smiles like a woman who has no idea what I'm talking about. I wish I'd brought one of middle sis' bunches of carnations as a thank you.

"Are you okay?" Mrs Singh asks a question that I suspect has been on her mind since I arrived at her door with an ugly, cried-out face.

"I am... it's just..." I don't know what to say.

Mrs Singh holds my hand and squeezes tight. Her hands feel both delicate and rough, a testament to her decades of hard work making dreams happen. "I know," she says. "It's not easy. Leaving home to get married is both the most exciting thing you'll ever do and the hardest."

With that, the waterworks return thick and fast.

"I know you want to get back to your flower wiring duties," I say to middle sis as we step into the car. "But do you mind if we have one stop off."

"What? A samosa chaat from Anand's for old times' sake?"

"Well no... but okay. Let's make that two stop offs."

I drive towards Sophia's house which is just minutes from Mrs Singh. I'm not exactly sure what I'm doing. I could knock on but I'm not convinced she'd answer. I don't think I could cope with the rejection.

Instead I decide to leave her a note. I find a pen in the bottom of my bag, but no paper. I open the glove box to find a handful of spare wedding invites we stored there when we were dishing them out, in fear that we might miss someone out on our drive-by.

I know she won't come but I can't leave things as they are. There's precious little space to write anything, so I have to put my PR hat on to think of something short and sweet. However, tapping my pen on my steering wheel, I draw a blank.

"I don't wanna rush you but, I'm terrified to think what they're doing with the bouquets at home," says middle sis.

Forget PR, I just write from the heart in a spare corner of the card: *Sorry I wasn't there for you like you had been for me.*

I stuff it through her letterbox and scuttle back to my car before heading off to the next important job, getting a round of samosa chaat for everyone at home.

SINCE GETTING BACK, I haven't been able to stop crying.

It's so ironic. I couldn't wait to get married and leave home. I was desperate to get out of this shared room. Now I'm actually getting married, I can't stop crying. Why was I in such a rush to leave home? Why was I so desperate to leave the only family I've ever known? Was it really so bad?

I know it's the next stage in your life to get married but now it's happening, now reality has dawned on me... I just want some more time at home. The house is warm with nephews and nieces playing downstairs in between making flowers and memories. Dad has resumed his casual smoking habit, laughing with uncle Tariq, who's come over this afternoon from the B&B where they stayed last night. Mum is cooking with auntie Rukhsana while my sisters are applying face masks. The home I so often thought was dysfunctional is actually... happy and content, the two things I never was during my time here.

I was such a shit these last few months. I gave everybody grief. They all took it, too. Nobody told me to shut the hell up. Well, apart from middle sis, and I think I deserved it at that point. Now I'm leaving this familiar place, where everyone knows my whims and moods.

"He's a nice boy," big sis says upon finding me in tears upstairs. "His family seem nice and it's not like he's a stranger. You know him, you want to marry him, and so you should be happy. This should be the happiest day of your life."

She hugs me before heading downstairs.

I am happy but I think I'm allowed to be happy *and* sad today. Yes, I'm happy that I'm marrying M. I couldn't be with anyone else. I'm not sad for going with M and leaving for London, I think that will be exciting. I'm sad for the happy home I'm leaving. The happy home that I took for granted because it was just... there. Life will go on. Obviously I'll visit. Mum will make her samosas. Yet it won't be the same. It won't be my single bed anymore. I won't make that same commute to work. I know I'm lucky, I've been told enough times. I know I've landed on my feet in so many ways. Yet I still feel like I'm stepping into the unknown. Yes, at times life here was mundane but it was *my* mundane. Mine. Not anymore.

In the midst of feeling all melancholy, I suddenly remember... I haven't watched that stupid webinar.

As I've got my room to myself for probably the last time in my life, I fire up my laptop, log onto the company Intranet and play the damn thing whilst continuing to sulk. Maybe this will be a welcome distraction from my mixed feelings of sorrow and joy.

Ten minutes in, it turns out it's not. It's just some cock-and-bull HR jargon about wellness in the workplace and something else airy fairy that hasn't quite captured my full attention.

"We're going to play catch in the garden. Do you want to come?" asks my adorable seven-year-old niece. "Mum said it might make you stop crying."

"Maybe in a minute, cutie," I reply. "I've just got to do some work."

"Is that why you're crying? Because you've got to work while we're all having fun?"

Bless her. "Yeah. I feel a bit left out."

"It's okay auntie," she says, sitting next to me on my bed. "I sometimes cry too. I cried the other day because mummy's got a baby in her tummy and I think I won't be her favourite girl anymore. Things might not be nice at home."

"Oh! Come here," I pull her in for a squeeze whilst also wondering if she'd done an unwitting gender reveal. "Things will still be nice. They'll just be different. Just think, you're not losing your mummy, you're gaining a new little friend. That's the best thing in the world. Right, I think I've done enough work, I'll come and play."

Bernadette did say it's more of a tick box exercise, so that's my box ticked. Just as I'm about to shut the laptop down, the boring webinar presenter shares a golden nugget: "Remember, it's all about mindset. If you think someone is out to get you, they will. Whether you think you can do something, or you think you can't, you're right either way. Essentially, how you perceive a situation can directly affect the outcome. If you see everything through negative eyes, things will seem that way. If you adjust that lens accordingly, you can make things more positive."

That turned out to be way more profound than I'd expected. *If you think someone is out to get you, they will.* The words echo over and over in my head. I could've done with hearing this back in February as that's pretty much the summation of my mind-set for the last nine months. I thought Bushra was jealous and purposely suggested a dodgy watch shop. I thought my sisters couldn't be bothered to help. I thought Julia was being a flake. I thought Sophia had ditched me for mum life. As for my own mum, my poor mum, she bore the brunt of it all. I'd created a negative narrative where it was all about me. I assumed the worst when everyone was doing their best. Except for the burly beautician, she was horrible.

When I head downstairs, mum's the first to greet me with the cordless in hand. "It's your mother-in-law," she whispers loudly, covering her hand with the speaker.

She still doesn't know how to mute the call.

"I know you busy and it be your last day home. How you feel?" asks my almost mother-in-law.

"I'm okay. A little nervous," I say, though regret mentioning the last bit.

"I understand but don't be. There's no need for nervous. I've said same to your mum, you'll soon know how we are, once you join our family. So I'll see you tomorrow?"

I guess that's her way of reassuring me. I appreciate the call, even if I still have a healthy amount of fear when it comes to my mother-in-law.

AS I STEP INTO BED for my last night as a single lady, I see a message from M:

Hey, you okay? I hope you're enjoying your last day at home. I've been busy sorting the wedding favours, which we'll distribute in the morning. Mum, my sister-in-law and sister have decorated the house with fresh flowers. I think you'll like it. I can't wait for tomorrow. I know it might be a mixed blessing for you leaving your parents' house but remember, you're not losing a family, you're gaining one.

I reply with my goodbye and try my best to get some sleep. It'll be an early start tomorrow with Kulsum arriving at 7.30am. Just as I turn over, I feel a funny groan in my stomach. The spicy sour chaat is repeating on me and... oh no.

Just as I think I've got away with it, little sis lifts her head up from her bed.

"Ewww, have you farted?" she asks.

I don't reply, I'm too busy pissing myself laughing under my duvet, hoping she doesn't notice my shoulders shaking with hysterics.

"God!" she huffs as she turns over to face the wall, away from me.

She'll miss me when I'm gone.

9th September

So this is it...

They're rolling out extra tables. How many people are here exactly?

In the sea of guests, I try to spot any familiar faces. It's like a Bengali Where's Wally.

"Have you eaten enough?" asks my big sis.

I can't very well say no as they're already clearing up the plates around me. We're at the final frontier now, where I'll be making my way down the makeshift wedding aisle, flanked by my cute honorary bridesmaids and their home-made bouquets. To give myself a sugar hit, I pull open one of the drawstring favour bags I was so stressed about, and un-wrap a peanut brittle. Bad choice, as I feel the caramel melding itself to my teeth. There's one chocolate left in the bag so I fold it into the band of my bouquet of roses, just in case I get hungry later.

"I'm good," I say to big sis between awkward, un-ladylike crunches of peanut. "I need a wee, though."

"Erm... okay, let's see how we'll do this," says big sis, acutely aware that my wedding lehenga does not come with a pee hole.

Mum's chatting with my mother-in-law (I can legitimately call her that now as I've just said I do to the Imam officiating our wedding). They seem to be smiling, almost giggling even. That makes me happy.

It dawns on big sis that she's going to have to take one for the team. "Come on then lady, let's do this."

There's something strangely intimate, humorous and undignified about squatting over a toilet as your sister holds onto the hem of your lehenga for dear life to avoid any overspill. We both laugh, mainly to drown out the trickling sound.

"It's nice to see you laughing, lady. You've been a bit of a miserable so-and-so of late," she says.

"I know. I didn't mean to be. I'm sorry if I've been giving you grief."

I don't think I've ever apologised so much in my life.

"So how am I going to... wipe?"

"Gosh lady, I don't know. I wore a saree at my wedding, this is all a bit new to me."

"Just do a jiggle dance to get rid of any droplets!" shouts a more experienced voice from outside the cubicle.

"Erm... thank you!" big sis shouts back, before whispering to me: "Who was that?"

"Well, there's 600 people here so I have no idea whatsoever," I reply.

Peeing in pairs, sleeping in carrier bags... it's been a week of firsts, and lasts. We both know it as between the giggles big sis sheds a tear.

"Right, are you ready?" she asks, dabbing at her eyes with a square of papery toilet tissue.

"Yes."

STANDING BETWEEN THE two pillars of the pretend altar, I can get a good look at everyone attending. They've all stood to attention. We've totally copied this from the church weddings we've seen in movies.

"Right, don't walk too quickly!" whispers big sis. "And don't stare at him as you're walking," she says, gesturing with her jewel tikka adorned head to the stage where M is stood, waiting like a prince for his princess (or at least that's what I'm envisioning. I can't blooming well tell as I'm now nervously looking down).

As we take slow and steady steps, with some false starts as I bump into the kids in front of me who are taking the instructions to walk slow to a whole new level, my eyes dart furtively from side to side at our guests. All whilst trying to remain coy and covert. It's not easy being a nosey bride.

To my surprise, Naila's here. I wish she'd have come over to say hello. She wasn't at the mehendi, so did she drive up by herself just for my wedding? She's stood next to uncle Tariq and auntie Rukhsana. I don't see her hubby there. Correction - I don't see a white man next to her so assume he's not here. That's okay. Baby steps.

Word passes that I must stop walking. I think they're taking more photos of us standing in procession.

"He's not ready yet," whispers middle sis, assumingly referring to M. I'm not sure what he has to get ready for. He's not walking anywhere. Still, at least this gives me more time to be nosey out of the corner of my eye.

"You look gorgeous!" shouts Fiona, with an enthusiastic thumbs up. It's the best kind of heckling.

I see Julia, with whom I'm guessing is Miles by her side. I raise my eyes for a better look and Julia smiles at me, nodding to confirm my assumption. It's like we're telepathic or something.

"Okay, come forward, very slowly," Rashid instructs us.

I take his advice to the extreme, taking such ridiculously slow steps that I might as well be going backwards.

Then I spot Sophia. She's come with her hubby Adnan, who's cradling baby Imran, though he's grown so much since I've seen him that he now looks more like a toddler. Sophia, clad in a simple navy blue salwar kameez devoid of any decoration, smiles widely at me as our eyes meet. We're metres apart so can't speak, but in the moment it seems like we both have an understanding - that there's much to discuss.

I'm instructed to take a right, along with my entourage, to climb the four steps onto the stage. I'm inching closer. I'm now glad my skirt is a little shorter than it should be. If it flowed past my feet, I'd probably trip on my heels as I climb the stairs. Instead, I can move more elegantly than I ever have before.

And then, for a moment, I look up. M is looking at me, trying to hide his smile. That's when I realise, none of this really matters. The taals. The bloated guest list. The chocolate fountain that never was. The sodding favour bags. The lehenga. Okay, maybe the lehenga matters. But definitely not the favour bags.

Because at the end of the day there he is. And here I am.

Books by Halima Khatun – have you read them all?

The Secret Diary of an Arranged Marriage

Winner of the 2021 Bookbrunch Selfie Award for Best Adult Fiction...

A British-Bengali girl looking for Mr Right. A motley crew of men, some hoping it's them. A mum on a mission to match make. And an age-old tradition with a twist. Welcome to the world of the arranged marriage.

The Secret Diary of a Bengali Bridezilla

And I thought finding a husband was hard...

One couple. Three months. 600 guests (most of whom I've never met) and LOTS of opinions. Welcome to my big fat Bangladeshi wedding.

The Secret Diary of a Bengali Newlywed

The one that got Booktok talking...

New husband. New city. New in-laws and new expectations. Welcome to my life as a Bengali newlywed.

No One Ever Asks Mum

THE SIDE OF THE STORY you never hear...

A mum on a mission to matchmake. A daughter with ideas of her own. A suitor that threatens to tear them apart. When it comes to arranged marriages, you never hear the perspective of the mother of the 'bride'. So now it's time.

Enjoy this book? Want to read more? The power is in your hands...

Firstly, thanks for taking the time to read my book. It makes my heart happy knowing that people are taking pleasure from my words. It motivates me to write more. I want my book to be read as far and wide as possible, and key to making this happen is having great reviews from readers like you.

Reviews are the most powerful tool in my arsenal when it comes to getting attention for my books. I'm not represented by a global publishing house and I don't have a huge marketing team and endless budget.

But I have something better, that money can't buy – a committed and invested readership. And I rely upon this most important asset, to spread the word.

If you've enjoyed this book, I would be grateful if you could spend just a few minutes leaving a review. It can be as short or as long as you like.

There's more to the story... free reads for you

I hope you enjoyed this story. But wait... there's more. As I mentioned, this isn't your average romcom. It's got people talking, challenged perceptions, and hopefully shown that we're not so different after all. As the series grows I'd like you to be part of my tribe, so I can share exclusive content, free reads, and get your opinion on future book covers, etc. Would you like to join my tribe? If so, sign up to my mailing list here: https://www.subscribepage.com/halimakhatun-books.

About the Author

Halima Khatun is a former journalist (having worked for ITV and the BBC), writer and PR consultant. Since she was a child, she knew that words would be her thing. With a lifelong passion for writing, Halima wrote her first novel - a coming-of-age children's story - at the age of 12. It was politely turned down by all the major publishing houses. However, proving that writing was indeed her forte, Halima went on to study English and Journalism and was one of just four people in the UK to be granted a BBC scholarship during her postgraduate studies. She has since written for a number of publications including the HuffPost and Yahoo! Style, and has been featured in the Express, Metro and other national publications. Halima also blogs on lifestyle, food, travel and parenthood on halimabobs.com. This is where she also shares updates on her novels.

Printed in Great Britain
by Amazon

84301525R00228